KING'S ASSASSIN

Angus Donald was educated at Marlborough College and Edinburgh University. He has worked as a fruit-picker in Greece, a waiter in New York and as an anthropologist studying magic and witchcraft in Indonesia. For twenty years, he was a journalist in Hong Kong, India, Afghanistan and London. He now has two children with his wife Mary and he lives and writes in a medieval farmhouse in rural Kent.

Praise for *The King's Assassin*:

'Set against the rebellion that led to Magna Carta, this fantastic novel, dark and sad in places, thrilling and colourful in others, challenges Hollywood's interpretation of Robin Hood'

Sunday Express

THE KING'S
ASSASSIN

ANGUS DONALD

Typeset by Palimpsest Book Production Ltd,
Falkirk, Stirlingshire
Printed and bound in Great Britain by Clays Ltd, St Ives plc

Papers used by Sphere are from well-managed forests
and other responsible sources.

MIX
Paper from
responsible sources
FSC
FSC® C104740

sphere
An imprint of
Little, Brown Book Group
Carmelite House
50 Victoria Embankment
London EC4Y 0DZ

SPHERE

First published in Great Britain in 2015 by Sphere
This paperback edition published in 2016 by Sphere

1 3 5 7 9 10 8 6 4 2

Copyright © Angus Donald 2015
Extract from *The Death of Robin Hood* copyright © Angus Donald 2016

Map drawn by John Gilkes

A CIP catalogue record for this book
is available from the British Library.

ISBN 978-0-7515-5198-3

An Hachette UK Company
www.hachette.co.uk

www.littlebrown.co.uk

For my father Sir Alan and my son Robin,
who are quite different from their fictional namesakes
and much more important to me

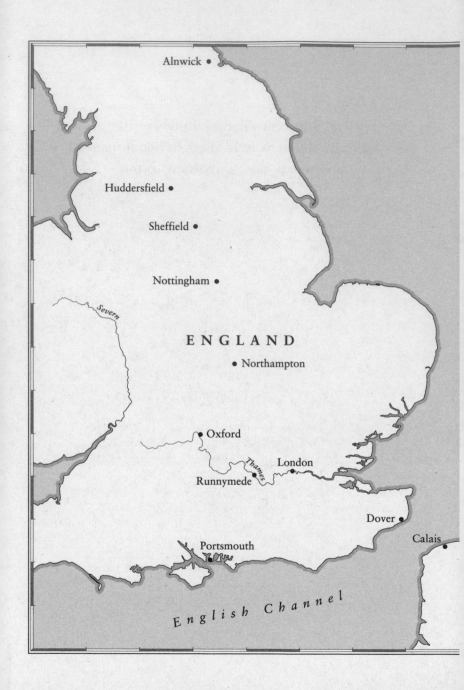

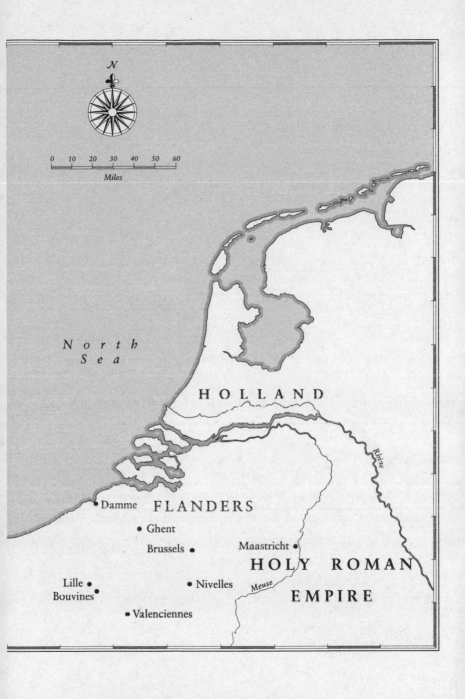

Part One

I, Brother Anthony of Newstead, take up this quill, this parchment and ink-pot at the behest of my brother in Christ, Alan Dale, in the winter of the Year of Our Lord twelve hundred and forty-five, meaning to set down the tale of his deeds and those of his companions long ago in the time of King John. The words are entirely Brother Alan's, who for ten years has been the senior monk of our scriptorium here at Newstead Priory and a venerable ornament to our godly fellowship, and I only attempt to transcribe them as faithfully as I can. His fingers can no longer securely grip a goose quill, and his health grows ever more feeble, which is natural at his great age – he is now three-score years and ten, he tells me proudly – and lately his eyes have grown foggy after years of labouring over our precious books and scrolls.

Brother Alan keeps to his cell most days, particularly when the ground is frozen to iron, and he is mostly abed save for a few hours each day, when I lead him out into the garden to allow him to smell the wind and feel the pale sun on his withered cheeks. It was Brother Alan who taught me to make my letters when I first came to Newstead as a novice nine years ago and it is no great hardship for me to take down his testament for posterity, indeed I see it as a debt that I owe him. We work at night, mostly, when my duties in the abbey are done, with Brother Alan speaking slowly from in his cot, swathed in blankets – for he feels the cold in his limbs and his many old wounds ache in this harsh weather – and myself faithfully copying down his words. We manage a few sheets every night before he falls asleep and I pray that his strength will hold out until his tale is done.

This is not entirely for unselfish reasons on my part. Brother Alan's words are a window on a time before I was born and, although many of the events he relates are shocking to me, I must confess that I feel a most unchristian thrill at these stirring tales of battle and bloodshed, of brave men and bold deeds. It is, indeed, an honour to have even such a small part in their transmission from his memory to this page.

Brother Alan is very near to death now, I fear. He has been sickening these past three years and yet some force, some strange and powerful energy, keeps the flame of life alight in his body long beyond the time when in another man it would have been extinguished. Prior William, our lord and master, says Brother Alan's longevity is a miracle and has

4

graciously given his blessing to this undertaking, this recording of his long life. I believe he too enjoys the tales as he insists on reading my manuscripts almost as soon as the ink is dry.

Like the Prior, I too long to hear more of these adventures that Brother Alan relates, particularly the tales of his lord, his friend, his brother-in-arms, the Earl of Locksley. For this story is about him as much as Brother Alan – about the former woodland outlaw who used the law to give justice to an unjust land; the rebel who brought a King of England to a table at Runnymede and made him submit to the will of the people, the fighting man who fought for peace, the nobleman that the common folk loved – and feared – in equal parts. The man they called Robin Hood.

Chapter One

The coast of Flanders was a black line across the horizon, the dividing barrier between deep-blue sea and paler sky. I sat in the prow of the snake boat, my sun-scorched face lightly kissed from time to time by cool dashes of spray, and fiddled with a loose silver wire on the handle of my long-sword Fidelity. We had been nearly two days in that damn boat; two days of the sun beating down mercilessly on our heads, the plank boards digging into our buttocks hour after hour, the crack of canvas sails above, the wild cry of wind in the rigging, the rush of live water against the wooden sides. Two days of eating stale bread and leathery salt pork; two days of drinking fishy-smelling ale, pissing, shitting – and vomiting, in rough swell – over the side. But God had been good to us; there had been no great storms to drench us, nor vast waves to dash the ship to pieces and drag our iron-clad bodies down into the deep.

And neither were we alone. On either side of the vessel as far as the eye could see were hundreds of ships like ours: long, low, lean, single-masted vessels crammed with fighting men, weapons, shields, food and stores, as well as bigger craft – galleys and busses, cogs and even a river sailing barge or two making the perilous crossing to the low lands across the German Sea from England. There were nearly five hundred vessels in all, I had been told, and some seven hundred knights, as well as many hundreds more men-at-arms, archers, crossbowmen, servants and squires – even a few women, hardy young trulls and big matrons with forearms like farriers, who followed a host wherever it went and provided the services that fighting men always require: cooked food, clean clothes and a willing body to warm the blankets.

We were a seaborne army. An armada. And we were going into battle.

I was in fear. I must admit it: indeed, I was terrified. This was not my first time going into the storm of battle, nor yet my twentieth, but the fear had come down on me that bright morning like a vile fog, like an invisible plague drawn inside me with my breath that was now eating away at my guts, gnawing away the strength of my bones. I was convinced that I would be butchered in the coming conflict. I could clearly see the sword cut that would smash through my guard, cut through helm and arming cap and crush my skull; I could feel the prick of the spear as it thrust into my chest, bursting apart ribs, crushing my organs. I could taste the searing pain, the gush of blood, the weakness and wrongness of it all, and the cold, slow slide into black.

I shook my head, trying to banish these visions of bloody disaster. I was a brave man, I told myself: be brave. But I had never had it as bad as this, never, not in all my long years of soldiering. I had fought many times, I'd won and lost, I'd been wounded and captured, I'd been tortured and condemned to certain death: but I had never felt as plain, ordinary, brown-your-braies frightened as I did that bright May morning off the coast of Flanders as we approached the estuary of the Zwin river and the port of Damme in the Year of Our Lord twelve hundred and thirteen.

It must be my age, I thought. For I was no callow lad, I was a seasoned man-at-arms of eight and thirty summers, wise in war and versed in the ways of men – a knight, indeed, with a manor to my name, a dozen fine scars and the beginnings of a belly – not some green sprig going into his first skirmish. I had called upon St Michael, my personal protecting angel, in half a hundred fights, and he had almost always warded me with his long white wings. But where was he this sunny morning? Where was my holy guardian that day as the wind swept us remorse-lessly across the flat blue sea towards our enemies, the mighty legions of Philip Augustus, the King of France? My spine ached, my belly felt cold and sickly, my left hand trembled, and I had to make a fist to mask the shameful physical manifestation of my cowardice.

I looked to my left at the nearest snake boat, some thirty yards northwards, and took a little comfort in the sight of a huge red-faced man with fat blond plaits on either cheek standing by the mast, one massive arm curled around it. He looked invincible. He wore a knee-length mail hauberk that seemed a little too tight across his vast chest, leather boots and gauntlets reinforced with strips of iron, a long dagger hung horizontally at his waist and a gleaming double-headed axe rested on one brawny shoulder. He saw me looking and cupped a hand to his mouth.

'We'll soon be amongst them, Alan, don't you worry,' shouted Little John, his words reaching me easily from the neighbouring ship over the howl of wind and sea. 'It's going to be a rare brawl,' he bellowed. 'Nice and bloody, you mark my words!'

I wrenched up a suitably carefree grin, as befits a man of war, and waved cheerily at him – but my guts were churning and I had to look away from his honest red face. How did John do it, in battle after battle, how did he find such joy in death? He had taken appalling wounds in his time; he had felt the Devil's stinking breath on the back of his neck. How could he still see this bloody business as a jolly game?

9

In that brief moment, I hated my old and trusted friend. I wanted to see him humbled; laid as low as I by fear and weakness. Immediately, I chided myself for that ignoble thought. John was John, and in the mêlée I knew he would take a sword blow meant for me – just as I would for him. If only I could master my fear. I glanced behind me and my eye alighted on a youth who *was* going into his first battle. It must be ten times worse for him, I thought, as he knew not what to expect. But, if he was as afeared as me, he was doing a far better job than I was in concealing it.

He was a handsome lad of eighteen or so, with light-brown hair and a long, lean face. He was dressed in an expensive hauberk of the finest mail and a domed helmet with golden crosses incised into the steel. His weapons, too, long-sword and dagger, were of the finest quality. And his shield bore the fierce depiction of a snarling wolf in gold on an azure field. But it was his face that made me pause every time I looked into it. But for his eyes, which were a rich dark blue, he was the spitting image of his father Robert Odo, Earl of Locksley, the man who was my own lord and master and who had persuaded me to undertake this very voyage into battle.

Miles Odo looked entirely unconcerned about facing mortal combat for the first time. True, he had been trained by some of the best swordsmen and masters-at-arms in Europe, former Knights Templar for the most part, since he was old enough to lift a sword tip off the ground. But, as far as I knew, he had never faced an opponent who was genuinely seeking to kill or maim him; nor had he ever faced a storm of arrows and crossbow bolts that plucked away the lives of the comrades all around you at the whim of Chance. A half-smile adorned his smooth young face, his brow was unwrinkled, though a dimple crinkled his cheek when he saw me watching him; he looked like a carefree young blade on a pleasure cruise – in pursuit of wine and women, not pain and slaughter – and by that placid cast of face I knew that he was as petrified as I was, or perhaps even more so. For he wore exactly the same expression his father had always donned when things were at their worst.

Robin's nonchalant words to me at the quayside at Dover, before we parted and he made his way to his own ship, echoed in my ears: 'Keep an eye on Miles, will you, Alan. Marie-Anne would be most upset if anything were to go amiss . . .'

It might have sounded as if Robin was unconcerned about the safety of his second son. But I knew him better than that. He had been commending Miles into my care, asking without asking that I watch over him like a mother hen in the coming storm of steel. And I would, fear or no fear. For the debts of honour I owed to Robin, and the love I bore for him, were bigger than all the terrors of the world. We had fought together on more than a dozen battlefields from the Holy Land to the fields outside his home castle of Kirkton in Yorkshire. He had saved

11

my hide so many times I could not count them. I would look out for his younger son as if he were my own.

Miles's elder brother Hugh, who was Robin's heir to the Locksley lands, was in the lead ship, a proud high-ended cog, with his father and William Longsword, the Earl of Salisbury, the leader of this seaborne expedition.

Hugh was a very different man to Miles. Where Miles was tall, fair and willowy, Hugh was shorter, dark and strongly built. While Miles was whimsical, dreamy and prone to laziness, though a dazzling fighter with sword or dagger, Hugh was studious and level-headed, a talented horseman and a dogged if unimaginative swordsman. Although they were separated in age by four years, they were very close, devoted to each other, and to insult or injure one was to bring down the wrath of the other.

I swung my legs over the bench so that I was facing back down the ship and face to face with Miles.

'Here, lad,' I said proffering the hilt of Fidelity. 'See if your young fingers can fix this loose bit of silver wire. Can you tuck it under there, under that loop . . .'

Miles bent his head over the weapon for a few moments, his nimble fingers tucking and tugging. The ship's captain altered course slightly, the sail cracked like a breaking branch, a rogue wave slapped the ship's side and a salty packet of water leapt up and dashed itself against the shield on my back and over my neck, sending freezing trickles down my back under my iron mail. I tried not to shiver.

'It is a truly wonderful sword, Sir Alan,' said the lad, handing it back to me, the loose end of wire neatly out of sight. He was right: a blue sapphire set into a ring of silver made the pommel, the long silver wire-wrapped grip allowed it to be wielded with one hand or two, the cross-guard was thick squared steel ending in two sharp points, which I used as a weapon almost as much as the yard-long shining steel blade.

'It's certainly an old one,' I said. 'I killed an evil man for it before you were born. But it has served me well over the years. Very well.'

There was a silence between us, as we both admired the play of light on the naked steel. Then the young man cleared his throat a little unnaturally.

'Sir Alan,' he said, 'is it true what Father says about you, that you have killed many, many men?'

I squinted at him in the bright sunlight, shrugged and said nothing.

He had the grace to colour at this gaucherie.

'I mean no disrespect, Sir Alan,' he said. 'Nor do I mean to pry into your affairs. I merely wanted to ask . . . I just wondered what it feels like, you know, to kill a man. To take everything he has – and will ever have.'

I thought for a moment. Facing battle, he deserved to hear the truth.

'It is hard,' I said truthfully. 'It is very hard the first time.' My mind went back to a woodland glade in England more than two dozen years earlier, and a dead knight on

13

the ground by my feet, a boy not much older than I was then, with his neck broken by my blade. 'It feels wrong,' I said. 'Like the worst sin imaginable. But it does get easier each time you do it. Much easier. Then it becomes no more than something that you have to do, a task, a labour, something that must be accomplished.'

He looked me straight in the eyes, his deep-blue eyes in his father's face.

I said: 'There will be killing aplenty today, lad, and we will do our part. But I want to ask a favour of you, a boon, if you will. When we go in, I want you as my shield-man. Will you do that for me? Sir Thomas Blood will be on my right, as usual.' I nodded over to the far side of the boat where a short, dark-eyed warrior in full mail was putting a final edge on his sword with a whet-stone. 'But I want you on my left. In the thick of battle, I want to know I've got a good man on my shield-side. Will you do that for me? Stick by me; guard my flank?'

Miles nodded and gave me a beautiful, beaming smile. 'I am deeply honoured, Sir Alan. You can rely on me. To the death!'

I nodded and swung my legs back over the bench to face forward again. I wondered how soon he would realise that the 'favour' I had asked of him – that he stay close by me on my left-hand side – was in fact no more than a ruse to ensure that he was under the protection of my shield in the coming fight.

And I wondered what he would say when he did find out.

14

No matter. There was grim work ahead and no time for niceties. And I would not be able to look Robin in the eye – or Marie-Anne – if their son was killed under my protection. I'd see him safely through this blood-bath or die trying.

The land had jumped a little closer and I stood up from the bench and looked out under a hand. There were sandbars visible, patches of lighter blue amid the turquoise, and I felt the snake boat shift direction slightly as the captain, a dour man called Harold, guided our vessels between two of the larger ones. But I could also make out the spindly masts of ships ahead by the smear of coast. Many, many ships spread right across the wide mouth of the estuary, with more concentrated at the centre where the river debouched brown from the muddy flatlands. As we came closer, I could make out the masts and rigging of hundreds, no, maybe more than a thousand ships, seemingly stacked against each other. In the late afternoon sun they looked like a great tangled forest in winter, the trunks and limbs bare of their leaves. My God, I thought, this is the whole enemy invasion fleet. Right here. All of it. King Philip's whole force is spread out before us, riding at anchor, or drawn up and beached on the sandy shore as carelessly as if they were in the port of Harfleur.

Our lead ship, a big cog with a high castle-like fighting platform at each end, and which flew the lions of England from the mast, was signalling to the fleet. I thought I could make out Robin on the deck of the vessel with his back

15

to me, conversing with a knight in glittering mail. Robin's long green cloak fluttered behind him in the north-westerly breeze. He was pointing upwards to where coloured pennants, tiny at a distance, were being hauled up the mast. A hundred yards behind the lead ship, I followed the line of his pointing finger, and could easily make out the message the flags revealed. We knew our orders, we'd been thoroughly drilled in the flag codes and, as they fluttered cheerfully in the salt-tanged air, their daunting instructions were startlingly clear.

I turned back to the body of the snake boat and addressed the score of men-at-arms sitting eagerly on the benches – men in mail and leather, bowmen, spearmen, swordsmen, helmeted and helmless – and said: 'It seems, lads, that we are not going to waste any time. No scouting, no hesitation, no parley. We go straight into the attack this afternoon. We are going in to take, burn or sink any French ships that we can. Lace up, men, and draw steel. Battle is upon us. May God Almighty go with us!'

I fumbled for my gauntlets, which were tucked into my belt, and in doing so I looked down at my naked left hand. The shaking had completely stopped.

My hand was as steady as a stone.

Chapter Two

As I pulled on my stiff gauntlets, reinforced with fat strips of iron sewn into pouches in the thick leather, and flexed my fingers vigorously to try to loosen them, I remembered the last time I had worn them, not much more than a month ago, and wished I had taken the time to dry and oil them properly before they'd been put away.

I had trotted up to the gates of my estate of Westbury in the dusk of a Sunday in mid-April, having ridden hard from Portsmouth the morning before. I was greeted at the wide-flung gates of the manor compound by Baldwin my steward and, to my delight, by Robert my son, a tall, shy, and strikingly handsome boy of eleven. I had pulled off the heavy war-gloves, tossed them to Baldwin with a warm smile as he gathered the reins of my horse, and scooped the surprised boy up in a vast bear hug.

After a long absence, I was home.

The subsequent evening had been one of merriment. Robert, once he had overcome his diffidence, had been keen to tell me everything that had happened to him since I had left for the south of France some years before and to show me his new treasures: a hunting dog called Vixen, an over-excited lurcher puppy in truth woefully lacking in discipline; a new hunting knife that one of the few Westbury men-at-arms had made for him; a rock that glittered like gold; a phoenix's feather, or so he claimed; and a genuine unicorn's horn, which on closer inspection I recognised as once belonging to a mountain goat – despite Robert's fanciful insistence that he had seen the legendary beast with his own eyes and hunted it to death with Vixen.

I partook of a delightful supper with my son and heir, served by Alice, Baldwin's younger sister, a plain, competent unmarried woman of thirty or so years who ran the manor household with her brother with a silent competence and grace. We ate a thin venison stew and bean pottage and a sallet of wild leaves – a rather meagre feast for a returning lord, I remember thinking – and for an hour or so afterwards he and I had made not-very-tuneful but perfectly joyful music together – he on the shawm, a flute-like instrument that he had learnt to play, after a fashion, in my absence, and I on my old vielle. Then

18

Baldwin, on the pretence of bringing me a cup of hot, spiced wine, interrupted our play and tugged me away. He insisted on speaking to me about the manor accounts. It was late for such a task and I had only been home for a few hours, so I was more than a little puzzled by his insistence. I could tell that something was amiss and so I packed Robert off to bed and he went, reluctantly, after extracting a promise from me to go riding with him in the morn.

As Baldwin and I burned a cheap tallow candle and pored over the rolls, the gauntlets lay on a window sill in the hall where my steward had left them and that, I recall clearly, was the last I saw of them before packing for the voyage across the sea.

For the news that Baldwin had for me drove everything else from my head.

I had been away from Westbury, from England, for some years, involved in that bloody carbuncle on the honour of Christendom, the hounding to death of the Cathars of Toulouse and the pillaging and destruction of their lands, but even in the far south of France I had been dimly aware of events in England during this period.

Baldwin filled in the close details: King John's sheriffs had been rapacious in their quest for silver for their royal master, and none less so than Philip Marc, the current High Sheriff of Nottinghamshire, Derbyshire and the Royal Forests, who had dominion over a huge swathe of central England. Marc was a mercenary, a low-born Frenchman from Touraine who had risen in King John's service over the past ten years through his utter loyalty to the King and his savagery in dealing with the King's enemies. And among that number were included those landowners who the King claimed owed him money. I knew Marc slightly from my days in Normandy, and liked him even less. The number of the King's 'enemies' had, I gathered, risen greatly in the years I had been away. After the loss of Normandy some nine years before, John had made increasing demands on any man of even moderate wealth. Tax after tax, relief after relief, as these demands for silver were known. And these extortions – there is no better word for it – were backed up by the full force of the local officers of the law. Indeed, no fewer than six times had the King declared 'scutage', an arbitrary levy on men of knightly rank and above, in the time that I had been away, and not a week before my return a full *conroi* of the sheriff of Nottinghamshire's mounted men had come to Westbury in mail and helm, swords drawn, and had demanded a payment of fifty marks from Baldwin.

Fifty marks! In a good year, the revenues of Westbury in total might have amounted to fifteen. Under good King Richard – and he was no sluggard at milking the country for money for his wars – I had paid two or at most three marks each year. Fifty marks was a veritable fortune.

My poor steward, with only a handful of men-at-arms

to protect the manor, was outnumbered and overawed. When the knight in command, some fat-faced deputy sheriff, backed by a dark-skinned mountain of a sergeant – a demon, if Baldwin was to be believed – had threatened to burn the place to the ground if some payment in silver were not made immediately, Baldwin had believed it was his duty to protect the manor as best he could and had surrendered all the coin that Westbury possessed to the King's enforcers: a matter of twenty-six marks, more than three hundred silver pennies, a couple of small barrelfuls. The sheriff's men had taken the silver and ridden away – but they swore that they would be back for the balance in due course.

'I am so sorry, Sir Alan,' he said. 'But I did not know what to do. With you away . . . It was not their first visit, nor yet their second or third. And each time they take something and their demands increase. I did not know what else to do, sir.'

I soothed him with the best words I could find, but my head was reeling. I had sent that silver to Westbury, as and when I could, and I had received occasional reports from the manor about Robert's progress and a tally of the rents and so forth. But nothing for many months. I had believed that all was well, that I might return to Westbury to find the place moderately well stocked with produce and with a goodly store of cash to tide us over lean times. I'd been wrong.

Baldwin showed me on the big parchment rolls that

in the past year the sheriff's taxmen had requisitioned from me six milk cows; a dozen black pigs; a pair of oxen; two riding horses; eighteen bushels of wheat; twelve bushels of barley; three of rye; five big round yellow cheeses, and, of course, twenty-six marks of sterling silver. As the rolls proclaimed, Westbury was near destitute. Almost its entire portable wealth was now in the sheriff's hands – and still, Baldwin told me, he was demanding more.

I had heard, even down in the war-torn County of Toulouse, that the King was squeezing the country like a ripe plum in his greedy fist, and I had even expected that, as a knight, I might have to pay a small amount to the crown for my lands. But I had not foreseen this pillaging of my goods and chattels.

Baldwin tried to give me comfort. 'Sir, you are not alone. Most of the knights in the north – even the great barons – have suffered in the same way. I dare say all over the country there are good men doing as we are and looking with dismay at their rolls and wondering how they shall maintain their dignity over the coming year.'

It was not much comfort, to be honest. Westbury was penniless, I was near enough a beggar for all my title and lands, and the sheriff wanted more.

Baldwin looked as if he would weep at any moment, so I hid my growing anger.

'Calm yourself, Baldwin,' I said. 'If the sheriff's men return we will defy them. Tomorrow or the next day, Sir

Thomas Blood will be arriving with two dozen good fighting men and the carts and baggage. Once they are installed at Westbury, we will shut the gates in their faces and dare them to attack. My men have fought halfway across Europe; they will not be cowed by a few Nottingham Castle braggarts. I'll warrant that if needs must we can hold this place against them till Judgement Day.'

The look of relief on Baldwin's face warmed my soul.

'They have only preyed on us because all the fighting men were away,' I said, slapping the old fellow on his thin shoulder. 'They thought we were weak. Maybe we were. We are not now. I'm here to stay and I swear that they shall not have another penny, not a slice of bread from me, not a cup of stale ale. Rest easy, old friend.'

'But in the meantime, sir, how shall we eat . . .'

'Sir Thomas is bringing stores with him – rough-and-ready travelling fare, twice-baked bread, hard cheese and some wine. It will serve for now, and Thomas has silver, too. Enough to replace the farm beasts, at the very least. We shall not starve, Baldwin, never you fear. And I will ride to Kirkton tomorrow to consult with my lord of Locksley. He will know what to do.'

I rode north with young Robert the next morning. It was a fine fair spring day, sunny but brisk, with a blue sky garlanded with wisps of cloud. Robert was in a fine tearing mood, galloping ahead of me on the dry road, causing his horse to rear, then circling back to urge me to greater

23

speed. He was proud of his riding skills, as well he might be, for they were excellent for a lad his age. But we took our time, walking the horses often to rest them and discoursing happily in the saddle about my adventures in the south and Robert's fancies and dreams. It was approaching dusk as we rode up the steep track from the Locksley Valley to the castle of Kirkton high above.

We rode past the church of St Nicholas and I nodded courteously at the ancient priest, half-dozing on a bench in the evening sunshine on the south side of the house of God, which overlooked the valley. The old man lifted a hand in blessing but did not move, and Robert and I made our way quietly past him through to the little grave-yard and up the gentle slope to the castle's wooden walls. We were admitted without fanfare by the porters, who seemed uninterested in the two dusty arrivals. Once inside the gates, I saw that we had arrived in the middle of a celebration.

Almost the whole population of the castle, and a goodly number of the folk from the village that sprawled beneath its walls, had assembled in the courtyard – several hundred people in a rough circle around the edges with a large space in the centre. It seemed that they had been there some time, perhaps all day, for stalls had been set up offering sweetmeats, cakes and ale around the inside of the castle walls, and the crowd displayed a jolly holiday mood. On the walls of the keep, a squat tower at the rear of the courtyard, a dozen bright flags flew proudly from the battlements, and a gaggle of nobility in silks and furs stood on the parapet watching the space below.

Two men in full mail stood in the centre of that space, both armed with sword and shield. Their faces were partially obscured by their helms, which were plain steel domes, with cheek guards and nasals. One was short and stocky, the other tall and thin: by the springiness of their steps as they circled each other warily I could tell that both were young and extremely fit.

I stepped down from my horse and quickly lashed the reins to a post, and then Robert and I pushed our way to the front of the crowd to watch the bout.

The taller one attacked first, and by God he was fast. He took two steps, feinted a lunge at his opponent's head, and whipped the sword down to strike at his foeman's forward thigh. The stockier fellow made a slow high lateral block, to counter the feint, realised his mistake and just got his shield down in time to stop the blade cutting deep into his thigh. He was given no time to recover, for the tall fellow was already striking again, a diagonal cut at the head followed up by a thrusting pommel strike that rang off the side of the stocky man's helmet like a church bell. It was a move I had never seen before; utterly original and devastatingly effective.

The shorter man staggered comically away from the blow, which must have partially stunned him; and the slender fellow let out a peal of boyish laughter.

It was then that I realised that the two men sparring

in the courtyard were Robin's sons: Miles and Hugh. I glanced at my own boy, standing beside me; his eyes were shining with excitement, his two fists clenched white as bone as if he too might shortly be called upon to defend himself.

The crowd were cheering, calling out advice: some of it helpful, some absurd, some of it quite obscene. Robin was standing with both hands on the parapet of the keep, flanked by two men I did not recognise, and looking down impassively as his two boys battered away at each other. Hugh had recovered himself by then, which was just as well, for young Miles was subjecting him to a blizzard of strikes, each as fast as a darting kingfisher, a dazzling display of his sword-skill. Metal flashed in the spring sunlight, white chips of wood flew from Hugh's shield, and the sword clanged once more against his brother's helmet as it skimmed its pointed dome. But Hugh did not go down. He hunched himself under the onslaught, and his blocks and parries were exactly precise, a classic defence – standard, tried-and-tested moves and would have filled any master-at-arms's heart with joy. Miles struck fast and hard, often in the most unexpected combinations, but Hugh's bulwark was solid; every time Miles's sword licked out, there was Hugh's battered shield ready to take the blow, or his blade to make the block.

And I could see that Miles was tiring.

For any man, no matter how strong and fit, tires after only a short while in the fury of combat. No one can fight at full pitch for long; and wiser, older warriors know that if they can survive the initial onslaught, their enemy will be weakened, and they will surely have their chance. Hugh was no grey-beard, he was in his twenty-fifth year, but he had the patience and wisdom of a man twice his age.

Miles's sword strikes were still coming fast as a viper's tongue, and equally as deadly, but they were met with a stolid determination that smothered all his energy and flair. And slowly, gradually, Hugh began to show his dominance. He stopped a lightning vertical cut at his head and stepped in, turning his ringing block into a half-decent lunge at his opponent's eyes. Miles, utterly surprised, only just managed to jerk his head out of the path of the blade.

And the tables were turned.

Hugh attacked: a strike on the right with sword, a punch forward on the left with shield; a feint at the head, a slash at the ankles. They were all well-worn, proven manoeuvres, the kind of moves that were drummed into all fighting men from the first moment we entered the practice-ground. They were utterly predictable. I could hear the echo down the long years of my own first sword-master, a grizzled outlaw called Thangbrand, bellowing out the numbers of the sequence. And yet, they were drummed into us all because they *were* effective; they were taught to generation after generation because they worked. Miles might affect a young man's contempt for the traditional combinations, but he had his hands full trying to counter them. Hugh bored on, stubborn as an ass; pushing Miles back and back across the courtyard with his dull, age-old technique, until, as perhaps Hugh had hoped, Miles made a mistake.

The taller boy took a gamble. Instead of stopping Hugh's sword blow to his left shoulder dead with his shield, absorbing the impact of the blade, and counter-attacking with his own sword – which would have been the usual response – he closed in and tried to shield-punch his brother's fist as it grasped the hilt of the swinging sword, down and away. The idea clearly being to make him drop his sword or at the least to open his older brother's body, and leave it defenceless against a wicked lunge to the belly.

But Miles mistimed it; he came in too close and moved too fast. The very top of his shield struck Hugh's hand, rather than the centre. Hugh kept his grip. And while his sword was indeed pushed wide, he was not forced off balance. Miles, on the other hand, was – he stumbled slightly and the older boy merely pushed forward with his own shield, trapping his younger brother's sword against his own chest, and then gave a hard shove, knocking him to the ground with a clatter of wood and metal equipment. An instant later, Hugh stood over his brother as he lay in the dirt of the courtyard, sword tickling his chin, and Miles was forced to yield.

Miles looked stunned as he lay there, then for a fraction

of a moment, insanely angry. Then the fit passed and his face creased into a smile and he began to chuckle ruefully as his older brother held out a hand to help him to his feet.

Hugh's expression showed not one scintilla of triumph at his victory. He even looked bored as he pulled his brother up and gently slapped the dust from his back.

The crowd of holiday folk cheered wildly, most of them, though I heard one or two curse God and the saints in a most vulgar manner, and I noticed many crossly handing over coins and even purses to their neighbours. Robin strode across the courtyard, in a rich dark green robe with fur as the collar and cuffs, and jaunty feathered hat atop his handsome head. His face a beam of pure happiness.

'My friends, the hour is late, and we have seen some fine sport this long day. Our fighting men have spent themselves giving us all such fine exhibitions of their prowess, and now it is time for the revels of the day: for feasting and music and dance. More wine, ale and mead will be served, the cooks are roasting two whole oxen over the pits in the long meadow as we speak, and there will be food and drink for all far into the night. But before we give ourselves over to pleasure, I ask you to show your appreciation for my two sons and their skill at arms. Give me a cheer for Miles Odo, a gallant warrior . . .' The crowd dutifully cheered, but not with excessive heartiness . . . 'and for the victor in today's final match, Hugh

Odo, whose birth day this is, and in whose honour all this revelry is named. Eat, drink and be merry, my friends, and raise a cup to my heir while you do so.' The cheer this time was an unforced genuine roar of approval which rolled around inside of the wooden castle walls like thunder. I had not realised till then that Hugh was so much liked.

We started to push our way through the throng towards the great hall.

'Why does Hugh get a celebration for the day of his birth, Father?' asked Robert. He scratched his cropped hair. 'Why don't I get a feast on my birth day?'

'We always celebrate your birth on St Robert's day . . .'

'Which was two weeks ago,' said Robert. 'You were still in France. Baldwin took me to church, we had pease pottage and boiled turnips for dinner, no more.'

'Pease pottage is a fine dish. Many a boy would be happy to have it.'

Robert went quiet, and I was stabbed by a shaft of hot guilt. I had not, indeed, been a very attentive father. Too often away, too long away.

'I was thinking that it was about time that you had a decent sword . . .' I said.

'Oh, Father,' said Robert, his face opening like a flower, 'that would be so wonderful. One like Fidelity? A hand-and-a-half with a jewel set on the pommel?'

'Well, perhaps not quite like Fidelity . . .' I said.

And saw his face fall.

'I mean one that is not quite so old and battered,' I said quickly. 'But a new sword, yes! – a proper blade for a promising young squire.'

While Robert fizzed with happiness, I cursed my own weakness. After the sheriff's depredations, money was tight enough at Westbury without me promising to spend a fortune on a sword for a boy whose voice had not yet broken. But a promise is a promise and I made a private vow that I would visit a cutler's shop in Nottingham in the next few days where the proprietor was an old boyhood friend of mine – and not quite an out-and-out rogue – to see what could be managed.

I also decided that Robert must have some proper training at last. Seeing the skills that Miles and Hugh displayed reminded me of how remiss I had been with my own son's martial education. He must be trained as a squire by the best, the very best. He must be sent to a great household, the household of a knight famous for his prowess, where he would learn all the skills of a fighting man and proper conduct in war and out of it. And I thought I knew just the right man for the task.

I found Robin in the great hall of Kirkton amid a throng of knights and men-at-arms from the surrounding area and their ladies and elder children. I knew most of them reasonably well and it took Robert and me a good deal of time to work our way through the crowd, nodding, smiling, clasping a hand here and there, offering a few words of greeting. Finally we reached Robin, who welcomed me with evident joy.

'Sir Alan, I thought I spotted you in the crowd,' he said loudly, in a somewhat artificial voice, 'what a pleasant surprise.'

His odd tone indicated that he wished to give me some message. I had been with him at Portsmouth not a sennight before and yet he was treating me as if I was a comparative stranger. Something was wrong. Robin continued in his faux-jolly voice: 'Come take a cup of wine with me and my friends. You have come to wish Hugh joy on the day of his birth, I make no doubt.'

I said I had. And I offered my congratulations to Robin's oldest son, who was standing beside him, wishing the young man all the happiness of the day.

'Glad you're here, Alan,' Robin said quietly in my ear. 'Something has come up. Something – ah – very foolish. But I need you to help me quash it.'

'Hugh, perhaps you would be kind enough to take Robert to the tables in the upper field,' said the Earl of Locksley loudly, 'and show him where to get something to eat. You might swing by the stables on your way and show off your birth-day gift.'

'A horse?' I asked Robin.

'A destrier,' he replied, 'it cost me a king's ransom. But you should have seen the way Hugh smiled when he saw the beast for the first time. Worth every penny.'

The two youngsters departed through the crowded hall,

chatting in a friendly familiar fashion, Hugh's brawny arm over Robert's thin shoulders, for they had known each other all their lives and I knew Robert looked upon Miles and Hugh as something akin to cousins, perhaps even elder brothers. I looked beyond the two young men and found my eye alighting on two mature knights who stood out from the rest of the revellers in the solemnity of their mien. They were dressed as for a celebration in fine-cut cloth, but standing slightly apart from the multitudes in the hall, by the wall, each attended by a pair of armed servants. Alone out of the hordes in Robin's hall they seemed serious, guarded and watchful, aloof from the revelling.

One of the men, a tall, dark-haired man in a crimson-and-white cloak, with a long bony nose and bright blue eyes, saw me looking at him and inclined his head in greeting. He did not smile but I knew that I had seen him somewhere before and so I favoured him with a courteous bow. His companion, in a glorious golden cloak, saw where his fellow was looking and also greeted me with a cautious nod, before whispering in his friend's ear. I had the feeling that I was being discussed by these two solemn, yet gaudy fellows, a most disagreeable sensation, and I was just about to go over and interrupt their private discourse when Robin beat me to it. He plucked at my elbow and led me over to the two men.

'Sir Alan, you know Eustace de Vesci, of course, lord of Alnwick Castle, who fought so valiantly with us during

33

the Great Pilgrimage,' my lord said, indicating the dark man in the crimson cloak.

As Robin said it, I did dimly remember the man from those long-ago struggles in the Holy Land. He had been an indifferent warrior, I recalled, but proud as Lucifer. He had snubbed me once in Robin's company, I think, called me an upstart or some such. But then I had not yet been knighted by King Richard and was just a common man-at-arms, so I supposed I must forgive him. But there was another reason why his name was familiar to me, and I found myself looking at him strangely.

'Lord de Vesci,' I said, 'what an honour to make your acquaintance again,' and I bowed once more.

'And you must know Lord Fitzwalter, constable of Baynard Castle in London,' Robin continued.

'Ha!' said the second man; a ruddy, square-set knight with brownish-golden hair. 'Constable of a charred ruin. Didn't you hear, Locksley? King John had it burnt to the ground in January and slighted its walls for good measure. It's just a heap of blackened rubble now. They say the smell of smoke still lingers, months later. Not that I'd know, of course . . .' Fitzwalter tailed off awkwardly.

Fitzwalter and de Vesci. I knew their names. Even in the far south of France I had heard their infamous names.

'Ah, yes, Lord Fitzwalter, what a pleasure,' I said, staring at the man.

'Is there somewhere we could talk privately, my lord?' said Eustace de Vesci to Robin. He rolled his eyes towards

34

me. It was clear that he did not wish a guttersnipe such as me to be privy to their elevated conversations.

'Certainly, let us talk in my solar,' said Robin, pointing to a door set in the wall at the far end of the hall. 'Join us, would you, Sir Alan, I want you to hear what these gentlemen have to say.'

De Vesci scowled but he began to walk in the direction that Robin had indicated. Fitzwalter smiled blandly and began to follow his friend.

I halted Robin with a hand on his arm.

'What is all this about?' I said. 'What do these two villains want?'

'They want me to kill the King,' said Robin.

I stopped dead in my tracks.

'Come along, Alan, we should not keep two such desperate cut-throats waiting, should we?' said my lord.

Chapter Three

The solar was empty – but for a large bed on one side of the room and a small table at the other at which a tray with a jug of purple wine, cups and a bowl of fruit had been laid. Robin had clearly been expecting to entertain here.

While de Vesci and Fitzwalter pulled up stools to the low table and, at Robin's urging, poured themselves wine, I pondered what I had heard of these two men.

Eustace de Vesci was from an old Norman family that had been a power in the north-east of England for generations. He had married the illegitimate daughter of the King of Scotland, a woman of surpassing beauty called Margaret, and ruled his wide lands from Alnwick Castle, a great stronghold north of the Tyne. Like many of the barons of England he disliked and distrusted King John, but last year he had been accused of being involved in a plot to murder him. The plot had been betrayed and de Vesci had fled north to take refuge with his wife's kin in Scotland. He had been dispossessed of his lands by the King, and if John had been able to get his hands on him he would have been a dead man. Indeed, if John knew that Robin was now sheltering him in Kirkton, Robin's situation would be precarious, too.

I knew less about the second man. Robert Fitzwalter, once constable of Baynard Castle by the Thames, and still a power in London and in Essex, had also been named as one of the conspirators and he had fled to France to save his skin. Now, evidently, both were back in England.

Lord Fitzwalter crunched into an apple and jerked his chin at de Vesci. 'Go on, Eustace, no need to be coy. Set out your stall,' he said through a mouthful of mush.

Eustace de Vesci took a swallow of dark wine, looked from Robin to me and back again, and began.

'You know King John well, Locksley, I think. You were very close to him in Normandy, in the last days there. And before that, too, as I recall. And so I would ask you a question, which I hope you will answer in all honesty, as God is your witness.'

Robin said nothing. I helped myself to a cup of wine. The silence stretched like soft dough in a baker's floury hands. To my surprise, Robin broke it.

'Ask, then,' he said.

De Vesci looked down at his hands. 'Before God, my lord, do you think that John is a good king?'

'No,' said Robin. A short flat statement.

'Is he a decent, honourable, fair man, a man worthy of respect and loyalty from the ancient nobility of England?'

Robin didn't deign to answer that; he just gave a soft snort of contempt.

'Is John a man who will protect and guard his people, and give them justice as he vowed to do at his coronation?'

Fitzwalter interrupted his friend: 'We all know he is not. Get on with it, man!' And earned himself a scowl from his dark-haired companion.

'Very well, I must ask you then, Lord Locksley: is John a fit and proper King of England?'

Robin shrugged.

De Vesci leaned forward: 'You heard about William de Braose and his family?' he asked but did not wait for an answer. 'He was a good man; you knew him and liked him, I think. Well . . . our good William is now dead, hounded into an early grave by a vengeful King. And for why? They had been close, as close as brothers, the King and de Braose, but his wife Maud, a silly woman, gossiped that John had had young Duke Arthur murdered in Rouen, which is something that a great many people have been saying recently. And the King, when he heard, was very, very angry. He responded by claiming that de Braose owed him a vast sum of money, some say as much as a hundred thousand marks, a payment for the grant of his lands and fiefdoms. He must pay up, said the King, or forfeit all of them. When de Braose pleaded that he couldn't pay such a price, the King sent knights to take his castles and seize his person.'

Robin stared at him impassively but said nothing.

'William fled to Ireland,' de Vesci continued, 'but the King pursued him there, sending a small army of knights after him. But de Braose was a wily fox – and William the Marshal and other good men gave him shelter for a while – and he evaded the searches of the King's men and came back to Wales dressed as a filthy beggar. But he was betrayed soon enough and the King's men followed him there, too, swearing that if he would not surrender to them immediately they would find him and slaughter him in his stinking rags. Finally the poor man escaped to France; he got out of the country with nothing more than the clothes on his back, and he died there in Paris – sick, alone and in penury. Some say he died of a broken heart.'

De Vesci leaned forward and grasped Robin's forearm, which was resting on the table. 'Yet still John was not satisfied,' he said, his voice trembling with emotion. 'He seized all his lands, all his manors and castles. He even managed to capture his wife, Maud, whose blather was the cause of all this trouble, and their son. That woman, brave in extremis, it must be said, demanded a trial; she demanded to know what crime she was accused of. She asked to be allowed to speak her defence to the barons of England, and vowed she would accept their judgement if they found that she was guilty of any crime whatsoever. But the King refused and had her imprisoned, quietly tucked away in Corfe Castle in the deepest dungeon. He gave orders that they were to receive no visitors – and no food.

'She and her son lingered for weeks, but eventually they both died. The son, it seems, in his desperate starveling state gnawed on his mother's corpse before the gaolers dragged it away. Ate his own mother's decaying flesh – can you imagine what would bring you to that pass? He died soon afterwards, anyway. God rest them both.'

There was an awkward silence in the solar after de Vesci's impassioned speech. Robin looked down at his tightly gripped forearm. The dark man released Robin's limb but tried to lock eyes with my lord. Robin met his gaze but remained silent.

I had heard rumours of the de Braose family's sad fate, but I was thinking mostly about Duke Arthur and his miserable death at his uncle King John's hands. I had witnessed it personally in the dungeon at Rouen Castle. So had Robin.

He knew as well as anyone what a murderous creature the King was. But, to my surprise, my lord of Locksley merely said: 'So . . . John is not a perfect, stainless monarch. Name one that ever was?'

40

'Not perfect?' de Vesci exploded. 'The man is a disgrace. He is a cowardly murderer of women and children! Almost anyone would make a better king!'

'Tell me,' said Robin, 'how come you to be in England? I had heard that the King had exiled you both on pain of death after the last . . . uh . . . incident.'

De Vesci was taken aback, quite surprised by this turn in the conversation. By 'last incident', Robin clearly meant the last plot to kill the King. De Vesci had been leaning forward and speaking passionately; now he recoiled from Robin, scowled and fortified himself with a sip of wine. It was Lord Fitzwalter who answered for him.

'It is all due to the graciousness of His Holiness the Pope,' he said.

It was my turn to be bemused.

Robin said: 'I see. So John is prepared to submit to the Pope, and the price is your return, and something else . . . what else? The French invasion?'

'What?' I said. This was all moving too fast for me.

Fitzwalter smiled tightly: 'I had heard that you were a sharp one, Locksley. Very well. I shall tell you. But this must go no further for the time being.'

The blond man looked at me. I shrugged, then nodded my acceptance.

'You know that John is excommunicate, and England lies under an interdict,' Fitzwalter said, still looking at me.

'All Christendom knows that,' I replied, stung. 'But John cares little for the Church and its threats of damnation. He once told me, when he was drunk, that he doubted the existence of the Devil. I believe that he only just stopped short of telling me, the court, the world . . . that he doubted the existence of God!'

De Vesci crossed himself but kept his mouth shut.

'What you may not know, Sir Alan,' said Fitzwalter, 'is that the Pope has given Philip Augustus his consent and permission to invade England in the name of the Holy Roman Catholic Church and claim the throne for himself – and for Christ, of course. The French have raised a huge army, tens of thousands of men, two thousand ships, too, and they have the good opinion, not just of the Pope, but of much of Europe in their plans to cross the sea and remove King John by force.'

'Some people might imagine that you would welcome that,' said Robin.

Fitzwalter shot him an angry look. 'We would *not* welcome that, my lord. We would not welcome an invading foreign army on to these shores, laying waste, burning farms, despoiling the land, slaughtering the people. We would not welcome subjugation by France – England becoming the plaything of a capricious French monarch. We are English patriots, not traitors to our land. We had all that wanton destruction when the Conqueror came over in our great-great-grandfathers' day. The north was a wasteland for two generations. Who would welcome

42

that carnage again? That – my lord – is what we are trying to prevent.'

'You have not yet explained how you come to be in this country, returned so soon from exile,' I said quietly.

'Yes, I was coming to that,' said Fitzwalter. He smiled ruefully at me, embarrassed to have lost himself in his passion. 'So the French are poised to invade, and they have the blessing of the Pope. But King John, seeking as always to outmanoeuvre Philip, sent an envoy to the Pope some months back offering His Holiness the Kingdom of England as a papal fief. He is handing the country to the Pope as a gift, as long as he is allowed to remain King. The Pope has accepted, of course. And John will do homage for England to the papal legate in a week's time.'

I must admit I was speechless with outrage. King John was throwing away the country, handing it over lock, stock and barrel to a fat prelate in faraway Rome.

Robin clearly saw my consternation. 'It doesn't change anything significantly in England, Alan,' he said. 'Everything continues as normal – all that changes is that John now has an overlord . . .'

Fitzwalter interrupted him: 'And the French have been told that, on pain of excommunication, they must not invade the Pope's new territory . . .'

'As I said, nothing significant is changed,' Robin cut through his guest's words. 'The French have not abandoned their plans to invade. I have today received a message from William Longsword, Earl of Salisbury, summoning me and all my knights to a general muster to combat this invasion. The French are still coming.'

'What has changed,' Fitzwalter said sharply, 'is that as part of the arrangement with His Holiness, my lord de Vesci and I have been pardoned and restored to our lands and fortunes. We find that most significant.'

Robin got to his feet. 'I must return to my guests,' he said curtly. It was a barely courteous dismissal of the two rebels. 'If you have anything further to say to me, I suggest you say it now. I want you gone from this castle first thing in the morning.'

De Vesci drew a big, sharp breath. But Fitzwalter stopped him with a hand on his shoulder. Fitzwalter said: 'You are a man who has lived outside the law. You have done evil things, do not trouble to deny it . . . Now we ask you to do something evil again, but for a noble cause. For the cause of this country and her people, we ask you, quite simply, will you help us kill the King?'

'No,' said Robin, without hesitation. 'Putting aside the fact that I do not trust either of you, nor like you, I will not kill the King, nor be party to any plot against his life. And for one simple reason. I swore a sacred oath that I would be his man for ever. And I will add something else for you to consider. It is a relatively simple matter to kill a king, but you cannot kill the idea of kingship. If you kill this king, another will take his place. And will he be any better than John? Who knows? He will certainly be more distrustful, knowing that his predecessor was murdered by his own barons. If you kill John, another will be anointed, perhaps a far worse man . . .'

'But as his counsellors, we would guide the new king,' said de Vesci.

'I suspect you would seek to rule through him,' answered Robin.

De Vesci's face flushed. 'We would never presume . . .'

But once again, Fitzwalter stopped him. 'We have had our answer, Eustace.' Then to Robin: 'May I have your word that you will not betray us?'

'You have it,' said Robin. 'I want as little as possible to do with either side in this matter. But I will thank you not to come uninvited to my home again.'

Fitzwalter nodded. De Vesci offered my lord a sneer. And Robin turned on his heel and walked out of the solar and back into the hall.

The two men were making their way to the door of the solar when I stepped in front of them and stopped them with a palm held out flat.

De Vesci looked so angry I thought he might try to strike me.

'I'll do it,' I said.

'What?' snapped de Vesci.

'I'll kill the King for you.'

Chapter Four

As the snake boat approached the flat brown coast of Flanders, I stood in the prow with the wind at my mailed back and rehearsed in my memory the reasons why King John deserved to die. I had to do something to take my mind off the fear that gripped my body and was causing my legs to tremble like those of a man with the palsy. Foremost in my mind was Arthur, Duke of Brittany, who had been my prisoner and later my friend in Normandy. He had been cruelly murdered within my sight in the dungeon of Rouen Castle by two henchmen of John's, while the King looked on and laughed. I had executed the two henchmen years ago, but I felt that I owed it to the shade of my murdered friend to complete the sentence of death I had pronounced in my mind on all three of them that awful night.

This was the most noble unselfish reason for the murder, I felt. But there were other equally compelling arguments for the King's death. In my youth, John had tried several times to have me killed. Years later, at Château Gaillard, despite his promises to relieve the castle, the King had callously left us all to die – and many hundreds of good men, including some very close to me, had perished in that protracted and pointless bloodbath. Their souls must be avenged, too. And lastly, apart from his many crimes, there was the man himself: cruel, weak, lecherous, cowardly, suspicious of everyone, close-fisted even to his loyal men, a ravening beast to any who opposed him. If any man deserved to die, I thought, it was him.

I could feel the eagerness of the thirty men behind me in the snake boat. It was like the tension in a newly strung bow-cord. We were inside the jaws of the estuary by then. To the north, the empty mudflats and low sand dunes stretched away into eternity, with barely a living creature to be seen but for a few white storks flapping lazily across the empty brown marshland. The estuary was about a mile wide at that point and the southern shore could not have been more different to the opposite bank. The French ships were clustered in their hundreds along the shoreline, the ones nearest the land tethered to stout posts hammered into the mud, the outer vessels moored to the landward ships.

The nearest French craft were less than a hundred paces away by now, and the alarm had been raised by the enemy long since. They knew we were coming. How could they not? Our white-sailed fleet filled the estuary like a flock of sheep moving slowly down a narrow valley. But there was something curious about the activity aboard the enemy decks: there was too little of it. There seemed to be far too few men aboard for such a huge mass of shipping. I guessed that there might be as many as a thousand ships all crammed along the southern shoreline that led towards the quay at Damme itself, a couple of miles further upstream. And at the quay, I could see that the ships were five or six deep against the wooden platform. I could just make out, beyond the crush of shipping, the tall thin houses that lined the narrow streets of Damme and a single spire of a church. However, despite the mass of sea-going craft, there were no more than a few hundred unarmed sailors in sight – and no sign at all of the French troops. Where were their knights? Could they be hiding?

Some of the smaller vessels, the furthest from the quay at the mouth of the estuary, were cutting their ties, hauling up sail and attempting to escape, but the wind was still north-westerly, coming directly off the water on to the land, and the majority of the shipping was pinned there by it. A few, those smaller vessels on the very edges of the fleet that we had already passed by, were managing to slide away out to sea – with a good deal of furious oar-work. But soon enough our own fast, light ships, the ones we called sparrow-hawks, were lancing out after them, grappling, boarding and swiftly subduing their panicked crews.

We were now only fifty yards from the quay, the centre of the compact mass of enemy shipping. I was standing in the prow of the snake boat, with Miles at my left shoulder, Sir Thomas Blood at my right, and I pulled Fidelity from its scabbard, and hefted my shield. It was eerily quiet, beyond the creak of rope and the splash of sea on wood. Even the sharp cries of the French sailors seemed strangely muted.

I had been in several water-borne assaults before, and by now the air should have been thick with crossbow bolts and arrows, the enemy fighting men packed inside the ship's walls, but I saw only one lone missile flying out towards us as the fleet bore down remorselessly upon the enemy moored against the grey land. Even that single quarrel, loosed by a single crossbowman in the forecastle of a big round-bellied cog to my left, fell short and splashed into the water before the lead ship.

I looked left at the neighbouring snake boat and caught Little John's eye. My huge friend too was standing at the prow, round shield in one hand, axe in the other. He was evidently as puzzled as I was by the absence of our enemies. He gave one vast shrug and spread his arms in the age-old sign for 'I don't know'.

'Where are they all?' asked Miles from behind me. 'I can barely see a single man-at-arms. They are all just common sailors, no shields, armour, nary a sword between them.' I thought I detected a certain amount of relief in his voice.

'Don't let your guard down, youngster,' I said. 'It could be a trap of some sort. The knights may be concealed below decks.'

But I did not believe it myself, and my head felt dizzy from the reprieve. For I could see that the French sailors were to a man abandoning their ships, hundreds of nut-brown bare-legged men in baggy, dirty white smocks were fleeing, bounding across the decks of the closely moored vessels, leaping from ship to ship, streaming away over the wooden quay and disappearing into the town of Damme behind it. Our lead vessel, the Earl of Salisbury's flagship, had a dozen men aloft reefing its sails and the tillermen were turning the prow to spill their wind, and as I watched, it arced gracefully, slowed and came to rest with only the gentlest of bumps against the round-bellied French cog that seemed now to be utterly deserted. There was no sign even of the lone crossbowman who had loosed at us.

The scores of English fighting men crowding the Earl's ship gave a roar that came clearly to me across the water, and they surged on to the enemy deck, brandishing swords and axes, their steel glittering in the sunlight to be met by . . . nothing at all. The English men-at-arms flooded the enemy deck, the blue and gold fleur-de-lys was swiftly hauled down, and I caught a glimpse of Robin leaping up on to the quarterdeck, his sword in his hand, not a foe in sight and a piratical grin on his handsome face. Behind me I heard the cries of Harold, our ship's captain, to his crew, and, as our own little boat turned into the wind, lost almost all headway and glided up to kiss against the side of a low flat barge, I saw that our enemy vessel too was devoid of Frenchmen.

We tumbled aboard, laughing, for the only living thing to greet us was a one-eyed tabby cat that wound its way around my shins in the hope of a free meal. Trying not to squash it with a careless foot, heavy as I was in my mail and war gear, I led my men across the deserted deck and to the next vessel, a cog with higher sides than the barge, which was lashed to its landward side. We clambered up the steep sides with the aid of netting that seemed set there for that very purpose, and rolled over the top on to the deck of the higher ship, swords drawn.

And once again we found not a soul.

In the absence of their fighting men, the enemy sailors had all fled their vessels by now – indeed, I could see the last of them disappearing into the streets of the town some fifty paces away – and wisely in my opinion. Why risk slaughter or capture? Their role was to sail these craft, or guard them against thieves in harbour. It was not their task to die fighting a vast host of heavily armoured enemy knights.

I felt the blood in my veins cool and slow. There was no fight to be had today. I was light-headed with relief.

No fight; nothing but hundreds of empty ships.

But they were not empty.

'Sir Alan,' a voice called from the doorway of the cog's cabin, interrupting my thoughts, and I looked and saw Sir Thomas emerge, his dark face split by a smile.

'The knucklebones have rolled in our favour,' he said, and I saw that he was holding a pair of silver wine jugs in his gauntleted hands, a golden chain was around his neck. 'Chance smiles upon us for once!'

He lightly tapped the two silver jugs together to produce a musical chime. 'This ship was the property of a rich man, some baron or count. There is a big chest of coin below, a box of jewels, too – a treasury! Oh, the nights of pleasure I could have with all this! And there's fine bed linen, armour, weapons, a dozen barrels of wine, too.'

I looked down at the sailing barge tied below the cog and saw that a couple of my men were pulling back the oiled sheet that covered the hold in the centre of the vessel, and wrestling out huge sacks of grain. It came to me then, like a short hard slap, that we had just captured the entire enemy invasion fleet, with all its stores and provisions, all its wine and grain and cheese and meat and flour, and all the personal possessions of much of the nobility of France – and all without losing a single man. It was a genuine miracle. I could feel the Hand of God beyond a shadow of a doubt.

'Be a good fellow and take that off, Thomas,' I said, pointing at his golden chain glinting on his chest. 'And set a guard on the coin chest and the jewels as soon as you can. A reliable man. No, two reliable men, so they may watch each other. And keep an eye on the wine barrels, too. Nobody is to get drunk, Thomas. Not now. Later we can be as drunk as bishops – as drunk as the Devil on Good Friday. But not now. Understand? Good man. I must away and seek orders.'

I scrambled down the netting on the side of the cog, and jumped the last two yards to land with a puff of dust on the huge pile of mounded grain sacks in the hold.

I looked through the rigging of our snake boat, now empty save for Harold the captain, who sat grinning at the tiller, and saw beyond, skimming across the brown water, a little fishing gig, manned by six oarsmen, approaching rapidly from further up the estuary where the bulk of our ships were now inextricably mingled with the deserted French vessels. And I saw that Robin was seated in the bow, looking as happy as a hungry child with his own bowl of sweetmeats.

As I helped the Earl of Locksley to clamber aboard our snake boat, he was already talking, half-laughing, jabbering at me excitedly: 'I need crews, Alan, crews. Anyone who has ever crewed a ship, anyone who has ever been to sea, or sailed a river, or fished from a coracle on a mill pond – damn it, anyone who has ever got his feet wet when it wasn't bath day. Ha-ha! Salisbury's orders. We are to get these enemy ships to sea. As many as we can. Right now. Minimum crews; three or four men, whatever it takes. We must get these captured boats to sea – with all their cargo, oh yes, and get them back to England. There is not a moment to waste.'

'So we are all going home?' I said.

'Not all of us, not yet. First we get these French vessels to sea. The weather is perfect, not a cloud in the sky, they can be home by tomorrow morning – and we are all, all of us, considerably richer. But first we've got to burn that town yonder. Salisbury wants to make his mark. "We are not thieves," he says to me, the impudent devil. "We are not all Sherwood riff-raff out to steal the possessions of gentlemen. We are soldiers at war taking lawful booty from the noble pursuit of arms!" As if that ever made the slightest difference! The fool. Still, we are under his orders, and they are: get all these ships crewed and sailing back across the Channel, quick-smart; and then I'm to take my company and torch the town. It will teach them a lesson, Salisbury says. The half-royal idiot.'

Despite Robin's harsh words about our commander the Earl of Salisbury, the King's own half-brother, I could see that my lord of Locksley was in high spirits. As usual, nothing cheered him so much as a fat profit. It was slowly dawning on me that we had taken possession of more wealth in the past hour than many a man might gather in a lifetime.

I picked out the few of my men who I knew had experience of sailing the rivers of England at least and put them under the charge of John Halfpenny, a runtish fellow with wispy grey hair and a squashed-in brown face who had been a fisherman and had later served on the merchant ships that plied from Bordeaux to Portsmouth, bringing wine to our shores. They were to sail the captured cog home, and its valuable cargo, with all possible speed. He was a diminutive man-at-arms but utterly ferocious in battle. He wielded two hand axes with deadly skill, and threw knives for sport, too, when the Devil was in him. But he was a good man at heart and I knew that many of the others were a little scared of him. I took him aside, gave him his orders and told him the names of the eight men who would be his crew, and added I would personally flay him and nail his carcass to the mast if a drop of the wine in hold was drunk before it was handed over to the King's men in Dover. He nodded soberly. 'Aye, Sir Alan, I'll keep those thieving drunken bastards in line, never you worry.'

'I mean it, Halfpenny,' I said. 'You deliver that craft to England safe and sound, cargo intact, or it's your ugly head on a spike.'

The little man hurried away, brimming with good cheer, and bawling to his comrades to get aboard right now or face the fucking consequences.

Harold, the snake-boat captain, assured me that the barge we had captured, which was full of wheat and barley, could be crewed by only three men, and I gave him two young men-at-arms who claimed they'd been to sea before and bade him God speed.

All across the Zwin estuary, Englishmen were clambering over their new ships, tugging ropes, loosing sails, hallooing excitedly to their fellows, capering in the rigging for the sheer fun of it. In less than an hour, some of the ships were already under sail and were making their unsteady way under their unfamiliar crews out of the mouth of the harbour and into the broad blue ocean beyond.

We slept in the customs house at Damme that night; Sir Thomas, Miles and myself, along with our depleted squad of a dozen men-at-arms. I allowed a small barrel of wine to be broached with which to celebrate our new wealth, for Robin's company had captured and dispatched to England seventeen vessels of varying size. There were still hundreds of abandoned French ships in the harbour at Damme, but we simply did not have the crews to sail them home. But, you may be certain, we had made sure that we sent off the biggest ones that were filled with the richest cargoes. By my calculations, each of the dozen men now curled and snoring in their blankets around me was worth at least ten pounds of sterling silver – roughly what a working man might earn, with luck, in ten years. A fortune, in other words. So we had drunk wine in good cheer, more enlivened by our new wealth than the liquor, and feasted on a barrel of oysters one of the men had found and barley bread and fat smoked hams and peaches preserved in honey. The younger men, some of my own Westbury folk, talked of setting up as freemen with their own strips of land, and humbly asked if they might clear woodland on my demesne to begin this new life. I happily agreed. Others thought it might be more pleasurable and profitable to own an alehouse in Nottingham or some other town or port. Another thought the life of a travelling pedlar, a chapman, selling silk thread and ribbons, pins and needles from hamlet to hamlet, would be filled with adventure and the chance to meet willing women. So we passed the evening in delightful contemplation of our new lives as well-to-do men.

My last thoughts as I fell asleep were of Robert's sweet boyish face. I had packed him off before we departed for Dover to Pembroke Castle in Wales, the seat of William the Marshal, one of the finest knights I had ever known and an old friend of mine. It had wrung my heart to send him away, after we had been so long apart, but I knew it was the correct thing to do. Robert must train as a squire in a great man's household, and while I knew that William himself would not often be there, I also knew that his wife Isabel would care for the lad and that he would receive a first-class education in the arts of war from the Marshal's well-trained knights and men-at-arms. Still I worried about the boy and missed him sorely, and the thought of him afraid and alone in a strange castle kept me from slumber.

Our parting had been tearful with Robert pleading that I not send him away. I was firm, however, explaining that he must learn the ways of a knight and asking if he did not wish to be as brave and skilful as Miles or Hugh. Then I told him harshly that it was unmanly to snivel quite so much at his age. He must dry his tears. Try to be a man. It was for his own good, I said, hating myself.

To soften the blow, I had paid a visit to my cutler friend in Nottingham to purchase a new hand-and-a-half sword, a fine light blade of Damascus steel in a tooled leather scabbard. When I presented the new weapon to Robert on the day before his departure, telling him that as a squire in the Marshal household he would need a good blade, his eyes opened so wide that they nearly fell out of his head. He rushed at me and crushed me in a hug so strong I genuinely thought he would crack my ribs – my gift, I believed, had partially reconciled him to his fate. Yet, as sleep finally pulled me down, I wished with all my heart that it could have been I who tutored him in its proper use.

The next morning, we hefted shields, helms and spears, struggled into mail coats, those that had them, or leather armour or quilted gambesons, and mustered on the quay with the rest of Robin's men. We had set out from England with a company, or battle as it was more properly known, of two hundred men, but fewer than a hundred souls mustered on the quay that morning on the last day of May. We had sent off more than half our number with the captured ships.

My lord of Locksley addressed the remaining men: 'My friends,' he began, 'we had a good day yesterday.' His remark was met with raucous cheers. 'And we will have a better day, today. Our scouts have reported that the French army is some thirty miles away, besieging the town of Ghent, which is held by the forces of our ally the noble Count Ferrand of Flanders. This town of Damme is near deserted. It is at our mercy. The denizens, men-at-arms and townsmen alike, have fled.'

More cheers.

'Our sector is the south of Damme, the merchants' quarter, and we have orders from the Earl of Salisbury to disperse any enemy force we see and to burn that part of the town to the ground. However, before that, before we set the torches, we may lawfully confiscate any of the enemy's possessions and claim them as our own.'

The cheers were now deafening. Robin had just given his men-at-arms, many of them former Sherwood outlaws, permission to loot the wealthiest part of Damme.

We formed up in a double file, the men happily jabbering to each other, eager faces alive with joy and anticipation, men boasting of the riches they would take and the destruction they would wreak. As we set off through the warren of narrow streets in the north of the city, passing churches, chapels, abandoned shops and houses already ravaged by our compatriots, and marched over the big wooden bridge that crossed the wide slow river that divided Damme north and south, singing broke out in the ranks. I sang too, and lustily.

We had an empty town to pillage and burn.

Chapter Five

After so many years of warfare, as you might expect, I have picked up a thing or two. And here is one thing I have learnt: there are two baneful elements that always go hand in hand with armies and fighting men – disease and fire. I have noticed that more people are killed by disease on campaign than by the swords of the enemy, although, of course, you remember the men who died violently more clearly than those who merely slipped away from life in the infirmary or staggered off the road on the march to die in the fields. The second thing is that the most destruction caused by an army is not done directly by the men in its ranks – despite their most valiant efforts – it is done by fire. In enemy territory, a soldier sets fires by instinct; he steals, he pillages, he takes everything he can get his hands on – then he burns whatever he cannot carry away. There is a sound military logic to this: by destroying goods and crops and houses and shops, he is denying the enemy the comfort of food and shelter and he is directly attacking the power of the lord who holds the land. But there is more to it than logic. There is a wild destructive magic to fire that appeals to the soldier, perhaps to all men. I have never seen soldiers so gleeful as when they have orders to torch a town. Normally steady sober fellows – dutiful fathers, loyal husbands, obedient sons – all become devils with a firebrand in their fists. Their features contort; their hearts are hardened, they set alight homes much like their own with a hearty disregard for the owners, men not too unlike themselves; they fire ripe fields of crops, knowing themselves what an appalling curse a failed harvest is, and that the bite of famine will mean a slow and painful end for the common men who planted the seed. But they burn anyway, with a dreadful, savage joy.

And so it was in Damme.

After we had crossed the bridge to the southern part of town, we looted every house and shop to our hearts' content, and men emerged from these largely deserted buildings grinning, bearing bolts of cloth, chains of onions, live chickens, silver goblets, even a golden crucifix from a rich merchant's house . . . whatever took their fancy. One fellow, a big veteran archer called Peter the Vintenar, who had been with Robin and me at Chalus when King

Richard had been mortally wounded, carried a huge carved wooden chair, almost a throne, with him, humping it from house to house as he pillaged the interiors and set his torch to the eaves. I heard one of his mates ask him what he planned to do with the unwieldy item, which must have weighed a hundred pounds at least.

'Never had no chair growin' up,' he said. 'Just two stools and a bench in our house, and Ma had fourteen children. Sat on the dirt floor until I was twelve and big enough to fight for a place on the bench. When I get back home, I'm going to set this big ol' bastard by my hearth and sit down and never stir again.'

When the house or workshop was emptied of all valuables, the straw thatch was put to the torch, or fires were set in mounds of broken furniture, and we moved on, carrying our booty and singing as we went.

The wind had veered overnight and now came directly out of the north, and in such dry weather – it was another glorious spring morning – we had to work quickly, for one burning house set fire to its neighbour and so on. The heat soon became infernal. The smoke rolled thick and black through the streets; the flames danced orange in the heat-shimmering air. The men's faces around me were brick-red and greased with sweat from the inferno and from their own joyous exertions.

We met a few of the 'enemy', desperate householders and their servants who had not had the wit to flee and who foolishly tried to defend their own hearths with butcher's knives and long roasting spits against Robin's well-armed ruffians. They all died; some swiftly, some in terrible lingering pain. The Sherwood men dispatched them as soon as they emerged from their hidey-holes, chopping them down with their short swords or sticking them through with spears. The men and boys all died; I did not enquire too closely into what happened to their womenfolk.

Such is war.

I kept Miles close by me during the ravaging of Damme, partly to prevent any accident befalling him – the last thing I wanted was for some desperate householder to leap out from behind a door and brain him with an iron skillet – partly to prevent him witnessing anything too horrific.

It was he who first spotted the knight.

We were advancing up a narrow cobbled street on the edge of the town, Miles and I, with three or four of my Westbury men-at-arms. Miles tugged at my hauberk and pointed. There was a lone rider, none too rich by the look of him, but fully armed with serviceable shield, sword and lance. Our street ended in a crossroads, and the knight crossed perpendicular to our line. His horse's linen trapper, a bright-blue cloth that covered the animal from neck to haunch, was thickly spattered with mud and the horse's head was drooping with tiredness. It had been ridden hard and far.

I knew he was French for the simple reason that he had to be. By the Earl of Salisbury's decree we had brought no horses with us in the ships from England. Even the grandest English knight was to fight on his own two feet in this expedition.

So, if my first thought was he's French, my second was, he's not alone.

The knight stopped his horse at the centre of the crossroads. He looked directly at us for half a dozen heartbeats, then he whirled his mount, with great skill and speed, and made off the way he had come.

A scout.

I was already shouting for the men to assemble by the time his horse's haunches disappeared from view. 'The French are here! On me, on me! The enemy are upon us!' I dispatched Miles to spread the word that all men were to rally by the big bridge in the centre of the town on the southern side. Now.

I sprinted up to the end of the street to look after the departing knight.

The street the knight had taken led directly to the town's southern gate, some hundred paces distant. I could just make out the blue mud-spattered trapper of the horse as he cantered through it, and beyond the gate, across the fields outside the town, moving shades of dun and grey, splashes of colour here and there, greens and violets, reds and yellows, and the glint of metal in the sunlight. Thousands of men.

An army on the march.

*

We hurried back to the bridge in the centre of Damme. I was pulling men out of houses almost every step of the way, bawling that the enemy were coming, and we were dead men unless we could assemble to protect ourselves before the French cavalry arrived. But a soldier in mid-pillage is slow to take orders. One grey-haired fellow, a tall, one-eyed veteran mercenary in Robin's service called Claes, who was plunging away half-naked on a woman with her skirts around her waist, had the temerity to snarl and swing a fist at me as I pulled him off his paramour. I dodged the blow, stepped back, put a hand on my sword hilt and he was instantly sheepish and obedient – he was a good soldier, Claes, at heart, and we had known each other for many years. He was still tying his belt as I pushed him out of the door of the house, which I noticed as I left was already filling with greasy, pungent smoke.

The word had got out by now among our men that the enemy were coming and as I jogged into the open space before the bridge, some sort of marketplace with rows of upturned carts stacked against the walls of the tall thin houses, I could see dozens of our fellows already there by the riverbank and scores more come streaming in to join them from the surrounding streets.

We formed up on the southern side of the bridge, with our flanks secured on both sides by the wide slow river. Robin appeared, as if by magic, with Hugh, both grim and grey-mailed head to toe, and between the three of us we got the men into a reasonable shield wall, two ranks thick, forty men wide, with Sir Thomas at one end and Sir Roger of Sheffield, a middle-aged knight, at the other.

'Our scouts report the French in huge number to the south,' Robin said to me, tersely. 'Thousands of them. That's the bad news. But they must have marched all night to get here from Ghent. So they will be tired. That's the good news.'

Robin put a hand on my shoulder. I knew what he would say and I dreaded it.

'I need some time, Alan,' he said. 'I need time to get all our men, Salisbury's and the others, out of the town and back to the ships. There are hundreds of them scattered all over Damme and the harbour. And I need to use my rank to get the other knights to obey me.' He meant that they would not heed my orders. 'The only practical way across the river for a mile either way is at this point, this bridge,' Robin said. 'So Alan, my friend, can you give me an hour? Can you hold them off for me?'

I swallowed. 'Give me the archers, and I'll . . . I'll hold them as long as I can.'

'I'll give you ten archers.'

'God damn it, Robin. Give me every single one of the fucking archers or you can hold this fucking bridge yourself against the whole fucking French army!'

Robin looked at me oddly. 'All right, Alan, you can have all the archers. And Little John, Sir Thomas and Sir Roger – and forty men-at-arms. Hold them as long as you can, then retreat – fast. Don't get killed. Don't do anything stupid. Keep Miles close to you. Ward him well. I'll see there is a ship waiting for you at the harbour.'

Then he was away, running across the bridge, shouting for his squires, with a stern-faced Hugh running at his elbow, and a dozen men at his back. Miles was standing beside me. His arms drooping under the weight of his heavy shield and drawn sword. For an instant, his expression was unguarded, eyes wide with fear and hurt. He looked forlorn and abandoned. I felt the same. I looked down at my own left hand. It was shaking again – indeed, it was jumping like a leaf in a gale.

We made a tight, slightly bowed wall of men half a dozen yards from the southern side of the bridge. Two men deep; shields locked in the front, spears protruding in a bristling line of sharp steel; the shields of the second rank hard up against the backs of the first row. I grouped the archers, perhaps forty seasoned men, many of them former Nottinghamshire outlaws and men from the wild Welsh mountains, on the bridge itself. The structure rose slightly, perhaps a yard higher than the cobbles at its central point, which made it easier for the bowmen to shoot flat over the heads of their comrades. There was a space before the bridge about fifty yards wide by forty, and three roads leading in from the southern part of the town. Gusts of smoke billowed down these empty streets from the burning houses, cinders swirled in the air, and a light fog was forming that obscured sight further than sixty or so yards.

But I could hear the rattle of iron shoes on stone, and the cries of many men and neighing of horses, and I knew that the enemy cavalry was not far away.

Little John was strolling up and down the front of the shield wall. He was magnificently relaxed, the great double-headed axe propped casually on his shoulder, a thick round oaken shield held loosely in his huge left hand.

'Not a step backwards, lads, not one step without I give the order,' he was saying in a conversational tone. 'I swear – by Christ's big fat swinging cock – that I'll chew the bollocks off any man who breaks this wall. Bite them clean off, by God, and swallow them like sweet grapes. Is that clear, you miserable pig-fuckers?'

Then he pushed himself into the centre of the line, in the second row, and rammed his shield against the back of the centre man in the first line. 'Nice and cosy,' he said. 'We stay here nice and cosy and see off these nasty Frenchmen. We hold this bridge till Sir Alan gives the word. Then, it's home to England and a life of luxury. We're rich, boys, and once we've done this little bit of bloody business, it will be honey cakes, whores and hogsheads of ale for the rest of our lives.'

There was a cheer, but it was half-hearted. I could smell the fear-sweat on the handful of men in the pathetically thin line. Many, I knew, must wish themselves already in England. The enemy were coming, and in far greater numbers than we had. And our friends and comrades were even now embarking on to the ships and heading for home and safety. But we were here, and we had to hold the damn bridge.

I pulled Miles towards me, and Claes, the tall, one-eyed rogue, and three other seasoned men from the second line. 'You are the plug,' I said. 'Claes, you know the drill. If the line breaks, you are to come forward and fill the gap. You're in command of this squad. I'll help you if I can.'

And to Miles: 'Stay close to Claes; do exactly what he says. And keep your shield up, head down at all times. Don't try anything foolish.'

Claes nodded his grizzled head: 'We'll keep 'em out, sir, don't you worry. Right, boys, on me . . .' and he led his little section away and into a huddle.

I walked the few yards up on to the bridge where the archers were stringing their bows, strapping on wristguards, and inspecting their shafts for warping.

'Nice day for it,' said Mastin, the leader of Robin's bowmen, a sly thief from Cheshire who I'd known since I was a boy. He was a short, square, hairy man, as bald as a monk on top but furred like a monkey from his beard downwards.

I looked up at the sky. It was almost completely obscured by swirling grey smoke. The heat was monstrous. It felt as if we were baking in a vast oven.

'Well,' said Mastin, seeing my incredulous look, 'it could be raining. The wet plays merry hell with my bow-cord.'

I gave a grating cough that might almost have passed for a laugh, and slapped the older man on his brawny shoulder.

'No fancy business now, Mastin,' I said, 'just kill anyone who comes out of those streets and into the square, all right? We'll hold them off and you kill them. Clear?'

But Mastin was already drawing his long, very powerful yew bow, a yard-long, wicked-tipped arrow already nocked. I jerked around and saw a score or so of men-at-arms in boiled leather armour come dashing out of the smoke from the easternmost street that fed into the space before the bridge.

The arrow whirred by my ear and over the heads of our shield wall; one of the enemy men-at-arms was instantly skewered through the chest. At that distance, no more than fifty yards, the arrow easily punched through his leather cuirass and slammed him back against the white-plastered wall of a house, pinning him there. His legs kicked as he wriggled and tugged at the wand of ash that nailed him to the wall.

His comrades faltered, hesitated, some taking a few steps forward, others stopping and beginning to edge back. Some turned, shouted incomprehensibly into the thick smoke behind them.

'Feather 'em, lads,' said Mastin quietly. 'Don't be shy.'

There was a creaking sound like an old oak door

opening, as forty yew bows were drawn. A cloud of arrows fizzed over our heads like a flock of lethal birds. They lanced into the French men-at-arms; seven or eight dropped immediately, some struck several times. Another volley sped overhead, five more men dropped, and the rest of the enemy sprinted back into the smoke-filled lane behind them and disappeared.

'That the sort of thing you were looking for, sir?' said Mastin.

'Just so,' I said. And this time my laughter was genuine.

I walked down the short slope of the bridge to the shield wall and strode along behind the second rank: 'See how it's done, lads?' I bellowed so that every man in the line could hear me. 'All you have to do is hold tight. Keep the enemy off this bridge, maintain the line and let the archers do the killing for us. We've got the easy job. Just stand firm here for a little while and then it's home to England and—'

I stopped abruptly as out of the smoke curtain across the eastern road entrance, a mass of horsemen erupted like steel-clad monsters belching from the mouth of Hell.

It was only a *conroi* of French knights and sergeants – about thirty men – but they seemed like a ravening horde a thousand strong. They were all in mail, mounted on big destriers, with twelve-foot steel-tipped lances couched. They came straight at us at the gallop, their iron hooves clanging against the cobbles, their war cries echoing eerily loud through the hot, close air.

71

'Stand fast,' I shouted, hauling Fidelity from its scabbard. 'Stand fast, men.'

Over our heads the arrows were hissing again. They smacked into horse flesh and punched through mail, emptying saddles, causing the horses to rear and scream in pain and fear. A company of horses will not charge a firmly held shield wall – a truth that has been the saviour of men-at-arms on foot since our great-great-grandfathers' day. No horse will impale himself upon a palisade of spears. Not willingly.

The arrow flocks flew, again and again, the thrumming sound beating our ears. The carnage was appalling. The French horsemen died as they charged, plucked from their saddles by the wicked missiles, their blood-splashed mounts impaled by shaft after shaft and crazed with pain and fright, bucking and kicking their lives away. But that attack was not stopped. The lead horse of the *conroi*, a grey stallion, its rider long since swept away by the arrow storm, and dying on its churning hooves, kept on coming at us, impelled by the sheer force of its own charge. Dying, dead, its chest stuck deep with a dozen shafts, the huge beast collapsed five yards away from the shield wall, tumbled over its own forelegs and carried on forward – smashing into the two-deep wall of men, snapping spears like twigs and battering through, creating utter disarray in our lines and a three-man-wide hole in our defence.

A rider directly behind the dead horse, miraculously

unscathed by the barrage, put spurs to his mount and leapt the beast's corpse – and he was in behind our wall.

The Sherwood men began to die.

The Frenchman lunged with his lance and transfixed two men, running them both through as if spitting capons. Then, urging his mount further into the press of men, he began to lay about him with a mace, smashing skulls and dropping our spearmen like alehouse skittles. Brave Sir Roger broke out from the end of the line, charging him on foot, snarling, his long sword gleaming – and died. His skull was caved in by the swinging mace like a spoon tapping a boiled egg. Another knight was coming in behind that first Frenchman, threading his horse through the bodies; now he was through, chopping down men on the right of the hole in the shield wall, widening it with great sweeps of his sword.

The air was filled with stinging cinders and veils of grey smoke like silken drapes. I could barely make out the burning houses of the far side of the square. The two enemy horsemen towered over us, huge and immediate. I ran forward, Fidelity in both hands, swung and cut the blade deeply into the thickly muscled throat of the mace-wielding sergeant's horse. The blood exploded, splashing like soup across my face, but even as the animal dropped, screaming and spraying, the man on his back was swiping at my skull with his weapon. By the grace of God, I ducked just in time, the mace's sharp flange merely ringing across the dome of my helmet. But it was enough to drive me to my knees. I cuffed the hot blood from my face with my mailed sleeve, looked up at the sergeant as he loomed above me on his dying horse, his lethal mace raised at full stretch above him – and a bow shaft smacked deep into his throat, punching into the flesh, knocking him back and away.

The second rider was down, too, the horse bristling with shafts, a trio of our men hacking and stabbing at his prone body.

And suddenly there were no cavalry left to menace us – broken mailed men and bloody arrow-stuck horses were writhing, screaming, dying all across the open space before us – but our defensive line was in ruins, and Frenchmen on foot, dozens of them, were now once again pouring out of the smoke, running towards our shattered shield wall. Indeed, we had no wall left to speak of, just a few scattered dazed-looking men-at-arms and two loose clumps of terrified men huddling together – a gap of at least ten yards between the separate groups.

I heard someone cry 'Locksley!' and snatched a glance to my right.

Miles and Claes and the men of the plug had formed a meagre five-man wall and were marching forward in step into the gap between the clumps of survivors of the cavalry charge, their shields locked together, stepping over the corpses of men and beasts. Miles, in the centre of the plug, was shouting: 'For Locksley, for Locksley!' His face was as pale as whey, blue eyes glittering like wet sapphires.

The short bar of five men, as fragile as a sheep hurdle, came into position between the two loose groups of our spearmen, almost filling the gap just moments before the French footmen struck. I was bawling at the men, hauling them bodily into position, shoving them back into the wall, urging them to link up, lock shields with their comrades and brace themselves.

A huge blond figure in grey mail leapt out from the centre of our wavering wall and, howling defiance like a madman, he rushed out alone to meet the first wave of oncoming French infantry, his axe swinging, a shining smear across the smoky air.

Little John barged straight into the mass of advancing French infantry, cutting the leading man completely in half, the double-headed axe carving through guts, ribs and spine in a burst of scarlet. His back-swing decapitated a second man, the severed head leaping high over our coalescing shield wall and bouncing away and into the river. Spears jabbed at John, swords thwacked against his mail, but the big man was a whirlwind of flashing steel and gouting blood – he stopped the enemy charge against the feeble centre of the wall, stopped it dead entirely with his own heroic ferocity. His foes cowered back in fright, or went around him, and space opened up, a hole in the battle an axe-swing distant from Little John. The time he gave us with his lunatic bravery was just enough for me to re-knit the shield wall together.

But he was only one man.

Away from the giant and his gory sweeping axe, to the left and the right, iron mail shining in the orange light of the burning town, the French infantry came on, a hundred men at least in that one charge. They crashed into our wall, batting away our wavering spearpoints and hurling themselves at the line, lunging with swords over the top of the shield rims, stabbing at the faces of our terrified men. I saw Miles duck and take a sword thrust on his helmet, but his head came up swiftly and he killed the man with a beautiful overhand lunge that skewered the hollow of his neck below his Adam's apple and pushed the blade a foot out the other side. Two of our men fell, faces gashed, at the weak join between the five-man plug and the left-hand part of the wall, and once more our line was breached. I took two steps forward, shieldless, into the open space and hacked Fidelity double-handed into the shoulder of a mail-clad man-at-arms who was surging forward with an axe, and felt the jar of steel on bone all the way up my arms. He staggered, the mail split and bloody. I kicked him in the belly, shoving him off my sword, and he dropped. I killed another behind him with a straight lunge to the chest; and lopped the left forearm off yet another fellow beside him, his shield hitting the cobbles with a clatter. But my desperate attack had taken me beyond the line of the wall now and there were enemies all around me. Indeed, such was the ferocity of the French charge that the wall was broken again – no more than a chain of knots of struggling men, French and English, shoving, slicing, hacking, slipping on the blood-slick cobbles, screaming and dying.

This was the mêlée, pure and simple, every man for himself. And with their superior numbers they must prevail.

'Back,' I shouted, 'back to the bridge. John, John, get them back. Now!'

Over the heads of the struggling men, I saw more French footmen coming out of the fire-lit smoke, another two score, massing on the far side of the open space. John was heedless of me: he was surrounded by at least a dozen men-at-arms and he seemed to be fighting them all at once. I felt rather than saw Sir Thomas hurtle past me, and charge into the pack around the big man, reaping lives like a man possessed, and in two heartbeats I was there too, dodging a looping backswing from John's axe and dropping the nearest French man-at-arms with a cut to the hamstrings.

'John,' I shouted. 'We must get back! John!'

Instead we went forward. With Sir Thomas on his right and myself on the big man's left, we waded into the enemy, three men against a multitude. Chopping, hacking, slashing   killing and killing again. We ploughed into the French infantry, cutting into their ranks like an axe through a rotten tree stump. But I remember little of the details: screaming faces, the slap of blood, the jar of steel sword against iron mail. Then suddenly the press around us had melted away, and I was left panting with Little

John and Sir Thomas in an empty space. The enemy, by some miracle, was pulling back. My huge friend was covered in gore and filth from head to toe, his eyes were bright as pine torches and a white line of spittle lined his gaping mouth. But he finally seemed to recognise me and to grasp what I wanted him to do. Turning his broad back on his foes, now glaring at us over their shield rims thirty feet away, he helped Thomas and me herd our living men-at-arms back to the foot of the bridge.

The French were milling around the open ends of the streets that led into the square; summoning the courage for another charge or awaiting the order. And our bowmen were still killing them. A man or two dropping every few heartbeats.

We got our men back, about twenty survivors, to the foot of the bridge, and I formed them huddled in a jostling mass between the wooden railings, shields up, spears forward, our archers – as yet untouched – at the rear. We were packed in tight as fish in a net, but we still held the bridge.

The French were still denied the crossing.

Chapter Six

The cobbles in the open space before the bridge were covered with dead, wounded and dying; French and English jumbled in the ultimate comradeship of pain and blood. The red carpet of agony writhed like a single beast, here and there an arm flailing towards the sky, or a man lurching upright and staggering a few yards before collapsing again. The unending screams and moans of beasts and men scoured the air. I felt a shaft of fear lance through my guts. But for the grace of God, that could well be me out there, sitting in a pool of my own filth, mewling for a swift merciful death. But I could not indulge my terrors while there was still a task at hand. The enemy had not departed the field and we still had a bridge to hold.

Indeed, the French were again massing in the shadows on the far side of the square – ghostly figures through the greasy fog, their ranks massively swelled to several hundred footmen at least, by my reckoning. The tall shapes of formed bodies of horsemen behind. They feared our arrows, for sure, but it was only a matter of time before they roused themselves to charge. Then we were finished.

Miles had a bleeding cut on his face, just below the cheekbone, but apart from that he appeared unscathed. His eyes shone blue and his whole body was thrumming with a violent, nervous energy. 'We held them, Sir Alan, we held them.' He was almost jabbering at me. 'I killed him, I did it. I killed my man. He's dead as a stone!'

'Yes, lad, you did well, very well,' I said kindly. But I could give him only half my attention. Mastin was beside me.

'Well, that was most gratifying,' he said, and grinned at me through his wiry beard, 'but my lads are down to their last arrows. Thought you should know.'

I nodded dumbly. And my eye was caught by movement upstream, along the riverbank that led towards the great trading town of Bruges half a dozen miles away.

'When the shafts are spent,' Mastin was saying, 'we'll muck in with the rest, but our swordplay isn't much and the boys have no armour to speak of . . .'

'No, no,' I said, still not looking at him. 'You've done enough, Mastin. And I thank you. We've all done enough for today.'

My eyes were fixed on the riverbank a hundred yards downstream, where I could see a mass of knights and footmen, perhaps several hundreds, slipping into the river, some holding the tails of their swimming horses, others just taking the plunge and splashing their way across to the far side. On the bank, other men still in the saddle were urging horses down into the flow as well.

We were about to be flanked.

'It's time to go,' I said. 'Mastin, on my command, I want every arrow you have loosed at the enemy, then we'll all go together fast as we can.' I raised my voice: 'You hear that, lads: we will be taking our leave very shortly. On the command, "Retreat", you have my permission to run like greyhounds for the harbour.'

The cheer was more like a groan of exhaustion but I could see chins lifting with the thought of the harbour, ships and home.

Sir Thomas Blood was beside me. His face was a mask of splashed gore and his long-sword dripped. But he seemed unhurt. 'You are to lead them, Thomas,' I said. 'Get them to the harbour when I give the word. Oh, and well done, by the way.'

The young man smiled. 'Lady Luck was with us, Sir Alan – this time!' he said and began to push his way through the archers to the rear of the bridge.

'God's great dangling ball-sack, Alan, surely we can hold them a little longer. I've hardly got into my stride . . .' Little John actually looked aggrieved that we were going to quit this place of blood, suffering and death.

'If we don't go now, we will never get out alive,' I said, and pointed upstream where a few sodden French men-at-arms were already on the north side of the river. 'If they get behind us, we're done for. And I'm not going to die for no reason. Robin said hold as long as we can. We've done that.'

'I could take care of those half-drowned pip-squeaks all on my lonesome,' said John, jerking his chin at the French across the river. 'Just let me—'

'No, John.' I put my hand on his brawny forearm. 'It's time to go.'

'Mastin,' I said to the hairy bow-master, 'give them a fond farewell . . . Now!'

The bows creaked one more time and the arrows flew and were swallowed by the smoke. But I could hear the chink of steel tips on iron mail, hear shouts of anger and pain and make out the shapes of men writhing and falling.

I gave the order. Sir Thomas led the men across the bridge, pell-mell, sixty or so surviving Englishmen only an inch away from panic, sprinting across the cobbles on the far side of the river, plunging into the maze of streets, heading north towards the sea. Little John and I were the last two men off the bridge.

And Miles.

Robin's son was still consumed by the soaring triumph

of his kill, and his white, grinning, bleeding face was close by my left shoulder. It was clear that he took my command for him to stay close to me seriously. As the last of our men disappeared into the smouldering town, the three of us took one final look at the French cavalry moving forward at last in the smoke-filled square and then we, too, turned our backs and sprinted over the bridge after our comrades.

We ran for our lives. I could clearly hear the shouting of the horsemen behind us, the rage of fighting men denied their revenge, and the terrifying clatter of horses' hooves on the wooden slats of the bridge. For a moment, I thought we had left it too late and we would be ridden down. We flew down a wide street with tall timbered houses on either side, and shops, looted and abandoned, gaping open at street level.

A bald man in a bloody apron flew out of a doorway to my right, a butcher's cleaver in his right hand, a snarl on his lips. God knows how long he had been hiding, awaiting his chance. I had no time for thought, Fidelity licked out and plunged straight into his belly. The man was brought up short, impaled on my weapon. His face twitched in surprise and pain. His cleaver rung out sharply as it hit the cobbles. But I did not stop; I tugged Fidelity free from his falling body even as we charged onwards. I could still hear the rattle of hooves behind, and that if nothing else gave our feet wings.

We dodged into a smaller street at right angles to the

main thoroughfare, and immediately turned left into another even smaller lane, then bundled into the doorway of a large merchant's house, and stood there, our backs pressed against the wood of the door, stifling our wild gasps for air to listen out for our pursuers. A short thunder of hooves from the lane, the sharp cries of men, and then silence.

It seemed we had lost them.

The inferno had crossed the river at some point in the last hour and here, too, the air was thick with smoke. It was difficult to see more than a dozen yards in any direction. I gave thanks to God, for that smoke would serve to shield us from enemy eyes. We ran past a church in a small square, where a priest and two young clerics in black robes stood at the door. The priest pointed and shouted angrily at us in French but we paid no heed and hurried onwards. Dead men lay on the cobbles, and a beautiful pure white horse stood miserably with its head drooping, slick red and purple entrails hanging from its belly, dangling to the earth. Clearly there had been hard fighting in this part of Damme, too. Now I saw that there were mailed men ahead of us – French, I had no doubt – although where they had come from I had no idea. We turned right into a street of fishmongers – although no living men could be seen, the stink of their wares was in the air and slim silver bodies were scattered across the cobbles like discarded ingots.

Fishmongers must be near the sea, I reasoned. They must be.

We turned again, darting into a narrow lane, following the sound of seagulls and my own instincts as to where the harbour must be – and after a hundred yards found ourselves at a dead end. The lane ended in a high house wall, plastered and whitewashed, but unpunctuated by door or window. We skidded to a halt, turned and began to retrace our steps, running back up the lane with a sense of dread ballooning in my gorge. I was right to feel the fear, for an instant later a knot of horsemen appeared like wraiths out of the smoke at the mouth of the street. They blocked the road.

We were trapped.

One of the horsemen was decked in a blue surcoat, two in identical red and white; the three behind in black. The knights saw us, the blue horseman gave a shout in French: 'We have you at last, you English rats! There is nowhere to scurry to now.'

I felt Little John bristling beside me, hefting his axe, rolling his shoulders to loosen the muscles. It was six horsemen against three men on foot: no contest.

Nevertheless, I hauled out Fidelity and took a stance beside John and a double grip on the hilt. We would go down fighting; take as many of them as we could.

The lances of the six knights came down as one. The blue knight shouted: '*Vive le Roi! St Denis!*' and the other five took up the cry. '*St Denis! St Denis!*'

They put back their spurs and charged.

'Sir Alan, Sir Alan,' Miles was shouting at me. I took my eyes off the oncoming foe for a mere instant and saw Robin's son beckoning me with huge sweeps of his arm. He was standing beside a big square window set shoulder-high into the right-hand wall of the lane, opening into a house; the wooden shutter was wide open.

I shouted 'John!' sheathed Fidelity and took two quick steps to the wall. As I boosted Miles through the open window, I could hear the ominous clatter of hooves on stone behind me. I shouted to the big man again: 'John, over here!'

Little John glanced over at me, irritation written all over his battered red face. He was readying himself to take on the six knights, who were even now bearing down on him a scant thirty yards away.

He was readying himself for death.

'Come on, you great jackanape!' I shouted behind me and, with the help of Miles's reaching arms, I made an undignified scramble up the lime-washed wall through the open square and into a dim, low room. Once inside, I turned and looked out the window into the light at my huge friend – and I thought then, not for the first time, that John must harbour a death wish. For the blond giant still stood in the middle of the lane, axe cocked above his head, with the line of horsemen almost upon him.

John gave an enormous roar, like a wild bear untimely ripped from his winter slumber, and he began to run.

But he did not charge the line of galloping Frenchmen. Little John turned towards me, towards the black square of the window. He ran full tilt, bellowing: 'Out. My. Road.'

I just had time to shove Miles away from the window, and duck below the lintel myself, as Little John sprinted to the wall of the lane and dived up and through the square space, two hundred and fifty pounds of warrior hurtling into the small room that sheltered Miles and me, and crashing down on a small rickety wooden table in the centre of the room like a trebuchet ball.

I bobbed up, hauled the shutter closed, and slammed down the stout locking bar.

Leaving the three of us in utter darkness.

The sound of metal blades hacking against the exterior of the wooden shutter began only a few moments later. But John's curses and groans were louder still as he struggled to his feet in the wreckage of the table.

'God's great pus-filled bladder. All we do today is run away!'

Already there were chinks of pale light gleaming through the shutter, where the swords and axes of the French cavalry outside were splintering the wood. I could clearly hear their excited cries. I grabbed Miles by the collar of his mail coat and hauled him towards the far side of the small room, scrabbling for the door latch. And we tumbled through into another chamber, far larger than the first, filled with smoke and a grey sickly light. A hearth smouldered with an iron soup pot suspended above it. Platters and pans hung from the walls. A huge mounded fishing net sat in one corner. A few stools were pushed back against the wall next to a trestle table filled with dirty bowls, cups and half a loaf of rye bread. The door stood ajar and light spilled inwards and beside it stood a man.

He was old and frail, his body emaciated, his eyes huge with fear in his wrinkled face. He was dressed in the rags of a grimy once-white smock of the kind that the seamen of this land wore aboard their open vessels. It flapped about his white skinny bare legs. He held an old bread knife in his shaking hand.

'Go away! Go away, English killers!' he said in French in a quavering, reedy voice. The knife was whittled down to a thin, curved strip of iron from years of sharpening. He could barely hold it still in his trembling hand.

Miles gave a shrill cry; his long sword was in his hand. He raised it, rushed at the man and hacked downwards, the blade chunking deeply into the old fellow's skull. The ancient crumpled to the floor.

As Miles levered the bloody blade out of the grip of the dead man's crown, he caught my eye. His face was shining with battle joy, glowing in the gloomy shack.

'Another kill, Sir Alan! I killed another of the French rascals,' he said, his young voice barely lower than a girlish shriek.

I frowned at him. There had been no need to destroy

the old man. A hearty shove would have got him out of our path, perhaps even a word of command. I had no time to contemplate that now. Little John was at the door of the hovel, his wide shoulders filling the frame as he peered into the smoke-filled street.

'All clear,' he said.

We bundled out the door and found ourselves in another lane, almost identical to the last, except that – praise God – it was empty of enemies. And looking to my right I saw above the smoke blue sky and fleecy clouds – and through the murk the wooden walls and soaring masts of moored ships.

We ran, coughing in the ash-heavy air, down the lane, and there we were at last at the quay of the harbour. The muddy water of the estuary had never looked so inviting. I could see ships, a long line of them, each one crammed with our men making their slow progress away and out towards the sea. The lions of England flapped proudly from the masts. And fifty-odd burning vessels right across the sweep of water roaring like funeral pyres. Smoke from the burning town rolled across the bay in thick black banks. The quay itself was splashed with blood and strewn with dead men and broken weapons. There had been a hard fight here, too, it seemed.

It also seemed there would soon be another. A dozen French men-at-arms, a hundred yards distant, boiled out of a side street that opened on the far end of the quay. They saw us and began to shout and point.

89

There was no sign of Robin.

There was no boat to take us away to safety.

I scanned the wide quay. Burning boats, dead men and empty brown water. There was loot scattered all over the wooden planks of the quay: silver ewers, copper pans, legs of mutton, bolts of cloth, smashed barrels of ale. A huge throne-like wooden chair sat forlornly a dozen yards from me, and I saw the body of the big archer Peter the Vintenar lolling in it, his belly a mass of black blood, his eyes staring sightlessly. Our living men were all gone, that was clear, embarked on the last ships to leave the harbour of Damme. And Robin had gone with them.

There was to be no escape. No salvation.

I could see more horsemen now, too, a fresh *conroi* of cavalry in sky-blue surcoats, lances high. And more men-at-arms, this time a score of crossbowmen in green and red particoloured tunics.

The cavalry began to trot forward, lances dipping. I saw that the crossbowmen were busily spanning their bows. And then a low voice behind me, below me, from the brown water said: 'Alan, over here!'

There at the harbour's edge, in a tiny fishing smack, just coming into sight around the prow of a burning warship, was Robin, standing beside a wizened little sailor in the bow working the steering oar who was plainly terrified out of his wits.

'Ah, there you are, Alan,' said my lord. 'Where on earth have you been? This is no time for standing around gawping at the enemy. You've surely seen a few angry Frenchmen before. Quickly now. Jump aboard. It's time we took our leave.'

We watched the town of Damme burn from the quarterdeck of a slow fat cog that was so laden with looted treasure it could barely swim. Robin, Miles, Little John and I sipped goblets of delicious sea-cooled red wine as the ship wallowed out towards the ever-widening green-blue ocean, looking back at the destruction we had wrought. The death of a town is a terrible and strangely beautiful sight: the roiling black and grey banks of smoke, licked by blasts and gouts of yellow-orange flame; burning red embers riding paths through the air like fireflies; the taller buildings roaring like vast torches, the wall of flames reaching up to the dark shifting heavens. A holocaust of houses, a conflagration of the citizens' hopes and dreams, even houses of God merrily ablaze; whole streets sheeted with wave upon wave of dancing crimson destruction.

There was no sign now of the French troops. I presumed that the army and anything that could still move had retreated to the safety of the surrounding countryside as the whole town howled, billowed and burned.

'. . . and then I killed him, Father. Overhand lunge, a blow as deadly as any Templar's, and down he went like a wet sack of sand. I did it, Father! I killed him.'

I closed my ears to Miles's excited prattle and sipped

my cool wine. I recalled the feeble old man with the bread knife in the fisherman's hovel needlessly cut down by this eager boy. But I said nothing either to the lad or to his proud father.

Such is war.

Chapter Seven

Although William Longsword, the Earl of Salisbury, was half-brother to King John and in many ways resembled him, he had an entirely different and far more pleasing character: he was open-handed, honest, fair and brave, if perhaps not as bright as he might have been. Every man, even the lowliest camp servant, who survived the attack on Damme was well rewarded for the success of the raid. And, in truth, they were a depleted number, for our losses had been grievous: five hundred or so men killed in the whole army and a thousand injured and wounded. King Philip's response to our unexpected attack on Damme had been swift. His army had abandoned the siege of Ghent the moment he had heard that our ships were approaching Damme, and his men had ridden and marched all night to confront us at the port that morning. Our little action at the bridge had been a mere skirmish compared with the main fighting to the east and south-east of Damme, where the Earl of Salisbury's men had been caught completely by surprise by the French. The casualties, I'd been told, had been horrendous, as vengeful knights rode down the drunken, loot-happy English men-at-arms, killing at will. It had been a massacre. Our Sherwood men, it seemed, had got off lightly. Indeed, in later years I heard young Frenchmen saying that the battle of Damme had been a victory for Philip's brave knights who successfully drove the cowardly English into the sea.

That is a lie. The honours of battle must surely rest with our arms. We came upon the enemy by surprise; we seized the town and everything valuable in it – then we destroyed it; and we either captured, or burnt Philip's entire invasion fleet to the waterline. It would take months or even years for Philip to muster such a force again.

England was safe.

As our ships made landfall at Dover, and the exhausted army disembarked, the Earl had his stewards set out a trestle table on the very quayside and each man who came down the gangplank was given a handful of captured silver pennies there and then. And there would be more to come, the Earl promised, when the goods and captured ships were valued and sold. But the soldiers' satisfaction was palpable. The alehouses of Dover were thronged for three days and the sturdy whores of the old port, reinforced by their sisters from all over the south-east of England, had never seen such a time of plenty. My own share of the booty from the raid on Damme, which was paid over to me not at the quayside but within a month or two of my return to England by a clerk of William Longsword's household, was twenty-five pounds sixteen shillings and sixpence. My fortunes were repaired overnight. But I did not debauch myself in Dover, much as I was tempted to. For it was there that Robin received the news from the north.

A messenger, filthy with sweat and dust from the road, found Robin not long after dawn in one of the stables of Dover Castle, which had been turned into a makeshift hospital. My lord had been visiting some of his wounded men, bringing them wine and soup and dispensing the victuals along with lavish praise for their courage at Damme. I was a dozen yards away speaking to a Westbury man who had a broken leg, and I clearly heard the messenger's words.

'My lord, it is my duty to report that Kirkton has been attacked.'

Robin's face went white as bone.

'Has Marie-Anne been harmed?' He seized the man by the shoulders and looked hard into his face. I saw the messenger wince at the power of Robin's grip.

'The Countess has not been harmed, but the attackers have done considerable damage to the castle and some men-at-arms have been killed and injured,' he said.

'Tell me the rest on the road,' Robin said, releasing the man. Then: 'Alan, find Miles, Hugh, Sir Thomas and Little John, and gather a dozen fit men-at-arms. I want them all dressed, sober and in the saddle within the hour.'

We were on the old Roman road, pelting towards London long before noon. By nightfall we were in sight of London's bridge, and turning left off the road on to the south bank of the river. Robin announced himself at the shut gates of the Priory of St Mary's in Southwark and demanded entrance. He was immediately granted it, despite the lateness of the hour, and as we stepped down from our horses, a very fat little man in a black robe and tonsure came hurrying out of the refectory to greet us.

I knew who he was, even though I had never met him before. It was Henry Odo, a distant relative of Robin's, some sort of cousin, and my lord's protégé. Robin had mentioned Henry to me several times and it seemed that the young man was a clever fellow but with little money and few prospects. I knew that my lord had sponsored him during his clerical studies at the University at Oxford, and had subsequently arranged for his position as sub-prior in the Southwark priory. I also knew that Robin had corresponded with him regularly during the years we were in the south. Henry had supplied Robin with news and gossip about London and the country as a whole; Robin, on his part, gave Henry a generous stipend that allowed him to enjoy his vast appetites to his heart's content.

Robin embraced Henry briefly but that was as far as

his courtesy extended. 'What news of Kirkton?' my lord said brusquely.

'Welcome to St Mary's, my lord,' said the fat man. 'I have prepared some refreshments in the refectory, some fine Surrey ale, a rather wonderful Somerset cheese, delicate . . .'

'Come on, Henry, tell me what you know.'

Henry looked crestfallen and he glanced at the armed horsemen milling about the dark priory courtyard. 'We'll talk inside,' he said.

Robin said: 'Alan, if you would be so kind – get the men and horses fed, watered and bedded down and then join me in there.' He pointed to a large building to the left of the courtyard. I merely nodded at my orders and watched as my lord strode away with fat little Henry bobbing along beside him.

It was not far off midnight before I had arranged the comforts of the men and horses, and I was able to join Robin in the refectory. He was waiting for me at a long table with a jug of ale and a plate of bread and cheese. There was no sign of Henry. Little John had disappeared with Sir Thomas off into the stews of Southwark and I sat down alone with my lord.

'Have you ever noticed how even-handed Fate is?' my lord asked.

I knew that I was not expected to answer this question. So I merely poured some of the nut-brown Surrey ale into my cup and gave a sympathetic grunt.

'Fate gives with one hand – our great victory at Damme, for example, all the rich booty, our escape – then She takes with the other.'

'Do you know any more about what happened at Kirkton?' I said.

'I have discovered little more than we had from the messenger in Dover – that there were about thirty fellows, who came over the walls at dead of night. Thieves, by the sound of it. They killed three sentries and broke into the hall. Marie-Anne, mercifully, got herself into the keep in time, and with her man Sarlic they held the men off from the battlements. Killing more than a few, apparently. But the thieves ransacked the hall, tore it apart, Cousin Henry says, and pillaged the solar where we sleep, and they went through Marie-Anne's private chapel, too. Boxes smashed, floorboards prised up, mattress slit and rummaged, cushions ripped open, all the plates and bowls and boxes smashed to pieces . . .' He emptied his cup.

'But it is a strange kind of crime, Alan. And they were strange thieves, indeed.' He stopped, silenced by thought. I filled his cup from the jug.

A trio of monks came into the refectory, yawning and rubbing their eyes. They helped themselves to a flagon of ale from the barrel and slices of bread from the board, and seated themselves at a table on the far side of the big room, giving us no more than a brief nod of greeting. I realised that it must be nearly time for the nocturnal service of Matins.

'Why do you think them strange?' I said. 'Half of England must know that you were going to sea with the Earl of Salisbury to fight the French. You were away with almost all your men. Kirkton was but lightly held. There were clearly enough of them to take the walls and they were bold, adventurous fellows, and no mistake.'

I was thinking that it was the kind of madcap escapade that Robin himself might have indulged in in his younger days. Tweaking the nose of a mighty but absent earl, young blades stealing the chattels of a rich man in the dead of night.

'No, Alan, it is not right. It does not feel right. Do not forget that I know half the thieves in the north – some of them are my oldest, dearest friends. And those that are not my former comrades, surely they must know my reputation, surely they must understand that I will track them down and have my vengeance . . .'

'We have been away a goodly length of time, Robin,' I said. 'Maybe with the passing of years . . .' I just stopped myself from suggesting that perhaps the common people no longer feared him, that a new generation had risen without respect for his ferocity.

Robin twinkled at me as if he could read my thoughts, as I sometimes believed he could. 'I know that I have neglected my monstrous side of late, Alan. I haven't flayed a crippled beggar for, oh, many years, nor burnt alive a helpless starveling child in an age, but I did not expect to be chided for it, even silently, by you!'

I smiled coolly at him. We had had a number of clashes over the years, mostly about his cruelty or indifference to the suffering of others. But what he said was true – in truth he had become a little more mellow, kinder, even, in his middle years.

'We'll make a decent Christian of you yet,' I murmured.

Robin scowled at me. 'You would fail to pass for a court jester – even of the meanest sort,' he said icily. 'But I might take you into my service as a fool – purely out of pity at your lack of anything even resembling wits!'

'And I would serve you, my lord, for the same pitiful reason.'

He gave me a half-smile. He had never had any love for the Church, and never would. But we'd known each other too long for these word-jousts to have much bite.

He looked solemn once more. 'Alan, to return to the matter at hand: this business at Kirkton. If you will forgive my vanity, I am troubled by the fact that these villains clearly had no fear of me. Moreover, they did not act like true thieves. There were objects of value – a silver crucifix from Marie-Anne's little chapel, for instance – that they did not take when they left. What thief would do that? And Cousin Henry said something else that made me think. He says I have an enemy.'

'So what!' I said. Robin had always had enemies – what powerful man does not? I could think of a dozen men who'd be happy to see him humiliated or dead.

'Henry says I have a secret foe who hides in the shadows

plotting my doom. He does not say who he is, he does not know, but it is someone with power, or access to power. But ill words are spoken about me, poison dripped in the ears of the mighty; Henry says whispers abound, although he claims not to know what they are.'

I still could not take my lord's concerns seriously. 'Do you think this all-powerful secret enemy is the one who broke into Kirkton and tore up your best cushions, ripped the curtains, smashed all the earthenware cups and plates?'

I started to laugh.

'It's not beyond the realm of possibility,' my lord said, but he was chuckling.

'Perhaps he is a hungry potter who seeks to sell you new crockery!' I said.

'Or an ambitious cushion-maker . . .' he countered.

We were both roaring by now and it took a good while for our mirth to subside. The monks on the far table were frowning at us.

'I knew you would make me feel better, my friend,' he said, wiping his eyes.

I finished my ale and got to my feet.

'We will know more when we get to Kirkton,' I said, yawning, for the drink had fogged my mind and suddenly I yearned for my dormitory bed.

'No doubt,' Robin said. 'Unless some enterprising cabinet-maker has burnt the castle to the ground before we get there.'

*

101

The castle of Kirkton was miraculously intact when we arrived on the third morning after our late-night drink in the Southwark priory. We had ridden hard and fast but somehow news of our arrival had gone before us and Marie-Anne was waiting at the wide-flung gates to greet her returning husband and her two sons. She must have been in her mid-forties then, but she was still a troublingly beautiful woman and although there was a thread or two of silver in her chestnut hair, her blue eyes were still bright and shrewd and her waist was as slender as a young girl's. While she embraced Robin, then Hugh and Miles, and asked about their journey, I stood back and admired her. Once, long ago, I had believed myself in love with her but that feeling had softened into a warm and benevolent regard and affection, a love of some kind, no doubt, but no longer the fiery ardour of a young swain.

For a woman who had been attacked so recently in her own home she seemed remarkably calm and self-possessed. And despite all our merry-making at the expense of the unknown attackers it must have been a terrifying experience for the mistress of the castle to find armed men in her home at the dead of night.

When she came over to embrace me and welcome me to the castle, I looked into her eyes and asked her how it had been for her. She looked around quickly. Robin was deep in conversation with Sarlic, a tough former outlaw who was Marie-Anne's personal bodyguard. His arm was bandaged and hung in a sling across his chest.

Robin's two sons had disappeared into the stables with the horses, and Little John had made straight for the big barrel of ale on the far side of the courtyard set up by the pantry and was filling himself a vast wooden mug.

'It was awful,' Marie-Anne said. 'They were all in black clothes, and the night was dark, and they swarmed, Alan, they swarmed like rats over the walls and across the courtyard. Like a black tide of vermin. I have never been so frightened – I have not felt fear like that since I was a girl, since Murdac took me . . .'

Sir Ralph Murdac, may he rot in Hell, once High Sheriff of Nottinghamshire, had captured Marie-Anne a lifetime ago, held her at Nottingham and raped her. Indeed, though no man dared speak of it in public, Robin's eldest son Hugh was a product of that forced coupling. I had not thought of Murdac, that vile lavender-scented creature, in years. But for Marie-Anne, clearly, he lived on in her nightmares.

'Sarlic behaved quite superbly, of course,' Marie-Anne said. 'He was up and armed and ready to fight in a couple of heartbeats. He and his men cut us a bloody path right through them from the hall into the keep, and we got inside there safely and barricaded the door . . .'

I looked behind her at the big round tower that dominated the western side of the castle. I could see marks of scorching on the wooden walls.

'. . . and we kept them out without too much trouble. Sarlic's bowmen killed or wounded a dozen attackers. Any they could see in the darkness they killed. But they were all over the place. They completely ruined my hall and my solar. Our bed is in tatters, Alan, it has been ripped to pieces, the curtains, pillows, even the mattress . . . I don't know what Robin will say when he sees the damage they have done.'

'He will simply be happy that you are not hurt,' I said.

Robin had been right, there was something strange about the attack. Marie-Anne had said that these attackers wore black – it was the most expensive colour of cloth, worn by rich noblemen and some wealthier members of the clergy. To dye a woollen cloak a deep black meant that you needed to spend time and money on the repeated dyeings with expensive ingredients. Very poor people did not bother with dyeing their cloth at all or wore cheap brown russet garb.

These 'thieves' were rich men, I thought, or were in the service of a rich man.

I strolled over to where Robin and Sarlic were talking and the bodyguard nodded a brisk but cool greeting to me. For some reason, Sarlic did not care for me overmuch. I did not know why, but I had never let it trouble my sleep.

At a pause in their conversation, I said: 'These men, Sarlic, these attackers – did they seem to you to be well trained?'

He gave a short nod.

'To the level of a knight's skill?' I persisted.

The bowman looked unsure. 'Perhaps,' he said. 'Perhaps not. It is hard to say. But they had at least the skills of a decent man-at-arms, or a good squire.'

'What did you do with the corpses?' I asked. 'Are they already in the ground?'

Sarlic frowned at me. 'No, Sir Alan, it is a most curious thing. When we drove them off, in the darkness in the heat of battle, they stopped and made sure that they gathered all their dead and wounded and took them with them when they retreated.'

'What do you think their intention was, Sarlic; what did it feel like to you?'

The old warrior looked at me steadily for a long while: 'I would say –' he turned to Robin – 'and begging your pardon, my lord, for I know you have suffered a valuable loss of goods and chattels – that these men did *not* come to rob you.'

'What did they come here for then?' said Robin. 'Tell me, Sarlic give me your true and honest answer.'

'I would say that their intention was to cause fear. I would say that the intention of these men was to frighten my lady, the Countess of Locksley.'

Chapter Eight

I had sent word to Baldwin at Westbury that I would be a few days in Yorkshire with Robin and the very next day a rider from my manor appeared with a letter for me. It was a summons to a summer celebration at Alnwick Castle.

'To Sir Alan Dale, the knight of Westbury in the county of Nottinghamshire, greetings . . .' it began, and it continued, in the most flowery language, to praise my skill as a *trouvère* and prowess as a noble (ha!) knight. The letter took a dozen lines of closely written parchment to invite me to an outdoor feast to be held at the end of the second week of July on St Swithun's Day and implored me to bring my vielle and to treat my fellow guests to a display of musical virtuosity. The missive finished with the words: 'I hope very much that we will find the time amid the revelries to discuss an important matter of mutual interest.'

It was signed Eustace de Vesci.

I had not forgotten my promise to help de Vesci and Fitzwalter to kill the King. Nor had I changed my mind. I had merely been pondering how I might do it. For some reason, I had it fixed in my head that I must look the King in the eye as I killed him – some tangled notion about the sanctity of kingship or perhaps to soften the terrible crime of regicide in some way. I was not clear in my mind, to be perfectly honest. I would have liked most of all to have challenged him to a duel and killed him fair and square like a man, but that was clearly not possible. He was a damned coward but, more importantly, he was also the King of England and if he even knew I harboured thoughts about his death he would have me snuffed out like a cheap tallow candle. But if I could manage the task in any other way, I would rather not murder him like a thief in the night, creep into his bedchamber and cut his throat while he slept. I wanted to do it in daylight, for him to see my face as he died, and for me to say the words I had prepared in my mind for all the world to hear:

'This death is made in the memory of Arthur, Duke of Brittany, whose murder at your orders I witnessed with my own eyes. Arthur, thou art avenged!'

There was one other very significant factor in planning the death of King John. I wanted to survive the event myself. At John's court there were always dozens of knights and barons present, mostly armed, as well as scores of royal guards, bachelors of John's household, mercenaries loyal to him and other warlike men who were likely, at the first cry of 'Assassin', to cut me down in an instant.

It was no easy task, I may assure you, and in the days after I received the summoning letter to Alnwick, I gave the matter some serious thought.

Robin's mind, meanwhile, was preoccupied with the well-trained, richly clad 'thieves' who had apparently tried to frighten his lady.

One morning he took me with him, me alone, and we rode south into the northern reaches of Sherwood forest. He had told me not to wear anything too rich and gaudy but to be well armed. We rode fast all morning, with Robin leading me down narrow secret paths that even I, who had lived in the region for many years, did not know. Noon found us in a sun-lit clearing, apparently empty of life. And Robin stopped his horse, pulled a horn from his belt and gave two sharp blasts on the instrument. There was no response and, after a while, Robin put the horn to his lips once more. But before he could wind, I put a hand on his arm and stopped him.

My spine was crawling with a thousand invisible insects. For somehow I knew that we were no longer alone. I scanned the foliage around the edges of the clearing and although I could see nothing in the gloom of the woods except shapes and shadows, I was aware that many eyes were upon me.

'Do not touch your sword, Alan, or any weapon,' said Robin quietly.

'You all know me,' he said more loudly, his voice echoing around the open space. 'You know my name; you know my reputation. Show yourselves.'

And, accompanied by a rustling from all around us, a dozen armed men stepped out into the clearing. At least half of them carried rough ash bows with arrows nocked, but the rest had rusty swords, long knives, wood axes, even makeshift pikes, fashioned from old blades strapped to long staves.

'My lord of Locksley,' said a tall, very thin man, his face drawn with pain and his right arm swathed in a filthy bandage, 'you honour us with your presence. Put up your weapons, lads – it is Robin Hood himself, returned to us at long last.'

Robin got down from his horse, walked across the space to the tall man and enfolded him in a warm embrace.

'Godric, it warms my heart to see you,' said my lord. 'You know my friend Alan Dale, of course.'

I dismounted into a sea of smiling, grimy and oddly familiar faces – although I was certain I had never met any of them before in my life. It struck me then that I was looking at faces from my youth, the faces of the outlaws of my first terrifying days with Robin when I was no more than a penniless cutpurse on the run from the law.

Godric and his band welcomed us, and feasted us, after a fashion, on a thin stew made from a brace of wild hares, which in truth was mostly water and wild herbs. Robin had brought a sack of bread with him and a skin of wine, and the men – and now women and children, who appeared shyly from the undergrowth to join the throng – passed the skin around drinking greedily and fell on the loaves, tearing them apart and using the crusts to wipe their bowls clean of the last drops of the stew.

Then we all sat carelessly upon the grass of the clearing, while Robin questioned Godric about his doings, gently interrogating him about the possible identity of the 'thieves' who had broken into Kirkton. But it quickly became clear that neither Godric nor any of his people had the slightest idea about who could have been behind the so-called robbery. They had heard nothing and could offer no information at all about the identity of the attackers.

They were a poor, raggedy lot, lousy, very dirty and none too bright, but I could see that Robin felt completely at home with them. Indeed, his whole face seemed to change when he was talking with them, he seemed to become less careworn, less taut, and by some trick of the forest light a good ten years younger. Nevertheless, this band of outlaws did not seem either a very happy or healthy crew. Their skins were tight against their bones, their limbs were meagre and their eyes huge with habitual hunger; the children were for the most part stunted and sick.

Robin asked to see the wound on Godric's arm, and at first the man refused. But after a good deal of coaxing, Robin got the fellow to unwrap the filthy bandage from around his right arm. Uncovered, it was a fearful sight: the hand had been crudely cut off at the wrist some weeks ago, by the look of it, and although the end of the limb had been cauterised with fire, the wound was an ugly greenish-purple colour, oozing fluid, and I could see maggots writhing under the skin. The smell alone revealed the dire state of the infection.

'How did you lose it?' asked Robin. He took the last of the wine, added it to a bowl of boiling water and began very gently to wash the wound. Although Godric did his best to hide it, it was clear that even Robin's light touch was excruciating.

'I was careless,' Godric said through gritted teeth. 'It was in the deep woods near Mansfield and I had just run down a plump young hind with my two dogs. I thought I was alone and was beginning to gralloch the beast when I looked up and saw a Nottinghamshire deputy sheriff and a dozen of his men all around me on their horses. I suppose I must count myself lucky – caught red-handed with a King's deer, I could have been hanged on the spot under the King's damned forest laws. As it was, the deputy sheriff, a cruel bastard called Benedict, killed my dogs outright. He had his men slit their throats, Rollo and Blackie, right there and then. I had no chance to say goodbye or nothing. Rollo was wagging his tail right to the end.'

There were tears in the man's eyes but I did not think they were a result of the pain he was enduring.

'They took my hand, too. Held me down over a fallen tree and hacked it off with a sword. Said it was a lesson for me not to despoil the King's lands. Said they were upholding the King's law. But that Benedict, he was enjoying himself. Bastard.'

Godric had evidently finished his tale and Robin grunted sympathetically. But I was fascinated by the raw, handless limb. There but for the grace of God, I thought – once upon a time, I might have been this wretch with his putrefying stump.

'The wound is bad, my friend, as you no doubt know,' said Robin. 'It must be cared for properly if you wish to live. I want you to go to Kirklees, to the priory a few miles north of Huddersfield – do you know it?'

Godric nodded. 'But they will have no charity for the likes of me,' he said.

'They will. And the nuns there are some of the best healers in the country. Tell them that I sent you. Tell the Prioress Anna that you come in my name and I warrant that she will do her best for you.'

Kirklees. That was a name I had not heard for an age. And I had not been there for nearly ten years. I had thought I loved a woman, a radiant creature named Tilda who had newly joined the priory, and in the madness of my love I had asked her to be my wife. But I came to her with the blood of her father on my hands and she had scorned my offer and had sent me away with her insults ringing in my ears. Matilda Giffard – how I remembered her beauty: skin so pure and white it seemed almost like the palest duck-egg blue, glossy black hair, a heart-shaped face, wide mouth, small nose and blue-grey eyes. And her low, delicious, smoky laugh would arouse a dead man. I wondered if she still lived and if so whether the years had been kind to her. She would be nearly thirty now, and surely the bloom of her looks was long gone and she was now a dried-out nun, stern, severe, godly. A true bride of Christ.

It was time to go, but Robin seemed strangely loath to leave. He spoke with each of the men in the band, listening to their grievances, offering his solemn respect for the harshness of their lives, sometimes making a jest to raise a smile. As we collected our horses and made to leave, Robin slipped Godric a purse of silver pennies and told him that any man in his band, if necessity pressed him, might take a deer or two from his lands without fear of harm. Then he offered to take any able-bodied brave young man who sought adventure into his service as a man-at-arms.

Godric thanked him but demurred. 'We are people of these woods, my lord,' he said, embracing Robin once more, 'we are not warriors. We'd be sorely out of place in a fine castle. This is home; we shall not leave it unless the sheriff forces us out.'

As we rode back to Kirkton, both Robin and I were quiet, cantering easily side by side through the gathering darkness. My lord spoke only once. 'We have travelled a long, long road, Alan, you and I,' he said as we reined in to look up at the cheery lights of the castle on the crest of the hill. 'We can never truly go back down it.'

Three days after that afternoon with Godric's band, Robin asked me to accompany him again when he went hawking with his son Hugh. We had a good day's sport – a brace of mallards and a fat roebuck – but I could not help thinking of the hungry folk of the woods and that dampened my pleasure a good deal.

We were walking our tired horses down in the Locksley Valley by the river, heading west back towards Kirkton with the hunt servants, the dogs, the equipment and the silent hooded hunting birds trailing behind us, when Robin opened his mind to me.

'I cannot understand it, Alan,' he said, 'Godric and his friends have made enquiries from Derby to Doncaster and they report that everyone claims utter ignorance of the men who attacked us. I've even offered a reward. Nobody knows anything. I am at a complete loss.'

I too had been pondering the mystery.

'Have I told you about the sheriff of Nottinghamshire's

depredations on Westbury?' I said. 'His men stripped the place almost bare while we were away. His armed men forced their way in and took my livestock, grain, my silver . . .'

'You did tell me, Alan, and I am sorry for it, but could we discuss that later.'

'No, no, you misunderstand me, my lord. I can deal with it perfectly well on my own. I meant only to say that Philip Marc has been ordered by the King to raise money by any and all means in Nottinghamshire – by force, if necessary. I was merely going to ask you how things stood with you and the sheriff of Yorkshire.'

Robin stared at me in astonishment.

'You think . . . You think these were the sheriff's men?'

'I don't know,' I said. 'But it is a possibility, isn't it?'

'I used to get on fine with Roger de Lacy, when he held the office. Remember him from Château Gaillard, Alan?'

'How could I forget,' I said. Robin and I had taken part in the bloody siege of Château Gaillard some ten years ago, and Roger de Lacy had been the mule-stubborn but somewhat heroic castellan of the castle, under whose banner we had fought.

'Well, de Lacy went off to quell the Welsh a few years back. Then we had another fellow in the post, FitzReinfrid, who was harmless enough. But he was removed – corruption I think, or incompetence, or maybe he just fell foul of the King. I don't know the new man. I've been away too much in recent years. He's a Percy, I'm told; Richard, or Roger, I think, and he was appointed a few months ago.'

'His name is Robert de Percy, Father,' said a voice from behind us.

Hugh moved his mud-spattered horse up between Robin's mount and mine and the boy continued in his quiet confident voice: 'He is a young fellow, eager to make his mark on the world, and he has a good reason to hate us – or at least hate Mother.'

'What is this?' Robin had gone pale. 'Why would anyone hate your mother?'

'It might be nothing at all,' said Hugh. 'I am merely following up Sir Alan's thought that these villains who attacked us might be the King's men. De Percy came to Kirkton some months back – you were away in France – with a royal demand for tallage. Mother let him in the castle, and Miles and I entertained him as best we could. We gave him meat and wine, looked after his horses, housed and fed his men – and then Mother examined the demand for tax in close detail.'

'Why am I only hearing about this now?' said Robin.

'We thought it of little account,' said Hugh. 'The demand was for a preposterous amount, ten thousand marks, and Mother spoke to the sheriff quite sternly. She said that we had already paid our taxes for that year. And we had paid an additional amount in scutage for your absence from the King's host. And she said she had even made a voluntary loan to the King of several hundred pounds in silver. Then she showed him the receipts she had obtained from the clerks of the King's exchequer for all these payments and told him that his demands were outrageous, even criminal, and that he ought to be ashamed of himself coming to her home in this way and badgering a poor defenceless old lady while her husband is away at war.'

Robin smiled. 'Your mother is a fine woman, Hugh,' he said, 'never forget it.'

'I was very proud of her, Father. She sent him off with his face glowing with shame. And, just to be certain, Sarlic and his bowmen lined up on the castle walls as the sheriff was leaving, with a few of our local village boys kitted out with spare bow staves to swell the numbers a bit. Miles and I put on full armour and exercised with a dozen lads in borrowed hauberks in the courtyard. It wasn't a subtle message to the sheriff – but it was a perfectly clear one. We will meet any force with force.'

'He has not returned since?' Robin said.

'No, but word of his humiliation has spread,' Hugh said. 'I heard a jongleur in an alehouse in Sheffield singing a rude ditty about the affair. It describes Robert de Percy as a naughty schoolboy being scolded by a great lady for his greed. He will have heard it, too, no doubt, and I doubt he loves Mother much as a result.'

I was impressed by Hugh's tale. I could easily imagine Marie-Anne standing up to the young Robert de Percy, her blue eyes flashing as she scolded him like an errant child, finally dismissing him and sending him forth from the castle empty-handed, with his tail between his legs. For a brief moment, I wished that Baldwin had shown a similar strength of character at Westbury when the sheriff's men came to call.

'What do you think, Alan?' said Robin.

'I think she's a magnificent woman.'

'Yes,' said Robin drily, 'but if you could tear your thoughts away from my wife's magnificence, do you think this Percy creature could be behind the attack?'

'I think it's quite possible, even probable,' I said. 'He might hope to intimidate Marie-Anne into paying up, and at the same time have seized a few valuables as a compensation for his hurt pride. But there is no way of knowing for sure.'

'There is,' said Robin quietly. 'I shall pay him a visit with Little John. And I will discover whether this is the man who thinks he can bully my wife.'

There was something about Robin's tone that sent a shiver down my spine.

'Would you like to come with us, Alan?' he asked.

I looked at my lord and saw that his eyes were the colour of wet slate.

'I cannot come with you, my lord,' I said. Although what I truly meant was that I did not wish to. I did not wish to see Little John tear the skin from this ambitious lordling or rip out his fingernails in an attempt to get at the truth.

I said: 'I'm sorry, but I must return to Westbury to prepare myself for Alnwick.'

The moment I said these words I regretted them. I had said nothing of my invitation to Eustace de Vesci's castle, and nothing of my vow to commit regicide.

'Alnwick?' he said. 'Alnwick – oh, Alan, what have you done?' My lord was nothing if not quick off the mark. 'You have become entangled with de Vesci and those other fools, haven't you? What does he want of you?'

'Ah, ah . . . I am to play music at a feast there. That is all. A little poetry for his guests.' I'm not a natural deceiver and Robin, who was, shook his head in disgust.

'You are lying to me,' he said, not angry but rather sad. 'I think I know why. You have accepted the commission they offered me, concerning the King.'

He glanced behind him to see that the servants were out of earshot. 'Alan, do not be a fool. Do not do this thing. These people would use you. They will make you their tool and then allow you to shoulder the full blame for the crime. Do not do this deed, I beg you. You will bring disaster on us all.'

'I am simply going to Alnwick to make music,' I said stiffly. But even to my own ears the falseness of my words was horribly obvious.

Robin and I did not speak again for the rest of the ride home and, as my lies had made things uncomfortable between me and my lord, that evening I made up my mind to return to Westbury.

'Alan, may I speak with you?' said Marie-Anne that last night. We had finished our awkward supper, Robin had retired to bed and I was sitting by the hall fire with a cup of wine by my boot thinking how pleasant it would be to return to my own hearth.

The Countess of Locksley pulled up a stool and sat down next to me. She lifted an iron poker from the stand and poked at the logs ablaze in the hearth, causing a shower of sparks to rise and new flames to dance merrily. In the firelight, she looked even more beautiful than in the glare of day.

'I have never thanked you for Damme,' she said. 'For warding Miles during the fighting, and bringing him home to me safely.'

I grunted a less than gracious reply.

'As a father, Alan, you know what anguish can come even from contemplating the death of a loved one, a husband or child. How would you feel, for instance, if in a few years' time Robin was to take your Robert off to war and return without him?'

Her shaft struck home. Even at the thought of such a distant tragedy, my blood ran cold. I squirmed on my stool. I could see where she was leading me.

'Your father is dead, Alan, and your mother, too – may God keep their immortal souls – and I have often wondered if the reason you are so careless of your own life is because you believe there is no one who would mourn you if you fell. Is that the case? Is that why you are so brave?'

'I have never thought about it. I just do what is required of me, I do my duty to my lord as best I can. It is certainly not bravery . . .'

'I think it is, so does Robin. You must know that we both care for you very much – in all the years we have known you, you and Robert have become as much a part of our family as Hugh and Miles. You must know that we love you. You must know that we would be heartbroken if you were to perish. Do you know it? Do you?'

I mumbled some form of assent. I knew it. I could not deny it. I loved them too.

'And this is why, Alan, you must give up this foolish plan to murder the King. Even if you succeed you will bring war, death and destruction down on all of us who love you: myself, Robin, Miles and Hugh – and especially your Robert . . . If you fail you will die miserably in the worst kind of pain, but I expect you would risk that. But know this: if you fail, the King will also have his vengeance on all of us.'

I had to get away from her and her softly spoken good sense. I could feel my resolve to undertake this killing weakening, melting like a candle too close to the fire.

I lurched to my feet and bid my lady good night. As I stumbled away from the hearth, I found that my cheeks were damp with tears.

121

Chapter Nine

On my return to Westbury the next day, I applied myself to a host of different tasks that demanded my attention. I bought a large quantity of new animal stock in the market at Nottingham – horses, cattle, pigs and sheep – to replace those appropriated from me by Sheriff Marc, I consulted with Baldwin about some repairs and new buildings to be constructed in the compound, and busied myself over the next few days setting the manor in order.

In late June, the weather turned foul and Westbury was lashed for several days with a series of prodigious thunderstorms. I kept to the hall, mostly, poring with Baldwin over the manor accounts and looking for ways to make the prize money I had gained in Damme go as far as possible. I seemed to have spent a good deal of it already and the bad weather was threatening to ruin the harvest – something I dreaded more than anything else. For even a man such as myself, a knight with lands and livestock, the threat of hunger was very real, and one bad harvest could have me tightening my belt. For the common people of Westbury it could mean death by starvation, although I would not allow that to happen while I still had any means at all. This was why the sheriff's outrageous demands for tax-money hurt even the King's wealthier subjects: we all had hundreds of hungry mouths to feed apart from our own families. That is not to say that we landowners would feed our starving peasants purely out of Christian charity: the tenants who worked our lands were the ones who made our living possible, their rents and services kept us. A dead villein harvests no barley, as the saying went. We needed them alive and well and working our lands.

I was standing in the hall doorway one evening and looking out over the sheets of grey rain as they pounded my lands and battered the crops, when I heard a cry from the sentry above the gatehouse and saw two of my men-at-arms hurrying forward to swing open the double gates of the compound. To my utter astonishment, a slight bedraggled figure on a magnificent destrier cantered through the opening gates, and slipped, almost fell, from the horse's back.

It was Robert.

I walked out through the pouring rain to greet my son

with my brain bubbling with questions: what was he doing back at Westbury? It had been less than a month since I sent him off to Pembroke Castle to begin his training as a squire – why had he returned so soon? Had disaster befallen him? Where had he got such a fine horse?

I managed to curb my curiosity until I had the boy inside the hall, stripped of his sodden clothes, wrapped in warm blankets by the hearth fire and sipping on a cup of hot, spiced wine and munching a honey-cake. But something was clearly very wrong. All the while that Baldwin and I were ministering to his comfort and health, bearing away his dripping tunic and hose, swathing him in fresh dry coverings, Robert did not speak; worse, he did not respond to my cheery prattle about the foulness of the weather. Neither did he look me in the eye at any time. He showed few signs of life at all except when Baldwin tried to remove his damp braies, the linen under-shorts that guarded his modesty, and then he snarled at my steward – a kindly old man who had cared for him since he was a baby – and slapped his hand away with something akin to ferocity.

Finally, with Robert cocooned in blankets and when the hot wine had put some colour back into his pale cheeks, I asked him what was amiss.

'I did not care for Pembroke,' he said sullenly. 'There are beastly people there. I want to stay here at Westbury – with you, Father – I want to stay at home.'

'Tell me, what happened?'

Robert said nothing, he sat there sipping his wine and staring blankly into the flames. I asked him again, feeling my own anger beginning to stir.

Once more, my question was met by silence.

'Tell me at least where you got the horse.'

'I did not want to go to Pembroke,' Robert said. 'I told you so from the beginning; I did not want to go and you sent me anyway. This is all your fault.'

'The horse, Robert; who does it belong to?'

He shrugged. 'I had to get out of there. It was there, already saddled and bridled in the stables, so . . . I took it.'

'You *stole* a destrier from the Earl of Pembroke? You robbed your *host*?'

Robert again relapsed into silence. And realising I was likely to get no more out of him that night, I sent him to bed.

I stayed up late thinking. Part of me was intensely proud of my son. He had ridden across the country, hundreds of miles alone on a strange and powerful beast through lands populated by enemies, brigands, rapacious men of all kinds, and made it home all the way from Wales safely. Part of me was appalled at what he had done. I had asked England's most renowned warrior William the Marshal to take my son into his household as a favour and to train him as a squire and ultimately make him a knight, and he had repaid the Earl of Pembroke's kindness with the theft of a valuable animal and desertion from his post. I did not know what had happened to Robert but, whatever it was, it could not have been so bad as to warrant this disgraceful display of churlish behaviour.

The next day I beat Robert.

It tore my heart to do it but I beat him hard on the bare buttocks in my solar with an ash rod no thicker than my finger, and I was pleased to see that he tried his hardest not to show the pain. When it was over I felt a great wave of shame and disgust at my actions – who was I to punish a boy for thievery? – but I knew I had fulfilled my duty as a father. However, when I told Robert he had to return to Pembroke with the horse, he absolutely refused. He defied me with his face blazing.

'I would rather die than return to Pembroke,' he said, his face blotched with tears. 'I will cut my own throat before I ever set foot in that foul place again.'

And like a weakling, I gave in to his threat.

I sent the war horse back myself with a pair of Westbury men-at-arms, and a message to the Earl of Pembroke containing a humble apology for my son's behaviour. Robert stayed out of my way for several days, but within a week things had assumed a more normal state of affairs and harmony was restored between us.

Although Robert never gave me a full account of what had happened at Pembroke, as he relaxed into life at home, I did gather scraps of information about his experience there. He had not got on well with the other boys there – they had teased and taunted him for his fantastical tales of unicorns, phoenixes and other legendary creatures, and mocked his lack of skill as a warrior. Well, they were boys. And it seemed that the man responsible for training the squires, a Templar knight called Brother Geoffrey, who was also the Marshal's almoner, had been a hard task-master. It was evident that he had not been as kindly as he might have been to Robert – for the boy could barely speak his name without grimacing. This Brother Geoffrey, I guessed, had not been satisfied with Robert's efforts and had singled him out for punishment on several occasions, forcing him to labour harder and longer than the other boys. This was hardly surprising – the Templars had high standards, they were after all the finest warriors in Christendom, and I knew that their training routines were famously gruelling. Moreover, it was, in a way, my fault. I had been neglectful of Robert's military education – he was eleven, and in a few years he might be expected to fight in battle, and I had scarcely prepared him for that trial.

I determined that I would remedy my mistake and, ten days after Robert's return to Westbury, I introduced him to his new sword-master.

Sir Thomas Blood was Robin's man, sworn to his service. But he was also an old and trusted comrade of mine. At one time he had been my squire – and he had proved superlative in that role: quietly competent, caring for my war gear and anticipating my needs like the very best of servants. He was an extraordinary man, to my mind: brave as a lion and a talented warrior with sword, dagger and lance. Indeed, he had even invented a kind of unarmed combat, a set of throws and strikes, locks and holds, that made him almost as dangerous without weapons as he was with a blade in his hands. Robert could scarcely have a better mentor to teach him how to be the perfect squire and from whom to learn the deadly arts of the knight.

Sir Thomas was not, however, without his flaws. He had agreed to take a temporary leave of absence from Robin's service (with my lord's blessing) and come to live with me at Westbury not only out of friendship but also for the promise of a stipend in silver every month. This was not because he was a greedy man, in love with lucre for its own sake, but because he had a weakness for gaming and had been rather unwise. He loved to play knuckle-bones, the various games of chance that were ruled by the rolling of dice, and he would play whenever he got the opportunity with whomsoever would wager with him. And he seemed to lose all moderation when in the grip of his passion for the 'bones', as he called them; I had known him to wager as much as a hundred marks on a single throw. Thomas had had a long streak of bad luck with the dice since his return to England – so much so that he had been forced to pledge money that he did not have. Ashamed of his foolishness, rather than going to Robin to humbly ask for the money, he had borrowed from the brothers of the Temple in London, some of the richest men in England, who were always ready to extend credit to impecunious knights. He hoped to use the silver that I would pay him for tutoring Robert to make good these Templar loans.

Robert seemed wary of Sir Thomas when I brought them together and told my son that his military education would now be in the dark-haired knight's hands. He eyed Sir Thomas suspiciously, almost fearfully, and Thomas made no effort at all to ingratiate himself with the boy. He told him brusquely to arm himself and show him in the courtyard what he had mastered so far.

Robert's first lesson was far from gentle. Within moments my son was on his back in the dust of the courtyard, with Thomas standing over him coldly ordering him to get back on his feet. I began to feel the creep of misgiving. Robert was a sensitive boy – was this dour fighting man the right person to form him?

My misgivings increased a few days later. I had given Thomas a fat purse of silver on his arrival, at his request – he said he wished to make the first payment to the Templars – but the next night, a Saturday, he disappeared, and when he was absent at Mass in the village church on Sunday morning, I truly began to worry.

I asked Baldwin if he knew where Thomas had gone and he said he had last been seen heading for Nottingham, where he intended to pay over his stipend to the Templars' representatives in the town.

I found Thomas without too much difficulty in a filthy tavern at the base of the castle. He did not notice me at first as I came to stand beside him and three ill-looking fellows who were crouched over a square, high-sided tray, the dice rattling merrily inside its wooden walls. The leather purse that I had given him the day before was flaccid and empty beside him, and three silver pennies sat in a tiny stack before his place. Thomas threw the bones and immediately blasphemed in a surprisingly fluent and extravagant manner for someone normally so taciturn. His cackling neighbour, a balding rascal in a dirty scarlet tunic, leaned over and scooped up the little pile of silver in the blink of an eye.

Thomas was still cursing, a foul cascade of the filthiest language I had heard in an age, when he looked up and recognised me.

'Sir Alan,' he said, 'for the love of God, can you give me an advance on next month's wages? I beg you.' His eyes were bloodshot from lack of sleep and there was a pitiful wheedling tone in his voice that I did not care for at all.

'Get up,' I said. 'We are going back to Westbury right now. Our dinner awaits.'

'But, Alan, I have these fellows. I can feel it. I just need one more throw—'

'Sir Thomas, you forget yourself,' I said. 'Come on, now.'

As Thomas stood up, the bald fellow in the red tunic

said: 'Care for a throw, sir? You have the look of good fortune about you.'

I ignored the man and pulled Thomas towards the door.

'He owes us money,' said a second man, a tall, hulking fellow with a purple-and-white nose very like a turnip. All three of Thomas's companions were now on their feet. The foul air in the tavern seemed to chill as if night had suddenly fallen.

I put my hand on Fidelity's hilt. I looked at all three men, one after the other, squarely in the eye. 'You have taken all that he has,' I said. 'So I cannot think that he owes you any more. And we are taking our leave now.'

'He owes us another sixpence,' said turnip-nose. He too had a hand on his hilt, a long dagger stuck in his broad leather belt.

'I say he does not.' I knew I was a hair's breadth away from bloody carnage.

'Er, Sir Alan, I do actually owe them sixpence.' Thomas looked shamefaced, but also quite determined. 'I gave them my word.'

I looked at him in surprise. I had been expecting him to back me in this dispute without question. 'Let us go back to Westbury,' I said, 'we can discuss it there.'

'No,' said Thomas quietly and firmly. 'It is a matter of honour.' And to the fellow in the scarlet tunic: 'Will you accept my boots and cloak as payment?'

'Throw in your chemise, too,' said the man, smirking.

'Oh for God's sake,' I said, and fumbled for my purse.

I counted out six silver pennies and tossed them with a tinny clatter on to the square tray.

On the ride home, I told Thomas that I would be deducting the sixpence from his monthly stipend, and also that I would pay him his fee at the end of his time with us at Westbury, or if he preferred I would pay it directly to the Templars in his name.

'You think me a fool, Alan,' he said. 'But I do not always lose, you know.'

I shrugged. 'You are a free man, I cannot tell you what to do with your money. But if you ever take Robert to a place like that, you will answer for it to me.'

We rode the rest of the way in silence.

Chapter Ten

At the end of the first week in July, I set off on the nearly two-hundred-mile journey from Westbury to Alnwick. Marie-Anne's words a few weeks previously had struck a blow at my heart, but I had accepted de Vesci's invitation to his summer feast. And I believed that I owed it to the lord of Alnwick and his friend Lord Fitzwalter to at least meet and discuss the issue of the King's removal face to face.

I rode north from Westbury alone, leaving Robert in the care of Baldwin and a now chastened Thomas – and I told no one where I was going, not even them. The fewer people who had knowledge of this plot, even if it came to naught, the better.

I crossed the Tyne at the New Castle on the eve of St

Swithun's Day with my mind a little clearer as to my purpose. I would talk with de Vesci and Fitzwalter, I would entertain their guests with my poetry and music, and if we could come up with a plan together that seemed to offer reasonably good odds of dispatching John and allowing me to escape unscathed, I would agree to do the deed.

That night I was received by the monks at Newminster Abbey near the town of Morpeth and at Vespers in the abbey church I prayed earnestly for guidance from the Lord of Hosts. On my knees in the cold gloom of the church, I closed my eyes and whispered: 'O Lord my God, guide me in my indecision. I know that red murder is a sin against your Holy Name, and that my closest friends are urging me to give up this bloody task, but my heart tells me that I must do this deed in the name of vengeance. For Arthur and all the men who have died at the King's hand. Help me, O Lord, send me a sign, tell me if I should take this sin upon myself or pursue the path of peace that your son, our Lord and Saviour Jesus Christ, has taught us. Amen.'

The next day, as I was riding the last few miles through the lush green pastures towards Alnwick Castle, I received the sign that I had begged for.

I was cantering along the sunken road and came around a blind corner and reined in sharply as I saw a big, well-muscled man in peasant's garb with a long knife in his hands standing by the side of the road. Beside him was a dog, a huge beast with its hair on end, its mouth gaping in a savage snarl, and a white froth of saliva garlanding its long yellow teeth. I stopped a good twenty paces from the man and beast but still my mount began to bridle and cavort in fear at the barking animal. My heart was pounding too and I had my hand on Fidelity's hilt, ready to draw and fight – but the peasant made no move to attack me and I could see now that the beast, although it was growling and shaking its large head, was securely roped to a tree.

'Good day to you, sir,' said the man respectfully, and he tugged off his shapeless woollen hat. 'Don't be afeared of Betsy, sir, she's well secured.'

'What is wrong with her?' I asked, dismounting and tying my horse to a clump of alder bushes a goodly distance away on the far side of the road. The dog was still thrashing about on the end of the rope snapping her jaws and seemingly trying to bite the man. I came cautiously closer, hand still on my hilt. 'She looks like she has a demon inside her – or the Devil himself.'

'I don't know about that, sir,' said the man. 'I'm not a learned man, like a priest or monk – or a gentleman such as yourself. But I do know that Betsy's run mad, sir. You see, a while back she was bit by another bitch, who was just the same way as she is now, all frothy and snapping like a wolf, terrible afeared of water, too, and a month or so later she took the madness herself. There's no hope for Betsy, sir, it grieves mightily me to say. No hope at all.'

'What will you do with her?' I asked, keeping a respectful distance from the animal's teeth.

'Well, sir, I was aiming to end her with this here knife. But I can't get close enough without I risk getting bit. And if she bites me, I'm Hell-bound, too. But, well, you see, sir, she was a good and faithful dog, before all this, and to be honest I can't bear to leave her here all tied up to die of thirst . . .'

The man paused and looked at me imploringly. 'She was a good dog, sir. Loyal, faithful as anything. Would you help me, sir, of your mercy, would you help me to do the necessary with Betsy? If I distract her, perhaps you could . . . with your sword? You would be doing me – and her, I reckon – a great service . . .'

I agreed, and as the fellow dodged about just out of reach of the brute's jaws on the one side, calling her name, I came at the dog from the other. I swung with Fidelity once and took her head off with one fast sweep of the blade.

The fellow was absurdly grateful. As I cleaned my weapon on a clump of long grass, he said: 'You are a saint, sir, and I have no doubt God will bless you in all your endeavours.' I merely nodded at him, for I was thinking hard. 'I owe you a great debt of gratitude for old Betsy,' he continued. 'And although I cannot repay you . . .'

'Nonsense,' I said, 'you owe me nothing. In fact, I believe I owe you something for showing me the truth,' and reached into my pouch for a penny to give him.

136

For God had given me the sign I had asked for. King John was the mad dog and I had been called upon by the common people of England to release him from life.

The day of the feast was one of blazing sunshine and, as it was St Swithun's Day, the country folk said it boded well for the rest of that summer. After the rainstorms of June, I was pleased, for it now seemed that the harvest at Westbury and all across the land would be a bountiful one. I took the opportunity of good weather to dress myself in my finest clothes for the celebration: a new tunic of fine sky-blue wool, close fitting above the waist but with the new style of long, wide drooping sleeves and long flowing skirts slit in the front to thigh level to expose my new yellow-and-red striped hose. My hose came with thin leather soles already attached so there was no need for me to wear boots or shoes, and showed off admirably, I thought, the muscular length of my legs. I had a new hat for the occasion, too, a smart black piece, shaped like a cone with a rounded point and a rolled brim. For once, I felt that I was dressed in an appropriate fashion for a feast.

An area of gently sloping sheep pasture to the south of the castle walls had been set aside for the festivities, and once I had changed my clothes in the castle and had a brief wash, I strolled through a makeshift town of brightly coloured pavilions and gaudy tents with my vielle slung on my back. My mood was light, buoyant even, the 'streets' of this tent-town were thronging with men and women, mostly dressed as extravagantly as myself, and I bowed and smiled at the gentlefolk I encountered.

There were tumblers, jugglers, pipers and dancing dwarfs to amuse the knights and their ladies as they strolled about between the tents, and men and maids with trays of hot pies and sweetmeats, sliced fruit and honeyed nuts, and servants with huge trays bearing cups of light red wine from Bordeaux offered refreshments to the multitude. I recognised some of the revellers, with a Yorkshireman here and there, though not many, since these knightly people were mostly from Northumbria and Cumberland, with a scattering of nobles from the Scottish lowlands. For a moment I felt very far from home. But not for long. I took a cup of wine and an almond custard cake from a passing servant, and sipped and chewed as I passed among the peacock-coloured tents. I felt the sunshine on my face and a sense of well-being, merriment occupied my mind in that hour, not murder.

At a space between the tents I saw that tables and chairs had been laid out and a small crowd of ladies had gathered around a well-dressed, fair-haired man who was singing sweetly and playing a vielle rather well. I lingered to listen as he came to the end of a *canso* about a great lady who was loved by a lowly knight, a retainer of her lord. Their love could never be, he sang, and the knight eventually threw himself off a bridge into the river out of love for her. A charming piece, if rather silly, I thought, but well performed by this musician.

I applauded with the rest of them and then caught the eye of the fair, ruddy-faced man who was performing it. It was Robert Fitzwalter, I saw, and among the crowd, almost at the same time, I spied my host Eustace de Vesci, lord of Alnwick.

Fitzwalter was an instinctively courteous man, as I had noticed when we met at Kirkton. He made some adjustments to the strings of his vielle and then silenced the chattering assembly with the words: 'This next work is played with greatest humility as a homage to a far greater musician than I, and in memory of a noble king . . .'

And to my astonishment he began to sing:

My joy summons me
To sing in this sweet season
And my generous heart replies
That it is right to feel this way.

It was a *canso* that I had written long ago with King Richard of England. It had enjoyed a brief popularity many years ago, when Richard was freshly returned from captivity in Germany, and it had had a topical flavour, but I had not heard the tune for many and many a year. Lord Fitzwalter sang:

My heart commands me
To love my sweet mistress,
And my joy in doing so
Is a generous reward in itself.

I had already swept my own vielle off my back, praising
God that I had thought to put the strings in tune the day
before, and together we sang the last two verses of my
work, with myself playing and singing a slightly different
version of the tune that twined around with Fitzwalter's
lines to give a pleasing effect on the listener's ear.

We sang:

A lord has one obligation
Greater than love itself
Which is to reward most generously
The knight who serves him well.

And then:

A knight who sings so sweetly
Of obligation to his noble lord
Should consider the great virtue
Of courtly manners not discord.

There was much happy applause from the gathered ladies,
and several of them crowded around me with pretty
compliments and cooing noises of admiration, and I felt

my face begin to grow red at all the attention. Someone brought me another cup of wine and I allowed myself to be persuaded to play one more piece for the assembled crowd.

I gave them 'Lancelot and Guinevere', and had the ladies sighing; then '*Le Chanson de Roland*', which made more than a few of them weep, and then 'The Fox Lord and the Lady Rabbit' – a ribald tale of vulpine lust and woodland virtue – which made them all roar with laughter. Then I pleaded a sore throat and summoned another cup of wine, promising to play again after sunset in the great hall of the castle. And all the while, as I played my vielle and sang and flirted with the ladies, I could feel the eyes of my lords de Vesci and Fitzwalter upon me, weighing me, or so it seemed.

After I retired from the field of combat, a young man with long curled hair leapt up and began to play a small shrill flute while his legs kicked out in some sort of manic new dance. I gathered up my vielle and bow and sauntered away from the crowds, mostly to get away from the young man and his screeching instrument, but also because I knew that Fitzwalter and de Vesci would surely follow me.

And so they did.

Chapter Eleven

A short while later, I found myself sitting on a gold-painted X-shaped stool in a rather hot and stuffy cloth-of-gold pavilion on the outskirts of the tent-town, quite close to the southern postern gate of the castle, being offered yet another cup of wine – but this one iced and of far better quality than the common swill I'd had before.

The wine-bearing servant disappeared and de Vesci, Fitzwalter and I were alone in the pavilion with just the shadows of the two men-at-arms outside staining the silken door flap to let us know that we were guarded.

'May I cordially welcome you to Alnwick Castle,' said Fitzwalter, raising his cup of wine to me.

'Thank you, my lord,' I said.

'It is my castle and I will do any welcoming,' snapped de Vesci.

'Very well,' said Fitzwalter soothingly. 'Bid our guest a warm welcome.'

De Vesci seemed to realise the absurdity of welcoming me for a second time and so he said nothing, merely sat there on his stool and stared sulkily into his wine cup.

Fitzwalter sighed at his companion's gracelessness and he leaned forward and asked how my journey from Westbury had been and whether all was well with my household. He asked after young Robert by name – which made me sit up, for I had never discussed my family with him before, and I realised what I should have grasped long before when he began playing 'My Joy Summons Me' – that Fitzwalter had made thorough investigations into my background and circumstances.

And he did not wish to conceal the fact.

I was not unduly perturbed that these two rebels had made enquiries about me. It was a sensible thing to do if we were to embark on such a dangerous enterprise. Indeed, I would not have believed that they were truly in earnest if they had not.

De Vesci stayed silent, fidgeting on his stool, but Fitzwalter made a few more sallies about the crops in Nottinghamshire, and we were discussing the blissfully fine weather like a pair of old gossips when de Vesci blurted out: 'So – will you do it?'

I caught Fitzwalter's eye and we both winced at de Vesci's crassness.

And so, partly out of playful cruelty, I said: 'That remains to be seen.'

'You gave us your word at Kirkton,' said de Vesci. 'Do you not intend to honour it? Have you lost your nerve?'

'Hold up, Eustace,' said Fitzwalter, putting a hand on de Vesci's arm, 'let us not put the cart before the horse.'

He looked at me: 'Since the subject has been broached, why don't we let Sir Alan tell us what he thinks of this perilous affair and then we can all say what is on our minds. Then we can proceed in an orderly manner. What say you, Sir Alan?'

I smiled at Fitzwalter: 'Thank you, my lord.' I took a deep breath. 'I have given this matter some thought and it is clearer than ever to me that King John must die. And I am prepared, for reasons of personal honour, for vengeance and for the good of the whole country, to do the deed myself.'

I tried to banish from my thoughts Marie-Anne's concerned face and continued: 'There are, however, to my mind two obstacles to achieving this. Firstly, since we must assume that the King is well guarded, we must consider how I might approach him with a drawn weapon in my hand and strike him down. The second obstacle to achieving this task is . . . well, that I do not wish to throw away my life in this or any other cause. I am prepared to take a risk, but I do not wish to be a martyr. You asked before, my lord, about my son Robert. I will not die and leave him at the mercy of a country torn by civil war. And the death of the King will, I believe, have that result.'

I paused and looked at my co-conspirators.

Lord Fitzwalter said: 'Let me say this – I will personally guarantee your son's safety if you die in this cause. I will ensure that he is educated and trained to the highest level and that he inherits your lands and has the strength and support to hold them. I swear that I would guard him and guide him as if he were my own son.'

'Thank you, my lord,' I said. 'That is most generous.' And I was indeed touched by the man's words. 'But I fully intend to survive this affair and look after Robert myself, if it is all the same to you.'

'We could poison him,' said de Vesci. And for a fraction of an instant I thought he meant my son. Then reason returned.

The dark man continued: 'I know an apothecary who would make us a fine tasteless powder. You add it to wine or food and the King would die some days later. The signs of the poison working are similar to the bloody flux – the constant flow from the bowels, the feverishness, the wasting away. If you were to administer the poison, no one would know it was you who had laid him low.'

Both Fitzwalter and I were silent at this. I did not like the idea of poison – but I could not exactly say why. Perhaps it was the lingering death, the secrecy of it, the underhanded devilry of the method. I would not be able to make my speech about Duke Arthur, I could not look into John's eyes and tell him why he was dying. And why he deserved to die. But poison, in truth, would achieve our ends admirably.

'I can see that Sir Alan does not favour this method of killing,' said Fitzwalter. 'And I am with him on this matter. Poison is a woman's weapon and not something that a man of honour would ever contemplate using.'

'A woman's weapon, pshaw!' said de Vesci. He looked quite offended by his friend's words. 'If Sir Alan is so concerned about risking his precious neck, then poison is the obvious answer. He can slip into the kitchens, sprinkle a little of the powder on some of the serving platters . . .'

'And how many others would die?' I asked. 'The King does not eat from one platter alone. All share. He offers the choicest cuts to his favoured men. Would you see them dead, too?' De Vesci shrugged. That made up my mind. 'I will not use poison,' I said. 'I will kill him with cold steel, face to face, and I will put my trust in God to guard me afterwards.'

'I have had a couple of thoughts that may be valuable,' said Fitzwalter.

He got up from the stool and went over to a chest on the far side of the pavilion; he bent, lifted the lid and extracted something.

'Give me your left arm, Sir Alan,' said Fitzwalter. I saw

146

that he was holding something that resembled an archer's bracer, the sleeve of leather laced to the left forearm of a bowman to reduce the lash of the bow-cord against the soft skin on the inside of the arm. But this was no ordinary bracer. It was bigger for a start and I could see that something long, thin and black was attached to the surface of the leather cuff.

I stood up and extended my left arm, and Fitzwalter pushed back the wide, bell-shaped drooping sleeves of my tunic and slipped the object on to my forearm, pulling the laces tight to secure it in place. Now, strapped firmly to my left forearm was a narrow leather sheath containing a slim steel killing dagger: a misericorde.

It was the weapon of an assassin.

The misericorde was a long, black, cross-shaped weapon made entirely out of steel with a slim blade about ten inches in length. It was a beautiful thing to behold despite its sinister purpose. It was used in battle to give a merciful death to a badly wounded knight by punching the blade through the hollow between collarbone and neck, and down into the heart. It was a weapon designed to slide in between the joins in a man's mail or, if used with sufficient force, to punch straight through the iron links and into the flesh beyond. It was a deadly tool designed with one purpose – to kill quickly, quietly and with minimum effort. I had once owned one and used it for many years, but mine had been made of iron with a wooden handle fitted on the tang and the metal had become old and weakened over the years. It had broken in a duel ten years ago, causing me to be slightly wounded. I had not replaced it.

Rather unnervingly, Lord Fitzwalter seemed to know all about this: 'This weapon will never break in combat, Sir Alan; it is the finest blackened steel made by the Moors of Toledo with all their heathen magic, skill and cunning. I do not believe there is a blade of equal strength in Christendom – and there are few in the Muslim lands either. It is my gift to you – take it with my blessings, whether you decide to join us or not. Here, draw the blade and try the fit of it in your hand.'

The grip of the misericorde was made of linked cubes of black steel with rounded edges, like a row of Thomas's dice, and finished with a large spherical steel pommel. The handle extended beyond the sheath on the inside of my wrist and the pommel seemed to nestle in the palm of my left hand; the fingers curled naturally around it. When I dropped my arm, my sleeve completely covered the bracer, blade and pommel, and when I pulled the handle with my right hand the wicked black steel slipped effortlessly out of the sheath. It was the perfect implement for the task at hand. I knew that I could approach King John, seemingly unarmed, and then pull the blade at the last moment and plunge it into his cruel heart in an instant. I could not imagine a better way to bring a blade to within killing distance of my foe.

The drawn misericorde fitted comfortably in my right hand. The handle felt warm and silky to the touch and light as a feather. It was so beautiful that I could hardly take my eyes off it – the black oiled steel, the holy cruciform shape, the elegant lines of the long blade. I tested the edge with my thumb. It was as keen as a razor.

Lord Fitzwalter had been watching my face intently. I saw that he was pleased with my reaction to his gift. He said: 'I have also had an idea about where and when you might do this deed – that is, if you choose to – and also how you might reasonably expect to escape with your life.'

I slid the misericorde back into its snug sheath, dropped my arm back down to my side and tried to pay attention to what Fitzwalter was saying.

'You know the King wishes to give his realm, our England, to the Pope?'

I nodded. I had an almost overwhelming urge to draw the misericorde again, just to see if it was still as beautiful as before, but I controlled myself and looked into Fitzwalter's honest ruddy face. He was still speaking of his regicidal plans.

'The King means to ratify his homage for England to the papal legate, one Master Pandulf, and he means to do this in three months' time on the ides of October in London at St Paul's Cathedral. All the barons of England have been summoned to attend the ceremony. It will be a great event, a charter sealed with a golden bull. Even

149

those barons who do not love John will attend with their knights and servants to witness the affair. Eustace and I will be there, of course. At a great feast, the King will try to placate his enemies with fair words and promises, and perhaps to cow us with his pomp and majesty, and also to make a public demonstration of the Pope's support for him at the same time. Are you following me, Sir Alan?'

'St Paul's, London, ides of October . . . yes, I follow you,' I said. But, in truth, I was distracted by the gentle weight on my left forearm.

'The charter is to be sealed and witnessed in the court-yard outside the cathedral. Imagine the scene: there will be great men and their entourages everywhere, the King will graciously pass among us, a word of praise here, a smile of acknowledgement there. He will be confident, secure of his victory. The Pope, and therefore God, is on his side. And all must see this. In the crowd of milling barons and knights, it should be relatively simple for you to come close to the royal person. Then, without warning, a commotion breaks out on the far side of the courtyard – some of Eustace's men will cause a loud disturbance, a fight, men cursing and struggling. All eyes will be drawn to them. And you, you strike, swift as a snake . . . A body of my men will be right behind you, seven or eight big knights in mail bearing shields, we think that is sufficient, for the task. You approach the King – attention is drawn away by the diversion, you strike, he falls, and you immediately turn around and pass though the crowd of our mailed knights, and away. If any man sees you kill the King, and seeks to follow you, our men will block their path with their bodies, their shields, they will trip them, stumble and knock them to the ground, cause even more confusion. We think seven men, eight or nine to be sure, will be sufficient unto the task. More would seem like a threat and might draw the eyes of the King's loyal men on to us. A waiting horse and groom will be just round the corner, there is a stables owned by a former servant of mine within fifty yards. He is a good man and he will see you saddled and on the road north as quick as thought. What do you say?'

He had my full attention by now. I could see his stratagem playing out in my mind. I would whisper to the King my message about Arthur just before the blade slid home. I could imagine John's astonished and then terrified face as my steel dug into his flesh and found his heart. Then I would turn, push through the gang of Fitzwalter's armed men, and they would obstruct any pursuit while I slipped away.

'Well, my lords, I think that—'

De Vesci interrupted me: 'Remember: the first act of any new King would be, of course, to ennoble you, Sir Alan,' he said. 'And, grant you great wealth. And, should you wish it, he would give you the hand of a suitable heiress, a royal ward, very young and beautiful, rich as a queen . . .' He was smirking at me in a most unpleasant

151

way. 'I hear that you are without a wife at the present time. How would you like a wrigglesome bed-warmer, just fourteen and in the prime of her looks? How would you like to be Lord Westbury, perhaps even the Earl of Westbury?'

I did not like his tone. And clearly neither did Fitzwalter. He glared at de Vesci and said: 'Sir Alan does not do this grave thing for gain, Eustace. He does it purely in the name of his personal honour and for the good of his country. Although, naturally, there would be advancement for all good men under the new rule.'

I had in fact been almost ready to agree to their plans, until de Vesci's crude attempt at bribery. Instead, to irritate him, I said: 'I will have to think on this.'

De Vesci's face was black as a crow's wing. 'While you think on it, Sir Alan, remember this – if we are successful in removing the King and replacing him with a more suitable monarch, and you have not helped us, or you have hindered us, or even, God forbid, you have betrayed us, there will be dire consequences. Think on this, Sir Alan: you are either with us or you are against us!'

'Consequences?' I said. 'Oh, no! Please, spare me from any consequences.' And I began to laugh. Great gales of mirth erupted and I laughed right in his thin ugly face. This fellow with his vague bribes and his silly attempt at bullying had sailed straight past offending me and beyond into the calm seas of the ridiculous.

'Get out, get out this instant!' Fitzwalter had de Vesci

by the shoulders and he was hustling him towards the tent flap. 'Get out, you cloth-brained imbecile.'

'But, Robert, this is my pavilion. This is my land, by God's bones!'

I was almost doubled over with merriment by now. Mainly because de Vesci was resisting Fitzwalter's force, digging his heels into the turf beneath his feet and pushing at the other man's chest with his palms. But Fitzwalter was stronger. He knocked de Vesci's arms aside and wrapped his own around his friend's chest.

'Get out, you cretin, before I take my sword to you!' And Fitzwalter bodily lifted de Vesci off his feet and shoved the protesting lord of Alnwick Castle out of his own tent and into the arms of the two men-at-arms beyond the flap.

As I struggled to compose myself, wiping the tears of laughter from my cheeks, and Fitzwalter got his breath back from his brief struggle with our host, a servant nervously poked his head through the tent flap.

'More wine,' growled Fitzwalter to the man. 'And be quick about it.'

'I can only apologise for that boorish fellow,' Lord Fitzwalter said a few moments later. 'We cannot always choose with whom we must ally ourselves.' We had resumed out seats in the gold-painted stools and were enjoying yet more delicious cooled wine. 'To think that a man like you would be swayed by the offer of a title

153

and a wealthy marriage; or even moved by de Vesci's silly threats. It is quite absurd.'

'I think if you tried hard enough I could be persuaded to accept the burden of great riches and a grand title,' I said.

Fitzwalter and I caught each other's eyes and smiled.

'And, it is true, my wife is dead and I would welcome another – if she were pretty and to my liking and if she freely chose me and were not forced to marry against her will. I could be persuaded to undertake that burden, too, I believe.'

Fitzwalter chuckled. 'You will be handsomely rewarded, my friend, do not concern yourself on that issue. Money, land, titles, whatever you desire. But may we get to the business; how do you see the plan? Would it work, do you think?'

As I rode south the next morning, I realised that I had not in fact agreed to undertake the murder of King John. It had merely been assumed between Lord Fitzwalter and myself that I would do the deed. And I would do it – not for titles and a rich heiress but as Fitzwalter had said: for my honour, for the memory of dead friends, for justice, and for the good of the country. Also, by the time I left Alnwick Castle, I had been convinced that I could kill John and get away free and clear. I had made one change to Fitzwalter's plan. I had insisted that de Vesci's men play no part in the distraction that was to draw attention away from the King at the moment I was to strike. I insisted that Fitzwalter's men organise the distraction, which was to be a cat-fight between two hired prostitutes, as well as providing the blocking force to cover my escape – I did not trust de Vesci. That is not to say that I thought he would betray me. It was his competence that I did not trust. His crude bullying and cajolery marked him out to my mind as a man of low acuity, not someone to whom I would care to entrust my life. He was a blunderer. If he or his men got the timing of the disturbance wrong – as I feared he would – or if it was not loud enough or compelling enough to draw all the eyes of the crowd, I might be left facing the King with a drawn blade in my hand and all the armed knights in the service of the King of England looking on. If that happened, I was a corpse. So Fitzwalter had finally agreed that de Vesci would have no part of the affair beyond providing the money for any expenses that might be incurred – the man was, it seemed, extraordinarily rich and used to having his own way, which might account for his graceless manner. Indeed, as I bade my sullen host farewell the next morning before setting out on my journey, after a little prodding by Fitzwalter, de Vesci handed over a heavy purse of silver for any expenditure I might make on the journey home, which was generous, and he did his best to wish me a good fortune and God's blessing until we met again in London in three months' time.

Chapter Twelve

I spent the rest of the summer busily engaged in the affairs of Westbury. Baldwin and I embarked on a series of building works. With the help of the men of the village, when the crops had been harvested and were drying in my barns – it was indeed a bountiful harvest, praise God – we improved the fortifications of Westbury, strengthening the main gate with new oak cross-timbers, and reinforcing the wooden walls around the whole compound, with laths of ash and hazel. But the greatest project of all was a tower that I began to build of stone in the north-west corner of the courtyard, abutting the wooden palisade. It was not much to begin with, merely a grey box of granite twelve foot by twelve with a small iron-bound wooden door but no windows on the ground floor.

The master mason that I employed to undertake this task assured me that at a future date (when I could afford it) I could extend the keep upwards and make it a properly impressive fortification. But just the first two storeys took two months to build and when they were finished, the season was late, and the weather was becoming too wet and cold to set mortar, and I called a halt to the work. That was my excuse; indeed, the true reason was that the fearsome cost of men and materials had far exceeded my expectations and I did not want to reduce Westbury to beggary just before the winter. However, when it was finished, though I scarcely had a penny left to my name, I did feel like a proper knight with a proper stone keep. It looked just like a miniature castle, in fact, squat and strong, imposing. I filled it with a month's supply of dried food, barrels of water and wine, boxes of clothes, tools and firewood, and a collection of weapons and armour.

Sir Thomas Blood truly began to earn his keep that summer too. He made no more visits to Nottingham alehouses to gamble, as far as I knew, and he dedicated himself to Robert's education. Every day just after dawn he took my son out into the courtyard, rain or shine, and began to tutor him in the arts of shield and sword. Robert was not a complete novice. He had received some training from myself and from other passing knights, friends of mine who were kind enough to spare a few hours in his instruction, but for a boy of eleven he was well behind other lads of his age and class, and I could see why they had teased him so unmercifully in his brief time at Pembroke Castle.

Sir Thomas began with the basics, teaching the boy to step and cut, to block and parry with sword and shield, and I watched them sometimes after breakfast as they fought their mock battles, with fond memories of my own long-ago education in the skill of arms. Occasionally, when I was not engaged in the rebuilding of the palisade or getting in the way of the masons at their work on the tower, I would take an old dull blade and put the boy through his paces.

God knows that I loved my son with all my heart and soul, but I cannot lie to you and tell you that he was a gifted soldier. He lacked the aggression necessary to make a fighter. When I urged him to attack me, his blows were weak, even limp. I was puzzled by this at first and when I questioned him he said that it was because he was afraid of hurting me. When I dared him to try, and knocked him down to make him angry, he responded, not as I had hoped with a spirited attack but with childish tears and a refusal to spar any longer with me.

Sir Thomas was made of sterner stuff than I. If Robert made a mistake or displeased him in some way, he punished the boy by making him run in full armour (an old cut-down suit of my mail) with sword, helm and shield and a sack filled with sand on his back around and around the court-yard sometimes until the boy was sick with exhaustion.

It would be fair to say that Robert hated Sir Thomas. Loathed him. But Sir Thomas was implacable, and when the knight gave an order, my son jumped to obey it. One afternoon, when Thomas was working the boy very hard – he was learning unarmed methods of disabling an armed man, as I recall – the teacher knocked his pupil down one time too many and Robert curled into a ball on the ground and began to bawl his eyes out. I had been watching and leapt to my feet, feeling that I should comfort the lad – but almost immediately I sat back down. The boy needed, most of all, to be tougher. Mollycoddling him would never answer. Though I may tell you that standing by and watching your only son being repeatedly hurt and humiliated – even in a righteous cause – is a trial that is hard to match.

Sir Thomas calmly ordered the lad to stop his cater-wauling and get up and fight like a man. And to my surprise, after a moment, Robert did shamble to his feet, wipe the tears and snot from his face and adopt the crouched fighting stance that Thomas had taught him. It occurred to me that, if not a great warrior, perhaps we might make a decent man of Robert yet.

And if my son did not shine as a fighting man, he did have other qualities that I discovered with great pleasure over the next few months. We played chess a few times that summer. And at first I barely concentrated on my moves, having so many other things to occupy my mind. The first time he beat me, I thought it must have been luck. Second time, I thought I must have made a serious blunder. But when he began to beat me easily, every time without fail, even when I tried my hardest, I knew that without a doubt he was my master at this game. It is a strange feeling for a father, to be bested by his son: and not altogether unpleasant. He was, I soon realised, as quick-witted as any boy I had ever known; but he also had a facility for invention, for thinking things that other boys – even other men – could never imagine in a lifetime.

It happened that Little John was passing through Westbury, returning from some errand of Robin's in the south, and he dropped in to give us his news and to find out how we were faring.

Over a mug or three of ale, Little John told me that the King was more determined than ever to recover Normandy. But the King knew he could not defeat the French on his own. His strategy was, in fact, not a bad one, Little John admitted. The King planned to mount an expedition to Poitou and attack Philip's men along the line of the River Loire. This would force the French King to come south from Paris and defend the territory he had captured from the Angevins, and then the second blow would come from the north. From King John's allies. He had been sending barrels of silver and military help to the counts of Boulogne and Flanders all year and supporting his nephew Otto, the Holy Roman Emperor, in his struggles against rival claimants to the title, too.

'He might have bought himself some support in Flanders and Germany,' chuckled Little John, 'he's sorely lacking in aid from home. Hardly any bugger heeded him when he called for English fighting men for the Poitou expedition.'

'Are they not sworn to aid him?' asked Robert, who was serving us the ale.

'They may have sworn a mighty oath, youngster,' said Little John, 'but that doesn't mean they'll honour it.'

And Little John was right. He told us that a group of northern barons, led by my new friends the lords de Vesci and Fitzwalter, had issued a joint proclamation declaring that though they held their lands from the King of England, and duly owed him military service for it, they had no obligation to fight in his wars outside his kingdom.

'But that's nonsense,' said Robert. 'English knights have been fighting abroad for their kings since the days of the Conqueror!'

'Quite right, youngster,' said Little John, looking at Robert in surprise at his shrewdness. 'But the barons are like anyone else. They like to back a winner.'

While he was with us, I asked Little John to give Robert the benefit of his years of combat experience and, with Sir Thomas's permission, the big man and my little son spent an afternoon in the courtyard working on ways in which a man on foot could defeat a mounted knight. I did not witness the display – I was on the far side of my lands helping to pull a ewe out of a patch of marshy ground in which she had been mired – but that evening over supper Little John surprised me by saying: 'He's a rare boy, your Robert.'

I asked him what he meant – bracing myself for John to say something derogatory about my son's lack of martial skills.

'He can't fight worth a damn,' said the big man, 'but you know that already. But he does have a wise head on his shoulders for one so young. I was showing him how a spearman can dismount a knight, the old leg-heave method, when he said something extraordinary. He said: "Instead of pushing him off the horse, Uncle John, why don't you pull him down? If you had the right sort of hook, you could pull him down like a bundle of hay off a wain."'

'You can't go into battle with a hay-hook,' I said. 'You'd look ridiculous, and you couldn't really harm the knight when he was down. Are you sure he understood what he was talking about? He is very young, after all.'

'Oh, he grasped it completely. And it's certainly worth thinking about.'

I merely shrugged and then our talk turned to other matters.

Two days after Little John's departure, the alarm was raised by the lookout on the new tower. It was now the highest point in Westbury and gave a view of the surrounding flattish countryside for miles. The man-at-arms spotted a column of horsemen approaching on the road and imme-diately rang the big hand bell attached to the flagpole to alert the people in the courtyard below.

I was pleased by the way Westbury reacted to the alarm. The big wooden gates in the front of the courtyard were speedily closed and double-barred with thick oak beams that lay snugly in iron brackets on either side of the portal. Every man-at-arms was rousted from their barracks or from the hall and mustered on the walls and on the roof of the tower. Our bowmen – a dozen men, sadly, no more – filed up on the right and left of the gatehouse, and strung their staves. A score or so of men-at-arms – mostly veterans, but also a handful of recruits from Westbury and the surrounding villages – manned the walls all around the palisade, while ten spearmen with heavy shields massed in the centre of the courtyard prepared to repel the attackers if the gate was breached. Baldwin marshalled the servants by the base of the tower; he was ready, if I ordered it, to start filling the keep with extra food, blankets and provisions and to get everybody inside in the time it takes to say an Our Father.

All this happened smoothly, with the minimum of fuss, and for that I had Sir Thomas to thank. He was captain of the guard at Westbury as well as Robert's tutor, and he had insisted on running drills for all the fighting men at least once a week from the very first day he had arrived. He was well liked by the men, many of whom had fought with him in the south. And those who did not like him feared him enough to obey his orders without hesitation.

I was standing atop the walkway above the gatehouse, with Robert beside me, both of us in mail and helm, when Sir Thomas arrived beside me to report: 'The full garrison is turned out, sir, forty-four men and all ready for action. Orders, sir?'

'Let's see who they are first and what they want, agreed?'

I put a hand on Robert's shoulder and looked down at my son. He was beaming with joy to be there with me, mailed, sword on his hip, ready for battle as my squire. I had forgotten how exciting an armed confrontation like this could be for the young.

I opened my mouth and roared: 'No one is to loose an arrow, launch a spear, throw an axe or make any other move unless I command it. Do you hear me?'

And the men of Westbury gave me a cheer of assent in return.

The column of horsemen was fifty paces away by now and I could see banners borne by some of the leading horsemen and the gaudy surcoats of the riders. They came armed for war, there was no doubt about that, and I had a fairly good idea who they were and what they desired.

A herald trotted forward of the pack and stopped in front of the palisade: 'These gates are to be opened immediately by order of His Royal Highness John, King of England, Lord of Ireland, Duke of Normandy and Aquitaine, Count of Anjou, Poitou, Maine, Touraine and

Mortain, loyal and most Christian servant of his Holiness Pope Innocent III—'

'I see no king among this company. Who usurps the King's name?' I bellowed.

There is a ritual, a formula to these encounters. Meaningless, of course, but I did not see any reason to deviate from it. I was counting their spears, judging the quality of their men and their mounts. A hundred and four, I made it. I was impressed.

'I do,' shouted a commanding voice from the mass of horsemen now a stone's throw from my gates, and a big imposing man in full mail with a black-and-gold surcoat astride a pure white horse rode forward. He had short-cropped grey hair, a strong square face and his left eye was blind and milky and a scar ran down from it almost to his jaw. His right eye was a fierce pale blue, and he stared up at me without a shadow of trepidation or doubt.

'I am Philip Marc, High Sheriff of Nottinghamshire, Derbyshire and the Royal Forests, and I serve King John, who is lord of all in this realm.'

I knew who he was, of course. Two men had emerged from the lines of cavalry behind him and took up positions either side of the sheriff. One man I also knew, a fat knight of good family and bad character; the other I had never seen before. He was a veritable giant. An enormous fellow, with dark skin the colour of old saddle leather, broad flat nostrils above a huge red mouth and black hair that curled in a hundred tight whorls on his head. The man was taller even than Little John and a good deal wider, too, with small, mean button eyes glowing in the rolls of fat on his angry-looking brown face. His horse was no destrier or palfrey – it was a heavy carthorse, as high as a man at the shoulder and perhaps twice the size of a normal horse. I knew this man-mountain, too, by reputation at least: he was the demon that had so frightened Baldwin. And yet he was truly no demon. He was just a man, albeit a vast man, from the forests of Africa to the south of the desert lands of the Moors. I had seen many men like him, although none so big, in the Holy Land and in Spain on the way home from the Great Pilgrimage.

'What can I do for you, my lord?' I said to the sheriff, still looking over his companions.

'You can open these God-damned gates, sir, and you can open them this instant, or you may call yourself a traitor to King and country.'

'You come here with men arrayed for war and demand that I open my gates, sheriff. But I shall not do that. The last time you King's men came inside my walls you stripped it bare of food and livestock and silver. You shall not enter. I defy you.'

'You can fight us, sir – if you feel inclined to test your luck – but I would advise against it,' said Sir Thomas, in a calm, powerful voice. 'I would suggest that you take yourselves away from these gates with all possible haste – because, if you do not, in about twenty heartbeats, I am going to begin the slaughter of your men.'

Sir Thomas made a hand signal and the archers, almost at the same time, all nocked arrows and drew back their cords to the ear.

Philip Marc smiled, a crooked little grin. He seemed not the slightest bit dismayed. 'Hold hard there, my good man,' he said. 'Let us not be hasty.'

He grinned insolently up at me. 'There is another choice, Sir Alan,' he said.

'And what would that be?' I said.

'We could talk,' said the sheriff. 'We could behave like Christians.'

I made Marc send his cavalry back a good half-mile before I opened the gates. And then, under an agreement of truce, I allowed him and his two companions to enter the courtyard, before slamming shut the gate and barring it securely again.

However, I could see no reason to be churlish. For all that the sheriff had come to me in force he was still the lawful representative of the crown and I was not, at least not yet, an outlaw. It crossed my mind that my plot with de Vesci and Fitzwalter to kill the King might have been betrayed, but while I watched carefully, I saw no sign of it on the faces of my guests. I had Baldwin organise a trestle table and benches to be set up in the courtyard and I told Robert to bring out ale and bread and cheese. Nothing too fancy, but not insultingly mean either. Philip Marc sat down, entirely at his ease, took a piece of bread and accepted the cup of ale poured by my son. The dark-skinned man-mountain ate and drank nothing and chose to stand at the south end of the table, and I was glad of it. I did not think the bench would have taken his colossal weight, and his height and bulk created some welcome shade.

The fat knight sat down opposite Philip Marc, next to Sir Thomas and, as he cut himself a huge chunk of cheese, I said: 'Well, well, Benedict, I have not seen your ugly face for a long while – but I see you have not lost your appetite.'

Sir Benedict Malet glared at me. I knew him for a glutton who put his own greed ahead of the needs of his men – I had discovered it when we had been at Château Gaillard together ten years before. I also knew him for a coward and traitor.

'Very true, Sir Alan,' he responded through a mouthful of cheese crumbs. 'I believe I have not seen you since the day you murdered my friend Sir Joscelyn Giffard, the lord of Avranches.'

'It was a fair fight,' I said hotly, 'a duel. He spilled my blood that day, too.'

'He did not choose to fight you – yet you killed him. That is cold-blooded murder,' said Sir Benedict, cramming a hunk of bread into his mouth.

I put my hand on my hilt, snarling. Truce or no truce, I would not be called a murderer in my own manor. Not by the likes of Benedict.

'Gentlemen, gentlemen,' said Philip Marc, 'a little decorum. We are here to talk business, not to cut each other to pieces. We can do that later, if it proves necessary.'

Sir Benedict carried on chewing but his stare was poison.

'I see you have already met my esteemed deputy sheriff, Sir Benedict Malet. And that big fellow over there is Boot, he is my . . . let us say my factotum.'

I was in no mood for pleasantries.

'Tell me what you want here, Sheriff,' I said brusquely.

'I should have thought that was obvious – I want what most men want. I want money. Your money, to be exact. Benedict has a bit of parchment somewhere – it is your bill of accounting. I expect he will show it to you if you ask him prettily . . .'

Benedict made no move and I said nothing.

'No? Not interested in the details?' said Marc. I could tell he was enjoying himself. 'Well, from my memory there is the matter of twenty marks or so outstanding for this year's taxes. And the King declares a further scutage of – oh, let us say fifteen marks – no, I feel generous, we'll call it ten marks.'

I stared at the sheriff in silence. Sir Thomas shifted on his part of the bench. I saw that he was staring up at Boot with an expression close to awe in his eyes.

No one spoke. So Marc said: 'Well, if you would like to hand over the thirty marks – or twenty pounds, if you prefer – then we will be on our way and there will be no need for any further unpleasantness.'

'That's it?' I said. 'You are demanding thirty marks – an outrageous sum which you know I cannot give you – and that's all you wanted to talk about? You could have shouted that up from outside the walls and saved everyone a deal of time and trouble. If you think you can take this manor – go ahead and try. I have powerful friends who will come to my aid. I wager we can hold you off till they come. And so . . . oh, just get out, will you, get out and take your fat friend and your factotum with you. Go!'

I got up and shouted for the servants to open up the gates.

'Oh dear, oh dearie, dearie me, I am becoming so absent-minded in my riper years,' said Philip Marc.

The doors of the castle had swung open and my grooms brought over the three horses of our guests.

'There was one rather important point I forgot to mention . . .'

Philip Marc swung up on to his horse.

'Is that your boy there? A pretty lad. He serves at table well: neat and quiet. I like that. You must be proud of him.'

I said nothing. Robert took a step closer to me. I could feel his presence behind my left shoulder.

The sheriff said: 'Well, here is the thing. The King must have his money. He is adamant. And I am empowered by him to use any means – I say any means at all – to raise it. So here it is: if you do not pay thirty marks in silver to the crown within the month, I will have my large friend Boot here tear your son's head from his shoulders. Boot! Show the gentlemen!'

I looked up at the sheriff with the blood draining from my face. He was sitting there smiling down at me from the back of his horse. Had he really just threatened my son's life? In my own home? I turned to look at Boot. He had not moved from his position standing by the table. But he had grasped the edge of the trestle board with one vast hand. The top surface was an inch thick of seasoned oak. He squeezed the wood and seemed to rip it sideways as if it were no more solid than a loaf of rye bread, and before my very eyes that huge dark man tore a chunk the size of a trencher from my table.

The giant tossed the piece of wood at my feet, turned and lumbered over to his carthorse. As the three of them rode out of the gate, I looked down at the object at my feet. I could see the impressions of Boot's broad fingers indented in the wood.

I did not pay the sheriff. I could have done, I suppose. I could have sold everything we had at Westbury and gone to the Templars or the Jews to raise the rest of the money. But I decided I would not give way to menaces, no matter what. Besides, it could have been no more than an empty threat. The King's chief officer in Nottinghamshire must surely balk at murdering an innocent child. The other great men of the county would not stand for it. I decided that the sheriff must have been testing my mettle, trying to put fear into me, and I determined that I would continue to defy him. Nevertheless, it is a hard thing to hazard your only son's neck and I did not sleep much in the next few weeks.

I kept lookouts stationed on the tower night and day. And Robert never left Westbury without a guard of at least half a dozen armed men. But I did not wreck myself and Westbury to pay over the sheriff's spurious tax demand. As the weeks and then the months slid by I heard nothing more from Philip Marc and his minions. And with the passing of time, my mind grew easier.

I did hear that the King had summoned his mercenaries and ridden north with a host determined to confront the northern barons over their refusal to serve him in Poitou, but on the road from London the Archbishop of Canterbury, Stephen Langton, a godly man, I had heard, and an honest one, had persuaded him that force was not the answer and King John had turned around and headed back south. I took that as a good sign. I heard nothing from Robin either that summer and I was loath to contact him as we had parted on less than cordial terms. That was bad, but I knew that if I saw him he would try to persuade me to abandon my plans for the King's removal.

The day of the ceremony at St Paul's drew closer and I grew more and more skittish. I practised drawing and stabbing with my misericorde for hour after hour until the sweet black blade seemed to leap into my hand – I had decided that I would make a frontal attack, plunging the blade into John's belly from the fore and then forcing it upwards to slice into the heart and lungs. It was a sure way of killing a man, I knew from long experience, and if I kept my body close to the King's while the steel went in and I shoved it upwards, I would be shielding my blow from many eyes.

In the week before the ceremony – in the drizzly, dreary start of October – I practised the blow so many times by day that I dreamt about the strike at night. On one occasion I caught sight of Thomas watching me seize the blade and mime the cut, but he said nothing and merely smiled, nodded approvingly and walked away. At the beginning of the second week of October, I handed over responsibility for the protection of young Robert and Westbury to Sir Thomas and his men-at-arms. Baldwin helped me to pack a satchel of fine clothes – I would need to fit in with the nobility of all England at the ceremony – and another of food and drink. I hung my sword from my saddle, strapped the misericorde to my left forearm, donned cloak and hood and, once again without squire or servant, I set off south on the road to London.

I had a King to kill.

Part Two

I write these lines in haste and in secret. Disaster has befallen us. Prior William has been reading these pages eagerly, collecting them from me as soon as I have finished them and burning the candle half the night to read them in his private apartments. But when he summoned me not an hour ago, his rage was as mighty as a winter storm at sea: an assault of sound and fury on all the senses. He said that he'd had no knowledge that Brother Alan was so deeply involved in the plot to murder King John, our own dear monarch Henry of Winchester's esteemed father, and he has forbidden both Brother Alan and myself to continue with our task lest we give encouragement to others who seek to lay rough hands on royalty. I think I understand why. Prior William has hopes that our good King Henry will make him a bishop one day – he has long had his eye on the diocese of Durham – and he fears that tales of regicidal plots emanating from Newstead will not win him royal favour. I pleaded complete ignorance of the conspiracy against King John, as well I might, for this came to me, too, as a revelation. Although in truth, from what I have heard of the character of Henry's royal father – by all accounts a most cruel and evil man – I cannot condemn Brother Alan for his long-ago actions.

Prior William went to see Brother Alan in his cell and berated him for a host of crimes, including *lèse-majesté*, treason and the sacrilege of regicide. He told Brother Alan that unless he showed the proper contrition, and did penance for it, he would burn in Hell. I know because I happened to be just outside the door of the cell with the dinner tray when it occurred and I heard every intemperate word.

However, despite Brother Alan's advanced decrepitude, great courage yet burns within his papery, skeletal frame. He told the Prior that he would be judged for his actions on the Earth by God alone, and not by some easily outraged pipsqueak of a churchman. And Prior William near had a fit of apoplexy. He threatened to turn Brother Alan out of this House of God, tonight, to freeze his old bones in the snows – but my old scriptorium teacher would not be intimidated. He told the Prior that at his advanced age, and having lived the life that he has, he no longer feared death, even in the slightest degree – and if the Prior wished to have his ancient carcass expelled from the monastery for some episode long in the past that he knew nothing about, well, that was his privilege, but that he must thereafter look to his own conscience.

God will judge you, too, he said.

Despite this provocation, Prior William stopped short at taking this extreme step, and contented himself with damning the old man and all his works, and in forbidding me to continue with my scribblings. Brother Alan's tale must remain untold, he thundered, until the Heavens fall and the seas turn to blood, and for my part in this disgraceful affair I am to be allowed no more than bread and water for my sustenance for one whole month.

I am a man of God, I do so long to be His obedient servant, and to serve my lord Prior to the best of my ability and with an honest heart. And so I will accept his punishment and humbly restrict myself to bread and cold water for a month. But I am a disobedient man, too, a weak and foolish fellow, for I cannot rest until I have heard the rest of Brother Alan's tale. And so I visit my old friend in secret, when I know the Prior is in conclave with others, and when Brother Alan tells me of his deeds, I fix his words in my memory, with only a few notes on a small slate, and commit them to parchment afterwards in the privacy of my own cell.

God will no doubt judge me, too, for my wickedness.

Chapter Thirteen

I arrived in London the day before the ceremony in which King John would do homage for the kingdom of England to the Pope's representative, Master Pandulf, the papal legate. I had been to St Paul's Cathedral before, of course – what visitor to London hasn't? – but I wanted to do a thorough reconnaissance of the cathedral and the surrounding area to get a feel for the ground.

I could not be certain where John would be at any particular time, except that it was likely that the King would spend some time greeting the gathered lords and bishops in the courtyard after the service of thanksgiving inside the cathedral – it would be dangerously rude not to acknowledge them, as many would have come from the furthest reaches of the country to witness this grave event.

As I strolled around the courtyard, which rang merrily to the sound of hammers as workmen erected a huge purple-canvas-covered wooden dais on the south-eastern side of the space where the actual ceremony of homage would take place, the enormity of what I was contemplating weighed on my mind. This man John, though a murderous coward and a treacherous snake, was God's anointed representative on Earth. He was the King of England! The Lord God Almighty had decreed that this man should rule over all of us, and who was I to flout His law? On the other hand, if God did allow me to slay the King, then God must approve of my actions. John *was* evil, he surely deserved to die. God must know this. Mayhap the Lord of Hosts guided my steps. I was in His hands, I told myself, and took some comfort from that.

Nevertheless, I went inside the cathedral to pray for guidance and ask God if the course I had chosen truly had His blessing.

I was just getting up from my knees, when my eye was drawn to a pair of women by the shrine of St Earconwald. In truth, it was only one of the women who attracted my eye: she was tall, slender and graceful, and I could tell without even seeing her face that she was lovely. The second woman was shorter, stout and a good deal older, but both were dressed alike in white robes with a black surcoat over the top and a square black headdress. They were Cistercian nuns.

The shorter woman turned towards me; she was hanging on to the crook of the taller woman's right arm as if she were an invalid and needed the younger woman's support, but when she saw me and the direction of my gaze, she glared at me – a look of such ferocity that I was taken aback. The older woman immediately released her hold on the younger and turned full face to me, like a warrior facing an attacker – her countenance was leathery and square, almost manly, with a sharp hooked nose, a dark hairy shadow on her upper lip and small, brightly burning black eyes. The hatred blazed from her: if she had been a man I would have braced myself for a blow.

Then the tall woman looked directly at me for the first time and I could see that I had been right – she was almost impossibly beautiful: glossy sable hair, a pure white heart-shaped face, wide red lips and happy blue-grey eyes.

'Greetings, Sir Alan,' Tilda said, 'how lovely to see you again.'

At the sound of her voice, low, rich and smoky, my stomach dissolved.

I strolled with Matilda Giffard down the long nave of St Paul's Cathedral. Behind us walked the short, angry-looking nun – who was revealed to be Anna, Prioress of Kirklees – craning her neck forward and desperately trying to hear what was said between Matilda and myself.

Anna of Kirklees had thawed a little towards me when Tilda told her my name and that I served the Earl of

Locksley. I knew that the previous earls had been generous to Kirklees and that Robin had continued the practice of patronage to that particular religious house. I asked after Godric, the outlaw Robin had sent to her, and the prioress told me that they had had to amputate a large part of his suppurating arm but they had managed to save his life. I thanked her on behalf of Robin and she managed a grim smile – but it was clear that she did not trust me with her beautiful companion and, as we walked slowly arm-in-arm down the length of the cathedral, she watched over our intercourse as a hawk watches a field mouse.

It was Tilda who suggested that we take a wander together to admire the beauty of the most famous cathedral in England and, to be honest, I was surprised by her friendliness. The last time we had met – at Kirklees Priory some ten years ago – the air had been thick with insults and imprecations. But it seemed that I had been forgiven. I asked Tilda what she was doing in London.

'Oh, the prioress has been invited by the King to witness his homage to the Pope. All the heads of the great religious houses – bishops, abbots, priors . . . oh, everyone – will be coming. Anna asked me to be her travelling companion and I was happy to accede to her wishes. It is exciting, isn't it? All the nobility of England coming here. And for such a good reason, too. I feel sure, now the Pope is our overlord, that must bring England closer to God. Don't you agree, Alan?'

I mumbled something.

She laughed. 'Why, Sir Alan, you seem shy all of a sudden. Surely you cannot have been thinking of our last meeting, when I behaved so abominably. You must allow me to apologise for all the vile and stupid things I said. I was angry with you over the death of my father – I was angry at the whole world in those days. But I have found true contentment now in the love of Christ. I hope we can put all that unpleasantness behind us, Alan, and be good friends again. Just like we used to be. Do you think you could be my friend?'

When a gorgeous woman gazes into your eyes and asks if they can be your good friend, I defy any red-blooded man to say no. I certainly could not. Tilda might have been a bride of Christ, but I was floundering in her lovely blue-grey stare and, I confess, my thoughts were turning in an altogether unholy direction. I'd had her – once. And, by God, nun or no, I wanted her again.

We strolled along the aisle of the nave, and enjoyed the hurly-burly of the London crowds – for St Paul's was as much a public meeting place and market as it was a House of God – and I told Tilda what I had been doing over the past few years, my adventures in the south, and she seemed most impressed. I told her about young Robert's progress as a squire, and about my plans for Westbury and the tower I was building there. I even told her of my tax problems with Sheriff Marc. As we reached the end of the aisle, where workmen, making a terrible din and filling the air with white dust, were

184

engaged in the construction of another bay on the end of the nave, we turned and began to head back east towards the choir.

Tilda said: 'I believe you have grown up, Sir Alan, all this talk of your son's education and building works in your home – and taxes! God save us all from taxes and the sheriff's boundless greed.'

'You have had your own problems with these demands for money?' I asked.

'By Heaven, we have,' said Tilda with a flash of anger in her eyes. 'Robert de Percy, the sheriff of Yorkshire, is a veritable beast in human form. He and his men thunder into the priory on horseback, issue dire threats and, although we try to accommodate them as best we can, times are hard. We give them what silver we can spare and they thunder away – only to be back a few months later with a fresh demand for an even greater sum. The prioress,' Tilda jerked her head backwards to the lady stumping along at our heels, 'my lady Anna, is at her wits' end. We have no more money put by; indeed, we were hoping to ask the Earl of Locksley if he would be so good as to make us a loan, just to keep the sheriff from the door.'

I was suddenly seized by a quiet rage. I thought about the 'thieves' who had broken into Kirkton, sheriff's men trying to intimidate Marie-Anne; and the same violent fellows terrorising Kirklees Priory and the good and holy women there as well. I thought about Philip Marc, our

Nottinghamshire sheriff, threatening to have his monster tear off my son's head if I refused to pay. I ground my back teeth. The same story was repeated again and again, all across that land. And the source of all of this intimidation and injustice was one man – the King. The King who exhorted his sheriffs to gather increasing quantities of silver from a land already groaning under the weight of his demands.

I was now more certain than ever that the King must be removed. Once again God had answered me.

'I dare say Robin will help you,' I said. 'And, as I am to dine with him today, I will mention your request and press the issue with him. But you may also find that, after tomorrow, Robert de Percy and all the other sheriffs and royal bullies will no longer be the blight on this land that they have become. I am sworn to secrecy and cannot say more,' I said, 'but, trust me when I say your troubles may suddenly, and very soon, be over.' I gave her a significant look and tapped the hilt of my sword.

Tilda told me I was a courageous man, she even kissed me lightly on the cheek and said that, if ever I happened to find myself in the vicinity of Kirklees, I must be sure to visit the priory. 'It has changed quite a bit since you were last there, Sir Alan,' said Tilda. 'We have extended the herb gardens to almost twice the original size. And the new infirmary – almost as big as the church and stone-built – is the wonder of the county. We do God's healing work there . . .'

'Sir Alan Dale,' said a deep male voice behind me, 'is that you?'

I had heard that St Paul's was the heart of London, the place to meet people and exchange gossip. I had heard that you would hear all the news of England if you spent enough time there and would run into everyone who was anyone if you idled long enough in its precincts, but I had not seriously believed it. Yet here was another old acquaintance met by chance that same morning.

'Sir Aymeric de St Maur, God's blessing on you,' I said to the tall, elderly, broad-shouldered man standing a yard away. 'You're in good health, I trust?'

'As good as Our Lord and this pestilential city will allow me,' said Sir Aymeric. 'Yourself? You look fit, Alan – heard you were consorting with Cathars and heretics and other undesirables. But you are back, I see, and apparently unharmed.'

Despite his words, Sir Aymeric de St Maur was smiling at me. We had had a number of run-ins in the past, and he had at times been friend and foe, but I respected the man, and admired him, for all that we did on occasion end up on opposite ends of the battlefield. Indeed, I liked him and I suspected that he liked me.

'I have heard that your many talents, my lord, have at last been recognised by your blessed brethren,' I said. 'I hear that you are now the Master of the English Temple and lord of all the Poor Fellow-Soldiers of Christ in this

187

land. How does all that wealth and power sit with you? You seem none the worse for it.'

'Ha! You are pleased to jest, Sir Alan. I have far less power than you might imagine and recently a lot less wealth: King John has twice this year demanded that the Knights of the Temple make generous loans to him . . . But enough of my tedious affairs. What brings you to London, my friend?'

'The same as everybody, I would imagine,' I lied, waving a hand about at the crowds of well-dressed folk wandering up and down the nave, 'the King's homage to the papal legate tomorrow. But let me introduce you to my companions . . .'

The meeting dissolved into pleasantries. Sir Aymeric was courteous to the two Cistercian ladies, praising the healing work of Kirklees, but he seemed rather too distracted to give them their proper due. Eventually, when he was about to take his leave of us, he drew me aside.

'Would you give my lord of Locksley a private message from me, Sir Alan,' he said, looking grave. I agreed, and he said this: 'Tell Locksley that I wish to speak to him while he is in London about a most urgent matter. If he would care to call by the Temple at his earliest convenience, I would be most grateful. And be sure to tell him this – it would be to his great disadvantage to make it later rather than sooner.'

It was a summons from the Templars.

And, for a courteous man, it was couched in none too courteous terms.

I was due to dine with Robin that day but it was almost noon when I took my leave of the ladies and made my way down towards Queen's Hythe, where Robin was staying with a wine merchant friend of his.

The wine that was served with dinner was magnificent but my welcome into the presence of my lord was not. There were a dozen other noblemen at the feast, including William the Marshal, Earl of Pembroke, and William Longsword, Earl of Salisbury, the King's half-brother who had led us to victory at Damme. There were also several of the grander merchants of London. I noticed that all the noblemen gathered there were staunch supporters of the King – none of the discontented northern barons were present. Had Robin chosen a side? Had he chosen to take the King's part?

I must admit that we feasted royally: roasted venison and wild boar, and spitted hares and dripping capons, great baskets of bread, bowls of freshly picked sallet leaves, crayfish stew, lamprey pies, cheese, fruit, puddings, nuts and wine – and more wine. I ate and drank with the rest of my lord's guests, but I was placed as far away from Robin as was possible given my rank as a senior knight. Indeed, whereas I had once frequently sat at his right hand, I now occupied a place far down the table among the lesser men-at-arms. My lord was angry with me. That much was clear.

'He knows what you are up to, Alan,' Little John told me in a loud whisper, when I stopped the big man after the feast and asked him why I was being treated so coldly. 'He doesn't like it. It would be best if you abandoned your little plot.'

'Not you as well, John,' I protested. 'Surely you know why I'm doing this; surely you agree that the man is a royal turd who must be washed down the chute.'

'Oh, aye,' the big man said, 'I have no problem with you taking out the King. And I'm sure you can do it. But I have a problem with you going against orders to do it. Robin is my lord – and yours – and he says no to this. Now, I won't stand in your way, for the sake of our friendship, but don't ask for my help either.'

Robin was cold and formal when I finally got to speak to him alone, long after all his guests had left. After the dinner he had been closeted with some of the greater barons and merchants for several hours and by the time I was admitted to his chambers, it was growing dark. Robin looked ill-tempered and out of sorts. I repeated the Master of the Templars' message word for word so as to convey its rudeness and urgency. But Robin merely grunted and looked at me with apparent distaste.

'So now you are mixed up with the Templars, too, are you?' he said.

I frowned. 'I am not mixed up – as you put it – with the Templars. I am merely delivering the message of the Master, who is an old friend of mine. And I am offering

190

to take a reply back to the Temple tonight, if you desire it.'

'I have no reply for them.'

'Do you know what they want?' I asked.

'No, and I don't care. I have had enough of Templars to last me a lifetime. The last time I went to the Temple, if you remember, they put me on trial for my life.'

'They will think you churlish if you don't reply.'

'God damn you, Alan. Why must you always seek to tell me what to do? I will have nothing to do with the Templars and their plots and politics – I have enough on my mind as it is – and if you were a wiser man, you would have nothing to do with them either. And nothing to do with those other cowardly schemers, de Vesci and Fitzwalter. Can't you see that they are merely using you? You are acting like a fool!'

I lost my control then. My anger had been simmering ever since the humiliation of dinner and the long wait to see him, and it boiled over in that instant.

'You call Fitzwalter a coward – and yet he at least has the courage to strike at the tyrant. You, apparently, do not. Perhaps it is not he but *you* who is the coward!'

Robin's face was white as salt.

'Get out!' he said quietly. 'Get out of this house before I do something I regret.'

I was already wishing my words back in my mouth. I had called my lord a coward to his face. I wanted to say that I did not mean it. I wanted to apologise to him and ask for his forgiveness, but before I could speak, Robin, for the third time, even more quietly and infinitely more menacingly, said: 'Get out, Alan. Now!'

I found my legs moving as if under the control of another man, taking me out of the chamber and towards the front door.

I must have walked back to my lodgings in Friday Street, a house owned by Lord Fitzwalter, but I have no recollection of it. I must have taken myself up to the garret at the top of the house where I was staying and washed and undressed and rolled into my cot. I must have fallen asleep. The next day, I rose late, long after dawn, with a double sense of dread, and washed and dressed myself in my finest clothes: the striped hose with the leather soles, the sky-blue wide-sleeved tunic and black hat. I do not think I have ever felt quite so alone. I strapped the misericorde to my left wrist and checked that it could not be seen when my arm was lowered. I drew it once and practised the killing stroke: a thrust, and twist upwards of the blade to find the heart.

My own heart was beating like a tambour. I felt the fear of what I was about to do weigh like lead upon my soul. My palms were wet, my hands shook. I felt sick to my stomach. God give me strength, I prayed. Do not let me prove to be a coward today, of all days. But despite my milksop quaking and the terrible deed that lay before me, half of my mind was on what I had said to Robin the night before. I wanted to rush directly round to the merchant's house in Queen's Hythe and throw myself on his mercy, beg for a reconciliation, tell him that I must have been drunk or mad to say such a thing. But I could not do it. Apart from pride or my dignity or anything of that nature, I had not the time.

The killing hour was upon me.

Chapter Fourteen

As I arrived at St Paul's Churchyard, I could hear the glorious singing of the monks from the cathedral spilling from the arched windows and the great open door in the south transept. It steadied me somewhat, that holy music, and I wiped my damp palms on my tunic and willed myself to be calm. God is here, I told myself. He sees me, He loves me. He will guide my arm this day. He is my strength and my shield.

I waited with the mass of people south of the cathedral, twenty yards from the dais and its gaudy purple awning where the ceremony would take place. It seemed as if the whole world was gathered in that courtyard to catch a glimpse of the King: apprentices with glowing faces, joyful with youth and at having a day of leisure; poor knights perhaps hoping for a chance to impress the court; big London goodwives angling for a touch of the King's mantle or a blessing for a sick child, merchants, shopkeepers, butchers, barbers, sailors at liberty from their ships, country folk in white smocks and floppy straw hats, children, dogs and horses. The great nobles and their retinues were already inside the church but I looked closely at the sea of faces and saw to my relief a captain of Fitzwalter's guards, bold in a gorgeous golden cloak with half a dozen men-at-arms at his back and a pair of slatternly women giggling beside him, there on the far side of the dais. He saw me looking at him from thirty yards away and gave me a small discreet nod of acknowledgement.

Be calm, I told myself. You know why you do this. For poor murdered Arthur, Duke of Brittany, for my son Robert, so that he may grow up and prosper in a just and fair land not under the yoke of a tyranny, for England and all her people . . .

And yet . . . And yet. He was the King. And what I was about to do would echo throughout England, throughout the world. God Himself had set King John over us, and I was presuming to know the mind of the Almighty, to know that He willed this King's life to be cut short by my hand. For a moment I contemplated walking away, pushing through the crowds and out into the vastness of London. I would find a tavern and drink until I knew no more. I was no assassin. What had I been thinking? I was a knight – I hoped a man of honour – and

195

here I was, contemplating this foul murder of the highest in the land. My back was slick with sweat, my knees were trembling, I could not seem to stop swallowing my own spit. And where, where was the King? The singing had long ceased in that vast House of God. Why was he not coming out of the cathedral? Had he changed his plans; had he somehow got wind of the plot? Was he toying with me? For an instant I stepped out of my body and contemplated the sweaty, trembling wretch I had become, his gaudy holiday clothes covering his black assassin's heart, one evil man in a crowd of happy innocent folk. Enough, Alan, I told myself. Be a man, for the love of God. Do not think; just do!

And, at last, they were coming out. A blast of trumpets. A blaze of bright colour. A file of Flemish crossbowmen wearing the lions of England on their red surcoats were shoving the crowds back. And there was the King of England, John, son of King Henry, brother of lionhearted Richard, a sallow figure, short, stooped, with greying once-bright hair but eyes as dark as his soul. He was dressed in a long purple cloak with white ermine at the shoulders and a thin circlet of gold around his brow. The crowd gave a vast roar – Love? Joy? Hatred? Contempt? Who could say?

The Flemish men-at-arms cleared a path for the King, brutally forcing the people back with their big wooden crossbows, using the heavy T-shaped weapons like cudgels and leaving more than a few bloodied faces in their wake.

John strolled into the centre of the courtyard, in an area of empty space, serene, yet with a slight supercilious smile playing over his lips. Behind him, out of the church door in a flood, came the other nobles, dazzling in blood red and leaf green, sea blue and silvery white, black fur and pale silk, jewels on every hand and at the neck, glinting in the sunlight.

I saw Fitzwalter's captain of guards in gold and scarlet scanning the crowd for me, finding my face and starting to push his way towards me. There was Robin, too, in dark forest green, bareheaded and standing beside the papal legate, Master Pandulf, an austere figure in black with touches of wine-red at neck and cuff, and Stephen Langton, the Archbishop of Canterbury. Robin saw me, I know he did, but his eyes moved over me as if we were strangers. Then he turned his back and began speaking to the legate. Fitzwalter's captain was at my shoulder by then. A comforting golden presence with eight mailed men forming a dense wedge behind him.

'Ready, sir?' he said.

I could not speak. My tongue and throat had become knotted. I managed a curt nod. The King was ten paces from me moving slowly towards the dais inside a loose ring of crossbowmen. John deigned to speak to a few of the men in the crowd; smiled and waved at others; a woman threw a rose at him that landed on the royal chest before slipping to the ground and I saw him flinch, for a moment, utterly terrified. William the Marshal called out a greeting to the King and was rewarded with a raised hand and a wave. The King was five paces from me, almost at the steps of the dais.

'Now!' said the captain in my ear.

Don't think, Alan, just do! Do it, now.

I moved jerkily towards the King, my eyes fixed on his face. I heard the sound of women shouting far behind him and away to my left; felt a wave of movement in the crowd. A burly crossbowman stood before me, a bearded man, reeking of garlic, but his head was twisted away, searching for the source of the commotion.

The women's screams had doubled in volume. I saw the red-haired wench seize a handful of the other woman's hair. A slap rang out. Men-at-arms were moving in to separate the women. More screams and harsh male shouts.

The Flemish crossbowman was distracted; his eyes fixed on the struggling women and the knot of soldiers around them. I slipped easily past his shoulder. The King was a mere three paces from me, with nothing between us but air.

I ran over in my mind the words I planned to say to the King at the moment the misericorde plunged into his belly: 'This death is made in the memory of Arthur, Duke of Brittany, whose murder at your orders I witnessed with my own eyes. Arthur thou art avenged!'

I realised that my lips had been moving to the words in my head.

Don't think, Alan; just do!

The King's gaze flashed to my face. He opened his mouth. I took a step forward.

'There, Stevin, there. It's Dale. The assassin! Take him, man, take him.'

My right hand was at my left sleeve; I was a yard away from the target.

But before I could even touch the handle of the weapon a force like a charging bull slammed into my back and hurled me sprawling to the ground. I saw a garlic-stinking bearded face snarling above mine and smashed my right fist into it. I lifted my head, my belly and upper legs pinned by the dead weight of the crossbowman and another fellow crashed down on top of my head and torso, flattening me back to the earth. I kicked and punched, writhed, squirmed and tried to reach my blade, but in an instant both my hands were held fast. Then my ankles were seized. There were booted legs all around. I felt a kick smash into my ribs. The pinning body suddenly lifted from my head and I stretched out my neck, teeth snapping, trying to bite anything within reach, and saw the shadow of a black, wooden T-shaped object swinging towards me. It crashed into the side of my head and I knew no more.

I have been knocked out of the world before, God knows, more times than I care to count, and mostly I recovered soon enough without serious hurt after a little rest and quiet. This time it was different. Perhaps it was my

199

advancing age. Perhaps the savage blow from the crossbow stock to my head shook up my brains in some unusual way. Perhaps it was because over the next few days the beatings never seemed to cease and I was never allowed to properly recover my senses. In any case, I cannot fully recall the next section of my life.

I know that I was bound, hand and foot, and stripped naked of my holiday finery, like a hog ready for slaughter, that every passing man-at-arms seemed to take a delight in kicking my bruised and roaring head. I was blindfolded, too, for a while, or maybe I just became blind for a period for I remember blackness and noise and pain – an ocean of pain. The beatings continued and I think I was in a church at some point – perhaps the cathedral itself, although it seemed a far smaller building. I smelled incense and wax and for some strange reason frying bacon and orange blossom.

Time passed and I heard voices raised in anger. The King's, Aymeric de St Maur and William the Marshal, too. And that of Tilda as well, soft and comforting, and her cool hand on my brow – but dreams and reality could not be easily parted. I thought I was at Westbury, at one point, with young Robert weeping over my dead body, saying: 'Don't leave me, Father, don't leave me at the mercy of that man.' I was back in the Holy Land with the blazing sun beating on my face. I was in Sherwood, still little more than a child, and Little John was crushing my head between his massive hands, the pressure tightening and tightening like a vice, and he was saying: 'God's fat greasy bollocks, Alan, you've drunk up all the ale again. You must be punished.'

I was in a cage, a wooden box on wheels with oak slats for bars, jolting over ruts in the road, and the sound and smells of horses, a sharp golden light in my eyes and rough hands pulling me from a slick of my own blood and vomit and the garlic-loving crossbowman punching me again and again before allowing me to slump down to the green turf. And blackness, sweet night and the blessed absence of light and noise.

I came to my senses in blackness. I truly believed that I might be dead and in some limbo state between Heaven and Hell. I opened my left eye. The other seemed to be glued shut. The blackness was the same with that eye open or closed. But my hands and legs were free and I reached up and touched my face and felt wetness and rough scabbing, and what seemed like vast hard lumps and bags of swollen tissue all over my face. I had no idea where I was or how long it had been since the day of the ceremony of papal homage. My hands roamed all over my body, feeling the tenderness in every inch of skin, the cuts and grazes, the pulpy ache of bruises no longer fresh. But I did not seem to have any broken bones: that in itself was a mercy, or perhaps in the afterlife all limbs were made whole. I was cold, deathly cold. Shivering like a man with an ague. I realised I was naked as a baby. And wet all over. I did not know whether the dampness came from sweat or blood or my own piss – my swollen nose was blocked solid and incapable of doing its duty. My questing fingers groped about my body and I felt cloth. Hallelujah! A blanket, by the feel of it. Furry with mould, torn and damp, but good English wool. I pulled it around my shoulders and sat up. My head reeled – streaks of red and yellow and silver exploding behind my eyes. My empty stomach heaved and I had to lower my head or I felt that I would die. I lay down and pulled the blanket over my shoulders and left the world once more.

I believe it was thirst that awakened me, my tongue dry and swollen twice its size and rough as oak bark. But I was still in the same dark place on a hard floor with a mouldy blanket over me and nothing more to cover my body. I could only conclude that I was alive. I was too aware of the aches and pains of my body to have left it behind on the mortal earth. Cautiously, I got to my feet. Every inch of my body hurt from my poor beaten head down to my bruised toes. I felt a wall on my left-hand side, rough, unplastered stone. Using my fingertips as eyes in the inky void, I began to explore my new world. It was a cold, barren place: four rock walls, a smooth stone floor and a ceiling about a foot above my head. I found a big, cool earthenware jug of water and a small wedge of rye bread, old and hard as hatred. Nothing more except a small wooden door set into the wall near one corner, on which I could feel the cold iron bands and studs that fortified it.

I drank half the water and used a cupful of it to soften the bread and get it down my throat. Using a strip of the blanket dipped in the jug I managed to unstick my right eye, though it was still swollen and tender and I could see no more in the blackness than before. I sat back down on the blanket and began to think.

I was a prisoner of the King, that much was clear. But where was I? Still in London? I thought not. I had been on a journey in that hellish stinking wooden cage, at least a day and a night. I reckoned that had been real. Though I had no idea where I had been taken or even in which direction. I thought about the King's words before his guards had wrestled me to the ground.

They were the last thing I remember clearly: 'There, Stevin, there. It's Dale. The assassin! Take him, man, take him.'

The King had called me an 'assassin' and named me. He clearly knew what I had intended to do before I even attempted it. Which begged the question: why was I still alive? If the King knew I had meant to murder him, why had he not had me hanged out of hand? Or had my throat cut and my body dumped in the Thames. He had done something similar to Arthur of Brittany and on far less provocation.

My bladder required my attention. I groped around the black space once more, feeling with my fingertips at ground level and especially in the corners, and found what I was searching for. A round hole about six inches wide that

203

dropped straight down below the floor for at least the length of my forearm. It was a drain. And this, I reasoned, meant that this was certainly a prison cell. Probably in the guts of a castle. The drain was to allow the noisome effluent produced by the prisoners to be swilled away by the guards. I used it for its intended purpose. Then sat back down on the blanket.

How long had I been in here, I wondered. I felt my chin and upper lip. There was a good deal of bristle beneath the scabs and filth – four days? Five? I had been shaved clean by a chatty London barber the day before the ceremony of homage. The ceremony had been held on Sunday, the saint day of Edward the Confessor, the thirteenth day of October. I had spent at least one night on the road, beaten unconscious by – what was that smelly brute's name? Stevin? So we might assume two days' travelling. In a slow cart two days might mean fifty miles. Had I imagined it, or had I seen the sun getting lower between the pair of horses that pulled my wooden cage along the road? If so, we had been heading west. I was probably about fifty miles west of London. As I was King John's prisoner, it was likely that I was being held in the dungeon of a royal castle, or one held by his staunchest allies. I thought of the royal strongholds that I knew of fifty miles west of London. Oxford? No, too far. Windsor? No, too close to London. Then I knew it: Wallingford. A small but strong royal fortress a dozen or so miles south-east of Oxford.

I was in Wallingford Castle. And judging by my beard, it was Thursday, the seventeenth day of October. Or possibly Friday.

I cannot tell you how cheered I was by my reckonings. I believed that I knew where I was and the day of the week. Paltry foundations on which to build your courage, you might think. But they made a new man of me.

I got up and hammered on the door with my fists – hurting myself in the process; even my hands were torn and bruised, and I knew that I must have fought my abusers and landed some blows. I called out as loudly as I could for a guard. My voice was weak, little more than a croak. There was no response. The silence mocked me. A wave of raw despair closed over my head once more.

I drank more water. I slept some more, too, and dreamt that I was free and happy and back at Westbury with Robert. We were riding, racing each other, in fact, on horseback across a wide open meadow, with spring flowers crushed under our horses' hooves scenting the air and the sunlight in our faces, hot sunlight . . .

I opened my eyes into a blaze of light. The cell door was wide open and a squat figure holding a burning pine torch stood in the doorway. The light burnt my eyes, and I had to shield them with a hand. The figure advanced and I saw it was holding a long, thick club in its right hand. Without a word, the gaoler came forward and struck at my head, hard. I got my shoulder and forearm up in time to stop the blow smashing into my skull – luckily, for I think it might have killed me. As it was, the blow thumped across my shoulder and clipped the top of my head and set off a hellish screaming inside my skull. I was immediately knocked flat on to my back, sprawled helpless on my blanket.

'Want another?' The creature raised the club over me. The voice was light, boyish, but I confess I cowered. On another day I might have taken that club away and forced it far up the fellow's fundament. But I was weak, hurting and my whole left arm felt numb and leaden.

'You behave yourself, like a good little boy, and you'll get a nice, hot bowl of soup later, when we get ours. You give me trouble . . .' The shape lifted the club.

'Who are you?' I said. 'Where am I?'

The gaoler swung the club but I twisted away as fast as I could and the blow cracked agonisingly against my spine.

'Bein' a good boy means you don't ask no questions. That vexes me, see?'

I said nothing. The pain was making it hard for me to breathe.

'Now, you get up, up now, and you stand still.'

The guard prodded me with the club.

I thought: I swear I will pay you out for that, you whoreson bastard. But I did not dare say a word aloud, not a word. I hauled my battered body with considerable difficulty into a standing position.

It hurt even to stand.

'Now be still. Just there. Don't move a muscle.'

The squat gaoler disappeared through the open doorway. My eyes were a little more used to the light by now and I could see into the room outside my cell. It was slightly bigger than my chamber but similar in its stark lack of decoration and almost as empty. Stone walls, a table and a stool. The gaoler, I saw to my surprise, was a strongly built woman of middle years with long grey hair tied in a horse's tail at the back and clad in a sleeveless leather coat. A vast sagging bosom protruded from the front of the coat, hanging over her belly. A filthy skirt hung to her ankles. She had her back three-quarters turned to me, had put her club on the table and was filling a small, iron-banded wooden bucket with a rope handle from a wooden butt on the far side of the room.

She came back to the door of the cell and flung a bucket of icy water directly in my face. I flinched from the shock and took one pace back.

The gaoler screamed: 'Don't you move! Don't you fuckin' move!'

Then she seemed to gather herself and she said more quietly: 'Don't you vex me, Sir Knight. Get back on that spot there and stay deadly still! I'm to clean you up, they said. Clean you up nice and make you presentable. You've got a visitor, they say. So don't you vex me.'

I returned to the spot by the door that she had indicated, the water streaming down my face and naked body. The gaoler returned to her butt and refilled the bucket.

I stood quite still.

The gaoler drew back her arms to hurl the water. I braced myself. The cold water flashed towards me. I reached out my left hand, pushing it straight into the deluge, seized the rim of the bucket, more by luck than skill, for the flying water had blinded me, and hauled back.

The gaoler, still holding the rope handle of the bucket and utterly surprised, shot forward, and I punched her as hard as I could with my right fist.

It was not the best punch I have ever thrown. I was weak, dizzy, my body was battered and bruised in a hundred places, but it was a half-decent strike and – much as I hate to hit a woman – I felt a flare of bright joy as my knuckles crunched into her hard jaw and I felt the snap of bone. The gaoler staggered against the side of the cell, her legs wobbling beneath her. The empty bucket clattered against the stone floor at my feet. She shouted: 'Alarm! Alarm!' – a feeble cry, but it spurred me to action.

I stooped, picked up the bucket by the rope handle, and as the gaoler recovered slightly and straightened up, I swung it and the iron-banded weight smashed into the side of her head. The bucket disintegrated into a mess of metal hoops, splinters and kindling. She fell like a dropped stone.

I slipped out of the open door like a weasel. I had the club in my hand and came back into the cell to see that

the woman was still alive, even conscious, and was struggling to get to her feet, blood streaming from her ear.
She was a hard-headed bitch, I'll give her that.

I killed her, God forgive me, with one chopping blow
of the club to the crown of her head, putting a dent the
size of an apple in her skull. Then I stripped the long
leather coat from her corpse. Wrapping the mouldy blanket
around my loins – it was light green, I discovered – and
club still in hand, I limped to the door of the outer room.
I was but one pace from the door when it swung open of
its own accord. A crossbowman, a big bearded fellow,
stepped into the room. His weapon was held to his right
shoulder, it was spanned, a black quarrel in the groove,
and pointed directly at my heart. I saw that it was my
old garlic-eating friend Stevin – and behind him I could
see four or five other crossbowmen, and beyond them a
pair of men with long spears.

Stevin said: 'Put the club down this very instant or
you die.'

I could see his right hand tightening on the lever that
would release the cord and drive the quarrel through two
yards of air and deep into my chest. At that range, it
would have punched a hole straight through and out the
other side.

The club clattered to the ground.

'Over there, sit on your hands,' said Stevin, motioning
me with the crossbow to the wall of the chamber. The
other guards flooded into the room, jostling and gaping

at me. I sat against the stone, my poor bruised hands under my poor bruised thighs.

'Sweet Jesu, he's killed Jessie!' said one of the crossbowmen, peering into the cell at the gaoler's corpse, his face pale as milk.

Stevin said, over his shoulder: 'He is as vicious as they say. Tricksy, too, by all accounts. And not above murdering anyone in his path. I want men with bows on him all the time, every instant when he is not in the cell. Am I clear? Jan, Willi – you keep your weapons spanned and on him all the time.'

And to me: 'I would as soon kill you now, assassin. But you have a visitor who wishes to speak to you, so I shall forgo the pleasure. Now, get on your feet. You walk three paces ahead of me. If you walk too fast, I kill you; if you run, I kill you; if you slow down, I kill you. Am I clear? If you make any sudden move, I kill you. Yes?'

I was marched down the long corridor outside the cell and its anteroom with three quarrel points making my back itch. I walked as well as I was able, a decent speed, neither too fast nor too slow – but not from fear at Stevin's threat.

It seemed to me that I was a dead man already and it could only be an hour or two at most before I was in my grave.

Chapter Fifteen

I was marched along the corridor, and glancing right and left through open doors, I saw that there were at least four other cells with antechambers just like mine. Through one door I saw a larger room with a brazier glowing a dull red and manacles hanging from the walls. An emaciated wretch was strapped to a table in there, pale as a frog's belly, except where the irons had blistered his skin purple. His eyes were closed and I prayed that he had found his eternal rest. This was clearly a prison, designed specifically for holding men, punishing them, absorbing their screams. And, oddly, I was a little cheered by this. I had heard tell of such a place: known as Brien's Close after a fierce nobleman in the days of war between King Stephen and Empress Matilda, or the 'Anarchy', as that period of lawlessness is now called. And it *was* inside Wallingford Castle. I had been correct in my calculations. I would know where I was to meet my death.

We went up a set of stone steps and along another corridor: guardrooms on this floor, and kitchens, by the smell of it. Onion soup cooking. Then we came out of the building into the grey light of an October day and I found myself in a large courtyard perhaps a hundred and twenty yards wide. It was surrounded on all sides by high stone walls, with towers set into them. To my right was a vast mound of packed earth a hundred feet high and atop it a curtain wall beyond which I could make out a strong square tower, the motte. Directly in front of me was, of all things, a vegetable garden: a rounded square filled with neat rows of leeks and onions, herbs and medicinal plants; a section of apple trees and trellises of plums. For some reason, Tilda and the new herb garden at Kirklees sprang into my mind. I had never seen it and I never would. I would have liked to have seen Tilda one more time, too, before the end. But that was clearly not to be.

The crossbowmen closed up around me as we crossed the courtyard and the people walking about in that space, men-at-arms, servants, a monk or two, stopped at the sight of me and gawped. I felt painfully conscious of how I must have looked: a prisoner, filthy and bloody, bruised and cut, dressed in a dead woman's leather coat with a mouldy blanket wrapped around my middle. A drunken pair of knights guffawed at my state and pointed, slapping

212

their sides with mirth; a passing priest closed his eyes and began to pray as I shambled past awkwardly barefoot with my cloud of watchful guards.

I was herded, not towards the motte and the high tower at its summit, but to the far side of the courtyard, towards the open gate through which I could just glimpse a broad expanse of water – the Thames, I assumed. I thought for a moment about trying to run. The main gate was wide open, and if I could slip my wardens I might find a boat . . . But I knew it was futile. I would not get ten yards before I was skewered by a trio of lethal quarrels. And I did not want to die. Not yet. The perennial prayer of the condemned man: *Dear Lord, not now, I beg you, not now.*

My captors took me to a large hall on the far side of the courtyard, and bustled me inside. It was half-filled with folk – castle servants, men-at-arms, countrymen and women, dogs and even a couple of hawkers with their birds on their arms – and I was shoved roughly to the floor by the wall and told to sit quietly and wait. While Jan and Willi stood over me with their bows – I was gratified to see that they were very tense and seemingly much afraid of me – I rested my head back against the wattle-and-daub wall and closed my eyes.

'Good Lord, you look a mess,' said a voice. I opened my eyes and looked up at a tall man with cropped iron-grey hair, dressed in a rich scarlet-coloured ankle-length tunic. He had a long sword at his waist and an ivory crucifix on a golden chain around his neck.

213

It was Aymeric de St Maur, Master of the English Templars.

The Templar began issuing orders: 'Get this man a stool, now, and a cup of ale – for the love of God. And something to eat.'

Stevin and the others had disappeared, but Jan and Willi looked at each other, hesitating.

'Get on with it, you fools. Now!' Sir Aymeric's words cracked like a whip. 'I'll watch him. He will not run, I promise you.'

As Jan unspanned his bow, tucked his quarrel in his belt and hurried away to obey the words of command, Willi looked sick with fear, but he held his ground and kept his crossbow pointed unwaveringly at my head like a good soldier.

'Well, you've really done it now, Sir Alan,' said Aymeric in a kindly tone. 'They say you were all ready to cut the King's head clean off. Is that right?'

I said nothing and closed my eyes again.

'Answer me, man, we don't have much time. Were you trying to kill the King?'

I was spared from answering by the arrival of a pair of servants with a stool and a jug of ale. I drank it greedily and set it between my feet as someone handed me a bowl of oat porridge with a handful of raisins stirred into it. I sat on the stool and slurped the food and washed it down with the ale, and Aymeric de St Maur looked down at me with a silent compassion.

When I had finished he said: 'Alan, I know you are a good son of the Church, and if you are to be executed, I know that you will want to die in a state of grace. I can shrive you of your sins, I can guarantee you a place in the Heavenly Kingdom, and I would do it – but if you care for your soul, you must answer this question.'

I remained mute.

'Where is it, Sir Alan?'

I goggled at the man. What on earth was he talking about?

'Where is it? Tell me, Alan, and I will save your soul.'

'What?' I stammered. 'I don't know . . .'

Just then Stevin returned with Jan and a trio of cross-bowmen. He snarled and kicked the porridge bowl out of my hands, then he and another guard hauled me roughly to my feet and began to march me to the end of the hall.

'Tell me where it is, Sir Alan, I beg of you. There is no time. Tell me and I will save you—'

I heard Sir Aymeric's words clearly as I was hustled away, three big angry men pushing and shoving me onwards, nigh on lifting me towards a big carved chair on a dais at the far end of the building.

And there was the King.

John looked old. His face was pouchy and grey, his red-gold hair was streaked with silver, his belly had thick-ened and slumped around his middle like a wide belt of flesh. Apart from those few brief instants outside St Paul's I had not seen him close up for many years – and those years had not been kind. He looked at me as if he could taste something disgusting on the tip of his tongue.

'I should have you hanged, drawn and quartered,' he said. 'I should have torn out your innards and fed them to my dogs long since. You have been a stone in my shoe, Alan Dale; a mosquito that I have been too soft-hearted to swat; a beetle that I have neglected for too long to squash.' His voice rose to the ugly croaking that I remembered well. 'This is how you repay my extraordinary leniency? With this?'

The King held up the black misericorde attached to the archer's bracer that Fitzwalter had given me. He was shouting by now, quite purple in the face. 'You murderous, gutter-born turd. You presume to lay hands on *me*!'

I let the royal fury wash over me. I would die, for sure, and I only prayed that it would be swift. It would be soon, I knew. I prayed that I would be reunited with my love, my dead wife Godifa, in Heaven.

'I would tear the flesh from you with red-hot pincers' – flecks of royal spittle rained down on my face – 'I would have you trampled by wild bulls and thrown still breathing to the lions of my menagerie . . .'

Suddenly the King's fury seemed to be spent.

'But your *friends*' – he spat the word – 'your friends at court tell me I cannot kill you without the risk of the whole of England rising in rebellion. They say there is no proof of your intent and that you are innocent of any crime. I say they are wrong. What say you?'

216

I had almost lost the wits to speak. Almost.

If I were a truly brave man, I would have spoken the truth and damned him for a foul and murderous tyrant who richly deserved death at my hands. But I did not. And in such moments as these the mark of a man is revealed. I played the craven – I was craven. I did not actually beg for my life but I did the next best thing.

'Sire,' I said, 'I am innocent of any crime. I did not strike at you or harm you. At St Paul's I merely wished to ask you a boon, to crave your royal grace's blessing on a private matter. There is no proof of my crime because . . . because I am truly innocent.'

I am damned as a coward. And a liar, too.

'No proof?' shouted the King. 'I say this is proof enough!' And he waved the misericorde in front of his face.

'Give me that blade and I will gladly prove my innocence with my body against any man you care to name.'

'Oh, you would like that, wouldn't you? Oh yes. You have a name as a cold-blooded killer. No doubt you would like to add one more corpse to the black tally on your soul. But I will not risk one of my good men against you. No, no, no!'

The King looked at me. He seemed to be thinking.

'Was it Fitzwalter? Or Lord de Vesci? Or both of them. You were seen at Alnwick Castle not three months ago. Did you hatch your little plot with them? Tell me? Do you think we do not watch them – those creeping northern reptiles?'

I shrugged. 'I am innocent, sire.'

'You lie – and yet I have given my word to your *friends*' – again that word – 'that I will not harm you without sufficient proof. And I am a man of my word. So I shall not harm so much as a hair on your head.'

I looked at the King, unbelieving. Was this truly a reprieve? Then I saw that a horrible smirk was twitching at his wine-red lips. He repeated: 'I swore that I would not harm you – and I will not.'

He gave a little chuckle that froze my blood.

'Take him away,' he said.

I was marched back across the courtyard with my head spinning from the encounter. What did he mean when he said that he would not harm me? And why did this uncharacteristic clemency seem to amuse him so much? As we entered Brien's Close, down the stone steps, through the corridors, and back to my black stone cell, the awful answer began to form in my mind. I was shoved roughly into my prison and before the door was slammed shut, I noticed something that chilled me more than I can say: the corpse of the woman gaoler was gone and in its place someone had set the big water butt from the antechamber. It had been filled to the brim. The door banged behind me and, a few moments later, to my horror I heard the slap of planks and the sound of eager hammers driving nails deep into wood. And, as the blackness wrapped itself around me once again, I had the answer to the riddle.

Chapter Sixteen

I wept. I confess it. Unmanly as it must seem to all. I wept like a baby – for I knew how I would die in those hours after I was nailed securely into my dark and silent tomb. I had water – many gallons, enough to last me for weeks. But apart from the few spoonfuls of porridge in my belly, I knew I would receive no more nourishment in this life. I thought of Maud, the brave and foolish lady of William de Braose, and her son who were imprisoned in Corfe Castle until they expired of hunger; not killed directly by the King's men, but just as dead nonetheless. King John would not harm me, just as he had said, but nor would he give me my liberty until I was a lifeless husk.

So I wept. I prayed. I wept again. And I slept once

more, wrapped in a dead woman's coat and a mouldy green blanket.

What can I say about the hideous lifetime I spent alone in the darkness in that cell? It was a small freezing hell, lacking in all comfort save the water barrel – and believe me I drank my fill. I also washed myself from head to foot and dried myself on the blanket. I cautiously stretched my body and loosened my bruised and aching muscles as well as I could.

Over the next few days, I searched the cell with my fingertips, every bump, every crevice, every fold in the rock walls. There was nothing in there but myself, my blanket, my sleeveless coat, the water butt and the drain. And not a sound to be heard nor a sight to be seen. Most of the time I sat on my blanket and thought – I thought about, well, I thought about nearly everything.

My musings first turned to Robin. My lord. How bitterly I regretted our last words to each other. I had been a fool to have abused him so. I had called him a coward to his face, perhaps the worst insult one could throw at a fighting man. I knew Robin had been hurt – angry, too. After our estrangement over my foolish attempt to take down the King – how could I have been so bone-headed as to think I would succeed? – and my gross behaviour, I knew I could not expect him to come to my aid. Indeed, I knew no one was coming to my aid. I believed that he might have had words with the King on my behalf – he and perhaps the Master of the Templars, and perhaps William the Marshal, too, were my 'friends', as the King had so scathingly called them. I believed that they and Robin might have warned the King not to harm me. But my lord could do nothing, even if he were so inclined, to extricate me from my tomb. I was in one of the strongest prisons in the country, inside a powerful fortress. Even with a mighty army Robin could not ride to my rescue, and to raise the force required to take Wallingford Castle, Robin would have to openly side with the rebel cause – something I knew he would not do. But even if he did, even if he overcame his doubts about rebellion, why would he sacrifice his soldiers to take a stronghold just to free one man – a man who had so insulted him? He would not. Robin was not coming for me. Nobody was coming for me.

In my weakness and self-pity, I wept again.

A day or so passed. Even so soon, I began to lose my grip upon the surface of the world. My belly was soon empty, and I drank water, pints of it, to give it the illusion of satiation. I worked on my aching body some more, losing myself in the strengthening routines that all soldiers know. I lay full length on my back and pulled myself into a sitting position, time and time again until I fell back exhausted. I lay on my front and, keeping my body stiff, I pumped my full weight up and down using only the strength of my arms. I paced that tiny cell corner to corner to keep my legs from becoming weak: one, two, three, four paces, then turn, and one, two, three, four back to the far corner. I walked for hours, until sheer exhaustion, and a knowledge of the futility of my actions, led me to cower miserably under the damp blanket and seek the solace of sleep.

How we take our daily bread for granted! I dreamed of food at the beginning, I thought of it every waking minute, too, as my belly shrank and whimpered and ached. After four or five days, when my gut was calling piteously, I hunted insects and beetles, which must have come up through that stinking drain – and ate them, crunching them up or swallowing them down still wriggling. But soon they disappeared, or were all eaten up, and there was only my empty insides shrieking at me for nourishment. I retreated into the land of dreams, for there I could eat my fill: I must have recalled every feast I had ever attended, I relived every pie, every dripping roast, every fragrant bowl of creamy pudding. I tormented myself with thoughts of the meals I would never enjoy again. I made up lists of what I would eat in Heaven – roast pork was the centrepiece of the feast, a whole gleaming piglet with rich wine gravy and the crackling, crisp and salty. But there would be fresh baked bread too with a slathering of yellow butter and soft crumbly white cheese and crunchy apples. And nuts and wine and singing and laughter.

But all pain eventually comes to an end. My hunger raged like a furnace for some days, perhaps a week, and then, as if burnt out, it subsided to a vague cold feeling of loss, an emptiness that was always present but duller than the agony of before. I began to die. And also to think clearly without the distraction of my belly.

I thought about Goody, my beautiful dead wife, with whom I longed to be reunited in paradise – but not yet; I thought about Tilda, and our one night together long ago in Normandy. I thought about Robert, about his sweet face screwed up in concentration over the chessboard. Then I thought about Westbury. I wished once more to be riding free on my own lands, with my hounds and huntsmen, with Robert and perhaps Robin and his sons for company. If I ever emerged from this dark place, I vowed to myself, I would never take the feel of sunshine on my face for granted again, nor the feel of a running horse between my legs and the wind in my hair.

I thought about Lord Fitzwalter and wondered if he, too, and Eustace de Vesci as well, were sitting somewhere in the darkness, with an echoing belly and nothing ahead of him except madness, despair and death. I doubted it. Robin had been right. I had been used by him and de Vesci. They had gulled me like a child into this mad scheme that, now that I truly considered it, had had scant chance of success.

I thought, too, about King John's words before I was taken: how he had called me assassin before I had even drawn the misericorde. And in the clarity of my own head, in the silence of the cell, and in the deepest part of my soul I knew I'd been betrayed. Someone had informed on me to the King. Someone had told him that

223

I was planning his murder and told him when I would strike – for the King had been expecting me. He had surrounded himself with his Flemish crossbowmen, Stevin and his mercenary ilk, and they had been primed to locate and intercept me.

But who could it be?

Fitzwalter and de Vesci knew of the plan – but why would they betray me? They wanted me to succeed. And the only other person who knew that I meant to kill the King was Robin. But he would never inform on me to the King. Would he?

I believe that my soul left my body in that deep dark place. The days passed with no marking them, no day, no night. I drank the water. I hunted anything that scuttled in the darkness and I dreamed: of food and revenge, or the smell of sweet flowers; of the taste of Goody's kisses. My beard grew in fuller, my skin became loose. And my soul left me for hours at a time. I found myself at one point looking down on my sleeping body from above. The cell was filled with a weird blue light and I could see every inch of that square stone box with absolute clarity.

I had ceased to exercise my body by then. I had not the strength to force my muscles to work. And when my soul rose out of me, I looked down at the wasted body, the bearded head pillowed on the rolled leather coat, my bony shoulders almost poking through the green blanket.

I wanted to be gone. I was tired of the cold and the darkness. I was tired of being alone. I heard the Voice of God calling me, calling me by name, and looked upwards towards a great, warm golden light . . .

'Christ's foul flapping foreskin – the stench in here would stun a bull,' said a deep and familiar voice. Then an enormous sneeze. And there was light. A harsh, burning dazzle that seared my eyeballs and made me whimper in fear and pain.

'Just get him out of there, John,' said another voice, equally familiar. 'Gently now. You'd best pick him up and carry him.'

I was lifted from the hard floor and borne out of that cell by powerful arms. I knew I was dreaming. I heard the second voice, close to my ear, saying: 'Alan Dale, I swear you're the most inconvenient, ungrateful, insolent, mutton-headed oaf that I have ever had the misfortune to take into my service.'

I ate soup, nothing more, for three days. And not too much of that. There was no roast pork with crisp crackling and wine-gravy. Robin knew, as I did, that to feed a starving man rich food will kill him as quickly as the hunger itself. After three days, I began to drink milk and took my first piece of bread.

Robin and Little John had taken me out of Brien's Close and installed me in a small shed – an abandoned blacksmith's forge to be accurate – on the south side of

225

the castle. There was no subterfuge, none of the cunning tricks that Robin was so well-versed in. No ruse at all. It was not bribery, nor yet force of arms. Robin had arrived with a small escort of thirty Sherwood bowmen and a royal warrant ordering the constable of the castle to surrender my person immediately to the bearer of the parchment without delay. Then he insisted that suitable accommodation be found for my recovery under the rough care of Little John.

I was only dimly aware of what was happening. I was sleeping half the day and all the night, but when I did manage to rise and stagger to the door of the stable and look out one afternoon, I was amazed to see the whole place was filled with men-at-arms in different coloured surcoats swaggering about the courtyard as if they owned it. On the far side of the castle, high on the square keep atop the motte, I could see two dozen flags flapping in the grey air. A gathering was in place. Beside the royal standard, the lions of England, I could see the banners of a handful of barons whose arms I recognised: William the Marshal, the Earl of Salisbury, the earls of Norfolk, Essex, Oxford and Hereford, Lord Fitzwalter and de Vesci were there too – even a white banner with a black wolf's mask on it, which was Robin's own device.

Little John, who was about some business of his own in the castle that day, returned at dusk. The big man was carrying a heavy sack that clanked as he walked. 'You'd best get your rest tonight, Alan,' he said, and gave a sneeze like a trumpet blast. 'For there will be some hellish noise tomorrow.'

'From the gathering?' I asked. 'There seems to be some sort of conclave in the castle of all the great men of England.'

'No, not from all those high and mighty folk up in the keep – from me,' said the blond giant with a smile. And he emptied out the sack he was carrying on the straw of the floor and began to sort through the twisted lumps of iron that it had contained.

I had not the strength to ask what he was about. My incarceration had left me with a fever and a hacking cough, and I returned to a pile of straw with a cup of mead, and after I had drunk it I coughed myself to sleep. I awoke late in the night, or rather very early in the morning, to find that Little John had built a huge fire in the abandoned forge and seemed to be piling shovel after shovel of black charcoal on to the flames. I thought he was trying to be sure that I was warm enough, and I was grateful for his solicitousness, for the nights were cold and damp and it seemed to me that I was getting sicker rather than stronger.

I found out what he was really doing the next day. He had set up an anvil and found a set of hammers and tongs from somewhere, and not long after first light he began heating various pieces of metal in the cherry-red fire, hauling them out when they glowed, and beating them with powerful strokes that seemed to drive a spike through my temples.

'Told you there'd be some noise,' he said, grinning over his shoulder.

'Do you have to do that?' I shouted to the big man.

'Have to. Got to beat it while it's the right heat. Can't wait around for it to cool. Why don't you go and stretch your legs? Robin's in the stable just now.'

Little John turned back to his hellish hammering.

I got down another cup of mead and ate a piece of bread with a sliver of cheese. It had been five days since my release and I was a little shocked at how feeble I still was. I pulled on the clothes that Robin had left for me and, shivering like an ancient and coughing like a Cornish tin miner, I ventured out into the drizzle of the courtyard.

I found my lord of Locksley in the stable about a hundred and fifty yards from the forge on the extreme far side of the courtyard. Once again, as I staggered across the open space, I received a barrage of looks of astonishment and contempt. 'God damn you all,' I thought. 'When I am well, if any of you dares to look at me like that, I will cut you a new shit-hole.'

I was exhausted by the time I arrived at the stables to find Robin overseeing the shoeing of his favourite horse, a blood-red mare called Eva.

Robin took one look at me and said: 'Damn it, Alan, what are you doing out of bed? You need to rest and sleep and take some soup. This is no time for gallivanting about the castle. Get back to bed.'

'Couldn't sleep,' I said, and gave a cackling laugh.

'Well, sit down here and have a sup of ale at least. Are you hungry?'

I shook my head but gratefully sat down by the water butt. I happened to catch my reflection in the surface of the water and nearly expired of shock. An evil old man stared back at me. My hair, which I usually kept cropped short anyway, appeared to have disappeared from large patches of my head, the bald skin showing cleanly through. My beard, normally a lightish brown, which I had not yet had the strength to shave off, was streaked with lines of white. My face was that of a grandfather – but covered with scabs, old yellow-brown bruises, half-healed cuts and fresh pink scars.

No wonder the men-at-arms in the courtyard had stared at me. I was, at that time, not far off forty and I looked double that age.

I turned away from the reflection.

'Tell me what is going on at the castle,' I asked my lord.

He was peering at his horse's off hind foot, which the farrier had lifted and held between his two legs.

'What?' said Robin. 'Oh, everyone is here. We were summoned, all the great and the good – and the bad, too, for that matter. It's the same go-around as at St Paul's last month, of course – but you won't know about that.

My apologies. The northern barons are here, the rebels, the undecided, the malcontents and the genuinely aggrieved, along with the King and the men who are still loyal to him, or who desperately need him; and the bishops and archbishops, the whole merry cavalcade. All the nobility of England, more or less, is here at Wallingford. That's why you're sleeping in a forge.'

'But what are they here for?'

'They are here to try to prevent the whole country falling into another Anarchy,' Robin said grimly. He murmured something to the farrier, pointing to a curl of yellow hoof that required clipping.

'More, please,' I said holding out my cup.

'Yes, I'm sorry,' said Robin, straightening up and bringing the jug over to me. He filled my cup and said: 'It's the same old thing at the root of it, Alan. Put simply, the King wants to get back his lands in Normandy and France. To do that he needs the barons to go to war, he also needs money to pay for the war. In raising the money for his wars, he has taxed the country until it is bled white, and then asked for more. The barons resent this – my God do they resent it – and that is fair enough; you and I both know what it is like to have a sheriff constantly hounding you for silver.'

I thought of Philip Marc's visit to Westbury and his threat to have his huge monster tear the living head from my son.

My thoughts must have been written on my face, for

Robin suddenly said: 'Last week, Alan, I sent Hugh to Westbury with twenty Sherwood men. And I hear that Sir Thomas Blood has been drilling your own folk like a moon-crazed sergeant-at-arms. You can set your mind at rest. Between the two of them they will keep Robert safe.'

'Thank you!' I would have said more but I was cut off by a vicious fit of coughing. It took an age for me to recover myself.

Robin waited patiently until I was still again and quiet. 'Where was I? Oh yes, the King wants the barons to fight for him in France. As you know, many of them refused his call to arms. So the King can fight them, or he can talk to them and try to persuade them to follow his banner abroad. The barons want an end to harsh taxation, to the practice of mulcting every man at every available opportunity, of putting men into debt with arbitrary fees and taxes and then imprisoning them till they pay up or die. And a host of other things besides. They want their grievances addressed before they will consent to fight.'

'But how can they trust the King?' I said. 'He will say one thing today and another tomorrow when the battle is fought.'

Robin frowned. 'I don't want to burden you with the details now, Alan, I can see that you do not have your full strength yet. But suffice it to say, an agreement has been struck and many of the barons have now agreed to take part in the King's expedition to Poitou after Christmas and to fight at his side to help him recover his lands and titles in France. Other men have agreed to go to the Low Countries under the Earl of Salisbury and to fight there.'

'Who in their right mind would volunteer to fight for this King anywhere in Christendom?' I said. 'What sort of idiot would trust John to keep his word?'

'This sort of idiot,' said Robin quietly. 'I have agreed to follow Salisbury to Flanders again. And you are coming with me. I'm to take a strong force of spearmen and bowmen and we are to attack France and win Normandy back for King John.'

'For God's sake – why?' I was near exploding. Instead I coughed like a dying man. 'Have we not served the wretched fellow long enough? Have you forgotten Château Gaillard and the men who were uselessly slaughtered there? Why, Robin, why?'

'Because,' said my lord slowly, 'among other things, that was the price demanded by the King for your freedom.'

I was speechless.

'So you, my old friend, had better rest and eat and get back your full strength. We have another war to fight in the spring.'

Chapter Seventeen

I did not become stronger that winter. I became more and more sickly. Something in that experience of incarceration had got hold of my soul and seemed determined to drag me down into the pit. Perhaps the Devil felt that I owed him a soul because I had escaped certain death in that dank cell. In any case, when Robin, Little John and the Sherwood men left Wallingford Castle two days later they had to bear me in a covered cart pulled by two horses. Beside me on the bed of the cart, as I shivered and coughed and slipped off for hours at a time into a hellish delirium, lay my weapons, my sword Fidelity and the misericorde that King John's men had taken from me. Quite how Robin had recovered them from King John, I never discovered – perhaps they had merely agreed that

I would need them in Flanders – but I was grateful that my lord had been so thoughtful. As well as my personal weapons, I lay beside a bundle of long oak staves with sharp and curious iron attachments at both ends: the fruits of Little John's noisy work in the forge.

Before we left, as I lay coughing on a bed of straw, Little John demonstrated his new poleaxe: the inch-thick oak staff was eight foot long, two foot taller than I, and at the top was socketed a one-foot spear blade. Below the spear part was welded a single axe blade on one side and a curving hook on the other. At the other end was a sharp iron butt-spike.

'This is the perfect weapon for the foot soldier,' Little John told me. 'And I have your boy Robert to thank for the idea. Do you remember when he suggested some sort of hook to pull a knight off his horse? Well, with a few modifications, this is the result of his thinking. It is very cheap to make, simple to keep and use, and is devastating against enemy cavalry . . .'

The big man demonstrated that the poleaxe could be used as an ordinary quarterstaff, blocking sword blows, keeping the enemy at bay, and striking with enough force to brain a man; then he demonstrated how it could be used as a spear – both ends being sharp enough to punch through mail; and then, after leaping about the forge with the poleaxe, whirling the weapon about his body, he showed me how it could be used as an axe, cutting at a man eight feet away, say a French knight.

'This is the part that Robert can take credit for,' said Little John. 'The hook!' He mimed gaffing a knight's mail with the hook behind the axe-head and hauling him down from the back of his mount before dispatching him with the butt-spike.

I'll admit I was impressed. Footmen hate cavalry and are most often terrified of them. An armoured man high up on the back of a horse is frequently out of reach of the man on the earth and can rain down blows that are very difficult to answer. But once a knight was pulled down to the ground in the thick of battle he was easy meat for even poorly armed infantry to engulf and destroy.

'When you are back on your feet, Alan,' said John, bringing me a bowl of hot leek soup and a cup of wine, and tucking the blankets in around my wasted body, 'I'll give you a few lessons. You'll get the hang of it in no time.'

It was nearly the end of November when we left, a season of wet and cold, a bad season to be travelling, for the roads had quickly become quagmires in the autumn rains and the wheels of the cart that carried me became stuck in holes and ruts at least three or four times a day and had to be lifted out by strong backs. I discovered from Robin that I had been in that starvation cell for seventeen days. That might not seem so much, a little over two weeks, but the toll on my body had been enormous. Despite several days of care and hot food, I was as frail as I had ever been, my arms and legs like sticks, the skin falling in loose folds over my belly, I had lost much of my hair and several teeth. But it was the damage to my insides that I feared the most. Something evil had got into my lungs and I often seemed to be drowning in phlegm. My chest hurt and I found myself panting like a hound. When I was not in the fever-lands of the dark night, I coughed almost continuously.

Robin, Little John and the Sherwood bowmen left me at Westbury, with Baldwin fussing about me, but I don't remember much of our parting. My lord was returning to Kirkton to begin planning the spring campaign and to start raising and training troops for the expedition. Hugh said that he was happy to remain at Westbury until I was fully recovered, and he and Sir Thomas had plainly been working hard on the training of my men.

Robert was pleased to see me but dismayed to find me so weak and ill. So I forced myself to get out of bed to watch a demonstration of his prowess in the courtyard. He and Sir Thomas Blood went at it with sword and shield, around and around, and while I could see that there had been considerable improvement, I could also see that he was still far from a warrior. I applauded him lavishly nonetheless and the boy seemed pleased to have gained my admiration.

Robert asked if I would care to go hunting hares with him and his favourite hound – a long, lean, wire-haired black lurcher bitch – but I declined and asked Hugh to take the boy out in my stead. Merely sitting on a stool and watching his swordplay for an hour had exhausted me. I slept for a whole day and a night afterwards.

At the beginning of December, a letter arrived from Lord Fitzwalter. I read it alone in my chamber by the light of a brazier. It began with the usual flowery greeting, and some compliments about my courage and a hope that my health and strength were recovering. And then it said: 'It grieves me to tell you, my friend, that you were betrayed in the matter that took place at St Paul's. We have discovered a spy amongst Lord de Vesci's men-at-arms who is in the pay of the King.'

None of this surprised me. I had known since my capture and incarceration that I had been betrayed. And at Wallingford the King had admitted that he had spies in de Vesci's castle. The letter continued: 'The wretch is even now screaming under the knives of de Vesci's gaolers and we will have the whole truth out of him. But you may assure yourself that he is guilty. We caught him listening at the door of de Vesci's chamber and found a sack of the King's silver under his pallet. Your sufferings will be avenged, my friend, and I hope that will be a comfort to you.'

In fact, despite what he had done to me, a part of me shuddered to think of the poor man on the rack in some godforsaken dungeon in the bowels of Alnwick Castle. I hoped his end would be swift.

Fitzwalter concluded his letter with an invitation to come to Alnwick again as soon as I felt stronger so that

I could be suitably rewarded for my pains and to discuss our future plans for the good of the kingdom.

'By God,' I actually said out loud. 'He means to have me try again!'

I screwed the letter into a ball and hurled it into the brazier. I had no intention of ever having anything to do with Fitzwalter and de Vesci and their plots again. Neither did I bother even to reply to his invitation.

A couple of weeks later, and with my lungs no better, I roused myself again for the Christmas festivities. It was a wet feast, and somewhat subdued. The rain had been falling for weeks by the day of Our Saviour's nativity, and I had hardly the strength to preside at the long table in the hall sipping watered wine while my household and the tenants from the village of Westbury made merry, singing the traditional songs and playing the old games while gorging on roast goose and smoked ham and drinking themselves insensible on vats of strong Christmas ale.

In January the snows came and blanketed the countryside, making it as pristine as a freshly laundered nun's habit. And still I languished, coughing weakly, sleeping for most of the day and night, eating little, sweating pints despite the winter cold.

I was dying. I was sure of it. And red anger burned in my breast at the knowledge. Had I survived the horror of the cell in Brien's Close only to cough myself into the grave at home in Westbury? I would not allow that to happen. This would not be the way I would meet my Maker. I was determined to will myself better.

I forced myself to rise each day at dawn. I took a large cup of wine with breakfast and forced down meat and bread, though I had no desire for it at all. Indeed, I would often vomit it back up again a few moments later. But I persisted. I walked the courtyard swathed in furs, and on one occasion tried rather ineffectually to swing the poleaxe that Little John had left for me. I was quickly exhausted and, trembling with fatigue, I ordered hot broth for dinner that noon with raw eggs beaten into it.

Baldwin's sister Alice was an invaluable nursemaid to me at this time. She brought me strengthening possets of herbs, oats and wine of her own devising. She wiped the night sweat from my body and changed the stained linen sheets of the bed. She sat with me for hours as I raved and saw visions, and when I was lucid, told me of the doings of the manor and the gossip of the village. But, comforting as it was, it was not her womanly presence that I craved. I had another woman in my mind, and I could not shake the image of her from before my eyes. I wanted Tilda.

In March, when the weather was milder and a weak sun had at last emerged from behind the iron wall of clouds, I determined to act. I rose, dressed warmly, strapped Fidelity to my waist and my misericorde on my left arm and ordered a horse to be saddled for me. As Hugh, Baldwin and Alice looked on, full of anguished concern,

239

and with a pair of young, strong Westbury men-at-arms for company and protection, I rode out of the gates of the compound and set out north on the road to Kirklees Priory.

It was a foolish thing to do. By mid-morning on the first day I was so weak that I nearly slipped from the back of my horse. My two men had to ride on either side of me with a hand ready to steady me in the saddle. I had told Baldwin and Hugh, as my reason for the journey, that I had heard good things said of the healing powers of the nuns of Kirklees and particularly the prioress Anna, and I told them that I was certain that I could only recover from my long illness at her hands.

The truth was that I wanted to see Tilda. But that journey in the brisk March wind nearly did for me. Not that I remember it all that well. I slipped in and out of consciousness for three days on horseback – for we travelled almost as slowly as men on foot – and by the time we reached the mill at the furthest part of the Kirklees lands I was tied to my horse, sagging in the saddle and three parts lost to the world.

The next I knew I was in a small cot in a bright room with linen sheets and blankets over my body, and a pretty nun, a stranger, was sitting beside the bed. Seeing me awake, she gave a squeak of surprise and rushed away to fetch a superior.

I looked about me. It was a clean, whitewashed room with a large crucifix on the wall opposite my bed. I lifted my head and felt – strange. I was weak, yes, and still thin as a weed. But the pains in my chest had gone. I gave an experimental cough and hacked a big ball of yellow-brown phlegm into the earthenware bowl beside the bed. I could hardly believe it. I felt – better. It was surely a miracle, a blessed miracle. I said a quick prayer of thanks to the carved figure of Our Lord in his Passion on the wall opposite. Then Prioress Anna was standing beside my bed, giving me a grim smile and putting a hand on my brow to feel for heat.

'We are very pleased with you, Sir Alan. By the grace of Our Lord and the skill of my nuns, I think we have got the better of your illness. How do you feel?'

I sat up fully in the bed. Apart from a slight dizziness, I felt wonderfully well.

'How long have I been here, Mother?' I said.

'You came here a little over two weeks ago, Sir Alan, and you were, I would say, about a slender half-inch away from death. But the sisters and I have worked night and day physicking you with infusions and purges and . . . well, here you are, and we are all pleased with your recovery. I was sure, at one point, that you would be gathered unto God. Absolutely certain. But you have a great healing strength in you, sir. I congratulate you on it.'

'I can only say, from the bottom of my heart, that I thank you, Mother Anna. I would like to thank Tilda, too, if I might.'

The prioress frowned at me. 'Tilda? Our Matilda? The sub-prioress is not here. She had been in Canterbury at a convocation with the archbishop. She is representing our house – I am far too busy to travel to these silly affairs. She will be returning soon, though, I devoutly hope and pray. Now you must rest yourself and in a little while I will ask the sisters to bring you some barley gruel.'

I was somewhat deflated to discover that Tilda was away and had had nothing to do with my cure, but I was pleased to hear that she was doing well in her vocation and had been entrusted with such an important task. And the joy in finding myself alive and nearly well was an ample compensation. I drank cold spring water and ate with pleasure for the first time in months. I attended Vespers in the priory church and gave thanks to God, once again, for my recovery. The next day I ventured out of the infirmary and walked for an hour in the famous herb garden. Two days after that I even took my horse out for a short canter over the priory lands.

There was still no sign of Tilda and I began to think of returning to Westbury. I was stronger and while I knew the journey would be tiring I believed I was fit enough to endure it. So I gathered up my clothes and weapons, and tracked down my two men-at-arms. They had been enjoying the company of the young nuns a little too much, as far as I could see, for there was a good deal of whispering, giggling and sighing from the circle of novices around them when I found them at last in the chapter house and told them they must take their leave. Rather sulkily they agreed to return with me to Westbury.

We saddled the horses and said our goodbyes to the prioress and the sisters. Just as I was thanking the lady for the kindness she had shown me, and about to mount my horse, a party of a dozen riders cantered into the courtyard, and there, a little travel-stained and flushed, and yet just as radiant as ever, was the woman whose angelic face I had spent so many hours contemplating.

Tilda stepped off her horse and immediately came over to greet me.

'Why, Sir Alan,' she said, 'you look so pale.' She grasped my hands in her warm ones. 'And you're so thin. What ails you?'

I began to tell her of my long illness and her eyes clouded with worry.

'But you are well again now?' she asked.

'Welcome home, my dear,' said Anna, from my shoulder. 'The sisters and I – we have all missed you.' And there was something about the older woman's voice that made me turn and look at her. Her face was flushed, her eyes were glittering as if she were containing a rage that was on the verge of being unleashed.

'Mother Anna, how wonderful it is to be home again,' said Tilda flashing her beautiful smile at the older woman. 'I am so happy to see you.'

She turned her beam on me: 'And to see you again, too, Sir Alan.'

'Sir Alan and his men are leaving, Tilda, so I am afraid you must bid him farewell. He doubtless has many affairs at home that he would like to attend to.'

I was about to say that I would be happy to spend more time at the priory, recovering my strength, when I caught the prioress's red-hot glare and stopped.

'Sir Alan, you cannot leave until I have given you something,' said Tilda. 'Do say you will not go until I have had time to fetch it. I will not be long! Do wait!'

She rushed away into the chapter house without another word.

The prioress leaned into me and said quietly but with an air of finality that brooked no arguments: 'Sir Alan, I think it is high time that you left us.'

She tried for a friendly smile, but the fixity of her face made the expression a hideous grimace. 'Having the presence of your young men here at Kirklees has caused some disruption among the younger sisters, and I would be most grateful now that you are well if you would take them from our precincts. I'm sure you understand. It has been a pleasure having you as our guest – but it is time to go.'

There was not much I could say to that. I was being ejected. While we waited in silence, I fiddled unnecessarily with the buckles on my saddle, scratched my head and patted my horse's neck. By God Tilda was taking an age!

I remarked on the weather to the prioress. It was, I said, very spring-like.

'It is spring, Sir Alan. Doubtless in your delirium you have failed to notice it.'

I could think of nothing further to say and ordered my men to mount up, before climbing a little stiffly into the saddle myself.

At last, Tilda emerged from the priory's main door. She was holding an object wrapped in a length of linen cloth. It was something hot. I could see wisps of steam leaking between the folds of the covering.

'To help you regain your strength, Sir Alan. You must eat plenty of meat, as much as you possibly can. This pasty is filled with good fat pork and healing spices – and has just come out of the cookhouse oven. Eat it all up and you will soon be as strong and brave as ever.'

I thanked Tilda for her gift and shoved it into the saddlebag. Now I too was eager to be away. The prioress's glare was making my spine itch. So, giving a wave to all the nuns, and myself giving Tilda what I hoped was a meaningful look of love, the three of us took our horses in hand and galloped out of the priory gates.

Chapter Eighteen

On leaving the priory, I rode south directly to Robin's castle, pausing only twice to attend to calls of nature, for my body was still weak and my bowels were in a fearfully loose state. It was a journey of perhaps a little under twenty miles, a gentle day's ride when I was fully fit, but I arrived at Kirkton feeling almost as wretched and fatigued as I had been when I left Westbury. I slid off my horse and stumbled into Miles, who had come out to greet me.

'Drunk, Sir Alan? At this time of day? I like a cup or two of wine myself, it cannot be denied, but never when I'm out riding.'

I growled a curse at the boy, pretended to cuff his head – then hugged him. It was a pleasure to see the cheeky imp, if the truth be told, and his handsome, cheerful face was tonic to my soul.

'I'm here for the night, Miles, and two men-at-arms – you'd better tell your father to deck the halls with garlands of roses and prepare the fatted calf,' I said.

'He's out with the troops on exercise – but he'll be back at nightfall, I'm fairly sure. I'll tell Mother you're here.'

Marie-Anne greeted me in the hall and, sensing my weakness, immediately guided me to Robin's chair – a vast throne-like object that would have suited a king more than a moderately wealthy northern earl. She sat down in the only slightly smaller one beside it. I was grateful to be seated, though, and happy to talk to one of my favourite women in the world over a cup of wine. I told her about my illness and how I had been cured at Kirklees. I may have mentioned Tilda's name once or twice.

'Oh, Alan,' she said, 'surely you are not getting any ideas about that one.'

I told her I did not know what she could possibly be talking about. But I felt my cheeks glow red anyway.

'She is a bride of Christ – not for the touch of lustful man,' my lady reminded me sternly. 'And after what happened last time when you asked her to marry you, you can't be making the same mistake again?'

'Matilda and I are just friends,' I said stiffly. 'We share a mutual fondness and regard for each other, nothing

247

more.' I shifted uncomfortably in Robin's hard chair. 'I would never encourage her to break her sacred vows of chastity,' I lied.

'Hmm,' said Marie-Anne. 'Kirklees is not so far away from Kirkton, and you know, Alan, I hear strange things from there. I hear that among the sisters, at least, chastity is not as strictly enforced, nor as highly valued, as discretion.'

I looked at her blankly. It was Marie-Anne's turn to blush.

'Never mind about that, Alan. My advice would be to put Tilda from your mind. She is far too beautiful – dangerously beautiful. Find yourself a nice, plain country girl. A good soul, hard-working. It doesn't need to be anybody grand. Take her to your bed, get married, have another child. It would do you good.'

I did not much care for the thought of some plain-faced country besom. She would be all rough hands, meaty thighs and ale-breath – and would likely get with child as quick as a wink and seek to claim the lord of Westbury as her husband.

Mercifully, our frank discussion was interrupted at that point by the arrival of Robin. He strode in, mud-bespattered and glowing with health, and cried out a merry greeting to me before pouring himself a cup of ale from the sideboard and downing the drink in one gulp.

'You are up and about, then, Alan,' said my lord. 'And clearly feeling strong enough to try and usurp my place.'

I realised then that I was sitting in Robin's throne next to his beautiful wife. I levered myself to my feet, apologising profusely.

'Sit down, Alan, I am only teasing. Sit down before you fall down. You look as if a strong puff of wind could carry you away.'

We shared an amiable supper together: Robin, Marie-Anne, Miles and Little John. Wine and laughter, good company and good food. Robin and Little John between them related how their preparations for the war were proceeding.

'We've got but a handful of cavalry,' Robin said. 'Twenty men, is all, and very few of them proper knights. I can't afford the extra horses and armour, to be honest. Some of the troopers are just men-at-arms learning to ride for the first time. But I am trying to get them into some sort of shape. We go out most days and practise our manoeuvres. But they are still quite raw.'

He turned to Miles. 'And where were you at reveille this morning? I checked your bed and you hadn't slept in it.'

'Ah, I had some business in Sheffield last night and I stopped there with, ah, a friend.'

'And which friend was that?' said Robin, looking at his son.

'I would be most shocked if you knew her, Father,' said Miles with a grin.

There was a short silence. Then Little John made a strangled snorting noise, a badly smothered guffaw.

'When we go out on troop exercise,' said Robin, 'I expect you to be present, correctly armoured and stone-cold sober. You're supposed to be a file leader, you're supposed to be setting an example to the other men. How do you expect men to follow you if you cannot be bothered to show your face at training? Next time, you will be there when you are called. Is that clear? Whether you have some unsavoury "business" in Sheffield or not.'

'Yes, Father.' Miles was outwardly meek. But I caught him giving Little John a sly wink when Robin's head was turned away.

'Is that it?' I asked. 'Twenty half-trained cavalry? It's not much of an army.'

Little John said: 'It's hardly worth counting the cavalry. But luckily we do have sixty archers, good men, old hands – you'll know a fair few of them from Damme and elsewhere; and I've got a hundred and twenty well-trained footmen, half of them armed with Robert's poleaxes, the other half with wicked long pikes.'

'That's more like it,' I said. 'The war really is on, then?'

'The King left for La Rochelle last month with a respectable force,' said Robin. 'A few of the barons went with him out of loyalty, and a large number of poor knights from the shires went, too, looking to make their fortune in ransoms. For our part, we're supposed to be ready by June. The Earl of Salisbury's taking us to Calais and there we are to link up with the dukes of Brabant and Lorraine, the counts of Flanders and Boulogne, and a strong German contingent under the King's nephew, Emperor Otto. If you want to know what all the tax silver John has collected has been spent on, it has gone to these princes. For months, years even, treasure has been pouring into Boulogne, Flanders, Lorraine and Brabant – and even into the Holy Roman Emperor's coffers – to ensure that they will join us in this fight against Philip. You know the overall strategy, of course?'

I nodded. 'It's the same as in the old days, isn't it? We squeeze Philip between two forces, one coming from the north, the men of the Low Countries and us, and the King coming in from the south-west from Poitou and Anjou. It's Richard's old plan.'

'Exactly,' said Robin. 'It all depends on King John doing his part in the west. If he can succeed in dividing Philip's forces, drawing at least half on to him, we can crash through from the north – maybe even take Paris. But I promise you this, Alan, if the King fails to rally support in Poitou, if he fails to win his battles, we will not be boarding those ships to Calais. If the King fails, and we are advancing down from the Low Countries, we will face the full might of Philip of France as he comes surging north. And that, my friend, will be the end of us all.'

'So all will depend on the courage and competence of King John as a warrior?' I said. 'How could *that* possibly go wrong?'

Robin looked less than amused. 'If the King fails, we

will not sail, Alan, I promise you. We will not leave these shores.'

The next morning I found myself in the courtyard of Kirkton just after dawn with a poleaxe in my hand and Little John excitedly demonstrating the blows, blocks and parries. The poleaxe felt as heavy as if the entire eight-foot length were crafted from iron, but I was determined not to show John my weakness. I had just, after several attempts, managed to complete a mimed hooking-and-stabbing manoeuvre to John's satisfaction, when we were interrupted by a rider, travel-stained and brimming with urgency, who rode into the castle and demanded to see Robin.

Half an hour later, I learnt the news: 'I've had a troubling message, Alan, from Cousin Henry in London,' Robin told me. 'The King has sent word to all his sheriffs that they are to double their efforts to raise money from all the shires.'

'The King needs more money – already?' I said.

'Yes, he has succeeded in bribing the Lusignans to come over to his side – all of them except Geoffrey, who hates him more than he loves money. The campaign is going well, apparently: he has taken Milécu, a small castle but a tough one near La Rochelle, and the Poitevin barons are now flocking in to do homage to him. But, I'm sorry to have to tell you this, Alan, the bad news is that your friend Philip Marc has boasted that he will raise an extra thousand pounds from Nottinghamshire alone by the summer to send to the King.'

I froze. To be honest, I had put the sheriff of Nottinghamshire and his threats to the back of my mind in recent months. Now my stomach felt like a hollow wine keg. A horrible premonition was forming in my mind.

'I have to go,' I said. 'I have to get back to Westbury immediately.' And without waiting for Robin's permission, I rushed out of the hall and went to find my two men. We were packed and saddled in no time, and as we sat on our horses before the gate, I bawled to the gate guards to open it and allow us out.

'My lord says no,' said the gatekeeper, looking up at me sullenly from where he stood holding my horse's head.

'Open the gate, man, and don't play the fool,' I said.

'I have orders from the earl not to allow you to leave, Sir Alan,' said this oaf.

'What! I must be away. Open the damn gate or it will be the worse for you.'

'All in good time, Alan, all in good time,' said a voice from behind me.

I turned in the saddle and saw Robin emerging from the hall in full mail, clad in iron links from head to toe. And behind him was Little John in an iron hauberk, with a long poleaxe in his right hand, and a stout kite-shaped shield in his left.

'You are far too old to be this impetuous, Alan,' said Robin.

I glowered at him. 'Open the gate, Robin,' I said, now beginning to warm with anger. 'Tell your men to open it now.'

'Did you really think I would let you go off to battle the sheriff of Nottinghamshire all on your own? Look at you – still weak as a kitten. You haven't even got a shield.'

'I'll manage well enough,' I said gruffly.

'If there is going to be a good fight, Alan, it's not fair for you to hog all the fun,' said Little John. 'Don't be so selfish!'

He handed the big, kite-shaped shield up to me.

'We're coming with you,' said Robin.

Chapter Nineteen

Robin took his whole troop of cavalry with him when we rode south for Westbury a quarter of an hour later, along with Miles and Little John. He said it would be a good field exercise for everyone, and indeed, he set them on a battle routine, riding in a double column with scouts on each flank and a pair of riders before and behind. They did not seem such bad soldiers to me, although some were clearly still uncomfortable in the saddle, and I had yet to see how they fared in a battle.

Once again I had been moved by Robin's generosity. He had his faults – God knows he could be self-serving, ruthless and cruel – but he was always, always loyal to his *familia*, those chosen few in his inner circle. I vowed to remember that, above all else about my lord. But I had bigger things on my mind than Robin's character flaws: the sheriff's threat to have his monster rip Robert's head off was paramount among them. Philip Marc and his loathsome toady Sir Benedict Malet wanted my money – I had refused it to them – and so far I had heard nothing more of the matter for several months. Indeed, I had not thought of it in weeks. But now it seemed blindingly clear that they would be bound to act: I had defied them, insulted them, and no man likes to take that humiliation without seeking revenge at some point. I only prayed that I would reach Westbury in time.

Robin drove his men hard, and I felt my weakness as a kind of constant guilt as we thundered along – if I had not been so ill, I would have been at Westbury preparing it for whatever lay ahead. If I had not involved myself in the plot against the King, I would not have become so weak. And I was still very feeble. I struggled to keep up with the other riders, even the novice horsemen, but the image of a headless Robert spurred my body onwards, forced it to conquer its frailty.

We reached the woods around Alfreton, a handful of miles from Westbury, at sunset and Robin called a halt for the night. I said that we should push on and reach the manor that night, but Robin stopped me.

'We need to know what the situation is before we go charging in,' my lord said. 'Hugh is there and Sir Thomas – and they will not let anything happen to Robert. Calm yourself, Alan, this is no time for recklessness. We sleep here and let the scouts do their work.'

In truth I was almost destroyed with fatigue. So after making a fireless camp in the deep woods and eating well from a basket of luxurious provisions that Marie-Anne had provided for us, I rolled myself in my cloak in a deep drift of leaves and slept like a dead man for eight hours. Robin woke me three hours before dawn with a cup of wine, a piece of buttered bread and a lump of cheese.

'They are there, Alan,' he said, before I had even scraped the sleep-sand from my eyes. 'I don't know who they are, but there is an armed camp halfway around Westbury. Maybe a hundred fighting men: knights and men-at-arms, mostly. But the scouts think they have not been there long, and the gates are still firmly closed to them. Westbury has not fallen, Alan.'

I sat up and immediately began to struggle into a borrowed hauberk that Robin had found me in his armoury the day before.

Robin said: 'This is what I think we should do . . .'

The Earl of Locksley's plan was simple but contained his usual measure of cunning. We could not hope to destroy a company of nearly five times our number, but we could sow confusion and panic and allow those two time-honoured military forces to even the balance. We were in the deep woods to the north-west of Westbury, near Alfreton, and the main enemy encampment, bar a few pickets, was spread out in a wide crescent shape to the south of the roughly circular walled compound that was my home, on the slope below its main gate. Little John and five dismounted men – the least skilled riders in the troop – would approach on foot as stealthily as they could and attack the western end of the enemy crescent. Their orders were to run into the camp, hopefully without being seen by the pickets, and to begin killing quickly and silently, slaughtering the sleeping men, and moving generally towards the centre of the camp. The alarm would surely be raised as soon as they began their bloody work and when the camp was astir, they would split up and fight their way to the main gate of Westbury where they should receive protection against their enraged enemies from the bowmen on the walls. Little John was big and ugly enough to be easily recognised by Sir Thomas or Hugh or any of the men inside the manor – even in the half-light of dawn – and so they should not be mistaken for attackers. But I was aware that the big man and his section were playing the most dangerous part in this operation – six men on foot attacking an armed camp of a hundred or so enemies. We could only hope that having six killers loose in the camp would make the direction of our attack hard to locate and so create shock and fear among the enemy troops.

Meanwhile Robin, Miles, myself and the remaining fifteen cavalrymen would circle round to the east of Westbury on horseback and when we heard the noises of alarm and Little John's fight begin in earnest, we would blow trumpets, make our war cries and attack as noisily as we could from the east. Robin hoped that the enemy – terrorised by assassins within the camp and faced with a disciplined cavalry charge from the outside – and whatever assistance the Westbury garrison could afford us – would flee the field.

'That is our objective,' said Robin, as we gathered in a loose group in the dark woods for a final conference before the attack. 'We want them to run south as fast as they can. Westbury is to their north, Little John comes in from the west; the cavalry from the east – we want them to run south. This is not about trying to slaughter every single one of the enemy –' I heard a muted cry of 'Spoilsport!' from Little John, which Robin ignored – 'this is about driving them away. Does everybody understand? Do not drift to the south, that is their exit route. Do not get between the enemy and the sheep pastures to the south by the river. We want them to run. If they don't, and it goes badly, head for the main gate. If the attack fails to drive them away, we need to be able to get inside the walls as quick as we can.'

Our movements shrouded by the grey blanket of the hour before dawn, I led the cavalrymen around the north side of Westbury, keeping a good three-quarters of a mile from the compound and travelling as quietly as we could. Little John and his section of men had departed a good half-hour earlier, as they were taking the shorter route round the west. I was glad that we were moving over my land, land that I had walked and ridden over for nearly twenty years, for I was able to select the quieter paths through the many thickets of vast bramble and along the tracks through the woodland that I had hunted since I was not much more than a stripling. Before long we were in place on the banks of the river, a mere two hundred yards from Westbury itself but hidden in a fold of land underneath a stand of beech trees. It was a favoured place to fatten the pigs and the beech mast was thick on the ground, muffling our horses' hooves. I stopped the troop, got down from my horse and squirmed forward on my belly ten paces to the top of a small rise from where I could see the Westbury compound and the pasture lands before it. Behind me the pinkish stain on the horizon signalled the coming of the sun. But I shivered in the chill air.

I had been feeling the usual stomach-clenching fear before action, a dryness in my mouth and a tremble in my hands, as we walked our horses around the back of my home – but now that I could clearly see Westbury and the great smear of canvas tents staining the land in front of my gates, my trepidation was for the main part displaced by raw anger. How dare these men come to my home and threaten those whom I loved? I would hit them with all my strength; they would pay with their lives.

I made my way back to Robin and the troop and reported: 'Their horse lines are to the south, and I'd say, yes, there are at least a hundred men, maybe more, plus camp followers and servants. A few are awake, I can see half a dozen campfires alight, and there is a pair of alert sentries about fifty yards beyond the rise. But I see no reason not to ride straight over them.'

A hair-raising scream ripped through the air, the last agonised cry of a man departing this world. It was the awful music of a battle begun.

I could now make out Robin's handsome face in the half-light: 'I believe Little John has already begun the party,' he said. 'Let us join him in his revels.'

We came over the top of the dip at the canter, in a tight wedge, with Robin at its point and Miles and I directly behind him. Behind us came the rest of the troop; each man armed with helmet, shield and hauberk and a twelve-foot lance. I had no lance, of course, I would not have had the strength to wield it effectively, but I had the borrowed shield on my left arm, a steel cap on my head, and Fidelity's shining naked blade in my right hand. The two sentries between us and the enemy took one look at the pack of cavalry that appeared, thundering towards them, as if from nowhere, and immediately ran yelling in two separate directions. We let them go and moments later we smashed into the camp with our formation intact.

We shouted our war cries with all our might – myself bellowing 'Westbury!' – and came crashing in through a space between two big grubby white tents, our horses' hooves ripping the guy-ropes and their pegs from the ground. As the tents collapsed behind us, Robin drew first blood, his lance leaping forward to skewer a sleepy man-at-arms in a black surcoat who was standing by a fire rubbing his face in astonishment. He abandoned the lance in the man's body and drew his sword, and by then the troopers were in among the enemy killing and screaming like devils. I saw Miles put his horse at a pair of dismounted knights, one with an axe, the other half-dressed but holding a sword. The boy took the axeman beautifully, hitting him plumb centre and lifting him off his feet with the force of the spear, and the other jumped aside as the horse came past and slashed at Robin's son with his sword. Miles took the blow harmlessly on his shield, turned his horse as neatly as a dancer and without even bothering to draw his sword, rode the man down, crushing him with the weight of his destrier, shouting: 'Locksley! Locksley for ever!'

A young man came blundering out of his tent, dressed in hauberk and helm and carrying a long spear, and I slashed at him with Fidelity, catching his helmet with my blade and knocking him flat on his back. Between my horse's ears I caught a glimpse of Little John, his feet planted in the centre of the camp, whirling the poleaxe to devastating effect, keeping three armed men at bay, and then stepping in and disembowelling one of them with the axe-head, then, when a second man ran at him from behind, smashing the butt-spike full into his face with no more than a casual glance over his shoulder. I lost sight of him as my horse ran between two large black pavilions with scarlet trimmings. A long-haired fellow ran across my path, a knife in his hand, and I cut him down as I passed with a looping side-blow that sliced the top off his scalp like a boiled egg.

The camp was in disarray by now, tents collapsed, horses running free, men scrambling to get away from the deadly lances of our men. But these were well-trained troops and their recovery from the twin attacks was admirably swift. I found myself coming round the side of a tent to see three mounted men in black-and-white surcoats, two with long lances, one wielding only mace and a shield. They saw me and immediately spurred their horses to meet me. Three knights against one in my weakened condition – indeed, had I been in any condition – was no more than a form of suicide. Still, it was too late to play the coward and I took a firmer grip on my shield and spurred in to meet them.

They were but ten paces from me when, from an alley between the tents to my left, one of our troopers came galloping. He was a good man, brave as a lion – for, as far as he knew, he was taking on three knights on his own. His horse came charging in from the side, he shouted something and plunged his lance deep in the side of the leftmost knight, just under the armpit, almost certainly killing him immediately. His horse carried him forward and the second enemy knight, moving slightly out of his path, chopped his mace into my bold comrade's spine as he passed. I heard the snap of bone like a dead branch breaking.

The third knight, his horse pushed out of line by the attack on his flank, came at me, his spear flicking out towards my belly. I twisted in the saddle, my horse side-stepped and I felt the hard impact of the lance head as it skimmed past my hauberk and slammed into my mount's hindquarters. With my horse dying under me, I cut hard at the knight's neck as he passed, the blade crunching against mail. Then the mace-wielder was on me from the other side and I took a pounding blow on my shield, and ducked as another whistled over my head. I got the horse, just, to turn and face the two men, but she was staggering, jelly-limbed, and I recognised that she was finished. The lance-man's head was flopping loosely on his torso; I had broken his neck. He slid slowly, almost gracefully, from the saddle. But the fellow with the mace had turned his mount and was back and coming in on my right-hand side. I pounded my spurs into my horse's flanks and she gave a last lurch forward towards my attacker. Fidelity flicked out, a straight lunge to his chest, and the man on the charging warhorse impaled himself on my blade, the combined impetus of our two converging horses driving the blade through his mail, through his ribs and deep into the cavity beyond. I felt the force of my blow rocket up my arm, slamming me back against the cantle of my saddle, and I lost my grip on the hilt as his momentum carried him past me. His horse charged on for a dozen paces and then came to a halt, confused, the man on his back, his master, dead in the saddle with Fidelity stuck halfway through his torso.

My own horse collapsed at that point, and I had to be quick, kicking my feet out of the stirrups, not to be tumbled to the turf or trapped under his falling body. I managed not to crash to the earth, landed on two feet and staggered towards the dead knight and his forlorn destrier. I had no sword, only a shield, and I wanted Fidelity back in my hand as soon as possible.

I could hear the battle raging around me: screams and yells and the crack of metal on wood. That was bad. The enemy was supposed to be running by now. Instead they were fighting back.

A tall bearded man ran at me – I never saw where he came from – wearing nothing but a chemise and braies, but he had a long hand-and-a-half sword held in both fists. He attacked immediately. I took a heavy double-handed blow on my shield that had me staggering backwards, but I had no sword with which to respond. He cut at me again, a pounding chop that, while I managed to catch it safely on my shield, felt like a strike from a battering ram. A third strike skimmed across the surface of my shield and clanged off my steel cap, and I felt my legs fail me. Down on one knee and cowering under the shield, I endured a storm of blows aimed at my head and shoulders. I could see his bare legs clearly on the green turf before me.

I pulled the misericorde from its sheath on my left forearm, the black steel slipping willingly into my hand. I surged up with the shield, pushing his weapon aside, and punched forward with the blade, plunging it into the meat of his upper thigh. He gave a noiseless gasp and, looking at him over my shield rim, I saw that he was white as bleached wool with shock. I stepped in, knocking the sword away, and plunged the misericorde deep into his naked belly, cutting the blade sideways to slice through his intestines.

He fell to his knees, dying, with a look of astonishment written across his face.

I left him to die, slid the misericorde, still wet, back into its sheath, and went to recover Fidelity. By chance, our duel had taken us near to the horse and the dead knight, and I quickly pulled his corpse from the saddle and recovered my beloved blade. I had meant to take possession of the horse too, but the animal, perhaps spooked by so much death and blood, cantered away in a shower of earth-clods before I could grasp its bridle.

I looked about me and saw the shapes of men-at-arms on foot converging on me, left and right. The enemy were certainly not fleeing, and were closing in to finish us. I looked ahead and saw the familiar wooden walls of Westbury.

I hurled my battered shield away and ran towards them.

I would not have made it to the main gate of Westbury but for the skill and courage of the men inside. For I was chased like a deer the hundred or so yards from the enemy encampment by a dozen howling men on foot and a-horse. And I was not the only man running for cover. I saw two of Robin's troopers cutting their way clear of a mass of furious black-clad infantry; Little John surrounded by a sea of foes, slicing at them like a reaper, using his poleaxe like a scythe, and at last surging his way through a spray of gore and towards the gate and safety. There was Robin just by the main gate, with a handful of our troops; the gate was opening, men were slipping inside. Merciful God be praised.

Westbury had not been insensible of the battle taking place beyond the walls. The palisade was lined with archers and it was these men who really saved me. I was conscious of a dozen arrows fizzing over my head as I ran helter-skelter from my enemies up the slight hill towards the gates, dodging left and right and, occasionally snatching a glance behind me, I saw my pursuers staggering, smacked in the chest or leg by yard-long shafts of wood, falling away – and I was clear.

The main gate was opening wider now.

I had expected some form of sortie from Westbury, the cavalry sallying forth to drive the attackers away from the gates. What happened instead left me gaping in shock. The gate was wide open now, and instead of a swarm of Westbury cavalry only two horsemen emerged, clearly recognisable as Thomas and Hugh. They were in full armour, sword and shield, and mounted on big strong horses, but they were not charging pell-mell into the enemy ranks, they were pulling a huge hay-wagon, piled high with wood and straw, doused in oil and burning like the fires of Hell.

I stood by the gate with my mouth open and watched as the huge burning wagon, pushed by a dozen men-at-arms from inside the gates as well as pulled by Thomas and Hugh outside, rumbled forward, found its own momentum and rolled ponderously down the slope into the heart of the enemy camp. When the wagon was trundling forward, picking up speed, the two men cut the ropes that attached their frightened horses to the burning mass, and circled back to the gates.

There they were joined by the rest of the Westbury horsemen, and as many of Robin's men as were still in the saddle, and now they all charged, pouring out of the gates in a compact mass in the wake of the rumbling, spark-spitting, unstoppable inferno that was cutting a fiery swath through the enemy encampment.

That fire-wagon probably killed or injured no more than a dozen men who were unable to get out of its path in time, and Thomas's cavalry charge contained fewer than a score of riders, but the combination of the two, added to the arrows of the archers on the palisade, was enough. Confusion and panic had come to our aid at last.

The enemy ran.

They streamed away to the south, scores of men-at-arms and camp servants, knights, too, abandoning their tents, provisions, weapons and stores to get as far away from the chaos of the burning camp as fast as they could.

Westbury was saved.

Chapter Twenty

A little before mid-morning, I stood on the walls of Westbury in my borrowed hauberk with Robin beside me, and watched as the last of our foes disappeared into the woods beyond the pastures on the far south of my land.

Of all the joys of life, there is nothing like victory. And for the first time in months, I felt as happy and light-headed as a schoolboy released from his lessons. Westbury was largely unscathed and happily our casualties had been light – although only two of Little John's five footmen got back into the castle alive, and Robin's troop of twenty was now reduced to sixteen men.

I learnt from Sir Thomas later that day that the enemy had arrived the day before, and a knight who had identified himself only as Nicholas of Hainaut had demanded that the gates be opened to him. He intended to conduct a thorough search of the manor, he had said, and Westbury should submit or face the consequences.

Sir Thomas had immediately ordered the Westbury archers to loose, and the knight had been cut down in front of the gate by a blizzard of shafts. My dark-haired friend was not a man to waste time when battle was at hand: and he was perfectly justified in his actions, as the knight had come arrayed for war to his gates and had issued threats. There had been no formal or even informal truce agreement in place. However, the enemy, furious at the precipitate slaughter of their envoy, had made a concerted attack on the walls, fifty men-at-arms with ladders, supported by a score of dismounted knights, but they had been driven back without too much difficulty by the defenders. The money I had paid out to strengthen the palisade had been well spent, I considered. Hugh had distinguished himself in the defence of the western wall, where the main attack had fallen, slaying the enemy in droves and casting the ladders loose wherever they landed on the battlements.

I thanked Hugh and Thomas with tears in my eyes for defending my home. But Hugh surprised me by saying that he and Sir Thomas could not take the full credit for the success of their defence.

'You have Robert to thank for that,' Hugh said. 'It was his idea to use the fire-wagon, and I would say that that was the move that tipped the scales.'

Robert had been dispensing ale to the thirsty men-at-arms from a large jug – and the men were drinking deep. And he seemed strangely shy when I summoned him over to confirm Hugh's words.

'Is it true, Robert, that the burning wagon was your idea?'

'Yes, Father. I hope you do not mind the loss of the wagon. I chose the oldest one we had, the one I felt we could most afford to lose.'

I hugged him, then, too choked with pride to speak.

As we sat down to dinner that day, just after noon, Robert brought round the water ewer, bowl and towels to allow the guests to wash their hands, and I saw that he managed this ordinary task with aplomb. He had just taken part in his first siege, he had very likely saved Westbury with his quick thinking, and now he was fulfilling his duties as a squire, in a fresh tunic, hair combed, nails clean, as if nothing out of the ordinary had happened. His hand did not tremble as he poured the wine; he carved the meat – we were eating fat roast pork with crispy crackling, at my insistence – in neat, thin, even slices like a master butcher.

My heart swelled with love at the sight of him: so what if he was not the world's finest swordsman? He would make a fine knight, a fine man, one day.

When we had eaten, I rested for several hours – although I had not been wounded the battle had taken its toll on my still weak body and I found I could barely stand. But the next morning I rose early and went out to survey the battlefield and join in the clean-up. The whole of Westbury was already there, picking over the leavings of the enemy: villagers scooping up discarded items of clothing, searching for a forgotten purse or a silver buckle; even the dogs of the manor and the village were out, scouting for any scraps of bread and meat that had been left behind.

Although I was sure that they came from the sheriff of Nottinghamshire, I was more than curious to discover exactly who the enemy had been, for the name Nicholas of Hainault meant nothing to me. It seemed they had left behind some evidence of their identity: a particular kind of wooden overshoe found in the Low Countries, some thick, waxy cheese rind discarded in the midden, a broken shield painted with a device derived from one I had seen on a knight from Leuven.

We concluded that they were Flemings.

'Mercenaries,' said Robin without a hint of condemnation. He could not very well sneer, as he had been one more than once, and so had I.

'The sheriff of Nottinghamshire is hiring mercenaries to collect his taxes, is that not self-defeating?' I said. 'Any money he gets will go to pay his soldiers.'

Robert's lurcher bitch Vixen was sniffing my shoes. I ruffled her behind the ears.

'Not necessarily. They may well be already bought and paid for by the King, who is lending them out to his sheriffs while they await orders for the Continental campaign. It is actually quite a good use for men who might otherwise be idle.'

'You sound as though you approve of the King's tax-collecting methods,' I said.

'I don't object to taxes, *per se*,' said Robin. 'Do I not charge my tenants rent? Do not you charge yours? What your friends, my lords Fitzwalter and de Vesci, propose is an end to taxation – and that is absurd. They would have a pauper king, weak and easily controlled by men such as them. What I would end is the arbitrary use of force by the King to seize whatever money he wishes, whenever he wishes it, as if he were a greedy child. But the only thing that can truly check him, de Vesci and Fitzwalter would say, is armed force. Armies, battles, civil war. They want to use the ultimate force against the King. I would do things quite differently.'

I hung my head. I knew I'd been unwise and that Robin, at great cost, had saved me from the consequences of my foolish plotting with de Vesci and Fitzwalter. I was glad I had burned Fitzwalter's letter now and resolved never to have anything to do with either man again.

I found the corpse of my horse that afternoon, and spent a moment or two in mourning for that noble beast who had taken the lance blow meant for me. The knight's spear had plunged straight through the saddlebag and deep into the horse's lower bowels. I had seen men die from that kind of wound and knew that it was both

274

painful and foul, as faecal matter from the lower gut mixes with the blood and spreads all over the wound and the outer body.

I have seen some men-at-arms take five days to die from such a wound and in agony for all that time. It is in God's hands, of course. But I was glad that it had been swift for my equine friend.

I glanced inside the saddlebag to check for valuables and came across the pasty that Tilda had given me, fat pork and healthy spices in pastry. It had smelled delicious when she had given it to me in the courtyard of Kirklees Priory, but now, sadly, it was the very opposite. The lance had ripped it apart and the glorious pasty was covered in blood and the half-digested contents of the horse's belly. I dug out the sticky pieces from the torn saddlebag and threw them away.

I looked over the enemy's former encampment and into the pastures beyond and saw Robert playing with his lurcher. Throwing sticks for Vixen to chase and bring back to the boy. Yesterday he endured a siege and today he plays like a child, I mused. I was almost overwhelmed by a feeling of love for him. We had fought here on this ground to protect him, and lost comrades in that struggle. We had won, yes, but I had risked his life over a little money. How would I have felt if Robin had not helped me, if Sir Thomas and Hugh had not been so staunch, if Westbury had been overrun and Robert was taken, and God forbid, torn apart by the sheriff's ogre?

I found Robin later in the courtyard of Westbury, examining the new tower.

'It needs to be higher,' he said. 'You need to put a couple more storeys on top, and that way you will have the height to—'

I interrupted him: 'I can't afford it. I can't afford anything. I have almost no silver left and I've decided to promise to pay the sheriff what he wants, even if I have to mire myself in debt to do so.'

Robin looked at me. 'I cannot help you, Alan. The cost of arming and outfitting for the Flanders expedition has hit hard. I'd like to help, but thirty marks . . .'

'No, no, my lord,' I said. 'I do not ask it of you. I will borrow from the Jews or come to some arrangement with the sheriff.'

Robin said: 'Are you sure? We've taught him a lesson, I'd say. He should keep his distance.'

'I cannot allow myself to be permanently at war with the sheriff of this county. I would be made an outlaw – I may be one already – and I cannot hide my entire household in the forest for the rest of my life. I must live here, I mean to grow old here, and they will always know where to find me, where to find Robert. If we are to go to the Low Countries this summer, I would be leaving Westbury to the mercy of Philip Marc and Sir Benedict Malet. I must come to an accommodation with them, and as soon as possible – I will ride to Nottinghamshire tomorrow.'

'Do you want me to come with you? We could show a little force, it might help your negotiations.'

'No, I will go alone. I must appear humble, a penitent.'

'Very well,' said Robin. 'But keep this in mind as you wrangle with the sheriff. We depart for Flanders soon – and that expedition may well prove as lucrative as the attack on Damme. I make no promises, but your fortunes could well be restored by battle. One rich French knight captured and the ransom could change everything. Anyway, something to think on. If you are sure you know your mind, we will take our leave of you this afternoon. But, if you will permit me, I will send a message to Nottingham Castle, reminding the sheriff that you are under my protection and that if any harm comes to you they must answer to me.'

'Thank you, my lord,' I said, and gripped his arm.

Robin's departure with Little John, Hugh, Miles and all his men left Westbury much diminished. But the place appeared bigger, too, and seemed to echo with its new emptiness. Sir Thomas had disappeared after the battle – I suspected that I knew where. But I could not blame him for seeking his pleasures after facing the storm of battle and I pretended not to notice his absence. So we were an even further depleted company when we sat down to dinner: Robert, Baldwin and myself, with Alice serving the repast. Baldwin made an attempt to lift my spirits with toasts to our triumph and stirring tales of the attack on the walls which Hugh and his men had so bravely fought off. But I was in no mood for the traditional self-congratulations of victory. It felt more like a defeat. Tomorrow I would go with penitence and promises to try to appease the wrath of my enemies.

Chapter Twenty-one

When I reached the gates of the town the next day, I was half expecting to see the walls lined with armed men. And I halted long out of bowshot to try to gauge what sort of reception I would receive. As well as Robin's messenger, I had sent a man from Westbury to herald my coming. I had asked for an audience with the sheriff at noon, and I had added that I came under a flag of truce. I did not seek to be shot down as Sir Thomas had slain the Flemish mercenary Nicholas of Hainaut.

Nottingham seemed entirely normal. There were a few bored crossbowmen on the town walls, who ignored me, and I was stopped by only two sergeants-at-arms at the town gates who asked my business. I sensed no danger at all.

I was wearing no mail – just a blue tunic, black hose and riding boots, covered with a long grey cloak, but Fidelity was at my waist and I had the misericorde strapped to my left wrist. The sergeants did not attempt to disarm me, they merely summoned an escort of half a dozen men from the guardroom and gave them orders to escort me to the great hall where the sheriff was holding court.

I felt no qualms until I reached the inner bailey of the castle itself. And there, the first thing I saw, over by the old alehouse, was a square-built structure, a platform on four legs as wide as a cottage, with a high beam suspended above it, the whole business newly constructed of green elm beams.

It was a gallows.

The sheriff received me in the great hall of Nottingham Castle. I knew that hall well but that day it seemed different. The space was filled with men-at-arms, mostly French mercenaries, like their lord, but I also heard the English-sounding words of Flemish being spoken by more than a few of the mailed men who stood around, laughing and joking, swigging ale or wine, and pinching the backsides of the prettier women servants. The hall had the atmosphere of a campaign tent or a barracks: drunken familiarity and sweaty male camaraderie. It was a far cry from the stiff formality and hushed awe of the place when King John was in residence – but then this sheriff, this Frenchman, was a stranger in this land: he was an occupier, sent here by the King to prey on the people and strip as much wealth as he could from the English. As a foreigner, the sheriff must feel unsure, perhaps even unsafe, which was why he kept himself surrounded by his armed men.

Not all the men there were foreigners. I was greeted, if that is the word, at the door of the hall by Sir Benedict Malet. He treated me with his usual contempt: 'So you are here at last. Hope you brought cash,' was all he said before leading me through the throng to meet Philip Marc, who was standing at the rear of the hall surrounded by a pack of guffawing French men-at-arms.

It crossed my mind, briefly, that it would be a service to mankind if I were to draw my misericorde and shove it hard into Benedict's kidneys, but I restrained myself.

'Ah, it is the noble Sir Alan Dale. You have come to pay me the money you owe, I make no doubt.'

The half-dozen men-at-arms in the pack around the sheriff had spread out in a half-circle. They listened to our conversation and from the smirks and nudges that they gave each other, I had the feeling that they were expecting some entertainment.

'I have come to discuss the scutage demanded by the King.'

'It is the same. Thirty marks, I believe it was that we agreed. You have it?'

'As I said, I mean to discuss it with you. Like a Christian.'

'Good, let's discuss like Christians. But I am afraid I

have some bad news for you, my friend. The King has decided –' Marc looked sideways at the men around him, and they sniggered like naughty children – 'I say the King has decided that thirty marks will not do. Oh, no, when we last spoke the price was thirty. Now it is fifty marks. Yes, fifty. As I'm sure you know, he is quite an insatiable man.'

I dug the nails of my hands into my palms but said nothing. My face must have been a picture, for the men-at-arms fell about laughing when they saw my response to their master's words.

'Tell me, Sir Alan, how is your charming son – Robert, is it not? He is in good health, I trust?'

'He is well . . . well guarded,' I said through my teeth, 'as I believe we proved to you not two days hence.'

'Yes, I heard you had a little affray at Westbury. Attacked by masterless thieves and evil men from Sherwood, I hear. An outrage, by my faith. And you saw them off. Very good, Sir Alan. I am pleased for you. But you must be fatigued after all your exertions. Pray, rest a little, take your ease. I will discuss the fifty marks you owe me later this afternoon.'

'I am quite ready to talk now,' I said.

'No, not now. I have a little business of my own that I must conclude before I can satisfy you, some business of the law. That is ever my burden as sheriff. But before we get to that, I am told you are a singer, is this so? Yes? Then, if you are not tired you must sing for me and my men. We sadly lack for entertainment here at the castle. A few passing jongleurs, and most too frightened to perform. Sing well and maybe, just maybe, the King will see fit to reduce your debts, eh?'

'I should prefer to discuss the tax money now, sir,' I said, hanging on to my temper with all my strength.

'No, sir, you will sing. You will sing now. I have a great love of music, I am a most cultured man. You will indulge me and then, perhaps, I will indulge you, eh?'

'I have no vielle, sir. My instrument is at Westbury. I cannot sing without it. Perhaps if we were first to discuss the money . . .'

'I know where I can find a vielle,' said Benedict unhelpfully. 'There is a fellow in the alehouse below the castle who plays tunes for flagons of ale. He cuts a very amusing caper, too, while he plays. Perhaps Sir Alan would also care to dance while he plays. Should I fetch it, Sir Philip?'

I wished then that I had sliced up the fat bastard's kidneys. But it was too late. Benedict Malet was already pushing through the throng to fetch the instrument, and Philip Marc was clapping his hands and announcing to the whole hall that the famous *trouvère* Sir Alan Dale would entertain us with his celebrated music. Furious as I was, I knew that I had to do it: if I could please him – and God how I hated the weakness of my position that forced me to do that – then I might perhaps succeed in reducing the debt. But I felt no better than a whore.

The vielle was a poor specimen, old, warped and unvarnished, and the bow was worse, the horse-hairs split and bunched at the top. However, I believe I managed to produce a passable sound. I did not dance. But I did sing. Judging my audience of mercenaries, most three parts drunk, I sang the great lays of France: of Charlemagne; of Roland and Oliver; stirring tales of battle and death, of self-sacrifice and tragedy. I swear that even those rough foreign men-at-arms were moved. I saw the dark bulk of Boot in the back of the hall staring at me with his huge red mouth open like a fish.

To finish off, just for the sheer devilry of it, I told them I would play a *canso* that I had written with King Richard the Lionheart – the finest monarch I had ever had the pleasure of serving. I gave them 'My Joy Summons Me' – and I put my heart and soul into it. The hall was absolutely silent when I had finished.

I tossed the old vielle to Sir Benedict, who was gazing at me with mixed hatred and awe, and strode over to Philip Marc.

'Now, sir, I should like to speak about my debts,' I said.

The man was actually weeping. 'No, no, Sir Alan, we cannot talk of such sordid matters now,' said Marc, wiping the tears from his cheeks. 'I have a task in the bailey that I must oversee. But your music was . . . it was magnificent. And I thank you, thank you, Sir Alan. You made me feel . . . ah, but forgive my nonsense. We will certainly talk afterwards, we will talk in an hour or two, my friend.'

I followed the herd as it streamed out of the hall and

into the inner bailey. More than a few of the tough merce-naries pounded me on the back as they passed and offered me words of praise and, despite everything, I was warmed by their pleasure.

The crowd gathered around the huge gallows that I had noticed in the bailey. It was no longer empty. Six men were now upon it. Five of them were bound fast with ropes and ties and were secured to five wooden stools on the plank surface. I knew not one of the five bound men – but the sixth was Boot. He wore a black leather jerkin and a cloth hood that covered his face save for two eye-holes and a gap for his mouth, but there was no mistaking his size and the copper-brown skin of his bare arms. A priest also dressed in black climbed up the steps and on to the gallows platform, followed by Philip Marc and his lumbering hound Sir Benedict Malet. The priest began to pray aloud for the souls of the five men, but his mumbled words were drowned out by Sir Benedict, who produced a roll of parchment and began to read a list of five names and professions: they were townsfolk, shop-keepers, merchants, artisans, all citizens of the middle rank, some I gathered of not inconsiderable estate.

'You men have all been found guilty of evading the King's taxes, lawfully levied upon your properties, and by this contumelious action you have forfeited the right to the King's protection. In the name of the law, I sentence you all to death, may God have mercy upon your souls.'

I saw that Philip Marc was looking directly at me.

Good God, had this crude display been arranged solely for my benefit? I broke my gaze from the sheriff. The priest had ceased his mumbling. Boot strode to the first victim – and I realised belatedly that there were no ropes attached to the beam above their heads.

This was to be no hanging, no commonplace execution.

Boot grasped the head of the first man. The crowd fell silent; I could hear a strange sound emanating from the huge man's red lips, it was high-pitched, eerie, but I could clearly recognise a tune. The monster was singing. Stranger still, I recognised that tune. He was singing 'My Joy Summons Me'. I felt sick. What cruel mockery was this?

Boot's fingers closed around the first man's skull, his huge arms gave one swift wrench, and the man's spine snapped like a twig. The victim uttered not a sound – but the weird singing coming from the huge red mouth never ceased – the man's head lolled on his chest, the neck unmistakably broken. I felt fingers of ice crawl up my spine. The huge executioner stepped over to the second man, grasped his head and twisted, and once again snapped his backbone as easily as if he were a chicken for the pot. And so he progressed through all the condemned men, dispatching each in an instant, coldly, efficiently, like a man arranging a row of melons in some eastern market.

And all the while, in his high, whining voice, he sang my song.

*

I admit that I was shocked, and a little unnerved, by the execution. I have seen death many times, and a dozen executions or more – I watched my own father hanged by the neck as a child – but few have chilled me like that cruel display.

In something of a daze, I found myself in the hall with Philip Marc an hour later. The sheriff seemed to me to be in a fine, happy mood. He cut himself a thick slice of mutton from a joint on the sideboard, and munching it, he said: 'So, Sir Alan, to business – I am at your disposal. I hope our little display of justice in the courtyard has shown you the consequences of refusal to pay the King's taxes.'

I had planned to flatter and wrangle, to cajole and reason with the sheriff. But the sight of those five men meeting their Maker in such a brutal fashion drove all my soft words from my head.

Instead, I said: 'I cannot pay you. I do not have the money. Truly I do not.'

'No?' said Philip Marc, cocking an eyebrow at me. 'No, I see that you do not. But perhaps you can get the money for me, eh? Perhaps if I give you some more encouragement. With more incentive, as my clerks say, you might find it.'

I was perplexed by his words and frowned at the man. The sheriff gave a chuckle. 'But I must not be so obtuse,' he said. 'Malet!' he suddenly roared. 'Benedict, where are you, my plump gosling?'

From a door at the far end of the hall, Benedict Malet emerged, smirking nastily. Directly behind him came two men-at-arms, and between them I saw with mounting horror that they held the writhing body of a small boy. It was Robert.

I was on my feet and heading for the trio in an instant, when Marc stopped me with a few words. 'Take another step, Sir Alan, and the boy dies.'

I saw that one of the men-at-arms holding my son had a blade at his jugular, ready to slice deep.

'What is the meaning of this!' I roared at the sheriff. 'I came here under a flag of truce, on the promise that no harm would come to me . . .'

'And no harm shall come to you, my dear Alan, as long as you behave yourself. No harm shall be done to your son, either. On exactly the same conditions.'

I looked at Robert. His eyes were huge with fear. 'They tricked me, Father. It was a dirty trick. I got a message from you saying that I was to ride immediately to Nottingham, and to come without telling anyone at Westbury. It said you urgently needed my help. Oh, Father, I truly thought it was from you. I am so, so sorry.'

'It doesn't matter, Robert,' I said. 'It really is no matter.'

'I am afraid that I have indulged in a *ruse de guerre*,' said Sheriff Marc. 'I am afraid that I delayed you for a little while until you and Robert could be united here. I do hope you will forgive me, but I was not certain that you would clearly see the importance of paying your debts if we did not apply a mite of pressure.'

'I will forgive you the moment you release my son,' I said, trying to remain calm. 'I will pay the full amount as soon as I can, but only if you release him now.'

'Alas . . .' said the sheriff, 'I'm sure you can understand my position. I know that I would sleep more easily if I knew that young Robert was snug in a cell in my own keep. Guards, you may take the prisoner away.'

'Wait,' I said. 'Allow me to speak with him for a moment.'

The sheriff shrugged. As I walked towards my son, I saw that Robert was weeping freely and it was only with difficulty that I kept my own eyes dry.

'Be strong, Robert. Be brave and patient. I will get you out of this place as soon as I can. Dry your tears, son. You know that I love you. You must be a man, for me.'

I embraced him, then held him at arm's length to look into his face.

'Be brave and be patient,' I said. 'And I swear I will fetch you home.'

But the tears were still running down his beautiful face. 'Vixen died,' he said. 'She was a good dog; never hurt anybody. She fell sick and died this afternoon.'

I was not physically restrained. The sheriff's men did not even take my weapons from me. Yet, despite my longing to cut out his cruel heart, I knew that I could make not the slightest move against the sheriff or any of his men while he held my son in his power. Our negotiations were swiftly dealt with. I agreed to pay the sheriff ten marks of silver within the week. I agreed that I would pay him another ten marks at Lammas, the festival of the harvest at the beginning of August, and the third and final payment of the thirty marks at Christmas – the sheriff's teasing talk of fifty marks having been dismissed early in the discussions. I told the sheriff with all the firmness I could muster that I would not tolerate Robert suffering any harm or even discomfort. And if he wished to receive these payments this must be clearly understood from the beginning. I also told him, and Benedict Malet, quite calmly, that if Robert did come to any harm, I would spend my life in the pursuit of bloody vengeance on them both.

'My dear Sir Alan,' said the sheriff, smiling kindly at me. 'Why should I damage your boy? You have kindly agreed to contribute to my coffers. As long as you pay what you have promised, not a hair on the boy's head shall be harmed.' Then his look changed, darkened: 'But if you play me false, sir, if you miss your payments, even by one month, one week even . . . well, you have seen what Boot can do.'

'Snap!' said Benedict, clicking his fingers. 'Oh, poor little Robert.'

I rode back to Westbury in the lengthening shadows with my soul on the rack. The only crumb of comfort I could find was the sheriff's eagerness to acquire wealth. I believed he would spare my son while I was providing him with coin for his coffers. He would not kill the goose that laid golden eggs. But my most immediate problem was how to raise the ten marks I had promised by the end of the week. I did not have it. But I would get it somehow. The thought of Boot's big hands around my son's skull made me feel sick and shaky.

In the event, Robin came to my aid, as I had known he would. He sent me five marks in silver, eight hundred silver pennies in a stout leather sack. I sold two of my horses and with what I had left in my counting house . . . I was still a good way short of the ten marks that I had promised. My salvation came from an unexpected source.

Sir Thomas came to me as I was sitting at the long table in my hall, once again going over the rolls with Baldwin and looking for a way in which we could raise the remaining money from the estate. Without a word Thomas dumped two heavy linen sacks on the table before us. They chinked.

'As I told you before, Sir Alan,' Thomas said with not a hint of a self-satisfied smile. 'I do not always lose.'

I was overwhelmed by his gesture. 'How much is it?' I said, lifting one of the bags and feeling the weight of the coins through the linen.

'It is a little over two marks,' he said. 'And it is my gift to you.'

'I can't take your money, Thomas,' I said, trying to mean it.

'Yes, you can. And you will. I feel that I was partly to blame for Robert being deceived by the sheriff's message. He is in my charge and if I had been here rather than in the stews of Nottingham when it came, I hope I would have seen through it. It's my fault, and so I should make amends. Take it, my friend, with my blessing. I'd only lose it again next time, most probably.'

I was extremely moved by Thomas's contribution and extremely relieved. It meant that I now had enough to make the first payment to Philip Marc, and the next day I returned to Nottingham to fulfil my commitment.

I did not see either the sheriff or his deputy Benedict, for which small mercy I was glad. But I paid over the moneys to the sheriff's clerk and received a receipt for the payment. Then I demanded to see Robert.

After a good deal of argument, in which I made various threats that I could not truly back up, I was allowed by an under-sheriff, a blackguardly fellow who I had seen before in the circle of smirking mercenaries around Marc, to visit my son for a few moments to verify that he was indeed whole and hale. He was being kept in a cell in the depths of the castle, the door warded by two men-at-arms, and the corridor manned by half a dozen men-at-arms. Even the stairs leading down to the prison block were guarded by a pair of Flemish knights. With a sinking heart, I knew that even if I had the military strength, which I did not, there was absolutely no chance that I could break into the castle and free Robert by force.

However, I was relieved to see that the boy was cheerful and moderately well cared for. He had candles for light (an expense for the sheriff to bear) and a towel, water jug and a piece of lard soap for washing, and regular if rather dull food twice a day. The boy had made himself a chessboard, with squares scratched on the stone floor, and the pieces fashioned out of lumps of candle wax, and he told me that he spent the time thinking, praying and playing chess with himself, left hand against the right.

'I am being patient and brave, Father,' he said. 'I know you will get me home as soon as you can.'

I was not allowed to stay with him long, but as I was departing, chivvied rudely out of the cell by the Flemish under-sheriff, Robert said something a little strange. 'Can you give Sir Thomas a message, Father? It concerns a small matter that he and I have been arguing over for some weeks now.'

I said that I would.

'Tell him that I have solved the inherent weakness of the hollow phalanx: each side of the square must be made up of four blocks of men, each a discrete command with their own captain, so they can open and close individually like doors to let the cavalry out without the whole of one side being left open to the enemy.'

I had no idea what he meant but I promised to deliver the message word for word. And when I did later that day at Westbury, Thomas merely said: 'Yes, that should work, I think. He's a smart boy, your Robert, you should be proud of him.'

Well, I was, of course, even though I had no notion, in this instance, of exactly why I should be so proud. I was also relieved that Robert was safe and being well treated. For the moment. But I had scant idea how I would be able to find the next ten marks, which would fall due on Lammas day at the beginning of August.

The late spring that Year of Our Lord twelve hundred and fourteen was a fine one: days of brilliant sunshine and only the occasional shower to make the country seem fresh and alive. I was still weak and bone-thin but I set my mind to improving my body with a will. I joined Sir Thomas Blood in the courtyard every day at dawn and we exercised with sword and shield until mid-morning. Robert might be languishing in a prison cell but I had to make myself hard so that I could fight to free him. For I knew that the only chance I had of raising the money to make the next payment, and perhaps with luck to make the full payment to the sheriff, was to win riches in battle and, with God's help, perhaps take a rich French knight prisoner. For the enormous amount of money that I needed could only come from a fat ransom.

I exercised with Sir Thomas every day. I also made sure that I ate like a wolf, taking Tilda's advice and having meat and fish with almost every meal. My coffers might be empty but there was still plentiful game on my lands and the rivers were full of trout. To strengthen my arms I began a routine devised by Sir Thomas which involved lifting round river boulders above my head and setting them down on the ground again, before repeating the exercise over and over. Sometimes I would sit on the ground of the courtyard manoeuvring these boulders around my body, shifting the weight from the left side to the right, and then back again. It does not sound like much but my stomach muscles ached for days afterwards and my arms burned. After a few weeks I could see the rounded swell of muscles returning to my upper arms, chest and legs, and I began to feel strong again.

I trained hard for two months with Sir Thomas and the garrison of Westbury and by the time Robin arrived in early June with nearly two hundred marching men, I was almost as fit as I had been before my illness.

My first thought when seeing this host was to gauge whether it was powerful enough to take Nottingham Castle. I said something along those lines to Robin.

'It grieves me to tell you that I do not think so, Alan,' said Robin. 'There must be a thousand men-at-arms in the castle now and the sheriff's spies are everywhere. They would be forewarned and we would fail. Then we would be outlawed – both of us – the very fate you said you wanted to avoid by making this accommodation with Philip Marc. But I will risk it if you ask it of me. For Robert and for our friendship.'

I realised then that I was being foolish. Selfish, even.

'Is Robert well?' asked Robin, with genuine concern in his eyes.

'Yes, he is in good health and spirits,' I said heavily. 'And safe enough, I believe, for the moment. But I would have him by my side.'

'We will make things right when we come back from the war,' Robin said. 'Just keep your eyes out for a plump French count or a wealthy baron or two.'

Over a cup of wine in my hall with Sir Thomas and Little John, Robin gave me the news from France: 'Try not to fall off your stool with surprise, Alan, but it seems that the King has been victorious in Poitou.'

I managed to keep my seat but I was considerably astonished.

'By all accounts, the King has been quite brilliant in his operations,' Robin continued. 'He has taken his army down the Charente and back, and across through Angoulême and the Limousin. He has quelled the Lusignans, even Geoffrey, and taken castle after castle. The local barons have surrendered to him, all of them, and begged to pay homage in exchange for keeping their lands. Most of them served him in the past, or Richard before him, or their father Henry – he is in his ancestral lands, of course, playing the hero king, the noble lord returned to claim his own.'

'It hardly seems credible,' I said.

'Oh, it is true all right, I had the news from Cousin

Henry in London. The bells are ringing out for victory all, over the city, he informs me.'

'Where is the King now?'

'Having settled Poitou, he turned north in triumph; he marched straight through Anjou and has seized the castle of Ancennis on the border with Brittany. He stands poised to capture Nantes and threaten the whole of Brittany. It's a brave and clever move: if he takes the city he will have another port as well as La Rochelle from which to resupply his growing forces.'

'And what of Philip?' I asked. 'Surely he has not been idle?'

'That is the best news of all. Philip has summoned his knights, called up the militia of Paris and the lands around and all his nobles of Burgundy, Champagne and Normandy and – we think – is making ready to march south-west to confront John. William des Roches – remember him from Normandy? He's Philip's seneschal now of course – well, he is trying to hold back the King. But our John has the bit between his teeth. Des Roches is outnumbered, and it seems he has been outgeneralled, too.'

I remembered William des Roches, an aggressive knight with fiery red hair who, with Robin, had been instrumental in capturing Mirabeau a decade before. He had become quickly disgusted with John and had given his allegiance to King Philip, one of many barons who had done so before the fall of Normandy.

'Philip must march to support des Roches in the south-west,' said Robin, 'or send a significant part of his army to do the same – or he will lose not only Poitou but Anjou, Maine, maybe even Normandy. John, believe it or not, is actually winning!'

'Take a stone to Fidelity's edge, Alan,' said Little John, 'we're going to war!'

Part Three

My sin has been found out; my wickedness uncovered. Prior William has learnt that, against his express orders, I have been continuing with the transcription of Brother Alan's tale. Another brother, and I shall not sully these pages with the wretch's name, saw me writing upon my parchments, asked what I was about and informed on me to the Prior. And so our master under God summoned both Brother Alan and myself to the chapter house and in the presence of a dozen other senior monks of Newstead he pronounced his sentence.

We are both to be banished from the abbey. But first we are to do penance for our crimes. I am to be stripped and given forty lashes in the courtyard in front of all the other members of our house. It seems a harsh sentence for such a slight crime, but I must not complain. It is God's will, after all, and Prior William says I must be taught humility before I leave these precincts, so that my time here should not have been completely wasted. And I will try to be humble and accept my punishment and my fate. But I must confess I greatly fear the loss of my home and my place in the world. I do not know how I will live outside these walls. I am young, however, not yet thirty, and so there is time for me to find another path in this world. It is far, far worse for Brother Alan. He will not be beaten, at least. At his age and in his state of health, forty lashes – even four lashes – would most certainly kill him, and Prior William does not wish to have his death on his conscience. But he is to be immured in his cell for a month on bread and water, and then expelled from the monastery. And I think that may be the death of him. But even in the face of the Prior's wrath, Brother Alan showed no fear. He stood as straight as his weak legs allowed him and damned the Prior as a coward and a bully when he heard the sentence. 'I have survived worse prisons,' he said. 'And suffered under worse tyrants than you.' Then he turned his back on William and limped back to his cell on his own two feet to begin the punishment. I know he has also sent a message to his grandson, who is also called Alan, requesting a corner of his old manor of Westbury in which to live out his last days. But he has had scant contact with his family for some years and I suspect that that relative may not look kindly on the former lord of the manor returning to his hall. God preserve him.

My beating is set for dawn tomorrow morning. And I earnestly pray that I shall have the strength to endure it. May God be with me, too, now and for ever. Amen.

Chapter Twenty-two

We marched south in the morning, heading for Dover and the grand fleet under the command of William Longsword, Earl of Salisbury, which was assembled there. I was loath to leave Robert in the hands of the sheriff, but I knew I had no choice. The only way I could acquire the money to free him was through battle. But it felt terribly wrong to be leaving the country at his time of need.

'Whether you are in Flanders or at Westbury,' said Robin, somewhat brutally, 'you still will not have Robert by your side. He will be safe enough until we return with the money to claim him. Come now, Alan, I need you to train your mind solely on the campaign. *I* need you now, Alan, and I need all of you.'

That was all very well for Robin to say. He was accompanied by both his sons. Miles and Hugh were to act as Robin's aides, relaying orders to the different components of his army. He also had with him a dozen light cavalry – to be used mainly for scouting – and not quite two hundred infantry, sixty archers, and the rest men-at-arms equipped with swords, shields and long pikes or Little John's new poleaxes. There were also a dozen squires and pages, the sons of Robin's noble friends, and a handful of unarmed servants to ensure our comforts on the march.

We embarked at Dover and made the short journey to Calais in less than a day. The sea was mild as milk and the grand fleet – many of them former French ships that had been captured at Damme – took William of Salisbury and a thousand men, a goodly number of them Flemish mercenaries under their captain Hugh de Boves, across with not a ship nor a man lost. We also took with us a deal of money, tens of thousands of marks in stout wooden barrels, under heavy guard, for silver was the glue that would bind this alliance of English, Flemish and German armies and give us the collective strength to smash the French.

We had more news at Calais: King John was again triumphant in the south. He had taken Nantes in a brisk fight and had captured Peter of Dreux, the Count of Brittany, whose wife was the sister of the murdered Duke Arthur. Better yet, the knights of Angers had opened their gates to him without a fight and the King was once

305

more in the capital of Anjou, the home of his forebears. Philip and his son Prince Louis were marching south from Paris with a large army – and, praise God, the north was now unguarded.

Robin was quietly pleased with the way that things seemed to be going. 'The way to Paris is open, Alan,' he told me in his tent a week after our arrival in France. 'For once, John has not made a total mess of things. All we need now is for the Germans to join us and we can plunge into the heartlands of France at will.'

We were bivouacked about twenty miles south-east of Calais, in thickly wooded countryside near the hamlet of Saint-Omer. William Longsword, the Earl of Salisbury, had distributed his forces across the countryside with orders to ravage the lands to the south. These rich farms and manors on the flat, wheat-growing plains had once been the lands of the Count of Boulogne but Philip had annexed the territory two years before and declared them part of the loyal county of Artois. Renauld of Boulogne – a tall, powerful, black-haired man, with a reputation for reckless courage – was now our staunchest ally, having been granted lands in England and awarded an annual pension from King John. He and Longsword were very close, hunting together by day and drinking themselves into a stupor at night. Renauld, who had a personal grudge against the Dreux family over some disputed lands, was particularly pleased that Peter of Brittany had been taken.

'That'll serve the bugger right,' I overheard him say to Salisbury on the march from Calais. 'Nothing like some time in gaol to teach a fellow to mend his wicked ways.'

I could not but agree. I now looked back on the actions that had led me to my time in Brien's Close with a shudder. I had given my trust to two men – de Vesci and Fitzwalter – who had not lifted a finger to save me when our plot had gone awry. They and many other English nobles were conspicuous by their absence on this campaign, despite the assurances that had been given to the King at Wallingford. Indeed, among the more powerful barons of the land, only Robin had honoured his commitment to come to Flanders and fight for the King.

The news was not all good, however. I had just returned from leading a patrol south, foraging for food – which in truth meant descending on a farm with a score of armed men and carrying away chickens, pigs, sacks of corn, anything edible, to the dismay of the owners – when I heard loud voices coming from Robin's tent. When I pushed open the flaps, I found Robin and Hugh in the midst of a quarrel.

'We cannot go off piecemeal,' Hugh was saying. 'Our strength is in our unity. It is madness not to wait for the Emperor. We must all go to Paris together.'

'It is madness not to attack now, while Philip is busy in the south,' said Robin. His voice was louder than usual, for he was not used to being contradicted. 'We will miss our opportunity while Otto enjoys the charms of his new bride.'

'What is amiss?' I asked.

It was Miles who answered me. He was lolling in the corner of the tent on a camp-stool sipping a cup of wine. 'It seems the mighty Emperor is more of a lover than a fighter,' said Robin's younger son. 'He married his beautiful bride at Maastricht a few weeks ago and now he is refusing to march until he has spent a few weeks in her delightful company. He's childless, of course, and they say he hopes to secure an heir before committing himself to the perils of battle.'

'He is going to lose us this war unless he pulls his finger out,' said Robin.

'It's not his finger he needs to pull out,' said Miles with a dirty chuckle.

Robin ignored the remark. 'I say we should march now, with the forces we have at our disposal – with the counts of Boulogne and Flanders and our own men we must have nearly three thousand; if we go hard and fast we could be in Paris in a week.'

'Emperor Otto, together with the Duke of Brabant and the German barons, represents two-thirds of our full strength,' said Hugh slowly, with irritating calmness; he might have been speaking to a particularly stupid child, not his famous father. 'We dare not risk proceeding without them. We must wait.'

'War is risk,' snapped Robin. 'And war is about taking

your opportunity when it presents itself. Now is the time to strike, our weakness will be irrelevant if we're swift. What say you, Alan?'

I needed a little time to think so I walked over to the wine jug and filled a cup. The prospect of invading France with fewer than three thousand men appalled me. But Robin was one of the finest strategists I had ever known, his instinct for a bold, successful move was almost as sure as the Lionheart's had been.

'I will follow you, my lord, whatever you decide,' I said. 'But surely it is up to Longsword. What does the Earl of Salisbury say?'

Robin sighed. 'Longsword says we must wait for Otto,' said my lord grumpily. It was clear he did not relish losing a debate with his elder son.

And there the discussion was closed.

In the following weeks, we ravaged the former lands of the Count of Boulogne, with his enthusiastic encouragement. There was no sign of a French army, we avoided the small castles garrisoned by Philip's men and his allies, and took out our wrath on the countryside. We burnt farms, we ransacked mills and barns for grain; we herded sheep and cattle back to the army, which was spread across southern Flanders from Calais to Lille. And we waited for Emperor Otto to sire an heir on his new bride.

I rode out mostly with a force of a dozen mounted

Westbury men and Robin's few cavalry, and Little John, who was in unusually high spirits in those days.

'There is nothing finer than having a juicy county to pillage,' said John to me on a bright and beautiful evening in early July. We were sitting in an abandoned barn about ten miles north of the city of Amiens, and as it was too far for us to ride back to the camp that day, we were roasting a stolen sheep and preparing to bed down for the night where we were. The men were tired: they had been riding and raiding all day. Many were already asleep, curled in the old straw like dogs. At noon that day we had come across a strong French militia patrol – levies probably recruited from Amiens itself – and we had fought a bloody battle with them and lost two men before they retreated. Although we had been outnumbered and surprised by the enemy, Little John had charged his horse straight into their packed ranks without hesitation and had begun laying about them with his poleaxe with such ferocity that the enemy had shrunk back, disordered, dismayed. And when Sir Thomas and myself had spurred forward and joined John in the heart of the fray the French had broken and run.

'Unless it is a nice bloody battle,' said John, grinning like a village simpleton.

I could not agree with him. These days I seemed to be more terrified than I had ever been before by the prospect of violence and every time I was called to fight I had to force myself to ride into battle. I feared that one day my nerve would break altogether, like those unfortunate French militia today, and I would shy away from a mêlée or even run like a coward. I hoped that on the outside I still appeared to be a valiant knight, but on the inside, in truth, I was quaking.

'Do you ever feel the fear, John?' I asked. 'I mean, on the eve of battle or in the cold hours before the fight, not when the blood runs hot in action.'

Little John frowned at me. 'Of course I do, only a madman has no fear,' he said, surprising me. 'But the fear is the fun part. The fear is how you know you are still alive, Alan. Your heart beats strongly, you feel every fibre, bone and muscle of your body. You think: maybe this time, just maybe this time will be the last day of my life. I see more clearly, I feel the fresh wind on my face, I can smell the odours around me as if for the first time: crushed grass, the sweat of my horse, old leather polished to a shine. The wood of my axe handle feels smooth and fine, like some costly fabric. I am alive. I am in fear – but I am more alive than at any other time.'

'But do you not fear the coming pain, or death itself?'

'No one likes pain, sure enough. But pain is part of life too. If I were a peasant labouring in the fields would I not too feel pain, in my back, in my limbs at the end of a hard day? I would feel the pain of hunger in times of famine and, worse, the pain of humiliation after a long, slow trudge of an uneventful life. Or, were I the kind of

311

man to marry and have children, I would most likely feel the pain of witnessing the death of a child, or a wife in childbirth. There is no escape from pain on this earth, whatever path you choose. I choose the joy of battle; the comradeship of men of courage. That is an ample compensation for a little pain now and then. I fear pain and death, of course, and I want to live, Alan, but I want to live like a man – until I die!'

'The afterlife does not trouble you, then? The risk of Hell for the terrible things we have done in this life?' The last gleams of sunlight were lancing through holes in the barn roof and I could see the dancing motes of hay caught in the golden beams.

'The priests tell us we must suffer Hell for our sins. I have done evil things, sure, plenty of them. But I have remained true to my lord, and I have followed his orders without fail. I have lived the life of a warrior, never shirking my duty, never abandoning my comrades. And I think God must understand the way that a soldier lives, the things that he must do. If He made us as we are, He must see a purpose in our brutality, in the killing and the pain that we inflict. I remember old Tuck telling me that God always had a plan. I believe it. I believe I am God's instrument, though I do not know His purpose. And I have been a true man, all my long life. I have remained true to my purpose, to my lord. If God is just, He will understand that.'

I had never heard Little John speak so, and I was more

than a little moved by his simple code, his faith in a just God. I had hoped to speak to him of my fears and to take some comfort from him for my own unmanly feelings, but I could not.

'I do not want to die,' was all I could say on the matter. 'I love life too much to see death as anything but a terrible sorrow: I want to feel the sun on my face, a horse between my legs, to take a lamb, warm and slippery from its mother's womb, to eat and drink and laugh with friends, to feel a woman bucking in joy beneath me again, to see my son grow tall. I feel that I must live, I must survive, not just for myself but for Robert, for Westbury . . . and perhaps for Tilda.'

'The rumours are true then,' said John, grinning at me. 'I heard you had been mooning after her again! Do you love her?'

I blushed a little. 'I don't know,' I said. 'I think I do. I think about her more than I should. She is a bride of Christ and has forsaken the love of men.'

'If you don't know, then you do not truly love her,' he said. 'And I do not think she is the right woman for you. Not because she is a nun – you could take her away from that if you chose, but because . . . I don't know. She is just wrong, somehow.'

I frowned at the man. Tilda was as close to an angel as any woman I knew, she had clearly forgiven me for the death of her father and now even seemed more than a little fond of me. I did not care to have her disparaged, even by him. I opened my mouth to say something, but before I could speak . . .

'I have loved but once,' my friend said – and stopped. I knew what he was about to say. Little John had loved a man, a beautiful youth, in fact, called Gavin, who had died in battle in the south. It was a sinful coupling, the Church would have insisted, the priests claimed that congress between two men was a foul abomination, and yet neither Robin nor I had felt any need to condemn John for his choice of lover. I had been surprised, to be sure, to discover that this huge brute had tender feelings for a handsome young lad half his age, but once I had got over the shock and seen the real deep affection between them I could not see anything truly evil in the matter.

Little John was staring at the ground between his spread knees. I knew that he was avoiding my eye.

I said: 'Gavin was a fine man, we all liked and respected him, and we all grieved when he fell.'

'Grief . . .' said Little John. 'We spoke of pain before, Alan, and I have never felt the pain of a wound as hard as the agony of his loss. He was so perfect, so strong, so alive . . . Gavin. Even his name breaks my heart in two.'

I saw that John was weeping then. Fat, oily tears were rolling down his lowered face and dripping from his big battered nose. I was at a loss. I'd never seen my friend so lacking in composure. I shuffled next to him and put an arm clumsily around his shoulders.

'I would give my life right now,' said John, between

racking sobs, 'to spend one more day, just one more hour with him.'

I patted his vast back, not knowing what to say.

'You shall see him in Heaven,' I said. 'I am sure that he waits for you there.'

Little John looked up at me. His big shapeless face was wet and oddly patched here and there with white. He gave an enormous sniff, and cuffed his running nose.

'I think so too,' he said. 'Heaven – or the other place, I care not. Gavin waits for me to join him. I shall be happy again.'

After a little while, John recovered himself. He shrugged off my arm and stood tall, a dark giant in the fading light.

Chapter Twenty-three

We returned to the camp the next day, driving a mixed herd of beasts before us: a dozen sheep, goats and pigs, even a lone ox we had found grazing placidly in a meadow. An army eats a great deal and I knew they would all be in our soldiers' bellies before the week was out. Robin rode out to meet us as we approached the wood that was our camping ground.

My lord congratulated us on our successful raiding and then said: 'When you have eaten and rested, Alan, get your men together and all their kit. We are moving out tomorrow morning.'

He did not look happy about it.

'What news?' I said.

'Otto is finally on the march – and we are to rendezvous

with him and the rest of the German contingent at Nivelles.'

'So we are to head south – to Paris?'

'That is the plan. I just hope we have not left it too late.'

'Too late?'

'You might as well know, Alan. It is bad news, I'm afraid. King John has failed us. He was besieging a fortress called Roche-au-Moine, a few miles from Angers, when the French army arrived. It seems they squared up for a pitched battle: John had the superior numbers and I believe he could have won the day. But on the eve of the fight, his Poitevin barons deserted him, those who had paid homage weeks before. Ran away. Still John could have fought, and won, with a little determination, I think: Richard would have done so. But no, King John turned and ran too and scurried back to La Rochelle, his tail between his legs.'

'But he is still there with an army; he is still a threat to the French.'

'Yes,' said Robin heavily, 'you and I might very well think so. But Philip doesn't. He has left his son Prince Louis and a few hundred knights to keep the King occupied and Philip has now turned north with all the rest of his forces and he is coming up to face us as fast as he can. He is raising men as he marches, every town and commune must contribute its militia, poorly trained pikemen for the most part, but the French barons are rallying to his banner, too, and in numbers. They smell victory.'

'We have lost, then,' I said. 'Our strategy was to divide Philip's strength between the south and the north. If he ignores John in the south and comes at us with all his might, we cannot stand against him. Surely we must flee. Surely we must make for Calais and home.' I admit I felt a wash of relief at the thought, although the moment I felt it I realised that no battle meant no ransoms, and no hope for Robert.

'Flee?' said Robin, looking at me sideways. 'No, Alan. There is still a chance we can beat him – we shall beat him. Longsword is determined to fight, and so is the Count of Flanders. Otto will surely lose his throne if he does not beat Philip, so he is ready for a battle, after a fashion. The odds against us are worse, for sure. Philip will be stronger now, but with the Germans we are still more or less evenly matched. If we all play our parts well, we can still win. Never fear, my friend, you will still have the chance to capture your prize.'

Two days later, at Nivelles, I felt a little better at the thought of impending battle. A mighty force was assembled in the fields outside the town – a vast army of some nine thousand fighting men, plus all the usual accompanying non-combatants, priests, whores, servants and itinerant pedlars, many thousands of them. It was three weeks into July, by then, and a fine unbroken sunny spell made all the banners of the assembled knights and colours of their surcoats seem even more brilliant than usual. Gorgeous blues, pinks and oranges, vibrant reds and greens, bright gold and silver, iridescent silks and satins; everywhere was the glint of sunshine on steel and the confident bellow of big men's voices. Perhaps, I thought, despite King John's failure to keep the bulk of Philip's forces from us, we did still have the strength to overwhelm him. The German soldiers of Emperor Otto's retinue were particularly impressive: their knights' armour was of the very best quality, glittering links of polished iron that covered them from top to toe; magnificent soaring helms, set with bright ostrich feather plumes, sharp spikes or even spreading antlers; big kite-shaped wooden shields of oak rimmed with hammered steel, huge two-handed longswords, and sumptuous velvet cloaks in all the colours of the rainbow. The Emperor's picked Saxon bodyguard was even more awe-inspiring: huge, blond, muscle-padded men, some even of a size with Little John, with great shining war axes, long daggers at their waists, domed helmets with heavy nasal guards, inlaid with silver and gold, ruddy, English-looking faces, swinging plaits and beards as thick as briar hedges. Beside them Robin's men seemed puny beggarmen in their dull cloaks and patched hauberks, with their roughly made poleaxes and unwieldy pikes.

I had command of our little cavalry contingent, with Sir Thomas and Hugh as my lieutenants and Miles grinning insolently from the ranks. We numbered thirty-two men mounted on lean, fast horses and were lightly armoured compared with the grand knights of Germany and Flanders. In their heavy mail, elaborate helms and long steel-tipped lances, and mounted on their huge, aggressive mail-clad destriers, they looked the very epitome of arrogant lords of war, which of course they were – and I was glad I would not have to face them in battle.

Our duties were to scout out the land before the advance of the main force and to run messages between the disparate components of the allied army. And therein lay our greatest weakness: Otto's five thousand men were a disciplined group, his proud knights and the mighty Saxon guard taking their orders directly from him, but the rest of the army was composed of small groups of minor barons and their men – companies of no more than a few hundred knights and mounted men-at-arms under the count of this place or the lord of that town. Flemish men-at-arms from Brabant and Holland, from the towns of Ghent, Namur, Dortmund and Leuven, marched with French-speakers from Lorraine, Calais and Boulogne, plus a few Norman knights too, who had lost their lands to King Philip, and our few Englishmen, of course, as well. It was not even clear who was in overall command. Otto, the Holy Roman Emperor, held the highest rank, but the Earl of Salisbury controlled the purse strings – King John's silver jingled in every baron's pouch; the Count of Flanders claimed command on the basis that it was his county we were to be fighting in. The Count of Boulogne claimed the honour since he was clearly the knight of greatest prowess, and he offered to prove it with sword and lance to any man who denied it.

Robin's contingent of two hundred men made him one of the middle-ranking barons – no match in strength for Emperor Otto or the Earl of Salisbury, of course, but more powerful than some of the Flemish companies. Despite this, my lord wisely remained largely silent when the bickering began at the council meetings.

For three days at Nivelles, the commanders of the various forces argued about what was to be done. I attended Robin at these meetings, though I was too lowly to speak before the great men. Philip was somewhere in the north already, that was all that we knew for certain; he was rumoured to be at Péronne with a vast host, as many as thirty thousand men.

He was heading north-west for Calais, to slaughter the garrison and burn the English ships in the harbour and cut off any hope of retreat for us . . .

No, he was heading due north for Tournai to ravage and destroy the Flemish heartlands . . .

No, he was making straight for us at Nivelles, making a lunge north-east for the rich merchant city of Brussels.

In the end it was the Emperor's reedy voice that prevailed. He was a slight man, handsome in a girlish way with his reddish-brown hair curled into ringlets and dangling around his pallid cheeks. He was King John's nephew, and I thought I detected a certain family resemblance in the soft, voluptuous line of his mouth and weakness of his jaw. But he was the greatest lord of the German lands and he threatened to take his army and retreat all the way back to Maastricht if he was not obeyed without question and thus was opposition to his plans muted, if not completely silenced. So we marched for Valenciennes, where Otto planned to take up a position across the road to Brussels. There we would await the French attack.

As the army lumbered south-west on the road from Nivelles, my men and I ranged out far and wide hoping to catch a glimpse of the enemy. We saw nothing of him. At Valenciennes, we had news from the constable of the town's fortress. Philip had passed us in the night. He was now at Tournai, twenty miles behind us.

Once again angry voices were raised in council. The Earl of Salisbury suggested that we simply ignore Philip and his army and make a lunge south for Paris, which was now undefended. Robin backed him to the hilt. But the barons of the Low Countries were adamant that we could not leave Philip with a free hand to pillage their territories – there would not be a manor or market town unburnt from Bruges to Beringen. Robin pointed out that if we marched to Paris, Philip would be bound to follow us or lose his ancestral capital, but my lord was swiftly shouted down.

Otto made the decision again. We turned the army

322

around and began to march north following the trail of destruction left by Philip's advancing host.

I stopped at the little hamlet of Cysoing at a local tavern with about fifteen of my men, while the rest ranged out in pairs ahead to the north and on either side, east and west, searching for the enemy. On the road behind us, stretched out over several miles, was the allied army, more than ten thousand souls in all. Robin and his footmen were in the vanguard of the main force with the knights of Count Ferrand of Flanders a mile or two behind us.

The terrified man and woman who owned the tavern willingly brought out five loaves of bread, some lengths of dried pork sausage and a barrel of wine for me and my men, and I promised them a silver penny if they could tell me anything of the French. They were a stupid couple, I thought, made more stupid by fear of the armed men watering their horses at their trough and munching their bread and sausage, and they spoke only Flemish, which I did not readily understand, but they seemed to be telling me that there were soldiers in the wood yonder, about five hundred paces from their door.

It seemed unlikely since we had heard or seen nothing, but I flipped them the silver coin and, not a moment after the tavern-keeper had snatched it out of the air, I heard the drumming of hooves and saw Miles and his scouting partner John Halfpenny come pounding hell for leather down the road from the wood towards me.

Miles reined in sharply and slid lithely off his sweating horse. The boy was in a lather of excitement himself. 'They are there, Sir Alan, just up ahead in those woods. French knights, hundreds of them, maybe thousands.'

I still could not quite believe the youngster. He was a good lad but a little prone to exaggeration and, like his father, very fond of a producing a grand flourish. I could hear nothing, see no sign of movement ahead. I raised an eyebrow at John Halfpenny, a runtish, ugly fellow but a good and reliable soldier. 'It's true, sir. Horsemen, most likely French knights, in numbers. I saw a dozen of the buggers myself.'

'Mount up,' I called. 'We shall go and see what we shall see.'

I sent John Halfpenny back down the road with a message for Robin, and sent another man east to find Sir Thomas and Hugh and bring them up into the wood. Then my men and I saddled up and headed at the trot up the road towards the trees. I turned my head from my position at the front of the troop and shouted: 'We are scouts, just scouts – remember that. We look, we see and then we report back. No trying to be a hero, no trying for ransoms. We're merely having a look. Understand?'

From my shoulder I heard Miles grumbling: 'Told you, Alan, it's the French army. They're up there. Don't you believe me?'

I gave him a sharp look: 'I believe you, Miles, but I want to see for myself. What would I tell your father?

That I heard the enemy was there from one of my troopers but did not bother to check for myself?' I gave the signal and the whole company rose as one to the canter.

The woods were thick, tangled and dim even at noon on a bright sunny day. The road dwindled to a muddy track. Beyond it, I could see no more than a few yards through the dense trees and undergrowth on either side. There was no sign of the enemy, not a horse, not a lone man-at-arms, and I would have doubted Miles's and Halfpenny's account but for the fact that the track beneath us was churned by the passing of many hooves. Horsemen had been here, perhaps twenty riders, but no more. We pushed onwards into the wood. I gave the order for silence and we slowed to a walk. The trees were thinning now, it was becoming lighter and I could see patches of green pasture beyond the treeline. And then we were out the other side and looking at a broad expanse of green field stretching out to the northern horizon and a wide highway cutting across it from left to right, east to west, which I knew must be the main road from Tournai to Lille.

The road was filled with men, horses and carts.

Thousands of them.

I took in the scene in one long sweeping glance. The track we were on led out of the woods and then north-west across the pasture to join the main road at a substantial bridge by a tiny settlement – a few huts and a small wooden chapel beside a stand of ash trees. The bridge crossed a wide sluggish river – from my briefings with Robin and the Flemish commanders who knew this area well, I knew it had to be the River Marque and the hamlet of Bouvines. To my left, I could see detachments of knights, some mounted, some off their beasts allowing them to graze on the lush grass. And a group of perhaps fifty crossbowmen were sitting or standing, distinctive because of their huge shields. The river had burst its low banks here south of the bridge and beyond the resting enemy bowmen was treacherous boggy ground. On the far side of the bridge, about half a mile away, I could make out banners and thick marching columns of footmen, many thousands, tramping towards Lille. The bridge itself was packed with men on horseback, and I thought I could make out the golden lilies of France on an azure field, King Philip's own royal banner, in the middle of the throng. Tailing back along the road east was the rest of the French cavalry.

The first thought in my head was: we have them! More than half, perhaps two-thirds of the enemy, was on the other side of the bridge; on this side of the water, strung out along the road back to Tournai, was the rearguard, picked knights looking to defend the army from an attack from the east. If we could come up now with all our force and assault them before they finished crossing the river, we could destroy the rearguard – Philip's best knights – before the infantry could recross the bridge and come to their aid.

My second thought was never properly formed. I heard Miles cry out: "Ware right!' I twisted my head and saw a mass of horsemen galloping at us from the east, along the edge of the wood. French knights, a dozen men, lances couched, charged into us without the slightest warning.

A fellow with a green oak tree emblem on his black shield was yards away from me, his lance reaching out for my guts. I got my horse moving just in time. His lance-head crashed into my shield with shocking force, rocking me back painfully against my cantle, but the angle of the shield was such that the steel head merely sliced across its face. He shouted something to me as he thundered past, an insult, no doubt. But I had better things to worry about. I hauled out Fidelity with the speed of sheer panic, and managed to bat away the next rider's spear with the blade as it came at me out of nowhere. Others behind me were not so fortunate. I could hear screams, howls and the clash of steel on wood. A knight came at me swinging an axe; I caught the blow on my cross-guard, pushed it aside and punched my mailed fist straight into his roaring face. And they were all past me. I yanked my horse's head around and saw that our lightly armoured scouts were beset by a swarm of furious knights, chopping with swords, and stabbing with their lances. At least three saddles were empty and I could see the huddled forms of my men on the ground.

Miles had a French knight on either side of him and the lad was fending off savage blows from both left and right with his sword and shield. I spurred my mount forward a dozen paces and crashed into the rump of the knight nearest to me. The impact jolted the man, unbalancing him, and I saw Miles's sword flicker out and plunge deep into his eye. The second knight rode directly at me and I took his sword cut on my shield and returned the blow, cracking my blade laterally across his face, smashing into the nasal guard of his helmet and stunning the man. He reeled in the saddle and I smashed his spine with a round-house chop to the back of his mailed neck, striking an inch below the line of his helm.

I took an instant to look around me. We were only a dozen yards from the line where the pasture ended and the woods began. At least half my men were down, dead or mortally wounded. I saw one knight stop his horse and lunge downward with his lance at one of my scouts who was curled like a baby on the ground. Miles was at my elbow, grinning like a demon. Together we spurred at the bastard, yelling our cries, I cut at his arm, the one now holding the lance buried in my trooper's guts, a full-strength blow with Fidelity, and had the pleasure of seeing my sharp steel cleave his limb off at the elbow. The arm fell, still grasping the lance. Miles slashed him deeply across the mouth with his sword as he rode past and the man toppled, screaming, spitting teeth and gore, to the turf. The rest of the knights, half a dozen men, seemed to have drawn off, about thirty paces towards the river, but they were not down, not defeated – they were regrouping. Worse, I could see beyond them the grazing horses being mounted and at least twenty fresh men-at-arms gathering up the reins and cantering towards us.

'Back,' I shouted, 'back into the woods.'

There was nothing else for it but to run: we were scouts, not heavy cavalry, and we would be slaughtered if we stayed to hold our ground.

I gathered my stunned and battered men – those that still retained their saddles – and led them back into the shelter of the trees. Turning in the saddle as we entered the dark, dense woods, I saw knights peeling off the main road to our north and trotting down across the open pasture towards us. An icy fist gripped my bowels. We would be cut to pieces if we did not retreat.

And suddenly there was Robin and Little John and Sir Thomas and Hugh and a dozen other riders coming towards us along the path through the trees. Robin rode straight past me and up to the edge of the wood and looked out at the flattish green field, now littered with a dozen bodies, and half a dozen riderless mounts standing forlornly with their reins trailing. The French cavalry had formed up in a big *conroi* of perhaps three dozen men fifty yards away and they were staring at us over their horses' ears. They looked to be readying themselves for a charge against the treeline.

'I see you've started without the rest of us, Alan,' said my lord.

He turned to one of his riders, a one-eyed veteran of

a dozen battles. 'Claes, get back to the main column, sharpish. Give my compliments to my lord of Flanders and tell him the enemy is here. Tell Ferrand that if he hurries himself we can smash them, here, now. Then find Mastin and tell him to get the archers up here at the double! They cannot come too quickly.'

Robin's presence calmed me, I must admit, for I had been feeling the first tremors of panic. He had grasped the situation at once – and was instantly in control of it. My stomach relaxed, my courage flickered and flared like a fire with fresh kindling thrown upon it. But the next thing he said plunged my heart back into my boots. 'Right, the wedge! Form on me. Quickly now. We're going to teach those cavalry the proper respect for English arms.'

Robin's men made up in the cavalry configuration known as the wedge in under a dozen heartbeats, with my lord at the point, Little John and myself directly behind him, Hugh, Sir Thomas and Miles behind us, and the rest of the dozen or so of riders behind them. A trumpet sounded, and we were off, galloping up the slight rise towards the formed French cavalry about fifty yards away.

It was an extraordinary tactic, against all the rules of horse-warfare. We were charging uphill towards a formed enemy that outnumbered us two to one. We should have retreated into the wood and waited for the enemy charge. Only Robin – and perhaps the Lionheart – would have attempted it, but it worked, by God! Mainly, I think, because of the total surprise. I could see the astonishment on the faces of the French *conroi* as we barrelled forward in the wedge and crashed into their standing ranks. Robin's lance took a knight in the middle of the *conroi* plumb in the centre of his chest, hurling him from the saddle, and then we were in among them, hacking, stabbing, slicing with sword and spear. I lunged at a red-faced knight with Fidelity and he parried with his sword and punched at me with his shield, hitting me painfully on the shoulder and chest. But the move left his defences wide open and Hugh, who was right behind me, buried his lance in his guts. I lanced a second man straight through his shouting mouth with Fidelity, my sword-point bursting right out the back of his head in a shower of red. And suddenly I was through the *conroi* and out the other side in open space. The enemy was shaken but we had barely dented their numbers. However, we had cut right through their ranks and utterly destroyed their cohesion. Little knots of men were now fighting all over the southern part of the field. Little John's horse was killed under him by a lance to the chest – but the big man kicked free of his stirrups and leapt from its falling body and began to wreak havoc with his poleaxe. He was a whirlwind of sheer fury, smashing at riders with his axe, skewering them with the long spear-point. I saw him hook one knight with the curved claw on the other side of the pole from the axe-head, and haul the fellow with main strength from his saddle, and when the knight was sprawled on the ground, stamp once with his right boot, with all his weight behind it, on the man's mailed head, splitting the skull.

Sir Thomas laid about him with a cold and deadly precision, felling knights, it seemed, with every blow. Robin's face was flecked with blood, and as he killed his opponent with a lunge to the throat, he seemed deliberately to wipe the spattered gore from his cheeks as he pulled his sword arm back from the blow.

And then it was over. The French ran. At least half of them completely unscathed but utterly unnerved by our savage and unexpected attack. We cheered ourselves hoarse. For the southern part of the field was ours.

For now.

Chapter Twenty-four

We pulled back to the edge of the woods again and tended to our wounds and our weapons. The battle was not over – not by a long, hot summer's day. Word of our arrival had clearly been reported to the main column, and the crowds of men at the Bouvines bridge seethed with activity, like a wasps' nest smelling sweet wine. It seemed as if they could not decide whether to carry on with the march to Lille or stay and fight. I saw that King Philip's golden lilies were now on this side of the river by the little chapel. The road was still clogged with traffic. But the French had not forgotten us. Three fresh *conrois* of cavalry were forming up about halfway between us and the bridge – perhaps a hundred knights. And they would certainly not be scattered by another mad uphill charge from the handful of Robin's men still in the saddle.

Worse, the crossbowmen by the marshes had transformed into a disciplined column and were marching down the track towards the treeline. These bowmen stopped a bare seventy paces from us, they stuck their huge shields into the turf and, working in pairs, they began to loose their deadly quarrels into the trees; one would shoot, while the other reloaded his weapon behind the safety of the man-sized shield. As our men began to fall, we pulled back further into the trees, while the horses were led even further back into safety. Robin ordered every man to take cover behind thick trunks or fallen logs, but to hold his ground. The black bolts whipped and cracked through the leaves, an awful sound, and now and then an unwary man would cry out in pain.

'Where the devil is Mastin?' said Robin to me. We were crouching down behind a great fallen oak, peering over the mossy rim as the crossbowmen pelted us with their barrage. The French cavalry were now coming towards us at a slow, steady pace, walking their mounts, keeping their dressing, three hundred yards away and closing.

Very soon they would charge into the wood and we would be hunted from tree to tree and slaughtered like vermin.

'Here, sir,' said a Cheshire accent not ten yards behind us. And I turned to see the short, bald, burly shape of

Mastin, captain of Robin's archers, and behind him scores of men with long black bowstaves wearing dark-green cloaks and brown tunics that melded them perfectly into the woodland behind.

'Good man,' said Robin. 'Get your men either side of the track in cover. Half on each flank. Don't be seen. Don't loose until I give the command. Don't pay any mind to the crossbows for now. I want the cavalry. Hit them when they charge. Yes?'

'Oh yes,' said Mastin. 'I understand you perfectly, my lord. And you should know that his honour the Count of Flanders is right on our tail, sir, with hundreds of his knights. Eager as a boy in his first brothel.' He gave a low chuckle and was gone again.

As I watched the cavalry slowly walk their horses towards us, flinching involuntarily as the occasional crossbow quarrel rattled the branches above us, I was aware, without having to look, of dozens of stealthy men taking up positions in the trees behind us. A comforting sensation, the feeling of comrades at your back.

The French cavalry stopped a hundred paces away, three *conrois* still neat and squared, bold and bright with the colours of their surcoats, each lance upright and bearing a fluttering pennant. I could see the captains riding along the front face of the ranks, bawling encouragement and issuing last orders to their knights.

A trumpet blew, shockingly loud and close, and the central *conroi* was suddenly at the canter, heading straight down the track towards the wood, their banners flapping in the wind, the horses' hooves shaking the ground. Behind them the other two companies were following on, surging down the track after the lead *conroi*.

'Now, Mastin, now's your time,' shouted Robin.

And I heard the archer captain mutter, 'As if I didn't fucking know . . .' before his words were drowned out by the whirr of sixty shafts slicing through the summer air as one.

The arrow storm smashed into the front rank of the leading *conroi*, and all but one saddle was immediately emptied. The second rank too was almost entirely destroyed. And in the third only half the men remained in control of their mounts. The charging French knights went from a bold display of perfectly arrayed charging horsemen, the very flower of French chivalry, to a blood-drenched shambles in the space of a couple of heartbeats. Horses, punctured by many arrows, sheeted with blood, staggered sideways and crashed into their fellows, mad with pain, the big destriers biting and kicking, throwing the entire formation into chaos. Other mounts collapsed or cartwheeled forward, creating obstacles for the mounted men behind.

A second volley from Mastin's men scythed into the survivors, with no less awful results. It was as if a giant invisible hand had punched into the company. The first *conroi* was utterly ruined now, a lone French horseman charging into the trees, the only man left out of thirty brave knights. He was screaming, '*St Denis! Vive le Roi!*' and then was abruptly silenced. I did not see how he died.

The archers were still nocking, drawing and loosing death into the second and third *conrois* with an awful humming rhythm. By the sixth or seventh volley – I had lost count by then – the French formation was no more than a collection of scattered clumps of horsemen desperately trying to control their terrified mounts, only a handful of men still coming gamely at us. The ground was slick with blood and filth, and writhing, staggering, wounded men and horses were everywhere. Screaming flooded the air.

And into this carnage, into this bloody hell on earth, the Count of Flanders and his knights made their charge.

A thick column of knights at full gallop – some two hundred men and horses, perhaps, it was difficult to tell as they went by so speedily – poured up the track through the wood, pounded past us and burst out into the fields beyond. They swept the remaining French before them like a vast broom, slaughtering those who were not swift in their escape. The knights of Flanders smashed the last clumps of resistance with ease, cutting down the enemy with sometimes as many as three knights against one. The French died – or ran. There were few who were lucky enough to surrender. And, still drunk with the joy of battle, the Flemish knights turned themselves loose on the crossbowmen. They crashed through the thicket of

337

huge shields, slaying the footmen with great bloody sweeps of their swords, riding down others who tried to run. More than one courageous bowman turned and faced his attacker and managed to spit his mounted enemy with a swiftly loosed quarrel, before he was hacked into bloody chunks by the vengeful comrades of the bolt-struck Flemish knight.

It was soon over. And the men of Flanders roamed the field south of the bridge and the road, red blades in hand, victorious.

The Count of Flanders, wily Ferrand, was no amateur at war. His trumpets sounded the recall and, eyeing the bulk of French cavalry – untouched by this skirmish and still many thousands strong massing by the bridge for a counter-attack – his men trotted their blown horses to the treeline, where we cheered them again and again for their valour.

The wood behind me was now thick with our men. Robin was with the Earl of Salisbury, who had our infantry and the remainder of our knights. As I came up to him, I heard Longsword say: 'Otto is coming up, Locksley, round to the east, he's trying to find a place to ford a stream over there. But he is coming and we can beat them here. If we are quick about it.'

I looked out through the trees. The majority of the French infantry were still on the far side of the bridge, but I could see that they were turning and beginning to recross back to this side. And the French cavalry had quit the main road and were now arrayed in three neat blocks under rippling banners, south of the bridge, half a mile away, their mail and arms glittering in the bright sunlight. I looked to my left, along the treeline, and could see the first units of the Emperor's Saxon guard appearing at the edge of the woods, with scores of magnificent German horsemen before and behind them.

Salisbury was still speaking to Robin and pointing out at the field: 'We will make our line here, north–south, parallel to the river. The Count of Flanders and his cavalry, and the footmen of Hainaut, will form our left flank, just here, anchored on this treeline. They should be able to keep those French horsemen at bay for a while so we can form up. Otto and his Germans will take the centre – he insisted, of course – opposite the bridge and the chapel of Bouvines; and we will form the army's right, the northern flank: the Count of Boulogne, your fellows, and mine. Get your men ready, we will curl round behind Otto and his troops, when they are in place, and take our positions up there beyond the road.'

Ferrand of Flanders had his men well in hand after their superb charge and they began to move out of the trees and form up in ranks about three hundred yards from the French cavalry. Some of them were a little bloodied from their victory over the arrow-shattered French, but they were jaunty, confident in their prowess and their numbers. They sang psalms as they walked their horses into position. And behind them came the men of

Hainaut – big peasants in leather jerkins and steel caps and carrying the long pikes that made them so feared by cavalry.

Otto's men were flooding on to the field, and I saw the famous standard of the Emperor, an eagle mounted on a dragon and borne by a golden chariot, in the midst of a knot of horsemen. The German horsemen swarmed forward to take up their positions opposite the bridge, a little untidily, perhaps – they could not match the neat ranks of the cavalry of Flanders. But they seemed eager for the fight, and I knew as well that the Saxons who formed the core of Otto's force, coming up on the heels of the horsemen, were serious warriors who had sworn an oath to die, if necessary, for their Emperor.

Robin had most of his pike and poleaxe men out of the woods by now, as well as the cavalry we had left, and as they began to march behind the jostling masses of Otto's troops and up towards the road, I lingered to rally our stragglers, as Robin had asked me to. I took a moment then to stand in the saddle and observe the French lines as they were coalescing to our west.

Their right wing contained the cream of their cavalry, their boldest knights. These men had formed the elite rearguard that I had seen marching on the main road – was it only an hour ago? The hot July sun, high above us, told me so. It seemed like several days past. A thin haze of dust, stirred by the feet of marching men and the hooves of thousands of horses, hung in the air all across the field. But further north, in the French lines by the bridge, in the centre of their position, I could still make out the King of France himself, a tiny figure in mail with a silver helm, surrounded by no more than a hundred knights and a company of spearmen, but above him flapped the long red-gold standard, the sacred Oriflamme unfurled only in times of greatest danger.

Their centre was thin, but hundreds of their footmen were now surging back over the bridge to swell their ranks. As I rode north with my handful of stragglers, we passed the last of the Germans, still pushing and shoving each other into their places, and crossed the main road, which was now churned to a mire by the passage of hooves. I saw that the French footmen from the bridge had begun to spill out northwards from the main road and sprawl out into the fields beyond opposite our position.

The Count of Boulogne, who was out ahead of the main body of our troops with the Earl of Salisbury, began ordering our formation. He had few cavalry left – perhaps fifty knights in all – but some two thousand foot, mostly pikemen, including Robin's poleaxe men and archers. I saw that Robin was with them, and Sir Thomas, too, and they seemed to be arguing with Boulogne and Salisbury.

I spurred my horse towards them and as I approached I saw that William Longsword was nodding his head at something Robin was saying and that Boulogne was frowning but did not seem too unhappy.

As I came nearer, I saw that something strange was

happening to the troops: the infantry seemed to be fragmenting into companies of about a hundred men. Sir Thomas came up, intercepting my line before I came within a hundred yards of the commanders. He was grinning like a monkey – a most unusual expression.

'Robin wanted to surprise you,' he said. 'He said it would cheer you no end. But in the event it took a little while to convince those dull-brained old stick-in-the-muds Boulogne and Salisbury. Anyway, what do you think?'

I had no idea what Thomas was talking about and so I held my tongue and looked on dumbfounded as, with only a small amount of confusion, the infantry formed itself into a gigantic square, with five separate companies on each side, north, south, east and west, coming together to make an impenetrable wall of men. The strangest thing of all was that the cavalry, which might ordinarily be on either flank of a solid block of infantry or behind it, was placed in the centre of the square, with the archers and the commanders protected on all four sides by thick ranks of pike or poleaxe-wielding footmen.

'I thought you would be proud of him,' Thomas said, a little smugly.

'Robin?' I said.

Thomas looked at me as if I were mad. 'No, young Robert. This new formation: it's all his idea. Well, I helped him smooth out a few wrinkles, but it's mostly his idea. This is the hollow phalanx. He must have mentioned it to you. What do you think?'

I had no idea what to say. Robert had never said anything to me about a hollow phalanx, except to ask me to pass on that strange message to Thomas from his prison cell. But I would be damned to Hell before I admitted that my son did not talk to me.

'It looks, ah, nice . . . very nice,' I said. 'Very efficient.'

I was still trying to digest the idea that our formation in this life-and-death struggle had been determined by a twelve-year-old boy, when Thomas broke into my thoughts.

'Yes, efficient is exactly the right word. We have very few cavalry and they could easily be scattered by a larger force of horsemen, but now they are protected, along with the archers, within the hollow phalanx. When our cavalry wish to attack, the phalanx opens, one of the companies of infantry swings out like a door, and the cavalry make their sortie, slaughter the foe, then return to the safety of the phalanx.'

Thomas and I had reached the huge square by then, and just as he said the words, the company of Sherwood men on the southern side of the hollow phalanx did indeed swing outwards as if on a hinge, shuffling in their ranks with minimal pushing and shoving for former outlaws, to allow us to enter.

Once inside, I did feel the swellings of pride for Robert and his extraordinary idea. It was the perfect defensive position, near-impregnable, to my eye. And I realised that God had smiled on me when I had appointed Thomas as Robert's tutor: the knight was always open to new ideas – had he not invented his own form of unarmed fighting? And when it came to military tactics, he had clearly nurtured Robert's talent for original ways of thought.

While I was silently congratulating my son and his tutor, I rode to the front of the phalanx, the west wall, and looked out over the field of battle.

The first thing that I noticed was that the French infantry facing us across three hundred yards of empty grassy space was growing in strength. Indeed, all along the French line the numbers had swelled and I felt the first twinges of a deep unease about the hours ahead.

It seemed to me that our commanders, in their desire to fight a traditional battle, with the two sides lined up parallel with each other, had missed a vital opportunity. When we had arrived at the battlefield, more than half the French had been on the far side of the bridge. If we had attacked then, immediately, we might have fallen on the French rearguard and destroyed it and chased the rest of the French army all the way to Lille. I could clearly imagine how King Richard would have managed it: an immediate assault on the bridge and to Hell with the paucity of our numbers. But the Lionheart was dead. Now, all but a handful of the French were across the River Marque, and we were facing the full might of Philip's forces.

I chided myself for my cowardly thoughts. We were at least a match for the French in numbers – and perhaps we even had a slight advantage. And looking behind me I could see that units of the German Emperor's army were still straggling on to the field. I thought I could make out the flags of the burghers of Ghent a mile or two away and several others beyond them. We would soon be reinforced, I told myself. It's just another engagement, like so many you have seen. Be a man. Do not show the world your fear.

I remembered quite suddenly that it was a Sunday. God's holy day. I crossed myself and murmured a prayer to St Michael, begging him to come to our aid. I was sure that God would not wish his mortal creations to spill their blood on his holy day, and yet it was we who had chosen to fight here, not the French.

Far down in the south of the field a shrill trumpet sounded. Then another. I shivered despite the heat of that blazing day.

For bloody battle was upon us.

And God alone would decide who triumphed.

Chapter Twenty-five

Ferrand, the irascible Count of Flanders, had been waiting patiently for more than an hour at the far south of our line for his allies to align themselves correctly. The Germans were still in disarray, groups of knights moving about the centre, arguing over who should have precedence; proud noblemen from Cologne and Aachen disputing with wealthy burghers from the Flemish lands.

Ferrand evidently believed he had waited long enough. Without consulting any of his allies, he unleashed his knights in a full-scale charge against the enemy lines on the southern flank.

I must admit it was a magnificent sight. More than five hundred mailed knights in gorgeous surcoats, the pennants on their lances fluttering gaily as they rode, and a similar number of mounted men-at-arms, exploded from our left flank and charged across the three hundred yards that separated them from the enemy. At the last possible moment they lowered their lances to the horizontal, gave a huge shout and crashed into the enemy lines. Standing in my stirrups, half a mile to the north, I watched in awe, the hair bristling on my nape, as these superb warriors crunched through the first line of the French, the spear-points plucking men from their saddles, their huge horses crashing into the enemy mounts and sweeping all away before them. Their charge utterly destroyed the first line and carried them right up to the lance-points of the second.

I thought for a moment that Ferrand's men must drive the French to their destruction into the boggy ground behind them – but the French, too, were fighting men of the first water, and miraculously, it seemed, they held against the rampaging men of Flanders, absorbed the power of their charge, and sprang back to engage them in a furious mêlée. I was too far to see much of the individual combats but I received an impression of a bulging, shifting line of men and horses, rippling like a trout-filled stream, banners flapping, flashes of silvery steel, and surcoats and horse's trappers, all the colours of the rainbow; yet I could clearly hear the clang of metal on metal and the screams and shouts of the battling sides.

Then, in an instant, it seemed that the French had broken – scores of horsemen, hundreds perhaps, were running from the fight heading north to the bridge and the wide banners of the King and his men. Others ran south for the woods, horsemen spurring into the trees pursued by howling foes; an unlucky few were pushed back into the marsh and floundered there, helpless until they were cut down. I saw Ferrand himself, with only his standard-bearer and a trumpeter, his sword lofted high, in the place where the French first line had been, shouting for his men to re-form, the trumpet echoing his command. His bold knights, who were by now spread all across the southern half of the battlefield, dutifully rallied to his call; they left off their pursuit of the beaten French and trotted to his banner in their hundreds. Ferrand turned, his bannerman lifted his standard, and the Count led his knights, swords bloodied, horses spent, and more than half their number dead or lying wounded on the field, back to their original positions on our left flank.

It's time, I thought, time for Otto to attack in the centre. The whole French right had been savaged by the Flemings – if only the Germans would attack the centre with one great crushing advance, we'd have victory in our grasp.

The Germans did nothing. Unbelievably they were still dressing their ranks. The Saxon guard had now been granted the honour of the right of the line, and were making their way forward in a block, to claim their new position. It was almost as if they had not noticed Ferrand's dashing assault to their front and left.

I rode over to Robin, who was chatting with his two

sons in the centre of our hollow square, as unconcerned as if he were on a family picnic. 'Should we not attack as well, my lord?' I said. 'Count Ferrand has done well in the south – the enemy are reeling, scattered – we should finish the job.'

'You know very well, Alan, that I get my orders from Salisbury,' he said, pointing to Longsword who was sitting his horse a dozen yards away eating an apple. 'He gets his from Otto. We've been told to hold this ground. That is why we are in Robert's magnificent defensive formation – you do like it, don't you?'

I said that I did.

'Well, you should do, the trouble I had convincing Salisbury to make it. Anyway, he's been told by Otto to hold this ground and that is what we are doing. When Otto calls for a general advance, then we will all go in together.'

I had been thinking about the prospects of capturing a rich man for ransom; I knew that my best chance of that would come once the enemy was smashed. And I also knew that the time to smash them was now.

'But that is plain stupid, Robin,' I said, hotly. 'We must attack now. Time is crucial. They are on the edge of panic, almost ready to flee. I can feel it. One big push and they'll quit the field, cross over the bridge and run like hares for Lille.'

'I agree with you, Alan, I'm not blind. I know what Ferrand achieved down there – but orders are orders. I cannot attack the King of France all on my own. Moreover, I cannot take my own men forward and break up this position. We must all fight together or we are sunk—' He suddenly broke off. 'Look, Alan, look!'

My lord was pointing south-west at the bridge of Bouvines. I could see horsemen, many hundreds moving southwards, the French King's household knights, barons from Blois and Champagne, and the refugees from the mauling given to them by Ferrand streaming south to retake the positions they had been driven from no more than a quarter of an hour before.

I muttered some foul oath and commented on the waste of an opportunity.

'No, no, Alan, look at the bridge,' said Robin.

I looked. Tendrils of smoke were rising from the wide wooden structure. Now thickening to great black plumes. And here and there the orange flash of flame, columns of shining sparks rising in the still summer air.

'They are burning the bridge,' I said incredulously. 'They are destroying their only means of escape.'

'King Philip is giving a message to his men,' said Robin grimly. 'Do or die. Death or glory. They do not mean to leave this field alive unless they are victorious.'

The French cavalry were now back in their positions on their right flank. They were fewer in number, and their lines were a little ragged but, apart from that, and the strewn bodies of horses and men that littered the field around them, one could hardly tell that Ferrand had

struck them a blow at all. All that courage and blood –
all expended for nothing. Then my heart skipped a beat.
They were advancing. My God, the French on their right
flank were actually advancing. Their cavalry were moving
forward in three long lines of horsemen. The French were
going to attack Ferrand!

I craned over to look at the cavalry of Flanders on our
left flank. It was in utter disarray – believing they had
vanquished their foes, perhaps even thinking that their
part in the battle was over, Count Ferrand's men were
scattered over a wide area, some several hundreds yards
back from the front line, most unhorsed, some tending
their wounds or looking to their mounts' well-being, some
were eating, drinking, some even lying on the ground at
their ease.

Not for long. At the sight of the advancing cavalry,
trumpets began to sound and suddenly it was all a-scramble.
The knights of Flanders responded with admirable quick-
ness. Men were hauling themselves up into the saddle. I
even saw one fellow, dressed only in chemise and braies,
leap astride his saddle-less horse and snatch a spear from
his squire and ride forward. They were spurring towards
Ferrand's banner in the centre where by now a loose knot
of loyal knights surrounded the count. But they were too
late – a horseman at full gallop can cover three hundred
yards in twenty heartbeats – and the Flemings were not
formed to receive the appalling storm that was about to
fall upon them.

'I wish I knew what Philip said to his commanders,' said Robin at my shoulder. 'He must have put the fear of Hell itself into them.'

I looked at the bridge: it was now a mass of flame and smoke. There could be no retreat for Philip's men. Not this day. But the enemy seemed to have no notion of trying to escape. On their left flank, the first line of the French cavalry was now at the full canter, their line of lances sweeping down into position like the opening of an enormous fan. The pounding of their hooves was audible even here, a half-mile away.

The French line struck the thick crowd of men about the Count at the gallop and washed over it like a giant wave breaking over rock. The banner of the Count of Flanders, a black lion rampant on gold, was now at the centre of a crowd of hundreds of struggling men, Flemish and French, slicing, stabbing, killing, dying. But the second line of the French, and then the third, charged straight past the mêlée surrounding the Count and sliced into the mainly unmounted men behind him and his bodyguard, who were now hurrying forward, desperate to join the fray before it was too late. The French rolled over the Flemings, killing scores, hundreds of their unprepared opponents. Everywhere on our left, the men of Count Ferrand were dying, spitted by French lances, hacked down by long blades. The scrum of battling men around the banner of the Count of Flanders was thinning too, its convulsions less frequent, more sluggish. They were surrounded by a sea of French horsemen.

'Surely Otto must do something now!' I said.

'He's moving,' said Robin.

Indeed, at last the Emperor was stirring himself. I saw a rider heading up towards us in our hollow square, crossing the road – finally some orders – and ranks of German knights were stepping out from their positions in perfect formation. The knights flowed smoothly forward. If they turn now, I thought, and fall upon the French cavalry from the flank, they can destroy them utterly. But no, the German knights were pulling further and further away from the bloody mêlée on their immediate left, the death struggles of Count Ferrand's brave men, dying one by one around the black-and-gold standard of their lord. Instead, the Germans were heading due west, into the sun, heading straight for the French lines before the inferno that had once been the bridge of Bouvines.

They were making straight for Philip.

I could see why. The King had sent most of his household cavalry to bolster his right flank and make the surprise attack on Ferrand; he had weakened his centre, almost stripped it of knights, and now Philip was defended only by ranks of infantry, ill-trained town militia by the look of them. The Emperor's cold logic was clear – he aimed to leave Ferrand and his men to their doom and strike a crushing blow, perhaps the decisive blow, at the centre of the enemy with all his might. It was a cruel tactic, but not a bad one. If Otto could capture or kill the King of France the day was won.

The breathless rider from the Emperor was conferring with Robin, the Earl of Salisbury and the Count of Boulogne in the centre of our square. It was orders at last. Robin was bellowing for the archers, and a trumpeter was calling for the cavalry to form up inside the square. As our fifty or so horsemen swung up on to their mounts, I pushed my horse into the first rank next to Sir Thomas Blood.

'Ever tried this sort of caper before, Thomas?' I said.

He shook his dark head. 'Robert and I discussed it many a time. The theory is sound, I would wager my soul on it; now we will see if it works in practice.'

The Earl of Salisbury addressed the troops.

'The Emperor has issued us with orders,' he began, and I could see by his expression that he did not relish this subordinate state of affairs. 'He commands that we support his attack on the King of France with an assault on the French left – those infantry over there.' He was pointing due west at a half a dozen companies, spearmen and crossbowmen, directly opposite our position and about three hundred yards away. I noted that the late afternoon sun, low in the sky, would be shining in our faces as we attacked.

'We are to sweep them from the field – the Emperor has commanded it – and then to continue on and join his assault on King Philip himself by the bridge. That is

354

what Otto wants. But you are my men. You obey my commands. We shall attack the enemy – and if they flee we shall naturally ride on and join the attack on the French centre. Perhaps that will be the way of it. It is in God's hands. But I particularly desire you to listen out for the recall – it sounds like this.' He made a signal to his trumpeter, who blew a trio of jaunty notes, and then repeated them. 'At that signal you will disengage and return to this position and reform within the square. Do not dally. Do not stray. If you hear the recall, you return here instantly.'

He gazed over the ranks of silent horsemen, waiting for some comment. None came.

'Right, let us do this deed of arms for the honour of old England . . . and, ah, Boulogne, of course and, ah, no doubt several other places, too. My lord of Locksley, you are to remain with the archers and return them here when their task is done.'

The two central companies of pikemen on the western side of the square swung open, one going left, the other right, and through this human doorway marched Robin, Little John and his sixty-odd archers, heading towards the enemy lines.

Salisbury, Thomas and I and the rest of our cavalry trotted out on their heels.

As I passed out of the square I could see what an effective defence it was: a fortress of men, bristling with spear-points, a hedge of sharp steel on all sides. There was no cavalry on earth that could breach it, and I marvelled once again at the cunning of Robert's design.

'God grant me a rich knight,' I prayed silently, as my horse stepped out on to the battlefield. 'You know how much I love my boy. Grant me this boon, O merciful God, and I will praise you for the rest of my life.'

We walked our horses across the field in two *conrois* of about twenty-five men, in line, one *conroi* twenty paces behind the other. The archers had also split into two groups, ranging out left and right from the advancing horse. A hundred and fifty paces from the enemy ranks, about halfway between their lines and ours, we stopped. The archers strung their bows and began selecting their arrows. I saw Robin testing his bowstring and sticking a dozen bodkin points into the turf at his feet, so they could be pulled from the earth and loosed with maximum speed. But the sun was directly in our eyes; I could see little ahead but a fiery yellow blur: left and right, I could make out archers squinting and holding up hands before their faces to block the glare. Others were pulling their hoods far forward to keep the blinding light at bay.

I looked left. The German knights were now deeply into the enemy ranks around the King, hacking their way through the poor levies of the militia with their two-handed swords. Around the Oriflamme was a wall of steel and horseflesh where Philip's remaining knights, no more than a score or so, held back, waiting for just the right moment to charge: too soon and Otto's counter-attack might sweep back all the way to the King; too late and the infantry, who were soaking up the punishment from the German knights, would be no more than reeking meat.

Otto himself had not left his position in our lines. He and his Saxon guard looked on impassively three hundred yards away as his noble knights demonstrated their valour on the ranks of peasant spearmen from Orleans and Paris.

Beyond the German lines I saw, with a jolt of horror, that our left flank was no more. There was no sign of Ferrand of Flanders; and his men lay in bleeding heaps. Dozens of French knights, sagging in the saddle, spattered with gore and filth, picked their way among the dead and wounded on exhausted horses, looking for men worth ransoming. 'O God,' I prayed again, 'grant me my heart's desire.'

I was jerked back to my own situation by Robin's battle voice calling: 'Archers . . . nock.' The thirty men in the left-hand company smoothly fixed a shaft to the string. On the right a similar number of bowmen, under the captaincy of Little John, did exactly the same.

Robin shouted: 'Draw . . . and loose,' and with a sharp creak and a swish, a black cloud of ash shafts hurtled into the air, hovered for an instant, and fell like black thunderbolts from the sky.

For the first time in my life I saw the archers of Sherwood fail. Blinded by the sun, they could not judge the distance well, and a goodly number of the arrows overshot the company of spearmen in front of them and fell harmlessly

357

into the empty pasture behind them. Other shafts went wide and a few even fell short.

There were shout of anger on all sides. I heard Little John bellowing, 'Aim straight, you silly buggers – are you blind or just stupid!' and his words were met by a chorus of English complaint.

The enemy directly to our front, a company of spearmen in stiff leather jerkins and steel caps about two hundred men strong, jeered us and made obscene gestures. One man turned his back, lifted his tunic and showed us his naked arse.

On their right was another company of spearmen, but on their left was a company in mail covered by green-and-red surcoats, and bearing huge two-man shields. Robin's men were not the only bowmen on this field.

'Nock,' shouted my lord. Then, 'Draw and loose.' But the second volley was little better than the first. A few men in the enemy ranks had dropped, skewered by our shafts, but once again the bulk of the arrows had missed their targets. Looking out under my shadowing hand, I could see that some of the enemy were laughing.

'Enough, by God,' shouted the Earl of Salisbury. 'Trumpeter, sound the charge.'

The trumpet sounded, I spurred my horse blindly forward.

Longsword himself led the charge directly at the unbroken spearmen. And Robin, bringing his men forward at a run, managed to loose one last flat volley into their ranks before our horsemen crashed home. It was just enough. Two front-rank spearmen dropped in front of Salisbury's horse, victims of Robin's last desperate barrage. Longsword jumped his mount into the gap, his lance punching into the chest of the second-rank man behind. And we followed him into the breach. Twenty-five horsemen pouring into a gap two yards wide.

We smashed that spear company wide apart.

I slammed my lance into a standing man's shield, knocking him down, hauled out Fidelity and began to lay about me. I chopped down and split the skull of a man on my left, turned and hacked at the shoulder of a fellow on my right – but in a few moments there was nothing but empty space around my horse. The nearest man to me was Miles, who galloped past hunting down a running Frenchman with his lance.

The spear company had melted like snow in sunshine under the cavalry charge and the surviving men-at-arms had almost all sprinted for the shelter of the nearest formation of spearmen, some thirty paces to their right, and been allowed to squeeze through the ranks and into safety.

They defied us there, from behind their bristling ranks of spearpoints, knowing that our blown horses would not charge home. We knew it too. I wondered if Salisbury would bring up the archers. And doubted it. I sheathed Fidelity. We had pushed that company of two hundred spearmen temporarily off the battlefield and left a couple of dozen bodies on the turf – but we had not altered the balance of the battle in any significant way. And I had not had the merest sniff of a knight to capture.

To the south, I could see that the battle around King Philip had reached its frenzy. The German knights were now yards from the royal household guards, exchanging sword blows with some of the richest men in France. The Oriflamme still fluttered above the King's head, although I could not see Philip himself. The crowd of fighting men convulsed and writhed; mailed men, sheeted in blood, fell or staggered away to the accompaniment of screams and shouts, the flash of steel, and the spray of gore; men dropped like ripe fruit from a shaken tree, yet fresh knights still plunged forward eagerly to join the fray. Suddenly I heard a great shout go up from the Germans, a roar of victory, and saw that the Oriflamme had fallen.

My God – was King Philip dead?

This is where we must fight, I thought, we should join the Germans with all our strength and smash through the centre to the bridge. Killing penniless spearmen over here was pointless, not when the King of France himself and his greatest nobles were faltering a few hundred yards away. I looked for Salisbury or Boulogne – determined to urge them to join the Germans in the centre. But to my surprise and horror, I heard the trumpeter by the Earl's horse sound the retreat. Three jaunty notes, repeated.

Not now, I thought, not now. God send me a knight. Any knight.

Then I saw why. The crossbow company had formed

up facing left, facing the empty space where the spear company had been and where we now casually walked our horses amid the bloody bodies. They had planted their huge shields and the bolts were beginning to fly. Evil black lines fizzed through the air about me. I saw a man, one of Robin's cavalry who had helped me drive away my enemies at Westbury, take a quarrel under the ribs on his left-hand side. The foot-long black shaft punched through his mail and he screamed and slid from the saddle. One of Boulogne's men was hit in the face, the bolt tearing off half of his right cheek and leaving him with a hanging flap and his teeth showing white against the welling red.

The trumpets were still sounding the recall. And still I lingered, hoping against hope for a noble foe to come against me. As I looked behind me I saw that Robin's archers were already running from the field back to the safety of our square. It was no use. I turned my horse east. Most of the other horsemen were already heading in that direction. Hugh cantered past me. He shouted: 'Sir Alan, it is the retreat. The Earl commands us to go back! We must retreat.'

I nodded vaguely at him, yet still I hesitated. I looked over my shoulder at the centre of the French line and saw that the Oriflamme once more flew bravely above the knot of French knights – and was that a flash of a golden royal coronet that I could make out in the middle of the throng? Perhaps Philip was not dead, nor even faltering. Indeed, his knights seemed to have found a new blast of courage. They were advancing, expanding like a flower at dawn from the tight bundle around the King, chopping into the foe, thrusting him back. The militia infantry too seemed to have found a renewed energy – they battered the enemy with their spears from behind, killing the horses first, then dealing with their riders as they fell. The German knights – those who yet lived – seemed to have been stopped in their tracks. Indeed, many were now retreating: I could see several tall men in fine mail and elaborate helms, slathered in blood and limping back east across the field using their two-handed longswords as staffs to help them hobble.

Otto's cruel gamble had failed. Our left wing, to the south, Count Ferrand's men, had been abandoned to their fate – and now that body of men no longer existed as a fighting force. In the centre, Otto's attack had failed to break through to the King. On the right, we too were now all running back to the safety of our defensive square.

It was time to go. I was the last of our men on the field. I touched my spurs to my horse, and at that same instant, felt a jolt beside my knee like a blow from a quarterstaff. I looked down and saw the leather flights of a quarrel sticking two inches out from my horse's loins. The animal took two steps forward and stopped – an awful broken whinnying sound coming from its throat. I looked around. My comrades were already halfway back to the square, out of range of the wicked bolts. Another missile slammed into the inside of my shield. And another, both punching through the wood and leather and narrowly missing my left arm. I realised that I was the favoured target for a company of two hundred crossbowmen only seventy yards away. A second quarrel slapped into my horse's barrel, crunching through ribs and into the chest cavity – the beast kicked out and staggered, bellowing with pain; a black bolt slammed into her eye, burying itself into her brain, and she thumped to the ground, now mercifully beyond pain. I slipped from the saddle as the poor horse was collapsing, and hunkered down behind the bulk of her off-side, slipping off my shield as yet another black bolt cracked against the dome of my helmet. The entire company of crossbowmen seemed to be shooting at me, and only at me.

How I cursed my lack of haste. I had lingered on the field too long after the recall was sounded. And now, with only a dead horse between me and thousands of foes, I was paying the price. I could not run – I'd be dead before I took three strides. But if I stayed here the spearmen to my right would come out from behind their steel hedges and slaughter me. I was trapped. I was a dead man.

Worse, I had failed my son.

Chapter Twenty-six

There have not been many times in my life when I have had impotently to suffer the wrath of bowmen, but as I lay there behind my dead horse, listening to the meaty thuds as quarrel after quarrel juddered into the huge corpse, I felt a rising sense of helpless fury. This could not be my death: marooned in the middle of an empty battlefield, stuck like a pin cushion beside a dead horse. I could not die here and leave Robert to die alone, between Boot's powerful twisting hands, uncomprehending of his father's fate. I risked a glance over the saddle, a crossbow bolt cracked past my right ear, an inch away, but I had seen what I dreaded: a dozen spearmen emerging from the ranks of their company and jogging towards me, grinning like apes.

I was not going to die without a fight, that was certain. I waited until the running spearmen came between me and the bulk of the crossbow company – it was easy to tell when this took place for the cracks and whines and thuds of the bolts suddenly stopped – and leapt to my feet and drew Fidelity. The spearmen were twenty paces away. It was one man against a dozen; a lone swordsman against a pack of men with spears: there was only one possible conclusion to this fight. This was it. I'd had a good life. I prayed to St Michael to give me strength to die well – and to Our Lord to have mercy on my son and shield Robert from the sheriff's greed.

Time to fight.

I leapt over the dead horse and took my sword to the spearmen. I knocked the leading man's thrusting spear-shaft out of the way with my left forearm, and chopped Fidelity into the corner of his neck where the head meets the shoulder an instant later. He went down like a dropped sack of wet sand. The next man fell to a wide, lateral cut from my sword that crunched into his back. I was in the midst of them by now, jabbing, cutting and dodging the spear-thrusts as best I could. And they were giving me space, spread out in a loose ring about me, dancing in and making short hard jabs at my body, but staying well away from Fidelity.

'He's one old man, for Christ's sake, kill him now,' growled a big fellow with a face burnt red by the sun. I made him pay for those words. He hurled his spear at me, I twisted sideways just in time and the shaft grazed my chest – and I was on him as he scrabbled for the short sword at his waist. I had a foot of Fidelity's shining length in his guts before his own blade had cleared the scabbard. I ripped my sword loose, shouldering him to the ground as I passed, and began running back towards our lines as fast as my legs would carry me. As the hollow phalanx was nearly two hundred yards away, I knew I would never make it. But I had to try. A spear flew over my shoulder. A crossbow bolt cracked off my helm. I could hear the pants and shouts of the men on my heels. Then, a beautiful sight. A lone knight in full armour, helmet down, lance couched, dark green cloak flying out behind him, was thundering towards me out from our lines. It was Robin, for sure. I could tell by the way he rode, by the lines of his body as he crouched over his horse's neck.

The horseman hurtled past me and crashed straight into the group of running spearmen behind. I heard a scream as his lance went home, and another yell and the sharp sound of snapping bone. Then the pounding of hooves, and a young voice behind me: 'Alan, take my arm and get up behind me. Come now. Quickly.'

A spear thumped into my back, high over the shoulder blade, I stumbled forward, but I knew the point had not penetrated deeply and I blessed the silver I had spent on decent mail. I slammed Fidelity into the scabbard, grasped Robin's reaching hand and swung up behind his saddle. Glancing behind me I could see that only four spearmen were still on their feet; they were launching their spears wildly at us in their futile rage. We were moving fast by them, the horse carrying our combined weight with ease, and in a trice we were out of range. Safe.

It was not until we were back inside the square of pikes and poleaxes that I realised the true identity of my rescuer. As I slid off the back of the horse, I was astonished to see Robin striding over to me from the other side of the square, where he had been conferring with the Earl of Salisbury. I looked up at the young face on the horse above me and saw that it was Miles, ruddy, sweaty and grinning from the excitement. I stammered out my thanks but he dismissed it with a wave.

'Rather enjoyed that, to be honest, Sir Alan,' he chuckled. 'We must do it again sometime!'

Robin slapped me on the back, relieved to see me safe. I winced as his hand caught the place that the spear had struck.

'It's looking bad, Alan, I must admit it. But I'm very glad to have you back. If you are fit – are you fit?' I nodded.

He looked at his bloody hand.

'Then I want you to take command of this section of the phalanx wall. You in command, Little John as your second, all right? Hugh has the next section along.'

I nodded again. And saw that the section he was indicating was the southern one, and it was packed with familiar faces. Little John found me a poleaxe, and I tried a few experimental sweeps and lunges, to get a feel for the weapon.

As I was familiarising myself with the heft of the poleaxe, Hugh came up to me from the section immediately to the east of mine.

'You understand our role in the phalanx, Sir Alan, don't you? We stand firm and keep the cavalry out with these things,' he said, pointing at the poleaxe in my hands. 'We don't budge at all.'

I confess I did not like his tone. This was a boy who I had known since he was in napkins telling me how to conduct myself in war. 'I think I have managed to grasp the tactics, thank you,' I said with a certain edge in my voice.

'Have you?' asked Hugh. 'Because there is no room for individual heroics in the phalanx wall. We all fight together, you know.'

'How dare you lecture me on combat, you puppy!'

'I dare, Sir Alan, because I have just seen you ignore a clear order for recall and very nearly get yourself killed. You risked your own life, which I suppose is your prerogative, but you also caused my brother Miles to risk his, in order to save yours. And that I will not accept.'

'I did not force him to come out to save me,' I said, sulkily.

'He worships you, Sir Alan, you are his model. He would do anything, no matter how stupidly reckless, to earn your admiration. And I will not have it, sir. I must ask you to behave more responsibly in future.'

And he turned his back and stalked off to his section of the wall.

Well, he was right. I had behaved irresponsibly, and I knew it. But that did not make being spoken to like a naughty schoolboy any easier to swallow.

To take my mind off my scolding, I pushed my body through the packed ranks of our men and took stock of the battle from the outside of the hollow phalanx.

The first thing I saw was that the French were on the attack. It looked very much like a general advance, which was always the last throw in any desperate, hard-fought battle. All along the line the French were moving forward: barons, knights and mounted men-at-arms, spearmen, pikemen, crossbowmen, too, they were all converging on one point. Even the Oriflamme, and the household knights of Philip, even the King himself, were on the move – the whole French army, still several thousand strong, was coming forward, marching away from the burning bridge and heading towards our lines. With a shameful sense of relief – and a misplaced one, too – I saw where the hammer blow of the French attack would fall.

Philip was making for Otto.

Trumpets called. Noblemen from Burgundy and Orleans, Berry and Ponthieu, Champagne, Maine and Touraine, bellowed their war cries, thrust back their spurs. And many hundreds of cavalrymen charged at the centre of our lines where the Holy Roman Emperor's standard, the eagle mounted on a dragon, towered above the impassive ranks of the Saxon guard.

The French cavalry slapped into the first line of the Saxons. And were held. Those superb German warriors refused to give an inch of ground; they fought with magnificent courage, their big axes swinging like Death's own scythe, blood flying, men falling screaming to the ground. But still the French piled into their ranks.

It was the enemy crossbowmen who tipped the balance. Hundreds of them came forward in their pairs, two slight men with one huge shield between them, and from both flanks they poured death into the ranks of the Saxon warriors. Quarrels whipped and cracked into their files, slaying mighty men with one-foot iron rods and leaving gaps into which the French thrust their armoured horses, their lances jabbing. The Saxons died by the score. More brave men stepped forward from the ranks behind to fill their places. To no avail. The pressure from the French was unrelenting.

Before my eyes, the Saxon line bent, buckled – and broke, quite suddenly. A great shout went up from the French. And at the same moment, the Emperor's eagle-dragon standard tumbled. I saw that the Germans at the rear of the battle were edging back, and now, O sweet God, they were running. Otto was running. Even some members of the Saxon guard were throwing their shields and axes away and streaming east with the other men, a panicked herd of humanity all sprinting for their lives.

In the space of a hundred heartbeats the centre of our lines completely disintegrated. A few of the better men stood their ground, knots of three or four back to back, gore-slathered axes in hand, defying the enemy to the last.

The crossbowmen made short work of them, punching quarrel after quarrel into their flesh until even these brave men were felled.

The sun was little more than a hand's breadth above the western horizon, and I was able to survey the whole battlefield to the south of our hollow phalanx. Bodies littered the turf across the whole field, the stench of blood and ordure was so strong as to be almost visible. Great flocks of black crows wheeled in the air above, waiting for their chance to feed. Count Ferrand of Flanders and his men were gone; Otto and his surviving Germans were streaming away to the east. Only we – the couple of thousand or so men who owed their loyalty to the Earl of Salisbury or the Count of Boulogne – remained of the army that had boldly challenged the French King that day.

We were alone.

It is most painful to tell of the events of the next few hours, the last hours of that terrible dying day. The French surrounded us on all sides. Their horsemen were thick as

371

flies around a dung pile. The cavalry charged our ranks, again and again, one or two brave men making a dash for us. Or occasionally a dozen men under a bold captain, who hoped to make a name for himself by smashing our formation. But, while our men died in ones and twos, skewered on the knights' long lances, or their skulls crushed by a well-wielded mace, the French could make no hard impression on our hedges of steel. They were tired, after all, dog-tired; their horses were exhausted, too. Some of the French knights had been fighting all day – against Ferrand, then against Otto and now they came against us. Some of us, too, had been in the fray since before noon. But they could not get into our square. Neither could we escape.

I remember only fragments of that last terrible fight. One last desperate sortie by the Count of Boulogne and his handful of remaining cavalry: we opened our wall in the south, the section I had command of, and the Count and thirty men charged out and smashed a *conroi* of French cavalry that was dressing its ranks for a charge against us. The French were scattered – but other knights swarmed towards the fight from all corners of the field and Boulogne's men found themselves in a fierce mêlée, surrounded. French pikemen joined the fight, too, running in and spiking their long blades into our knights' backs as they fought hand to hand with the other mounted men. The Count and a scant eight horsemen managed to fight their way clear and make it back to the square

– but it was clear we would never have the strength to make a sortie again that day.

I fought beside Little John on foot for most of that last battle, in the press with one-eyed Claes beyond John on my left, Thomas on my right, and a dozen good men from Kirkton and Westbury all around me. The French came on, again, and again. We kept them out, fighting like men possessed, using our poleaxes to cut and stab at the horsemen above us, and hooking unwary knights to haul them from their mounts' backs and down to destruction. It was a weapon I came to love, in truth: efficient, deadly, evening the odds between a man on foot and the man a-horse. And with every strike of the pole, every grunt of exertion, I breathed Robert's name.

We fought magnificently, truly we did, but each enemy charge weakened us, and at every assault, bloodily repulsed, a few more of our men fell to their long lances. It was quite clear now how this nightmare would end. There could be no surrender, the French knights had made that plain, calling us mercenary dogs, vermin, taunting us with the prolonged execution that would face us when we were captured; and there was clearly no escape to be had.

In a lull between attacks, when I was dazed with exhaustion, my arms like lead after wielding the unfamiliar poleaxe for so long, the wound in my back burning like the fires of Hell, Little John came over to me with a canteen of water and wine.

As I slurped down a good pint of that sweet mixture

in one draught, Little John said: 'You know something strange, Alan?'

I was too tired to speak; I could only stare at him mutely over the rim of the canteen.

'I had a dream last night that Gavin was with us. It was so real, I felt I might have reached out and touched him.'

I grunted something and took another huge swig.

'He begged me to be with him,' said Little John.

That brought me up short. 'He spoke to you?'

'Yes, he asked me to join him in the light of God's grace. He said it as plainly and simply as I am saying it to you now.'

'It was a dream, John, a strange fancy of the mind on the eve of battle. I don't think it really means—'

I stopped suddenly. The unfinished thought instantly wiped from my head. For at long last I could see our doom approaching. Five companies of marching crossbowmen. The French had decided to take us seriously.

So began the duel of the bowmen. The crossbowmen formed up in five blocks all around our hollow square – although by now it was not the neat, box-shaped object it had once been. Now it was more a shrunken circle of desperate bleeding men, spear-points facing outwards like a gigantic hedgehog. The largest groups of crossbowmen were formed up in the south, the south-west and the west in blocks of about a hundred and fifty men each. Two

374

smaller companies of enemy bowmen took up positions to the north and the east.

They planted their huge shields. They spanned their bows. And methodically, calmly, with an absence of fury or any kind of passion, they began to kill our men.

Our Sherwood bowmen answered them, of course, but they were few in number by then, many having fallen in the phalanx walls, and they were sadly short of shafts. They had been shooting all day and some men had fewer than four or five arrows left in their arrow bags. But they killed crossbowmen as well as they could, shooting the enemy down when they emerged from behind their shields to loose at us. But it was cruelly one-sided. I saw Philip himself, briefly, back at his old command position by the bridge, and he seemed to be directing a large number of knights to their duties.

It was clear what was in the King's mind. For the knights – perhaps all the remaining able-bodied chevaliers of the French army, some three hundred horsemen – were forming up to the west, with the blood-red sun setting at their backs, in one huge company behind the crossbowmen stationed there. When the crossbowmen had weakened us sufficiently, when there were but a few hundred of our battered men still standing, the French knights would make one last glorious charge, crash through our wavering spear-wall and complete the day's slaughter.

The crossbowmen decimated our ranks, one or two men fell every heartbeat to the whirring black bolts. Our ragged hedgehog began to melt away like a snowball by a Christmas hearth. Men were dropping on all sides of our redoubt as the evil bolts sliced into our ranks from all corners of the compass. The whole circle of spearmen seemed to twist and shrink under the deadly onslaught, as bolt after bolt slammed into our ranks, and the screams of the wounded split the air again and again. There was nothing we could do about it except to stand – and die. Right beside me, I heard a shout of pain and a man stumbled into me and collapsed. I caught him and lowered him to the grass but he was stone dead before he touched the ground. It was Claes, a veteran of many of Robin's bloody battles, a good man now gone, with a black quarrel sticking from his one remaining eye. As I crouched over his body, the tears welling in my own eyes at yet another comrade ripped from this earth, I felt a hand on my shoulder and looked up into Robin's face.

'I'm not going to stay here and watch my sons die,' he said quietly into my ear. 'I'm not going to watch you or Little John or any more of my good men throw away their lives in this cause. It's time for us to go home.'

Chapter Twenty-seven

We ran. It was as simple as that. Robin spoke quietly with a dozen of his senior men. He had all the archers loose one last volley at the crossbowmen directly in our path. And we ran. The Earl of Salisbury must have caught wind that something was happening, for just before we made our move he called across the shrinking circle in the centre of our redoubt, asking Robin what was amiss. Robin did not deign to answer him. Instead, he gave the word of command and with a howl we charged out of our positions and sprinted directly at the crossbow company to the south.

Little John led the charge, with myself and Sir Thomas just behind him, and Robin and his two sons brought up the rear. Between us were some ninety of Robin's men-at-arms, bowmen and dismounted cavalry and even a few of the Earl of Salisbury's men who had either also decided it was time to depart or who had just been swept up in the movement of our running men.

Within ten heartbeats we were in among the crossbowmen – dodging between the huge planted shields and killing like fiends. Taking a bloody revenge for the carnage we had suffered at their hands. My wound felt like a red-hot poker being thrust into my back, but I gritted my teeth, determined to ignore the pain. I swung Fidelity at a man who was in the act of spanning his crossbow, bent over the weapon with one foot in the stirrup on the end of the bow on the ground, hauling back with both hands on the string. My blade caught him in the centre of his spine, chopping through leather, flesh and bone and dropping him in an unstrung mess on the ground. I killed another man, a lunge to the groin, even as he pointed his loaded weapon at my chest. He fell back as he pulled the lever and the string twanged and loosed the bolt high into the sky.

But Robin was shouting: 'On, on, make for the woods. Don't tarry, don't stop for anything. We must get to the trees.' For we were heading for the Cysoing woods due south of the battlefield, where the battle for Bouvines had begun several lifetimes ago. Night was falling, it was already a pinky-grey twilight, and in the woods, in darkness, we would be safe, or so Robin had promised. But before we could find safety in the trees we had a thousand yards to run across a battlefield swarming with victorious French men-at-arms.

I ran, snatching glances behind me, looking for enemy horsemen – for that is what I feared most, the galloping horseman and his long lance that would punch through my backbone as I ran. But it seemed that we had taken the French by surprise. The enemy horsemen were still forming up in the west, opposite the circle of desperate men that we had abandoned. Already there were several knights shouting and pointing in our direction, and it would not be long before we were pursued and brought to battle. I saw too that the Earl of Salisbury was rapidly filling the gap we had made in his circle of steel by our precipitate departure. He and the Count of Boulogne were grabbing men and shoving them into the space where Robin's men had stood. I blessed Robin then: I would rather die on my feet running, dodging, perhaps even able to strike a blow myself, than standing in a thin line of men patiently waiting to be felled by an anonymous crossbow bolt.

An instant later, I regretted my thoughts, for I could feel the thunder of horses' hooves through the turf below my flying feet, and looking back I saw that a *conroi* of cavalry fifty men strong was galloping down the field towards our fleeing men.

The wood was still five hundred yards away and our men were strung out in a line, knots of two or three men, perhaps a hundred yards long. I saw a man to my left running at me – a sword and shield in his hand, a dismounted knight, perhaps, or a squire. He shouted an invitation for me to stand and fight and for a moment I hesitated, and I swear to you, on my honour, that I looked to see signs of wealth about his person. He was a shabby specimen, his mail old and rusty, and I ignored his challenge and put my head down and ran, ran with all my might south, south for the woods and safety.

Two hundred yards to go. As I leapt over a dead horse in my path, a crossbowman popped up from nowhere and loosed a bolt at me from twenty paces away and – miraculously – missed. I ran on straight past him, legs pumping, sucking down the sharp air, feeling the red-hot pain in my back stab me with every stride.

A hundred yards now. The first of our men were now at the treeline. I saw Little John and Thomas charge a group of the enemy gathered there. John decapitated a French man-at-arms with his poleaxe, Thomas neatly disembowelled a second, and the rest of the enemy section ran like rabbits before their fury, heading west towards the marshes.

Little John stood next to an ancient oak shading his eyes with his hand and looking north towards our men as they straggled to him. Thomas was helping a wounded archer limp into the shelter of the trees.

I was thirty yards away from the woods, clear of the enemy now and with nothing but half a dozen corpses between me and safety. I turned and looked back up the field. Many of our men had not been sufficiently fleet of foot, or had lingered to take their revenge on the cross-bowmen. For those unfortunates, the cavalry were upon them. I saw a Sherwood archer ridden down with almost contemptuous ease by a French knight. He did not bother to use his lance, merely crashed his horse into the running man and trampled him under its churning hooves. Another man, a Kirkton cavalryman, now without a horse, dodged left and right, ducking under the following horse's neck, almost escaping before tripping on a tussock of grass, stumbling, and being dropped by a swung sword to his neck from a clearly irritated French knight.

And there was Robin fifty yards behind me, with Miles and Hugh, and another man-at-arms, running in a pack, all four of them carrying swords and shields – with three French cavalrymen hard on their tails. The enemy were no more than twenty yards behind them, long blades bright in their hands, their expressions wolfish.

Robin glanced over his shoulder and shouted for his sons to halt. They obeyed immediately. And all stood together back to back, shields high, swords extended, as the cavalry rushed at them, cutting at their up-held shields as they surged past. I saw one enemy blade slip through their defences and come back bloody. Then they were past the three men on foot. The man-at-arms who had been running with them either did not hear Robin's cry or decided to ignore it. When Robin, Miles and Hugh formed their back-to-back triangle defence, he ran on heedless – and was overtaken in a trice by a French knight who dispatched him cleanly with a lance-lunge through the small of his back that lifted him off his feet before dumping him dead on the turf.

The cavalry was not done with Robin and his boys. Not nearly. They circled back and made another pass at my lord and his boys, a clashing of steel on wood, and again I saw them bloody their long blades, and beyond these three knights, to the north, I could see a dozen more riders approaching, lances in their hands.

Robin was a dead man and so were his sons.

And I had a choice to make.

I could carry on running, following Robin's orders to run for the trees without stopping for anything. Or I could go back to help my lord in his hour of peril.

It is at these times that a man learns if he is a coward or not. Thirty yards way from me was Little John, the woods and safety in the growing darkness. Behind me was Robin, Miles, Hugh – my friends, my saviours, and almost certain death.

I hesitated. God forgive me – I could not make up my mind. I could not push myself into death; I could not run for cover either. My legs would not move. I seemed to be frozen in my abject cowardly state. I believe that I might still be standing there to this day if what happened next had not happened.

I heard a great shout from the treeline. Turned and saw Little John bounding towards me, his poleaxe in his hand, the cry of 'A Locksley!' on his lips. The big man hurtled past me like a force of nature, like a great rushing wind, and he charged straight into the nearest horseman of the trio raining blows on Robin and his sons.

The passing of Little John unlocked my courage. I took a double-handed grip of Fidelity and charged after the big man – to the rescue of my lord.

Thank God, for I could not have lived with myself else.

Little John lunged with his poleaxe, driving the spear-tip deep into the back of the horseman, splitting mail links and grinding the sharp steel into the flesh beyond. The horseman gave a howl and spurred away, but he was a dead man.

A second horseman rode directly at John, slashing at his head, but Robin and his sons had broken out of their back-to-back position, exploding outwards in a blur of steel and movement, and Hugh neatly lopped off the horse's forefoot with a single blow, causing knight and mount to tumble. Robin finished him as he sprawled on the ground. The third knight nearly had me, his sword blow from behind whistled over my helmet, but I twisted and caught him with an upward lunge that punched through the mail around his inner thigh and slid my blade up into the meat of his leg, scraping the long bone inside. He screamed horribly and rolled away from me out of the saddle.

Robin was shouting: 'Run, all of you, run! Alan, help Miles! Take his arm!' And I caught Robin's youngest as he staggered towards me, still grinning but with his side streaked with red and his face as pale as death.

There were more horsemen only twenty yards away, half a dozen knights in a pack, and beyond them a score of running crossbowmen. Little John stood facing his enemies, his long poleaxe held horizontally across his chest in both meaty hands, as if he planned to deny them further passage south with its wooden shaft.

Robin shouted: 'John, leave them, we must run!'

The treeline was fifty yards away, and a handful of Sherwood archers were nocking, drawing and loosing their last remaining arrows at the oncoming cavalrymen. I was hauling, half-carrying Miles towards the wood as fast as my churning legs would carry us. I turned my head, and saw Robin just behind me with his arm around the bloodied form of Hugh. Beyond them a feathered shaft smacked into the chest of the leading knight, spinning him out of the saddle and away.

Robin shouted: 'John, come now!'

For the big man was thirty yards behind – directly between us and the five advancing cavalrymen, facing the enemy, his feet planted. John looked over his shoulder at Robin. He favoured me, Robin, all of us with a long, happy smile.

He shouted: 'You go along without me. I'm tired of running. Besides, I haven't finished with these French fellows yet.'

And the big man charged straight at the oncoming

cavalry, his poleaxe swinging, a titanic roar of battle on his lips.

I did not see John die. It brings tears to my eyes even to remember those last few moments of his life. But he saved us all from the pursuing enemy and ensured that Robin and myself, Hugh and Miles, and all the rest of our men, made it safely to the treeline and into the darkness of the woods, and so I think that by his lights it was a good death. I pray that he is reunited with Gavin in Heaven or wherever their souls travelled to after their time on this earth. I wept that night, too, as we bound up our wounds and made a fireless, cheerless camp in the deepest part of the wood, sleeping in utter exhaustion wrapped in our cloaks.

A little before dawn, Robin and I ventured out, just the two of us. The victorious King had made his camp in the far northern part of the battlefield, away from the blood and the bodies, in a great enclosure surrounded by his baggage carts. I could clearly hear the sounds of drunken French revelry from a mile away, shouts, snatches of song, laughter, and see the merry twinkling of campfires.

In the cold grey light I could see little on the battlefield but the mounded forms of dead men and horses. There was no sign of the once-impregnable circle of spears, no sign of any remnant of the Earl of Salisbury's men – I found out later that Boulogne and Salisbury had been taken captive, as had Count Ferrand of Flanders earlier in the day, but that all the surviving common men-at-arms had been executed on Philip's orders.

We found Little John's body without too much difficulty a dozen yards from the place he had begun his mad charge, half-buried by a dead horse with a scatter of corpses beside him. His huge body had been hacked, sliced and battered in the most appalling way; there were three crossbow bolts in his chest and belly and his big skull had been staved in, but it was clear that he had fought as well as he had ever done, and taken a good many of the enemy with him when he went onward.

The fact that Robin and I were still breathing was the greatest testament to his self-sacrifice. And I can say no more of my old friend, except to say that he was a fine man, a superb warrior and, until the last, a true hero. *Requiescat in pace.*

Robin and I were both weeping unashamedly as we carried his body with us back into the woods. We washed it ourselves and wrapped it in green cloaks, sewn tight around his huge form as a shroud. And then we moved out, carrying all our weapons and gear and with four strong men carrying John's body – heading south through the trees, aiming to strike south and west for the coast and the hope of a ship for home. Our hearts were bruised raw, our heads fogged with grief, exhaustion and the awful knowledge of failure.

We had lost a great battle; we had lost a great friend. Such is war.

Chapter Twenty-eight

We walked south for many hours in the morning after that battle, to put some distance between us and the enemy knights, then turned north-west. All of us were hurting in some way or another and we were a miserable, raggedy crew on the march, hiding from any horsemen we saw and sleeping in the woods, under hedges or in lonely barns. My wounded back bled and bled and refused to close up, even after Thomas put a red-hot knife blade to the wound on the second night of our journey. Miles had a bad wound to his shoulder, a sword cut that had sliced deep into the muscle; and Hugh had been stabbed in the meat of his waist, and like mine, the wound did not stop bleeding for several days. Most of the surviving men had cuts or wounds, or punctures from quarrels, but we could not afford to move too slowly, nor rest long. God knew when Philip's cavalry might find us, and we were in no condition to fight them off. We had to march on – or die.

I do not think we would have got more than a dozen miles had it not been for Robin. He seemed to shrug off the fatigue of a hard-fought battle as if it were no more than a dirty cloak and on the road he was filled with a strange and manic energy. He was once more the young outlaw I had known in bygone days, carefree but cunning and filled with an almost supernatural vitality. Perhaps it was the loss of Little John that fired him to strive so hard to keep us moving, I do not know. Perhaps it was to ensure safety for his boys. But he was truly tireless, cajoling or bullying stragglers to keep up with the column – for if they were left behind they were dead men – ranging ahead to scout out the land and guide us to safer paths away from the dwellings of the local people. His eyes glowed like molten metal day and night, and though his face was more gaunt than ever, I never once saw him flag. He urged us onward, promising a safe camp and a decent rest that night if only we would march another few miles. His example was magnificently inspiring: even badly wounded men staggered on long past their limits, binding their wounds tighter and putting one leaden foot before the other with faces set hard against their agony. Once, when my own weariness and pain forced me to my knees by the side of the road, I found Robin at my side, his white face inches from my own.

'Come now, Alan, this won't do. I need you to set an example. What would young Robert say if he could see you defeated by this?'

Robert: that pain was worse than the wound by far. I had failed him. There would be no rich ransom with which to secure his freedom, and the feast of Lammas, when the next payment to the sheriff was due, was but days away. I was almost blind with despair but, for Robin, I straightened my spine and took another step forward.

Half a dozen men died of their wounds on that march. And it took us four brutal days to reach Calais, sixty miles of creeping through enemy territory, fearful of every man and wary of every village. But we made it, and all thanks must go to Robin for that feat. When at last we came in sight of the high walls of Calais town, I confess I sat down and wept.

Robin did not slacken his zeal even after our arrival at the port: he shed the outlaw persona that he had employed to bring us safely through hostile country and once more he was an English earl, a man of wealth and consequence. Within an hour of our arrival he had arranged hot food, wine and accommodation for all of the seventy-odd men-at-arms who had come through this ordeal with him.

He even took the time to secure a barrel of double-boiled vinegar to house the mortal remains of our dear friend. We had brought Little John's body every step of the way on that cruel march from Bouvines, and every fit man had done his share of carrying that burden, even I with my wounded back had done my part. But, by God, when we arrived in Calais, my old friend was smelling ripe.

Robin had insisted. And I was glad of it afterwards. He wished his friend's bones to lie in a place south of Kirkton called Hathersage – it was a manor that Robin had granted to a cousin of the big man long ago. That was typical of Little John: he had taken nothing for himself from Robin in all the long years of service to him. When his lord had wished to reward him – as he had me with the gift of Westbury – John had told him to give the manor of Hathersage to William Nailor, his first cousin, a farming man with a large young family. John asked nothing for himself but the honour of serving Robin. And he had died, as he had lived, serving his lord.

There were other refugees in Calais from the disaster at Bouvines, a handful of Flemish knights, one or two English men-at-arms who had run from the final massacre of the spear-circle, but not many. The Germans, of course, had headed north with their fleeing Emperor and we saw neither hide nor hair of them again.

The mood among those who had lived through the battle was sour: some blamed Otto for running, others said that it was Ferrand of Flanders' fault for recklessly attacking before the rest of the army was ready. Some men even blamed Salisbury and Boulogne for failing to come to the aid of the Germans when King Philip made his general attack on the eagle-dragon standard in the centre of our lines.

I was sharing a jug of wine and a loaf of sweet manchet bread with Robin and Thomas on the third night after our arrival at Calais – it had taken us three days to find a suitable ship and we were due to depart the next day – and I asked my lord why he thought we'd been so thoroughly beaten at Bouvines.

'There are always a thousand factors that decide the outcome of a battle: the weather, the morale of the two sides, whether the ground favours cavalry or footmen, what was in the men's bellies the night before battle was joined – strong wine, rich meats, or nothing at all – the sun shining in your eyes, the success of this attack or that one, a noble defence here, an act of cowardice there. But, in this case, I think that there was one over-riding reason why we were beaten. It was a failure of command.'

I frowned. 'Salisbury was not such a bad commander,' I said.

'He was adequate,' Robin agreed. 'But he was not in command of the whole army. No one was. Otto claimed it, but he never had the whole army in his hands, just his own Germans; Ferrand answered to nobody and did as he pleased; Salisbury and Boulogne resented Otto's usurpation of command and refused to help him in his hour of need. Philip was able to fight three separate engagements, three battles, in effect, against three separate foes and win them all one by one. That is the true reason why we lost. If we had had a good overall commander, well . . .'

Robin raised his wine cup to me. 'I should have listened to you, Alan. The honest truth is that we should never have fought that battle – at Bouvines or anywhere else. Philip was too strong for us.'

'I blame King John,' said Sir Thomas. I looked at him, a little surprised. For Thomas rarely spoke in company; he was, except in matters of war, a shy man.

He looked outlandish anyway that night, quite ridiculous. The first night we had arrived in Calais most of the men-at-arms had immediately sought out wine and ale and had quickly drunk themselves into a squalid state; indeed, Robin and I had had more than a few jugs of wine, toasting our dead friend Little John, and recalling his exploits with joy, laughter and more than a few tears. But Thomas had not joined us. He had disappeared at sundown and returned at dawn, naked and with only a filthy pair of braies wrapped around his loins. As was his practice after combat, he had found a knucklebones game in one of the dives by the harbour and this time had managed to lose everything he owned – his sword, his armour, even the clothes on his back. He came to Robin and me as we were breaking our fast, my lord and I both bleary and hungover, and confessed his foolishness.

Robin had merely laughed, but I was angry. I had dared to dream, when I found out that he was gone gaming, that he would return, like the last time, with a fortune that I could use to placate the sheriff of Nottinghamshire and his monstrous servant.

'I did think of Robert when I was at the bones,' Thomas had said to me earlier. 'I was three marks up at one point and I would have stopped and given all to you. But some malign devil made me throw one last time, and then again, and in the end, well, you see my situation now . . .'

Thomas was dressed in a garish assortment of ill-fitting rags. An oversized once-white chemise, now stained a pinkish hue, covered his torso, topped with a very short threadbare cloak of greyish-yellow wool. His hose were grey, too, but so baggy and creased from repeated washing that his legs looked like those of that fabled African beast, the oliphant. His belt was a length of rope and his shoes were crude clogs – lumps of wood hollowed out to make a space for the feet. Robin had organised a collection of spare clothing from the men and had even bought Thomas a new sword from a Flemish knight who had decided to enter a monastery and would have no further need of it.

'You blame John? How so?' asked Robin that night, looking at Thomas. 'The King was not even present at the battle.'

'He was there in spirit – and in blood,' said the knight. 'It was his army; he paid for it, his silver called it into

393

being; his brother Salisbury and his nephew the Emperor commanded the majority of it, and the other nobles were all in his pay. It was John's army and so he is to blame for the failure of our arms.'

It was quite a lengthy speech for Thomas. But I could see he passionately believed what he was saying. Moreover, he had not finished. 'If King John had commanded the army of the north, we might have won. All the knights there were beholden to him and honour-bound to follow his orders. There would have been a single commander, not three factions. He was not there, so he must take the blame. Also, his plan was to divide Philip's strength. He failed at that. He did not engage Philip's knights at Roche-au-Moine, he retreated—'

'Hold on,' said Robin. 'Be fair to the wretched man. His Poitevin barons turned tail and ran. Half his fighting men abandoned him.'

'And why did they do that?' asked Thomas, only to answer the question himself. 'Because they do not trust him. They do not love him, nor have they confidence in his ability as a commander. Why? Because they know him.'

There was a short silence after Thomas's words. I agreed with everything the man had said. It was Normandy all over again. The Poitevin barons had distrusted John, and with good reason; so they had refused him their support; indeed, they had joined the enemy. These barons were no doubt already preparing their embassies to King Philip, offering to do homage in exchange for forgiveness for their disloyalty and the right to keep their lands.

'He's right, Robin,' I said. 'The blame for the debacle at Bouvines, for everything – for the sacrifice of Little John, even, lies at the King's door.'

Robin looked at the two of us. He sighed.

'I know,' he said heavily. 'He is to blame – and all across England men will be having this same conversation. The King has gambled and lost – once more. He has taxed England, and taxed her again until she was bled white, and he has thrown the money away on this attempt to win back his lands. He has lost. And they will make him pay for it in England.'

'He deserves to pay,' said Thomas.

'So you, like Alan here, would kill him? You would murder the King?'

Sir Thomas said evenly: 'If I had known at the time that Sir Alan was making an attempt on the King's life, I would have helped him solely out of friendship. But I did not know and I did nothing. If another attempt was made I should give him all my aid, I'd give all my strength to the task, but this time out of conviction. John is not fit to be King. He should not rule our land in the way that he has done until now – with rapacious greed and no concern for justice or the rights of a free man. Imprisoning a baron here, stealing a knight's property there, selling his royal favour like a whore. John is no rightful ruler.'

'That is not the answer,' said Robin. His silver eyes were sparkling in the candlelight and he seemed gripped by a strange and powerful passion. 'Murder is never the answer, my friends. I might not have understood that in my youth, but I know it now. We must seek to curb the King, to make him subject to our will, to the law of the land. We shall have justice for all – from the King to the meanest commoner, I swear it. I mean to make England a country fit for my sons to live and prosper in. They and their sons shall live in a land free from fear of the King's wrath, free from the whims of greedy sheriffs, free to choose what they will make of their lives. And this, my friends, is how we shall do it . . .'

My lord began to speak.

We returned to Dover the next day, a day and a night of sailing, though the weather was as vile as the Devil could make it. After disembarking, sore and sick, we rested one night at the priory and began the long march north the next day. The stop in Calais while we had waited for the ship had done our men a power of good. They were rested and mostly recovered from the battle – although many of those with wounds we left in the care of the monks of the priory at Dover. Those men with very serious wounds had all died either in Calais or on the march from Bouvines. Some, those whose pain was very bad, and who requested it, had had a little help in their onward journey from Robin and me. This sad but merciful task had normally been the province of Little John and we felt his absence then like a dark hole in our lives.

I arrived at Westbury with a handful of my surviving men, weary to the bone and with a heart as heavy as lead. Robin carried straight on to Kirkton with his sons and I felt even more bereft by their absence, but Sir Thomas elected to stay at Westbury and keep me company for a few more days. That was kind of him, but the paramount emotion in my heart was not loneliness but fear. It was two days past Lammas-tide and I had nothing, not even a shilling, with which to pay the sheriff.

Baldwin greeted us at the gates and swiftly organised hot baths, clean clothes and plentiful food for Thomas and my men. It was good to be home, but the place seemed strangely empty without Robert's presence.

'What news, Baldwin?' I asked my steward after we had unloaded our gear and I had washed the dust of the road from my throat with a cup of well-watered wine.

'Ill news, sir,' said Baldwin. I saw that he looked to have aged a good deal in the few weeks we had been away. His hair was completely white now. 'The sheriff's well-built deputy, that Benedict fellow, came to the gates the other day with a dozen men. I would not let him in, as you instructed me, sir, but he did not seem to mind too much. He shouted up to me that it was Lammas and asked me where you were.'

I nodded. It was to be expected.

'I told him your whereabouts were none of his business – I hope I did right, sir.'

I said he had done exactly the right thing. But there was something odd about his mien, something sly and shameful. He would not look me in the eye.

'What else, Baldwin? Come on, man, spit it out.'

'He asked me to give you a message, sir.'

'And, what is it?'

'He said: "Tell Sir Alan that I am building a gallows."'

I rode to Nottingham Castle the next day with only Thomas for company. I was going to parley with the sheriff. I had a proposition to put to him.

I rode through the town of Nottingham and stopped my horse about three hundred yards away from the gatehouse of the Outer Bailey of the castle, outside a tavern I knew, just out of bowshot from the castle walls, and sent Thomas forward.

I stood by my horse sipping a cup of ale and watched Thomas ride to the gatehouse with a feeling of looming dread. If they accepted my proposition, I was most likely doomed. If they did not, my son Robert was. For the arrangement I offered the sheriff was as simple as it could be: my life for my son's. I would surrender my person until the money could be raised in exchange for Robert's liberty.

I waited an age – several hours, it seemed – while Thomas spoke with the gatekeeper and someone was dispatched to take the message to the sheriff. And as I waited, drinking another cup of ale and munching bread and onions, I thought about the sweetness of life and its brevity. But one thought was uppermost in my mind. I clung to it like a drowning man to a tree branch. Whatever happened to me, by my actions this day, Robert would live to grow into a man.

Sir Thomas returned eventually, he looked tired and very sad.

'It is agreed,' he said. 'Philip Marc is away – he's at Oxford now with the King. But Benedict Malet accepts your proposal on his behalf. We will do the exchange outside the gatehouse. You for the boy, and you must be unarmed. So if you truly want to do this you'd better give me your sword now and that misericorde up your sleeve. They will search you. I will give them to Robert.'

As I walked my horse slowly to the gatehouse, I said to Sir Thomas: 'You will do what I asked – to Malet?'

'If they murder you, he's a dead man, the sheriff, too, just as soon as I have my chance,' said my friend. 'Rest easy on that score. God go with you, Sir Alan – I pray that we shall meet again on earth – or in Heaven.'

I had only the briefest moment with Robert in the shadow of the gatehouse, time for one fierce hug, while Robert sobbed and begged me not to leave him again.

Robert was now nearly as tall as me, I noticed as I held his thin body to mine. He must be twelve years old, I reflected, nearly a man – and I knew that Robin and Sir

Thomas would ward him, and keep him from harm until he was strong enough to fend for himself. They would probably do a better job than I would. And that thought gave me the courage to walk through the open door of the gatehouse.

To my doom.

Chapter Twenty-nine

I was left in the same cell that Robert had inhabited in the very bowels of Nottingham castle – which seemed fitting. I was quite literally taking his place. But whereas Robert had been allowed the freedom of his limbs and given candles for light. I was shackled by the prison guard, wrists chained to ankles, stripped to my braies and chemise, and left in the dark. However, I waited for only an hour or so before Sir Benedict Malet came to visit me with a lantern and a greedy smile. That did not surprise me – for he was not the type to forgo the pleasure of gloating over my downfall. What did surprise me was that he brought a companion with him: a tall man in a long white cloak with his head shaved in the tonsure. It was a Templar.

Benedict's first act when he entered the cell with his

guest was to kick me several times. I twisted my body to spare my wounded back but caught most of the blows on my ribs. And, mercifully, Benedict quickly became out of breath from his exertions and stopped.

While Benedict wheezed and I lay huddled on the floor in my chains, riding the waves of pain, the Templar looked on impassively.

Finally, the man spoke: 'We have not met before, I think, Sir Alan. Although I have had the pleasure of your son's company.' The Templar gave a strange leer. 'I am Brother Geoffrey, I belong to the Order of the Poor Fellow-Soldiers of Christ and the Temple of Solomon. I also have the honour of serving William, Earl of Pembroke. I am his almoner but I also have charge of the training of his squires.'

I looked at him. This was the fellow that Robert had so disliked when he had spent that brief time at Pembroke in William the Marshal's household.

'I heard that you were hard on my son,' I said. 'But I will not hold that against you. I am sorry that he left the Marshal's household so precipitately.'

'He has weak blood. He will never make a knight,' said this man, and it occurred to me that I did hold his harshness to my son against him. But the Templar was still talking: 'I do not come to discuss your son's shortcomings with you. Indeed, I have one question to put to you, one question only.'

I stared up at him, waiting.

'Where is it?' the Templar said.

I was suddenly transported back to Wallingford Castle the year before, the time when I had been waiting to see the King, battered and bruised and fresh from my cell in Brien's Close. Sir Aymeric de St Maur, the Master of the English Templars, had asked me exactly the same question. And I was no wiser now than I had been then.

'Where is what?' I said.

Benedict stepped forward and kicked me once again, hard in the belly.

'Answer the man, you wretch,' the deputy sheriff said.

'I do not know what you mean,' I gasped. 'What is it that you seek?'

The Templar knelt down beside my head. He spoke softly, no more than a low murmur. 'You claim ignorance, Sir Alan? Perhaps a lapse of memory?' He grasped a handful of my hair and twisted it, turning my head painfully so that I was forced to look into his eyes.

'It was a long time ago, after all,' he said. 'Let me aid your recall. A fierce battle at the fortress of Montségur, in the county of Foix, far in the south, fifteen years ago. Does that stir your memory, Sir Alan? I'd be surprised if it did not.'

I felt a cold draught blow over my half-naked body; my scalp was on fire.

'You and your master challenged a company of Templar knights under the command of Guy d'Épernay, the Preceptor of the Templars of Toulouse. In exchange for your lives and freedom, Robert of Locksley gave over an object, a very precious object, to that knight. Do you recall now?'

I did. We had been at the mercy of the Templars after days of hard fighting, and Robin had exchanged an extraordinary object for our lives. He had given the knight Guy d'Épernay a beautiful golden chalice, decorated with precious gems, and had told the Templar that it was the Cup of Christ, the fabled vessel that had been present at the Last Supper and had also held the precious blood of Our Lord as it flowed from His body on the Cross. And he had lied. The chalice had, in fact, been fashioned by a Jewish goldsmith of Lincoln and had been part of a rich haul that Robin and I had stolen from Welbeck Abbey.

'You cheated us, Sir Alan,' said the Templar, giving my hair a tweak that brought tears into my eyes. 'You and my lord of Locksley gave us some bauble and retained the true relic. Can you deny it?' Although he kept his voice as low as before, it had taken on a tone of deep fury.

'You made fools of us. You made fools of our Order. For many years we guarded that cup – I myself have spent many a night kneeling in prayer before it, the cold stone biting my knees – and all the while it was a sham, a tawdry fake that you had the effrontery, no, I say the foul blasphemy, to pass off as the sacred Grail!'

I looked up at the man. Twin spots of red illuminated his pale cheeks.

'What makes you think that it is not the true Grail?'
I said.

'We are not without our sources of information,' said
this fellow. 'But we were ignorant for many years – many
years of falsehood, lies and ignominy, while you laughed
up your sleeves at us, and we were informed only recently
by a reliable source that you had perpetrated this foul
trick on us! Our agents have searched your master's home
very thoroughly – it is not there. And so I believe that
you must have it in your possession. So – tell me now.
Where is it?'

'It no longer exists,' I said.

At that, the Templar banged my skull painfully against
the stone floor of the cell. But at least then he released
my hair.

He stood up and wiped his hands on his gown.

'Sir Alan,' the Templar said, 'forgive me. I am much
given to wrath. But I am not an unreasonable man. I
believe God has caused me to be here at the moment
that you have fallen into the power of Sir Benedict. I
came to Nottingham on another matter entirely, at the
behest of my master and the King, but it seems to me
that the Lord has placed you in my hands. It may be that
I am your salvation, too. The Lord works in mysterious
ways, after all. I have spoken to Sir Benedict and on
behalf of my Order I have made him an offer for your
life. Tell him, if you please, Sir Benedict . . .'

'Brother Geoffrey has offered a delicious sum in silver

for your miserable life, Dale – far, far more than it is worth, far more than you owe us. And I am minded to accept. All he asks is that you tell him truthfully where this holy relic is that he seeks. I don't mind either way – either I receive a fortune in silver or I am afforded the pleasure of seeing Boot twist your head off in the morning.' He giggled.

Brother Geoffrey locked eyes with me, staring intently. 'So, Sir Alan, if you value your life at all, tell me – where is it?'

I shut my eyes tightly, for I fully expected to be punished for my next utterance, and said: 'What you seek has been destroyed. I swear it. It was utterly destroyed in the south years ago. The Grail no longer exists.'

'You gave us the false relic – our young informer was quite clear about that – you gave us an extremely valuable cup of gold encrusted with jewels – it was worth some hundreds of pounds. Your master would not have thrown away something so valuable only to destroy the true object. I do not believe you. You lie and your life-hope fades with your lies, Sir Alan. Are you ready to face your Maker?'

'No, not then – not at Montségur.' I felt the weight of exhaustion all over my body, I was tired of this Templar and this whole painful piece of mummery. 'It was destroyed some years later – in Toulouse. I saw it burn with my own eyes.'

'You lie!' Brother Geoffrey's wrath had returned and I

braced myself. But nothing came. The Templar said quietly: 'I know in my bones that you lie.'

'Do you require me, Brother, to send for my inquisitors?' said Benedict.

'No, thank you. Sir Alan, for all his blasphemous chicanery, is a brave man – I have heard this from all quarters, from the Master of the Temple himself. Sir Alan does not fear death, nor pain, and I believe that torture would not answer here. He will not give up his secrets. And, for my part I do not want that sin of blood upon my conscience. Well, there it is. I will make further enquiries with his lord, who may be more forthcoming. God will judge Alan Dale – and very soon I believe.'

'Torture is a sin?' said Benedict – he sounded disappointed. 'Well, if you have no further questions for him . . .'

Benedict came over and kicked me again, hard, on the side of the head this time. 'You have just cost me a great deal of money, Dale,' he hissed. 'That irritates me somewhat. But I console myself with the thought that you will not irritate me for much longer. For tomorrow you must answer for your many crimes. The sheriff would rather have your money. But he is in Oxford, and I do not think I will waste my time waiting for that. I will take your life, for my own satisfaction, and the debt will fall on your son's shoulders.'

I shouted, 'No!' and writhed in my chains.

'But, yes,' said Benedict. 'Think on this: Boot awaits

you with the sunrise and he shall tear your living head from your body – and your son shall pay every penny of the silver that is due. You will see the face of God, Alan Dale. At dawn.'

As the two men left the cell, and the darkness closed around me, I was vividly picturing Sir Thomas Blood with a naked sword in his hand and Benedict helpless beneath his blade. But it did not help all that much. I was going to die and nothing in the whole world was going to prevent that. I knew that Sir Thomas could not come for me – indeed, we had agreed that he was not to undertake any sort of rescue. Robert would need his strong right arm in the years to come and he must not throw his own life away in a useless attempt to free me.

And Robin, my thoughts and hopes turned to him, naturally. He had rescued me from similar dark places several times, not least from Brien's Close the year before. But he did not know where I was. And even if he did, I did not think he could organise a rescue attempt before dawn.

I will not burden you with my thoughts that long awful night as I lay on my side in the darkness. Suffice it to say that I wept a little, I prayed a good deal and I thought long and hard about my life, about Robert's future. I must have slept, too, for at some point in the night I became aware that I was not alone. There was a massive presence in the cell with me, on the far side of that space, and I imagined I could smell the strange spicy scent of a man's sweat. A huge man. For an instant, I thought it was the ghost of Little John come back to the world to sit with me in my last few hours and bring me safely through my time of death.

Then I heard the sound of singing. It was a high-pitched voice, sweet and pure as a cathedral boy's, and the song he was singing was 'My Joy Summons Me'.

My skin crawled and I was partially frozen in terror – for the last time I had heard that voice, singing that tune, the singer had been snapping the necks of his victims on a scaffold in the Middle Bailey. The giant Boot was in my cell and he was softly singing my death song.

I said nothing, I do not believe just then, stiff with terror as I was, that I was capable of speech. Boot sang on and on, quite beautifully, in his weird high voice.

Then he came to the end of the song and stopped. The silence stretched out between us and still I could not speak. I wanted to order him away, to curse him, to call out for help – but I knew that it would be useless. I thought: Does he mean to kill me here? There was not the slightest hint of dawn in the air, no noises from the castle, no chink of light. Just this great presence and myself in the darkness together.

Boot spoke: 'They want me to end you tomorrow, Sir Alan,' he said in good clear English, with only a trace of a Moorish accent. I realised that I had never heard the man speak before; indeed, in my mind he had always been a dumb brute, little better than an animal.

'I know it,' I said.

'The song,' the big man said, 'they tell me that you made it. Is this true or was it another man who gave this music to the world?'

'I made the song with my King, Richard of England, a long time ago in a land far away. We created the words together in friendship, but the tune itself is mine.'

'Then I can no more end you than I could end myself,' said this extraordinary fellow. 'But I do not know what now to do. This is my home, and my work is here – filthy, ugly work, it is true, but it must be done. And I like to think I make the passing of my charges as swift and easy as I can. I sing them your song now, every time, as they leave this earth. I believe it gives them one last small pleasure before the end.'

'I am sure it does,' I said. I did not know what to make of the man. But all of a sudden hope was flaming bright in my heart.

'You are a knight,' he said. 'You have lands, serving men – followers?'

'I do. Not many, I am but a poor knight. But I serve a great lord and he has many followers and would welcome more, if they were worthy.'

'I would not serve another man. But you . . . I would serve you if you were to teach me how to make this kind of beauty. Could you do that? I am not a wise man, nor a cunning one, but I feel music, I feel its beauty . . .'

'You would be most welcome in my service,' I said.

'And I would teach you to make and play the most beautiful music, but, alas, I am not in a position to do that – you know what my fate must be, whether it is you who dispatches me or another.'

I rattled my chains a little to make my point.

'Would you swear it? Would you swear that you would take me into your service? Teach me all you know?' he said. There was a wondering tone in his voice.

'If you can free me of these chains and help me to escape from this place, I swear that you will be the most valued of all my men. We will make all the music in the world together. But you must swear me your loyalty, as I will swear mine to you.'

'I swear it,' said the giant.

'As do I,' I replied. 'You are henceforth my sworn man.' It was perhaps the simplest and quite the most bizarre ceremony of the ancient act of homage I had ever witnessed; the sacred bond between man and lord reduced to its dry bones. Yet somehow it retained a power and majesty even in the darkness of that foul cell.

'Now, can you go and find a key to rid me of these chains?' I asked.

'We have no need of a key.'

I felt huge warm fingers brush my ankles and heard a tearing, wrenching noise and the squeal of tortured metal. An instant later my hands, too, were free of the shackles.

I stood tall in the darkness.

*

411

Boot led the way out of the cell with myself hard on his heels. The two guards, who were expecting Boot to emerge, leapt to their feet when they saw me at his shoulder. My new friend said nothing, merely seized both astonished men by their surcoats and smashed their heads together with a dull thump. The guards fell noiselessly to the floor. I stripped a surcoat from one of the men and took his sword belt, too. We walked up to the end of the corridor, where there was a little guardhouse at the foot of the stairway. I peeped around the corner and saw four men snoring on their pallets and we crept past, quiet as mice. We walked out of the sleeping inner and middle baileys unchallenged – it was still a good hour before dawn – and scarcely noticed, but at the gatehouse of the outer bailey a drowsy guard had stopped us and asked our business. I had said that I was returning to Westbury under Boot's supervision to fetch the tax money that I owed the sheriff. The guard had seemed unconvinced by this tale; he said that he had better call the sergeant and check it was right to open up the postern gate to us. Boot hit him once, a gentle tap to the side of the face with his huge fist, and he collapsed in a heap, dead to the world. By the time the sun was peeping over the eastern horizon, Boot and I were jogging along the track that led away from the town of Nottingham and north-west towards Westbury.

By noon, I was at home, dusty, panting and sore of foot. Thomas greeted me incredulously when I arrived at the gates of Westbury, and Robert rushed at me and hugged me with tears in his eyes.

'Oh, Father, I truly thought I would never see you again,' my son said. He looked fearfully up at Boot's looming form.

'What?' I said. 'Did you think there was a prison in England that could hold me?' I was feeling dangerously light-headed, almost giddy with happiness. 'I have friends everywhere, my boy. And if I don't have them, I make them: this is our new comrade Boot,' I said, and the huge man bowed low, quite elegantly from the waist.

'Boot, this is my son Robert. I commend him to your care for the next few days. And I charge you with his safekeeping.'

'I am honoured, sir,' said Boot. 'I shall guard him with my life. Do you care for music, little one?'

Robert said something about playing the shwarm, and I left my son discussing that less-than-exquisite instrument with my latest recruit while I began to rouse the manor for our imminent departure.

'Baldwin, we cannot stay here,' I said. 'The deputy sheriff will be upon us with all the force that he can command within an hour or so. Pack all that you can in haste and let us be away to Yorkshire – to Kirkton.'

With Thomas, Robert, myself and a handful of Westbury men-at-arms all fully armoured and mounted – there was no horse that could accommodate Boot's huge size and

413

no hauberk that would fit him – we headed north for Kirkton. I calculated that my son would only be truly safe from Benedict's fury if he were inside Robin's walls.

We marched within the hour. I had refused to answer their questions until we were well on the road, some fifteen miles north of Nottingham, and had stopped long after nightfall to make a dry, fireless camp in deep woods. As we munched bread and ham and passed around a large skin of wine, I regaled our company with the tale of how Boot had boldly rescued me from the sheriff's clutches.

The story seemed to embarrass Boot, and he excluded himself from our jolly congratulatory conversations, keeping silent throughout, but my own curiosity about this huge man who had saved my life got the better of me and I asked him to give an account of himself and how he came to be in England.

'I do not like to talk,' said Boot in his high, child's voice. 'I am not one of those clever fellows who chatters and laughs and jests and makes play with words, I am a simple man, but I will tell you a little about myself, Sir Alan, as it is fitting for a man newly entered into your service.'

I passed him the wineskin and he sank a good pint of rough red wine in two huge swallows. Our company was silent by then, every ear straining to hear what the giant would say next.

'I was born in a land far away, far to the south beyond the seas and the deserts, a land where the sun shines all day every day. I was born in a village, a poor place compared to Nottingham or other great towns of England, a place of small mud-walled huts and grass roofs. My father, who was a hunter, named me Kasa Vubu Ngbengu Mbutu in honour of his clan and the spirits of the forest – but the name is too hard for English tongues and so I am called simply Boot in your language.

'I was a big baby, and as an infant I grew even bigger, I ate more than twice the amount that my brothers and sisters took, and we were a poor family, very poor, and there were many hungry mouths. One day my father took me north to trade with the men of the deserts, the Moors: horse warriors with long robes and lighter skin and great curved swords. My father sold me to them when I had seen only five wet seasons and I never saw him or my mother or my brothers and sisters again.'

The Westbury company was entranced by Boot's tale. Not a man yawned or scratched himself or coughed, every eye was on the storyteller, a huge shape in the darkness talking slowly in his child's voice.

'The Moors did not keep me – well, they kept a part of me. They cut me, they cut away my stones – they took away my hope of manhood – and they set me to work tending their horses. But they feared me, even the poor ignorant slave that I was, as I grew taller than all the other boys. By the time I had seen twelve summers – about your age, Robert – I was taller than all of the men and far stronger too. The Moors admired at my size, but they feared me. They sold me again, this time to the Sultan of Oran, and I was housed in the palace and set to guarding the women's quarters.

'I ate and I grew, and soon I was bigger than all the other slaves, a monster they said, and my master sold me again – this time to a travelling man, who had a collection of human oddities like me – there was a pretty lady with a full red beard, a stupid youth with the face of a pig, and a pair of dwarfs who would tumble and turn tricks and make the audience laugh. This fellow – his name was Salim – took me north again, across the narrow water to the rich lands of al-Andalus, and there he showed off his charges at the courts of the emirs. I bent metal bars with my bare hands, I lifted oxen off the ground, I wrestled with local champions, two or three against one, and I was always victorious. And for this Salim was showered with silver, and I was given all the food I could eat and a warm bed at night. I learnt languages of all the places that I visited, the many kinds of Arabic and a little of the Latin tongue they speak there, and in the north of that land. I like languages, I hear the music in their rhythms. I heard the poetry in the language of Occitan, and I met for the first time the men who travelled from court to court playing their music.

'It was in the north of al-Andalus near the Christian lands that I first heard music, real music, music of the kind that Sir Alan makes. And I fell in love. I set myself to learn the language of these troubadours, as they called themselves, so that I could hear the songs of these men and understand them fully. I was a full-grown man by then, as you see me now, and though I could never know the love of a woman myself, I swam deeply in these songs of love and pain and loss. They called to something within me. I learnt to sing them in Occitan, in French as well, and I dreamt of bold knights and the fair ladies that they loved and yet could never have.

'Salim was not a bad master. I was a slave but he never beat me – he did not dare, if the truth be told – nor did he let me go hungry, less my strength be diminished. But I was not happy. One day I walked away from his encampment without a word of farewell. I wanted to see the lands of the infidels, as we called the Christian folk. I wanted to hear their music again. So I walked north.'

Boot reached for the wineskin and took another enormous swallow. It occurred to me that Boot was a man who would require a lord with a fat purse just to keep him in sufficient food and drink. But he would be worth every penny I spent on him, too.

'How came you to England?' I asked.

He shrugged. 'I put the sun at my back and walked,' he said. 'I crossed mountains, I swam rivers, I trekked through deep forest, I marched until my bare feet were hard as leather and my clothes no better than rags. I made my daily bread by the same tricks I had used with Salim – I bent iron, I fought the strongest men of each village for coin or food, sometimes I sang in the market for scraps of bread. But mostly I walked. In the land called Touraine, north of the great River Loire, a terrible war was raging. Englishmen and French were fighting each other, and I fell in with a band of mercenaries under their captain, Philip Marc. It was with his men that I learnt to speak English – for many among their number hailed from these shores. They fed me and I fought by their side – but I am not a true man of war. I am strong but even the strongest can be overcome by hard steel. I do not care for war – these people did things to their enemies that I will not repeat; and they forced me to do the same . . . But I never fully understood who we were fighting and why we must do these foul deeds. I was glad when Philip Marc and his surviving men were recalled to England by their King. I thought that meant an end to war, an end to the slaughter.'

I heard Sir Thomas give a low chuckle at that statement.

'Philip Marc is not an evil man – I know you will disagree, Sir Alan. He is a hard man who takes his orders from the King, nothing more. He gathers taxes, burns farms as a punishment and kills the enemies of his King, not from any pleasure in their deaths but because it is required of him in the role he must play.'

I did not agree but I remained silent.

'Sir Benedict Malet is another kind of creature,' said Boot. 'It was his notion that I should become the executioner of Nottingham. "If you want to eat, you black lump, you must follow my orders," Sir Benedict said to me. "When I say kill, you kill." And I did – indeed, in that way I am no better than Philip Marc. I snapped the necks of people each week and sent them to Heaven. I told myself that if I did not do the task then another man would – and I would be expelled from the castle and must return to my life of wandering. So I killed for him – I killed scores, perhaps hundreds, and at each execution, Sir Benedict would be there. He liked to watch the dying of the light in their eyes. It gave him joy. He would torment them beforehand, too, with talk of how I would make their deaths . . .'

Boot fell silent for a while. I thought of Benedict gloating over me in my cell.

'I am tired,' he said. 'I am tired from talking and from sorrow. I would sleep now: but there you have my tale. A half-man am I, his manhood cut away from him, a friendless man in a foreign land, a killer of innocents at the orders of others.'

It was Robert who spoke: 'You are not a half-man. You saved my father from the sheriff and for my part that makes you more a man than many I have known.'

'And you shall never be friendless,' I said, 'not while you are among us.'

Chapter Thirty

Kirkton was once again preparing for war when I arrived there the next morning, but on a muted scale. A few score foot soldiers were drilling in the green sheep pastures outside the walls – the men who had come back alive from Bouvines and a few new recruits, but pitifully few. A dozen cavalry were training on the slopes down to the river. That disastrous Flanders expedition had greatly sapped Robin's military strength and the failure of the army to gain anything in the way of booty had slowed the flow of young men willing to risk their lives as men-at-arms in his service.

Robin greeted me in the hall where he was playing chess with Hugh after dinner and it seemed he could sense at once that something was wrong. I told him about my imprisonment and escape from Nottingham and he looked at me gravely. 'That was a reckless thing to do, old friend, to put yourself in their power. Swear to me you will not do so again. You should have come to me first.'

I laughed, and said: 'Oh, I have learnt my lesson, my lord.'

Robin offered to house my entire following until such time as the threat to Robert and myself was ended – which was truly generous, for I had no idea when I might be able to return in safety to Westbury.

I thanked him and said: 'There is something that I must tell you that I learnt during my imprisonment.'

'Yes?' he said, looking attentively into my face.

'Do you remember when we came back from Damme and learnt that someone had attempted a robbery on Kirkton in your absence?'

'Vividly,' said Robin. 'A gang of enterprising cushion-makers, we thought.' And he smiled at me, remembering our joke.

'Did you ever question the sheriff of Yorkshire about it?' I asked.

'I did – I took Little John and some men and we bearded him in his lair. I broke into his chamber at midnight in York Castle. Cost me a fortune in bribes, and more than a few favours, but I got in there without much trouble. I asked him and he swore on his children's lives that he had nothing to do with it. I didn't hurt him, if that is what you are driving at; he was scared enough by Little John looming over him in the darkness with an axe. I asked, he said no, and I believed him. Why?'

'I think I know who those "thieves" were,' I said. And I told him of the conversation I had had with Brother Geoffrey.

'You think it was Templars searching for the Grail?' Robin scratched his fair head. 'Could be – they didn't take much of value as common thieves would. Yes, I can see that. Templars – or men who had been bought by them.'

'I also think that it was Templars who attacked Westbury after my illness, when we scattered them with Robert's fire-wagon. Philip Marc and Benedict Malet seemed to know little about the battle – and, come to think of it, when I went to Nottingham straight afterwards, none of their men-at-arms were marked by combat.'

'Yes, they too could have been Templars; they fought well enough,' said Robin. 'So I think we can take it that the Order is out for our blood. And a lot more will be shed if we don't give them the Grail. It's a shame we can't do that then, isn't it?'

I nodded. The Grail truly had been destroyed after a long war in the south. I had seen it burn. It no longer existed. Then I told Robin what else the Templar had said about his sources of information.

Robin gave a great heavy sigh. 'You believe this almoner

then, this prating, hair-pulling Brother Geoffrey, and his talk of an informer in our ranks. You think there is a man who is telling all our secrets to our enemies, who secretly wishes us ill.'

'It would not be the first time.'

'Indeed,' said my lord. Ten years before I had suspected that there was a traitor in Château Gaillard. Robin had not believed me. But I had been right.

'Why is there always someone who hates us and wears the mask of love?' said Robin sadly. 'Cousin Henry warned me about this, too. Do you remember? Come on then, Alan, tell me. Who is it? I know you have been thinking on this. I see it in your eyes.'

I looked at my boots. 'It must be someone who is close to us,' I said, unable to meet Robin's eye, 'someone who has or who has had contact with the Templars.'

'That could be anyone,' Robin said. 'Hell's teeth, my sons were both trained by Templars, Miles practically worships them, as many youngsters do – you surely don't think they could be traitors?'

Robin looked at me; his eyes glinted like drawn steel. 'Tell me that you don't think Miles or Hugh is in league with the Templars, Alan, and tell me that now.'

'I don't think it is one of your sons.'

'Who then?'

'I don't know,' I said, but I could not meet his gaze. And there we left it.

We settled in easily at Kirkton. Thomas continued his

423

training of Robert with sword and shield; Miles and Hugh, who had both been close to my son since his earliest days, joined them in their lessons, and when the training was done for the day, the three boys would slip out of the castle to roam the lands of my lord. They would return at nightfall, muddy and laughing, with Robert nearly dead with tiredness. I did not enquire too closely what their exploits were on these youthful excursions, but I trusted Robin's sons – well, Hugh, at least – not to lead my boy into too much danger.

After a few weeks at Kirkton, I took Robert off on an expedition of my own. We headed north, just the two of us, on a golden September morning.

'Have you ever thought what it might be like to have a lady living at Westbury,' I said casually, as we trotted along through the vast bosomy landscape of the dales.

'You wish to marry again, Father?' said my son.

'Maybe . . . maybe. We shall see. What would you say if I did?'

'I would not mind. If the lady were of the right sort.'

'And what sort would that be?'

'I would like her to be true. She must be pretty and kind and jolly – all those things – but I would like her best if she loved you and me and Westbury and our life there above all else. I would like her to love all of us with all her heart with a love that would last for ever and never fade. She must be one who would never leave, never waver in her steadfastness, always be there no matter what the weather or what assails us, in poverty or in wealth, war or peace. I would like her to be true.'

We were heading, of course, towards Kirklees. I had taken it into my head that Robert should be introduced to Tilda. I had not set my mind on asking her, once again, if she would be my wife. But I confess it was in my thoughts. I missed the comforts of a woman in my bed and while I knew that Tilda had her faults, I wanted her nonetheless; I wanted her more than I liked to admit. Each time I recalled our one coupling, usually late at night in bed, it set my loins afire. I could clearly imagine her at Westbury, caring for Robert and me, running the manor calmly and efficiently, offering love, warmth and good counsel. Much of the time Westbury was little more than an armed camp. I wanted it to be a home. Moreover, I had been conscious in recent weeks that if something were to happen to me, Robert would be all alone: though I knew Robin and Thomas would protect him, and their rough male company would be vitally important for his growth into manhood, I knew that he also needed to have a woman in his life.

About a mile or two outside the priory, we stopped at a tavern in Kirkburton to take a cup of ale and so that Robert and I might change our clothes into something less travel-stained as befits a visit to a lady. I was about to remount my horse and travel the last few miles to our destination, when I heard the drumming of horses' hooves on the road. As I stood holding our animals' heads, a cavalcade of horsemen thundered past, heading south away from the priory. I blessed my luck that my hat was pulled low and that Robert was at the back of the tavern using the latrine, for the face I glimpsed at the head of the pack of a dozen Nottinghamshire men-at-arms was the bloated visage of Benedict Malet.

A wave of cold fury washed over me, I found that I was actually trembling, gripping the hilt of Fidelity so hard that I felt my knuckles were likely to spilt the skin. For apart from the shock of seeing a man who had so recently threatened not only my life but my son's, it also seemed plain to me that Benedict Malet could only have been coming from one place.

Robert and I waited in the cloister of Kirklees Priory for what seemed an age. Finally Tilda appeared, sweeping in in her black-and-white habit, her normally pure white face a little flushed. 'Sir Alan, what a great pleasure to see you again,' she said, kissing me. 'And this must be Robert – such a good-looking boy!'

Robert began to make his bow, but Tilda seized him by the shoulders and kissed him robustly on both cheeks. 'My dear, you must forgive my impetuosity, but you are the very spitting image of your handsome father,' she said, smiling at the boy. 'The very model of a dashing squire. You will break all the ladies' hearts when you are older. What joy it gives me to meet you. Sir Alan has told me so much about you.'

Robert was wearing a pair of black silk hose and a scarlet velvet tunic that Miles had outgrown, his hair was freshly cut, his face and hands clean, and he did indeed look fine that day. I noticed with satisfaction that my son blushed and hung his head shyly at the womanly attention he was being given.

Matilda herself looked if anything even more beautiful than ever. The roses in her pale cheeks made her blue-grey eyes seem especially lively, her wide lips were red as blood. And each time she gazed into my face, I felt my heart give a little flip.

'I hope we are not taking up too much of your valuable time, my dear,' I said.

'Not at all, I was engaged in the herb garden just now, trimming back the summer growth, but life is so dull here at Kirklees. We mostly pray and work, pray and work; it is a refreshing treat to have a pair of dashing gentlemen pay us a visit.'

'Have you not already received visitors today?' I said.

'Why no, Sir Alan,' said Tilda, and she glanced low and to her left. 'We live quietly here at Kirklees.'

A trickle of ice-water chilled the inside of my belly. Tilda was lying to me.

'Have you not this day received a visit from Sir Benedict Malet?' I said.

Tilda looked directly at me. Something dark moved beneath the surface of her blue eyes. She did not reply to my question. Instead, she clapped her hands sharply and a novice nun appeared instantly on the far side of the cloister.

'Martha,' she said to the girl. 'Would you be kind enough to take the young gentleman to the kitchens. I think there are some of those wonderful honey-cakes left. And perhaps afterwards he would like to see our famous herb garden.'

I was reminded that Tilda was the sub-prioress, a woman of consequence within these walls. The novice trotted over to us and curtseyed prettily and, after a quick glance at me to see he had my permission, Robert followed her out of the cloister.

Tilda and I stood in silence for a while, my question still hanging in the air.

'I hope you are not going to be disagreeable, Sir Alan,' said Tilda eventually. 'But if you must know, yes, Sir Benedict did pay me a brief visit today. I did not mention it because I know that you and he are not the best of friends.'

'The man tried to kill me not two weeks ago; he threatened to kill Robert too.'

'Some misunderstanding, I expect—'

'It was no misunderstanding, by God. That man is a murderous wretch—'

'If you are going to bellow at me as if I were one of your rowdy men-at-arms, I shall have to ask you to leave,' said Tilda sharply.

I apologised, biting back the hot words that came

rushing to my lips. Don't be a fool, Alan, I told myself. Do not make a fool of yourself again in front of her.

She gathered her calm. 'Sir Benedict is my friend and he has been one as long as you, Alan. I think I have the right to see whomever I choose.'

She was right, she did. For much as I hated to admit it, I was already thinking of her as mine. She most definitely was not – at least, not yet. And although I could not bear her to spend any time with Benedict, I knew that I must not make the same mistake that I had made all those years ago and try to force her to bend to my will.

'Forgive me,' I said. 'I do not wish to quarrel. You must see whomever you wish to. Although I wish it were not him. Now, tell me how you have been,' I said, smiling at her lovingly. 'Are you well? How is life at Kirklees? Does it suit you?'

I spent a pleasant hour with Tilda, talking of her life as a bride of Christ. She liked it on the whole, she said, and she felt her life had meaning in the service of God. But she admitted that sometimes she longed for male company, for the freedom of the lay life and a break from the grind of religious duties. And I was privately encouraged by these words. I told her of the battle of Bouvines and the death of Little John and she seemed genuinely grieved by the loss of my friend. She asked after Robin and asked me to thank him for his many kindnesses to Kirklees. Eventually, I took my leave of her and she sent a servant to fetch Robert from the herb garden.

As she kissed me goodbye, I felt a strong urge, almost overpowering, to ask her to be my wife – indeed, I found it hard to tear myself away from her side – yet I restrained myself. There was no hurry, I said to myself, we would visit a few more times, Robert and I, and I would let the two of them get to know each other better. And then I would make my move.

As we rode home I asked Robert what he thought of Tilda. He was quiet for an uncomfortably long time, and then he said: 'I think she is truly beautiful, Father. I can see why you admire her so much. A very pretty lady.'

I was about to ask him more when he said: 'One thing is strange about their herb garden, Father. For a place where they grow supposedly healing herbs, there seemed to be a great many plants that are poisonous in the beds there. Martha warned me not to touch a good three or four of them: foxgloves, giant hogweed, several different types of nightshade . . .'

'They use them to cure people,' I said. 'They are famous for it. A tiny bit of poison can fight off the morbid humours efficiently, I believe. They certainly managed to cure me of my lung disease. If you like, I will ask someone to explain it to you who knows more about it than I. Or you could ask Tilda when we next visit.'

Chapter Thirty-one

All that autumn, Robin was as busy as a honey bee, travelling the country, criss-crossing England to visit and talk to every man of even the slightest rank. He rode from knights' manors to grand castles from Kendal to Kent, from Whitby to Wales and back again – and, most of the time, I went with him. Indeed, we were so busy that I found I did not have time to visit Tilda again that year as I had promised Robert.

Everywhere we went, Robin spoke with the landholder about kingship and the law of the land, about King John and what might be done to curb his excesses. He spoke about taxation and the cause of justice for all and about the ancient laws and customs of England. He was tireless. Indeed, I sometimes wished he had taken the pace a little

431

more easily, for after two months of ceaseless travel I was longing to return to Kirkton and take my ease for a few days. However, in mid-November, I found myself with my lord and a dozen men-at-arms as our escort, who were just as exhausted as I was, outside the walls of Alnwick Castle, walking our horses through the drizzle in the green pastures where my lords Fitzwalter and de Vesci had seduced me into their murderous designs. After so many weeks of consultations with lesser men, Robin had come at last to call on the two most powerful and influential leaders of the opposition to King's rule.

We were ushered into Alnwick Castle and straight into the great hall – an enormous room with a vast hearth in the centre of the space. A bonfire of half tree-trunks burnt in the hearth and the damp was further dispelled with a pair of yard-wide braziers at either end of the long room. Yet it was still uncomfortably cold and neither Robin nor I removed our cloaks or gloves as we were handed cups of hot spiced wine to sip by the castle servants.

As we waited, standing by the oversized hearth, sipping our warm wine and allowing our rain-sodden clothes to steam, I thought about the last time I had been here and the foolish risk that I had been induced to take by the two men we were about to encounter. I do not know if it was the hot wine hitting my empty stomach or just that I had been dwelling on injustice with Robin for so many weeks, but I felt a strong surge of anger against these men. I had been used, bent to their purposes and then discarded when things had gone wrong. I had been a fool but they had taken advantage of my good nature. Something of my thoughts must have shown on my face, for Robin frowned at me over his cup.

'Should I have left you behind?' he said.

'No, my lord.'

'You must be calm, Alan. Whatever is between you and Fitzwalter and de Vesci, you must forget it. We need them now. Only they can deliver the forces we need to accomplish our task. They have the men, we do not. If they once used you, console yourself with the thought that we are now using them – and for a far more noble purpose. Do not let your anger get the better of you, I beg you.'

'No, my lord,' I said.

Robin still did not look happy. 'Perhaps it would be better if I were to do all the talking. Be a good fellow, Alan, and just stay mute for the time being, will you.'

'As you wish, my lord,' I said.

'Ah, it is my lord of Locksley and the redoubtable Sir Alan Dale,' said a voice. We turned to see Robert Fitzwalter striding down the hall towards us, smiling in greeting.

Beside him walked Eustace de Vesci, who said rather coldly: 'What a pleasure to finally have you pay us a visit, Lord Locksley. We hear you have been making a good number of visits recently. Here, there, everywhere, we are told, whispering in corners, meetings in secret. I wonder you find the time to come to Alnwick – and you have brought Sir Alan with you. A double pleasure.'

'The pleasure is all ours,' Robin said. 'And when it comes to whispering in corners and plotting dark deeds, I would say that you are at least my equal in that field. However, I am glad that you should have heard of our journeyings, for it will give you some idea of what we are hoping to discuss with you.'

De Vesci scowled. He opened his mouth to say something.

'Gentlemen, gentlemen,' said Lord Fitzwalter, 'there will be plenty of time for discussion later: first, I insist, let us have some food, some wine, a little music, perhaps.' He clapped his hands and a dozen servants rushed into the hall and began laying a long table with plates and cutlery, baskets of bread and flagons of wine.

We ate pheasant and fresh trout and exchanged platitudes while a handless lout standing in a corner of the hall sawed away on a cheap vielle and murdered some better-known pieces of the *trouvère*'s art – none of them mine, I was relieved to hear.

My noble lords de Vesci, Fitzwalter and Locksley discussed the King's recent inglorious return to England; they idly chatted about the justiciar Peter de Roches's moves to supply and strengthen the royal castles across England – including Nottingham, which I learnt was to receive an extra contingent of twenty knights and two hundred men-at-arms. They spoke generally of the deep anger that many barons – and not just those in the north

434

– felt towards the King and his sheriffs. But they delicately refrained from discussing my disastrous attempt on the King's life and its consequences. Neither did we talk about the mismanagement of the Earl of Salisbury's campaign in Flanders and the shattering defeat at Bouvines. Nor did the subject of rebellion directly come up. I kept my mouth shut during the entire meal – except when I admitted food and wine – and neither de Vesci nor Fitzwalter made any comments to me, or about my silence. Yet that did not make me any less angry.

We were availing ourselves of nuts and fruit and a sickly yellowish wine, when a servant announced that a late guest had arrived. Next, a man in a long black cloak with a deep hood was escorted up to the table. The servants took away his cloak and hood and I was astounded to find myself staring at one of the last people on earth I might have expected to see in this wild northern rebel stronghold. It was his grace the Archbishop of Canterbury, Primate of All England, Stephen Langton.

We all rose from the table and greeted the paramount churchman in England as befitted his high rank. We kissed the huge onyx ring on his right hand and he was given a vast carved chair in which to sit while servants poured water to allow him to wash his hands and face and brought a plate of food and a large and very valuable Venetian glass filled with a deep purplish wine.

While the servants fussed around the archbishop, bringing him cushions, moving the red-hot brazier a little nearer to his chair, refilling his wine glass, I considered the new arrival. He was a tall, slender man in his middle sixties, I would guess, with a long, sharp nose, deeply cut lines in his handsome face and bright intelligent blue eyes. I was surprised to see him here, for he was a man of God, a personal friend of the Pope, and since John had rendered England up to Innocent the year before, I had assumed that he must be in favour of the status quo. Indeed, I was astonished to see him breaking bread with the King's enemies.

He saw me looking at him and returned my gaze.

'You are Sir Alan Dale,' he said. 'I saw you last year in St Paul's courtyard before the ceremony of papal homage.'

I admitted that this was so. His bright blue eyes bored into me.

'Tell me truly, Sir Alan, if you will, did you indeed intend to murder the King?'

Before I had time to answer, de Vesci and Fitzwalter both started speaking, their words tumbling over each other: '. . . all a misunderstanding . . . entirely a mistake . . . Sir Alan meant no harm . . . very unfortunate . . . some confusion . . .'

The Archbishop utterly ignored the rebels' protestations and continued to look calmly at me. When there was silence again, he raised one eyebrow.

I said: 'Yes, my lord, I would surely have killed him had I got close enough.'

The archbishop nodded as if he had expected this

answer. 'Tell me, Sir Alan, do you still feel the same way towards our royal lord and master?'

I broke my gaze from his. I took a breath and said: 'No, I do not. I deeply regret my actions now. My lord, the Earl of Locksley, has persuaded me that there is a better course, a more honourable and effective course to take than cold-blooded murder.'

The archbishop was smiling at me. 'That is good, my son, for I would not wish to consort with murderers. Had you answered differently, I would have left you, all of you, upon the instant. But Christ teaches forgiveness for those who truly repent, and as His servant I can do no less. God's blessings on you. I absolve you.'

I felt a lifting of my spirits at his words and a glow of warmth towards the great man. Fitzwalter and de Vesci were rendered as mute as I had been at dinner by the archbishop's words and it was Robin who picked up the conversation.

'My lord archbishop, I have been engaged these past months on a peculiar mission,' Robin said. 'I have taken it upon myself to question the leading men of England about their grievances with the King. If he will not hear them – and many tell me he is deaf to their entreaties – then I believe we must compel him to listen and to acknowledge the wrongs that they have suffered.'

'There are a great many men with grievances, that is true,' said the archbishop.

'Yes, my lord,' said Robin, 'and I was inspired by your

call last year for the King to renew the charter of the first King Henry – the old charter that guarantees the liberties of all free men under the crown.'

'I begged the King to renew it – he flatly refused,' the archbishop said with a rueful smile. 'He even threatened to have me exiled again.'

'Yes,' said Robin. 'Well, I believe it is time for a new charter. A charter that puts to the King all the complaints, all the injustices, all the wrongs of the land – all in one great legal document. He must set his seal to it, he must agree to be bound by it – or he will lose his crown. It will be a charter that he cannot ignore.'

De Vesci and Fitzwalter were leaning forward, their elbows on the tablecloth amid the scraps of the meal, listening intently to Robin's words.

Eustace de Vesci said: 'You would bind the King by law? The King? With a piece of parchment? What babbling nonsense is this?'

'It seems to be an original idea, that is true,' said Robin evenly. 'But perhaps it is not so outlandish. Consider this: if the King wishes his vassals to serve him, the King must be bound by an agreement with his vassals. The custom has ever been thus: when a man swears homage to the King, the King too has an obligation to his man. The King is bound by this obligation, by this custom. What is the law but a legal codification of our rights and customs? The point I am making is that the King is already bound by a law of sorts in the form of our ancient customs.'

The men around the table seemed unconvinced by Robin's argument. I had, of course, heard him repeat it many times before in a hundred halls across the land.

Robin tried a different approach. 'The King makes the law, surely, but where is it written that he should not himself be subject to it? If he is not, and he rules by whim and force of arms, he is no better than a tyrant. And how can any man rest easy in his bed if he knows that the King, if he so chooses, can steal that bed from under him, murder his wife and children, throw him in prison for debts conjured out of the air? The King must be subject to the law so that we can all be free of his tyranny.'

De Vesci said: 'I find it astonishing that a former outlaw should lecture me about the law of the land.'

To my surprise, Robin did not react to this insult. He smiled and said: 'You do not like my sophistry, very well. This is my last point: if you compel the King to agree to this charter, you compel not only him, but future kings and all their heirs and descendants – for ever – to behave in a way that you have determined. You will have changed the relationship between King and subjects for the better and for all time.'

My lord fell silent. De Vesci and Fitzwalter were looking at each other. The Archbishop of Canterbury was gazing up into the ceiling, perhaps contemplating Heaven. Finally, Fitzwalter spoke: 'What exactly would we put in this charter?'

Robin said: 'Whatever you wanted, within reason. I

have a list of grievances that I have collected from people across the country. What I propose is that, initially, we put everything we can think of in the charter, and we can work out the fine details later. We must have agreement from a dozen other magnates, a hundred other barons, before we can present it to the King. Why don't you tell me what you want?'

'First and foremost, we must protect the Church,' said the archbishop. 'If you want my support, that is my only condition.'

'Agreed,' said Robin.

The archbishop smiled broadly. 'By happy chance, I have brought with me three of my household clerks – all possessing fine legal minds – they are being fed in the servants' quarters as we speak. With your gracious permission, my lord de Vesci, I will summon them and they can begin to draw up this charter of liberties in the proper legal Latin. Is that acceptable to you all?'

Robin and Fitzwalter nodded. Our host Eustace de Vesci looked bewildered but said nothing and a servant was sent to fetch the three clerks.

Robin also disappeared to fetch a bundle of parchments on which he had written down the demands of the dozens of men that he and I had spoken with over the past few weeks. While I waited for him to return, it suddenly struck me that the archbishop's presence here was no mere accident. Robin, clearly, had invited him to make the long journey north from Canterbury, and he must have had a good reason to comply. I looked at Lord Fitzwalter; he too, I suspected, had had a hand in engineering this meeting with the archbishop. But I was also certain that this was all news to de Vesci. I had the distinct feeling, as I often did with Robin, that I was attending an elaborate performance designed to achieve a particular end. In this case it seemed to me that Robin, Lord Fitzwalter and Archbishop Langton were conspiring together to convince de Vesci – the richest and most powerful of the northern barons, and perhaps the most difficult man of them all – to join their schemes.

The remains of the feast were cleared away. A pair of candle-trees were lit and brought forward, for night was falling. And three men in dusty black robes with the tonsures of clergy were led to the table. I may not have been attending fully when their names were announced – or perhaps I have merely forgotten them – but in my mind they were nameless, drab, grey men. Clever, no doubt, perhaps even wise, but not with the kind of fire of spirit that would make them any sort of pleasure to be with. In my mind the Canterbury clerks were the fat one, the tall one and the small one – collectively, the three wise men.

The three wise men set out their quills, inkpots and so on, Robin handed them a fat sheaf of parchments filled with his own spidery black writing, and so began one of the strangest nights of my life.

*

441

Archbishop Langton began the session by saying: 'Despite the fact that he has made over England to the Pope, King John cares nothing for the Church – indeed, I have my doubts that he even believes in God. And, if I may, I would like the first article to which we wish to bind the King to be concerning the liberty of the Church of England. Is that agreeable to all of you?'

Fitzwalter said: 'By all means!'

Robin said: 'Certainly, my lord.'

De Vesci said: 'If you must.'

I kept my mouth shut, but what the archbishop did next confirmed in my mind that this was not the first time the Primate of All England had discussed a charter such as the one Robin had seemingly just proposed.

'Very well,' said Langton. He leaned towards the fat clerk, who seemed to be their chief, and whispered in his ear for some time. The clerk began to write on a sheet of clean parchment, with an impressive turn of speed, a sort of note form of whatever the Archbishop was saying in his ear.

Fitzwalter turned to Robin and said: 'So you have been taking soundings all across England?'

'Yes,' said my lord, 'for some weeks and months now.'

'And what do most people say?'

'There is some general support for the charter,' said Robin. 'But if there is to be a confrontation between us and the King, most of the knights and barons would rather wait to see who will be the victor before committing themselves.'

'I see,' said Fitzwalter. 'That chimes with what I've heard, too. And have you identified any particular grievances that people wish the King to address?'

'It's a strange mix of things,' Robin said. 'Many people are concerned about inheritance, the reliefs that heirs must pay the King to possess a dead relative's lands. The King has been charging thousands of pounds for this right, and people want it limited to a reasonable figure – say, a hundred pounds. Then there are the widows – they do not want to be compelled to marry by the King, just so he can reward his followers with their lands. There is a good deal of strong feeling about this. But there is a whole host of other matters, great and small: my friends in Sherwood want the forest laws made less harsh, even abolished, but that would take some doing; on the other hand, some people just want a few fish weirs in the Medway removed, which I think we can manage without too much difficulty. I've made a note of it all here.' Robin patted the sheaf of parchments before the three wise men.

The fat clerk cleared his throat, stood up and said in a low, quivering, portentous voice: 'We think it should begin like this, my lords . . . John, by the grace of God King of England, Lord of Ireland, Duke of Normandy and Aquitaine, and Count of Anjou, to his archbishops, bishops, abbots, earls, barons, justices, foresters, sheriffs, stewards, servants . . .'

'You can skip the usual greeting,' said Langton. 'Just read out the first article.'

'And speak up, will you,' said de Vesci. 'There is no need to mumble.'

The clerk began again, a little louder: 'First, that we have granted to God, and by this present charter have confirmed for us and our heirs in perpetuity, that the English Church shall be free, and shall have its rights undiminished, and its liberties unimpaired. We have granted and confirmed by this charter the freedom of the Church's elections. This freedom we shall observe ourselves, and desire to be observed in good faith by our heirs in perpetuity.' The clerk stopped and sat down.

'That sounds all right to me,' said Fitzwalter. 'You'll translate it into good Latin, in due course?'

The clerk nodded.

'It's a bit wordy,' said de Vesci. 'And you've got the bit about "our heirs in perpetuity" twice. If that's just the first article, this is going to be a very long night. I'd better get them to bring some more wine.'

'Perhaps, my lord, you might like to think about the articles you personally would wish to include,' said Robin to de Vesci, who brightened considerably.

'Good idea,' said Fitzwalter. 'I know what I want – I want the King's habit of demanding scutage whenever he damn well feels like it stopped – he can have it if he's captured in battle and we need to raise a ransom, or on other special occasions, but he can't just call scutage whenever he likes and wring the country dry. Oh, and I'd better get something in there about the rights of

444

London, or my merchant friends there will not be pleased at all.'

'I want a full pardon for any crimes,' said de Vesci, who was suddenly cheerful. 'Not that I admit to any. Ha ha! And I want to be able to move freely about the country – and abroad – without the King declaring me an outlaw. Not all of us want to have to sleep in the woods like a villein, Locksley! Ha ha!'

Robin smiled blandly but said nothing. And so the evening progressed with something almost approaching a spirit of celebration. Wine was drunk, articles were proposed, amended and then turned into fine-sounding legal words by the three wise men, who read them back to us from time to time with suitable gravitas. I stayed aloof from the discussions for the most part, but I marvelled at the way Robin had manipulated these men into willingly going along with his extraordinary plan.

After several hours of hearty discussion, Robin said to me: 'And you, Alan, you are awfully quiet – what is it that you want from the King?'

I said without thinking: 'I'd be happy never to have to go back to that gaol in Wallingford – to Brien's Close. I'd be happy if I never had to fear being seized and flung into prison and left to die by inches without the chance to defend myself or explain. It is a fate no free man should have to face.'

I looked hard at de Vesci and Fitzwalter.

De Vesci looked away. But Fitzwalter held my gaze.

'We wronged you, Alan, I know we did. We pulled you into our schemes and then abandoned you. There is no excuse, except that after we were betrayed we had to go into hiding for a few months ourselves to escape the King's wrath. But we were wrong, I admit it. We should have helped you. All I can say now is that I am heartily sorry. Can you find it in your heart to forgive us?'

I was dimly aware of the archbishop conferring with the tall clerk. I thought about his forgiveness for me at the beginning of the meeting. I thought what it would mean to carry a burning grudge against these two men for the rest of my life – or until I could take a suitable revenge. It was not worth it. Truly, it wasn't. I was not permanently damaged by my experience in gaol – Robin had saved me from that awful death and here I was now, hale and whole.

'I forgive you,' I said. 'I forgive you both for any wrong you have done me. Let us put it behind us and never speak of it again.'

'Well spoken, Sir Alan,' said the archbishop. 'Spoken like a true Christian knight.' He favoured me with his broad smile. Fitzwalter embraced me in a bear hug, and even de Vesci shook me limply by the hand and muttered something about regrettable events and no hard feelings.

'There is one thing I would say to you, Sir Alan,' said Fitzwalter, 'which perhaps I should have said before. You remember that we thought we had found a traitor in our midst, a fellow who had taken the King's silver to spy upon us?'

I did.

'Well, it seems that he was not the man who betrayed us at St Paul's. My men were very persuasive – I won't go into details – but he refused to admit that crime under indescribable pain. He denied it even as he died. So, it looks as if it was someone else who betrayed you. Perhaps someone in your own camp.'

I looked at Robin and raised my brows.

He nodded and said: 'I heard him, Alan. But we need to talk about that another time.'

'How does this sound to you, Sir Alan?' said the archbishop, and he waved his hand to the small clerk, who rose to his feet and read out in a strong voice the following words, words I remember as clearly today as then, words I hope I shall never forget: 'No free man shall be seized or imprisoned, or stripped of his rights or possessions, or outlawed or exiled, or deprived of his standing in any way, nor will we proceed with force against him, or send others to do so, except by the lawful judgement of his equals or by the law of the land.'

'That will do fine,' I said, sniffling a little and wiping my face, for my eyes, unaccountably, seemed to be blurred with tears.

Chapter Thirty-two

The next few weeks were frantic. The archbishop's clerks wrote out the charter in fine Latin and copies were circulated to many of the most powerful men in England. The earls of Norfolk, Essex, Oxford, Hereford, Hertford, Albemarle and Winchester, dozens of lesser barons and hundreds of knights all received copies from Robin with notes inviting them to contribute to the clauses contained within it and to the wording of the document: the charter was loose in the kingdom, it was discussed, derided, dismissed, but very often lauded in knightly halls from Penzance to Penrith.

Not all the barons of England were in favour of it – and few would publicly state that they had joined Fitzwalter and de Vesci's party, who were openly defying the King's officers by this point. I personally delivered a copy of the charter to the Earl of Pembroke – and William the Marshal, that grizzled old warhorse, a man who I respected enormously, gave me an embarrassing public dressing down, accused me of disloyalty to our divinely anointed King, fomenting rebellion and civil war, and tore the document up in front of my face. Were it not for our long friendship I think he might have offered me harm, or tried to imprison me and deliver me to the King.

Indeed, England *was* on the lip of civil war: John had returned to England in mid-October with a substantial army of Poitevin and Flemish mercenaries – he no longer trusted even those English knights who had agreed to serve him – and these foreigners he installed as sheriffs, bailiffs and foresters in all the counties where he still held sway, with orders to raise as much money as they could by whatever means they saw fit. It was tantamount to a declaration of war on his own kingdom. These foreign sheriffs proved to be as ruthless as Philip Marc in the collection of taxes – and while they caused great hardship, they advanced our cause immeasurably.

Men from all over England were now writing to Robin and contributing clauses that they hoped to see included in the charter, and most were accepted and swiftly incorporated by the archbishop's clerks. But one article that was proposed proved to be more controversial.

Lord Fitzwalter had been invited to Kirkton for Christmas. His grand fortress in London, Baynard Castle, had been destroyed by the King two years before and, while he had some lands and a small wooden castle at Dunmow in Essex, he had been residing with de Vesci in Alnwick for some time now. I believe he had had his fill of the boorish lord of Alnwick and sought a respite, which is why he was welcomed at Kirkton for the Feast of Our Lord's Nativity.

One evening in mid-December, Robin and Fitzwalter were wrangling over the charter as usual, going into great detail on the changes to the law of scutage, when the subject of guarantees came up.

'Even if we can get John to agree to this charter, is there any guarantee that he will keep his word afterwards?' I said, not meaning to stir things up but in a spirit of genuine enquiry.

'He would be perjured and the whole country would know it,' said Fitzwalter. 'His authority would be utterly destroyed if he broke his word. He could not do it.'

Robin looked at me. I shrugged.

My lord said: 'Our experience of King John has been that his word of honour means next to nothing. I think Alan has a point here. We need some device to keep the King honest after he has agreed to the charter. Otherwise he is most likely to agree to it and then repudiate it whenever he feels like it.'

'What do you have in mind?' said Fitzwalter. 'How does one ensure that a dishonourable King keeps his sacred word?'

'I think if we appointed a council to oversee the King,' said Robin, 'say twenty-five powerful barons and senior churchmen whose task it was to ensure that the monarch kept to his agreement and who were empowered by law to seize the King's castles and lands if he broke his word . . . That might work.'

'A Great Council of barons, earls, bishops and abbots, eh?' said Fitzwalter. 'To meet regularly, discuss the issues of the day, advise the King and keep him in check. You mean what the French would call a "parliament".'

'You realise,' said Robin, 'that if we include this Great Council clause we make it that much less likely that John will agree to it.'

'We are going to have to put a knife to his throat to make him set his seal on it anyway,' said Fitzwalter. 'Why not put a Great Council in the charter. I think it is a splendid idea . . . Why are you both staring at me like that? I meant knife to his throat in the figurative sense. I didn't mean to actually put a knife at . . . unless, Alan, you feel strong enough . . .' He grinned at me.

'No,' I said. 'We are not going down that path again.'

'I was merely jesting, of course,' said Fitzwalter. 'But do not delude yourselves, my friends, that this can be done with fair words, flowers and kisses. The King must be brought to heel and compelled to set his seal on this charter. By force.'

*

The King refused absolutely to countenance the charter. A version of it – including Robin's Great Council idea – was dispatched to Windsor Castle at Christmas, with a letter from twenty principal rebel barons, most of them northerners, including, of course, Robin and my lords de Vesci and Fitzwalter, wishing the King joy of the season and inviting him to consider their demands for the sake of the country.

The refusal reached us at Kirkton in the last days of December. It said that the charter was totally unacceptable – a crime against the King's dignity, an affront to all the laws and customs of England – and it reminded all the noble participants of the document that they had done homage to the King and therefore owed him absolute loyalty. However, he also summoned the rebel barons, under a flag of truce guaranteed by William the Marshal and the Archbishop of Canterbury, to St Paul's Cathedral in London on the sixth day of January to discuss the matter. John was saying no, and at the same time hinting that maybe something might be managed.

I did not attend the meeting at St Paul's between the northern barons and the King for the very good reason that I was not invited. And, in the event, I was glad that I had not made the arduous journey to London and back in mid-winter, for Robin told me later that nothing at all was achieved.

In February, I returned to Westbury after my long stay at Kirkton with Robert, Thomas, Boot and Baldwin and a strong force of men-at-arms – a hundred men belonging to de Vesci, enough men to defy the sheriff indefinitely, if he should come for me. And a few weeks later, there were once more armed men outside my gates.

The Earl of Pembroke, William the Marshal himself, rode up to the gates of Westbury on a mild day in the middle of March. He came in peace, of that I was sure, for he brought with him only half a dozen men-at-arms, enough to see him safe on the roads. He also brought with him his almoner, Brother Geoffrey.

As it was one of the first days of sunshine since long before Christmas, I was sitting at a trestle table in my courtyard, allowing the slight warmth to bathe my pale skin, while the Westbury servants turned out the hall, swept out the floor rushes and the cobwebs, washed and dried all the crockery, pots and pans, laundered the linen, aired the blankets, flung open all the shutters and allowed fresh spring air to circulate and flush away the dense fug of winter. Twenty yards from me, Sir Thomas and Robert were halfway through their sword practice, going at it hammer and tongs right across the yard and back again.

I greeted the Earl with considerable warmth, for I was very fond of him despite the unpleasantness of our last meeting. Brother Geoffrey I greeted coolly and it seemed that we both tacitly agreed not to mention that encounter. Whether the Marshal knew or not what had occurred between the Templar and me in that cell in Nottingham last autumn, I did not discover, but the situation was very different now. I had my own men-at-arms around me and a hundred spearmen belonging to Lord de Vesci. There would be no hair-pulling this time, no threatening interrogation.

I served the Marshal and his almoner wine at the table while his men were fed and their horses watered and given hay across at the stables. I called Robert over to greet the Earl of Pembroke and was most irritated to see that he was unwilling to come to the table. In fact, one moment he was in the courtyard sparring with Thomas and the next he had completely disappeared. I sent Thomas to fetch him and told his tutor in no uncertain terms that I expected my son to behave with proper courtesy towards our noble guest. Robert's theft of a horse from the Marshal's stable and his desertion from his post still haunted my conscience.

After an awkward wait, Robert did eventually appear. He bowed low to the Earl and his almoner and made a stumbling apology for his past behaviour, and the Marshal graciously said it was no matter and all was forgiven. And then Robert begged to be released to continue his training session with Sir Thomas and I had little choice but to agree. We drank wine and nibbled sweetmeats and watched Robert and Thomas have at it in the courtyard – and though he had made considerable progress in the past few months under Thomas's careful instruction, that day, to my irritation, Robert was particularly clumsy, even dropping his sword at one point. The Earl of Pembroke watched this dispiriting display without comment and, after we had spoken of the weather and the state of the roads, the Marshal came to the nub of his business.

'It's this damned charter, Alan,' he said. 'It won't do, you know. The King will never agree to it, not in its present form. He must be free to raise taxes from his barons – how else can he fight his wars? – and he will not be governed by this devil-spawned Great Council. He must rule ungoverned – he is the King!'

'It was his ungoverned rule that brought us to this pass,' I said mildly.

'God's blood, Alan, how can you side with this contumelious rabble? I know your master, my lord of Locksley, is an outsider, an outlaw, a natural rebel, if you like. But he is also a man of honour, you and I both know that. Why he should ally himself with scum like de Vesci and Fitzwalter is beyond me.'

'He has served King John loyally, despite everything, and with scant reward for his steadfastness . . .'

'Is that what he wants? A reward? If he would come over to the King's side, renew his homage in public, I'm sure we could arrange something. And for you, too, that unpleasantness at St Paul's can be forgotten. You could have more lands, a shrievalty, perhaps a lordship . . .'

'This is unworthy of you, my lord, to come to us with bribes.'

For the first time in my life, I saw the Marshal look

abashed. His face flushed and he looked away. Brother Geoffrey said nothing. Then William said gruffly: 'I do not much relish the role of beggar man, Alan, but I must think of the kingdom. You and your rebels will tear England apart. If you will not be reasonable it will come to war, civil war, Englishman killing Englishman, brother at the throat of brother. The Anarchy all over again. Is that what you all want?'

'The King must be curbed,' I said. 'He cannot continue as he has in the past. You know as well as I how he behaves. No baron with any spirit can abide it any longer. You talk of civil war: it is the King who is forcing war upon the country.'

'There is no hope of reconciliation, then?'

'I do not believe so, my lord. It is the charter or nothing.'

The Earl of Pembroke let out a great sigh. 'I thought as much. But you will make the King's offer to my lord of Locksley? Tell him he can have anything, within reason, that his heart desires if he will help to end this foolishness.'

'I will tell him, but it will not change his mind.'

The Marshal nodded. He rose from his bench. 'I can at least do some good while I am here. I do not like to waste a journey.' He stomped across the courtyard, shouting: 'Robert Dale, you sir, you hold that sword as if it were a goose feather! You want to kill your opponent, not tickle him. Here, boy, let me show you . . .'

As I watched Robert cut and lunge against imaginary

opponents to the Marshal's jovial exhortations to strike harder, for the love of God, the Templar spoke for the first time.

'You think you are safe here, with all your men-at-arms. But you are not.'

'Really?' I said. 'I believe my life is safer than yours at this moment.'

The almoner glared at me.

'You see that big fellow over there,' I said, pointing at Boot, who was stacking heavy sacks of grain in the far corner of the courtyard.

'The black brute? What of him?'

'That is the fellow who was to execute me that last time we met,' I said. 'He would have snapped my neck like a chicken at the sheriff's command a few hours after you left me. Now he willingly serves me. And at my word he would end you without a moment's hesitation, if I but asked him.'

'You think I fear death? I serve God and the Knights of the Temple. I am protected in this life and the next. I have no fear of your threats,' he said. But I saw that his hand had strayed very close to his sword hilt and he was eyeing my huge friend with a good deal of trepidation.

'You miss my point, Templar. I make no threats to you. I only wish you to know that I too have powerful friends. And I make this promise to you. If you and your Order will leave me in peace, I will leave you unmolested too. But if not . . .'

'The Order will have the Grail from you. We shall not rest, I shall not rest, until we have recovered it.'

'What I told you last time is Gospel true,' I said. 'I give you my word. The Grail is gone. It is destroyed. It is no more.'

The Templar was staring fixedly at Thomas and Robert, who were standing side by side and watching the Marshal demonstrate a complicated hooking manoeuvre with the sword. 'Our informant,' he said, and he seemed almost involuntarily to jerk his chin at the three figures in the centre of the courtyard, 'has told us otherwise.'

Brother Geoffrey looked directly at me, his eyes seemed to burn with rage: 'Know this, Sir Alan, neither you nor your master shall have any peace until you deliver the true Grail into my hands. I give you my word on it.'

Chapter Thirty-three

The Marshal, Brother Geoffrey and their men left without staying for dinner. Which was just as well as I did not think I could be civil over bread and meat to the Templar after what had passed between us. The Earl of Pembroke jested that he had to hurry back to the King's side before he did anything foolish, but before they rode off he asked me once again to convey his message to Robin.

I set off for Kirkton the next day, alone, leaving Thomas in command of the garrison at Westbury with orders to double the guard until further notice. As it happened, I encountered Robin around noon a dozen miles south of Kirkton, marching on the road with a company of a hundred exhausted young recruits, breaking them in, as he called it, with the help of Hugh and Miles.

As his sons ordered a break from the march and oversaw the distribution of ale and bread to the men, I conferred with Robin at a little distance from the rest of the company. I did not want what I had to say to be overheard.

'The Marshal came to see me,' I told my lord.

He nodded as if he had expected this news. 'Did he have anything to say?'

'Not really – he was looking to woo us to the King's side by offering inducements, lands, titles. I told him we weren't interested. As we agreed, I said it must be the charter or nothing.'

'Well done, Alan,' said my lord, 'but why then did you charge all the way up here to see me?'

'The Earl of Pembroke brought his almoner with him.'

'The Templar? The fellow who thinks we have the Grail?'

'Yes – and he's not going to give up his conviction easily.'

'I am beginning to seriously dislike this fellow,' said Robin. 'He's the one who tells us we have an informer in our ranks, isn't he?'

'He says the informer told him we still have the Grail.'

Robin sighed. 'We need to talk about this, I suppose. You think the person who betrayed you to the King is the same as the man who spills our darkest secrets to the Templars. Is that right?' My lord did not sound convinced.

'It would make more sense. I cannot believe we have two traitors in our ranks,' I said.

'And who do you think this master of deception might be?'

I looked at the ground beneath our horses.

'You rode up here to tell me this, Alan, you must have someone in mind.'

'I think it is Sir Thomas Blood.'

It pained me to say the name. But Robin looked puzzled.

'Why Thomas?'

'Brother Geoffrey all but pointed him out to me and said he was his informant.'

'Really?'

'Well, he was looking at Thomas when he was speaking of his source, and he indicated him with his chin.'

Robin was silent for a while. 'I'm not sure, Alan. It doesn't feel right. The Templar could be trying to misdirect us. I can't see why Thomas would do it.'

'For the most common reason there is: for money. Thomas loves to game, as you know, he plays knucklebones and he has debts – he owes the Templars a great deal of money. He might well have traded information for a remission of his debts.'

'Do you think he would do that?' said Robin, still looking doubtful.

'Remember his father? A Welshman hired to kill you back, oh, more than twenty years ago. He was in the pay of Ralph Murdac and came into your solar at night and I killed him in the dark. Could you forgive the man who killed your father? I couldn't.'

461

'But Thomas has always been the very model of loyalty. He has never once been anything less. I cannot believe it.'

'Thomas was with us at Montségur, he must have known about the false Grail and the trick we played on the Templars of Toulouse. He was at Westbury when I went to Alnwick to plot with de Vesci and Fitzwalter, and still there when I went to St Paul's to make my attempt on the King. In fact, he saw me practising with the misericorde days beforehand.'

'I cannot imagine Thomas doing that,' said Robin. 'Not Thomas. I'm sorry, but I cannot believe he means us harm.'

'Who else could it be?'

'Oh, Alan, it could be any number of people – a lot of folk could know about the Grail. How many men did we ride away from Montségur with – five, six, was it seven? One of them could have known about the switch and told a legion of friends – I can imagine old Claes, in his cups, regaling a tavern full of people about how he fooled the noble Order of the Temple, making his cronies laugh like donkeys. I did not expect it to remain a secret for this long. As for the person who betrayed your plot to the King – I would look to de Vesci and his people in Alnwick. Even if it was not the fellow they caught and tortured to death, King John could well have other spies in their camp. I truly think you have it wrong.'

I was silent for a moment. Perhaps Robin was right

and I was wrong. Was Thomas a good and loyal friend? Was I maligning an innocent man?

'This is the problem with traitors,' said Robin. 'We've had a few in our ranks over the years – I know that – but one can become over-suspicious, distrusting the innocent as well as the guilty. Do not say anything to Thomas, Alan, I beg you. Let us watch, see if we can catch him out. But don't do anything rash.'

On my return to Westbury, I watched Sir Thomas Blood day and night and I could see nothing suspicious in his demeanour. He trained with Robert every day, and whereas my boy had once hated him, it was clear that his emotion had been transformed into something close to adulation. The two of them were now close and even when they were not training, they seemed to spend a good deal of time together talking about tactics and strategy. Thomas's behaviour was always impeccable. He was liked by everyone at Westbury. It seemed that he had even turned over a new leaf.

'Sir Alan,' he said to me one day, when I was sitting in the courtyard after breakfast with my eyes closed taking some sun. 'Forgive my intrusion.'

If I am honest, I must admit that I had been taking a short nap. I opened my eyes and saw Thomas standing before me with a pretty young girl of about twenty summers. She curtseyed prettily and I lumbered to my feet to greet her.

'This is Mary,' said Thomas. 'She is Athelstan's daughter, from the village. And she has kindly agreed to become my betrothed in the summer. But we would both very much like your blessing on our union.'

'Mary, daughter of Athelstan, of course,' I said. 'My hearty congratulations to you both. And, of course, you have my blessing!'

'Don't you worry, sir, I'll look after him properly,' said Mary. And I noticed that her belly was a good deal rounder than a twenty-year-old farm girl's should be.

'It seems you will have more responsibilities soon, Thomas,' I said.

Thomas smiled. 'I'm ready for them, sir,' he said. 'Mary has made a new man of me – she has even convinced me to forsake the bones. I've made her a solemn vow on my honour. No more gaming.'

I believed him. I think it was his simple joy and evident love for Mary that convinced me that I had indeed been wrong about him. No man that transparently happy could have such a duplicitous heart. Robin was right. He was not the traitor – and I felt very relieved that I had not confronted him with my suspicions.

In early April, at dusk, Robin came to Westbury with Miles and Hugh. While the young men went off in great high spirits to drink ale in the pantry and make their boyish jests together, Robin and I took a sober cup of watered wine and repaired to the hall to talk.

But the first thing Robin said set me laughing like a loon.

'King John has taken the cross,' said my lord. 'He has vowed to ride to the Holy Land and free Jerusalem from the Saracens.'

'Oh, that is a good one,' I said, wiping tears of mirth from my eyes. 'King John as a warrior pilgrim! Tell me another.'

'It is quite true, Alan,' said Robin, but he too was smiling.

'If the Lionheart could not do it, I cannot imagine John managing that impossible feat,' I said. 'Besides, who would go with him? He can barely get his knights to fight for him on the other side of the Channel. Is he planning to go all that way on his own, carrying his own weapons and kit? Ha-ha!'

'Oh, I doubt there is anyone in England who thinks he will achieve it, but it is a clever move. As a holy pilgrim he comes under the protection of the Church.'

'Oh, yes,' I said, suddenly understanding. 'It means that if we attack him we are attacking the Church, attacking God, in effect.'

'Exactly,' said Robin. 'The Pope is now his strongest supporter.'

'So what does that mean for us, for the charter?'

'Well, your friend Fitzwalter is a clever fellow, I'll grant him that. He says if John is on the side of the angels, then we must be too. We must be at least as holy or even holier than him. He is marching south now with de Vesci and a dozen other northern barons – and he is calling his forces the Army of God. He proclaims our cause as the cause of the Church, too, as we are fighting for the liberties of the English Church. If John wants to play the pious zealot, we must play the same game.'

I recalled Archbishop Langton's insistence that the first clause of the charter of liberties should be a call for a free English Church, and remembered also my distinct feeling that the great prelate, Robin and Fitzwalter had been planning this long before our supposedly accidental meeting in Alnwick.

'So we are truly on the march, then?' I said.

'We muster at Brackley,' said Robin, 'in two weeks' time.'

The Army of God, which gathered in the last week of April at Brackley, about twenty miles south of Northampton, was a good deal less impressive than its name. Robin brought as many men as he could spare from the defence of Kirkton, some forty men-at-arms on foot and a dozen of them mounted. I brought de Vesci's borrowed men-at-arms south with me, returning them reluctantly to their rightful master, but that meant I was forced to leave a garrison of my own folk with Baldwin at Westbury and in the end all I could contribute to the Army of God was half a dozen men-at-arms and one knight – Sir Thomas Blood. Robert Fitzwalter's men – including Lord de Vesci's cavalry and contingents from other barons including the earls of Winchester and Essex and the Bishop of Hereford – numbered fewer than a thousand.

It was not much of an army with which to challenge a King.

However, when I voiced my concerns to Robin he seemed unworried. 'This will be all about momentum,' he said. 'Most of the barons of England support our cause, and will swiftly come to our banner if we are successful. But for the moment they are biding their time, waiting on the side of the battlefield to see who proves the strongest – us or the King. No baron wants to be on the losing side. We have to show them we can win. If we can take one or two royal strongholds, the lords will declare for us, you'll see.'

I also brought Robert and Boot with me to Brackley. I had heard nothing from Benedict Malet or Philip Marc, since my escape, but it seemed foolhardy to leave my son alone in Nottinghamshire with only a handful of men-at-arms to guard him. He would be safer with the Army of God. Boot watched over Robert while he was with the army like a mother hen, but my boy also spent a good deal of time with Miles and Hugh. I even came back to our tent one evening to find him playing chess with Robin.

'Your boy has an extraordinary mind,' Robin told me afterwards. 'I thought I was humouring the lad by playing a game with him and he destroyed me in a dozen moves.

He also has some very bold ideas about what this army should do. Even more surprisingly, I find myself absolutely agreeing with him.'

The castle of Brackley, a wooden motte-and-bailey fortress on a limestone knoll to the south-west of the town, was not spacious. The Earl of Winchester, whose castle it was, and his men were housed there with Fitzwalter, who was now grandly calling himself the Marshal of the Army of God, but the rest of us had to find accommodation in the town or encamped in the wide fields around it. The place had been famous for tournaments in King Richard's day, but to be truthful it had become something of a dismal backwater. And, as I recall, it seemed to rain hard continually for the whole time we were there.

On the third day, all the leaders of the Army of God were summoned to council in the hall of the castle and the collection of bedraggled knights, their cloaks sodden, and honking and sneezing from a cold that had already spread through the ranks from the grandest earl to the meanest churl, was less than awe-inspiring.

The King was at Oxford with a strong force of merce-naries and his half-brother the Earl of Salisbury, and a message had been sent to the King – an ultimatum, in effect – saying that unless he were to agree to the terms of the charter of liberties then the rebel barons would renounce their homage to him and a state of war would exist between the two sides. While we waited for his reply, the question on everybody's lips was: what should we do next? There were other groups of rebel barons in arms near Exeter and Lincoln, but the feeling was that it was up to the leaders of this water-logged rebellion to make a significant move. But what?

Geoffrey Mandeville, the Earl of Essex, was the first to speak at the council. He was a portly toad-like man with fat dewlaps that jiggled on either side of his chin as he spoke. But his tone was bold and he was clear in his mind what was necessary.

'We must confront the King at Oxford – get right up to the walls and show him our strength. He's a coward and he will be put in fear if we confront him boldly.'

I applauded his words but I was one of only a few. The rest of the barons muttered and mumbled and blew their noses noisily.

Lord de Vesci said: 'Utter nonsense, Mandeville, the King is far too powerful. Quite apart from his mercenaries – who alone outnumber us two to one – Oxford is a nest of royalists and a well-fortified and provisioned city. We have no hope of taking the place by force, nor of reducing it by siege. We have no siege train, for one thing. Not a single trebuchet or mangonel to bless ourselves with. We could find ourselves uselessly camped outside his walls for months. Then we would have to march away with our tails between our legs. We would look ridiculous.'

'We will look ridiculous if we do nothing and stay here,' replied Essex with a good deal of spirit. 'Half my men are already sick, by God, and sleeping in damp fields is not going to improve their lot.' But it was clear that the general opinion was against him and thereafter he remained silent.

'I'm sorry you don't like my hospitality,' snapped the Earl of Winchester. 'Perhaps you would prefer to leave my lands—'

'My lords, quiet, if you please,' said Fitzwalter. 'We need to come up with a plan, not squabble like infants. Does anyone have any other useful suggestions?'

'We put our trust in God,' said the Bishop of Hereford, folding his hands before him in the attitude of prayer. 'He is mightier than all the armies of the world, and the Lord of Hosts will deliver us from this tyrant – if it is His will.'

'Well, while the Almighty is making up his mind,' said de Vesci nastily, 'what shall we humble mortals actually do?'

Lord Bedford rose timidly to his feet. 'If you do not care for Brackley, I would willingly offer you my castle as a refuge – it is somewhat larger than this place and I have a dozen barracks for your men. Plenty of dry straw for all—'

Robin cut him off: 'It is perfectly clear what we must do – to me at least and to some of the younger men in our ranks.' He shot me a knowing wink.

'Yes, Locksley?' said Fitzwalter. 'What do you suggest?'

'We will win this contest only by a bold stroke. Only

by taking the bull by the horns will we persuade the undecided barons of England to rally to our cause. We must attack, we must win and we must do it quickly.'

'You would attack Oxford and the King there?' said Fitzwalter, frowning. 'That seems absurdly rash. I thought we were all agreed that—'

'Not Oxford,' said my lord, 'but London.'

There was a general gasp from the twenty or so men in the hall and immediately a hubbub of shouting, frightened voices. 'Outrageous!' 'Absurd!' 'We simply don't have the strength . . .'

Robin smiled serenely until the noise fell away and then said: 'Think on this, gentlemen: London is the richest, the most important city in England – a good deal of the King's governance takes place there. The merchants of the city are some of the greatest men in the country, richer even than the mightiest earl, saving your presence, Essex. The wealth of the nation's commerce is there. It is the beating heart of England.'

He quietened the rising tide of voices with an outstretched hand. 'My lords, I know it will be a hard task, but think: if we have London within our grasp, we hold the country too. If London is ours, the King cannot hold out; he must accede to our wishes. If we have London, we have the King in the palm of our hands.'

Even I was a little shocked by the boldness of Robin's plan. We had fewer than a thousand men – there was no way on earth we could capture a city with fifty times that

471

number of citizens. It was stronger than Oxford by far. And if we could not take Oxford . . . I wondered if Robin was truly serious. Was he playing some game?

If Robin was playing a game, I judged that he had lost. For the men in that room shook their heads, snuffled, coughed and quibbled. They muttered that he was deluded. They said he was courting destruction. The Earl of Winchester asked if he was drunk. 'It's young Robert's idea,' Robin murmured to me. 'A very good one.'

Fitzwalter quelled the agitated crowd of damp barons.

'I am the Marshal of this Army of God, and since quite clearly we cannot decide among us what we should do, it falls to me to make the decision. We shall not attack London, thank you, Locksley, we shall not beset the King at Oxford, but we shall strike. And hard. Northampton, not twenty miles from here, is held by no lord or earl but merely by a rabble of mercenaries under a French rascal named Geoffrey de Martigny. He's a paid man, his loyalty is to silver, let us go there and see if we cannot change his allegiance with a show of force.'

And so we marched to war.

Chapter Thirty-four

I had been a mercenary several times and so, for that matter, had Robin. And I knew well the contempt in which many noblemen held a *stipendarius*. But it still surprised me just how mutton-headed a proud knight can be, for clearly there are mercenaries and there are mercenaries – and the better ones, the ones that last in the profession, are as true as steel once they have taken their pay. It is a matter of honour. And any man who thinks that a mercenary has no honour is a fool or else he has never fought a proper war. Geoffrey de Martigny was as loyal to King John as any man – more loyal, indeed, than many of the well-born men who camped outside his castle, for they had taken oaths to King John and were now in arms against him.

Martigny shut tight his gates, lined the walls of Northampton Castle with a hundred crossbowmen and defied us. And for all that Fitzwalter had taken a necessarily bold decision in leading us here, it was in truth a sad mistake.

We were two weeks before the walls of Northampton, two dismal weeks of squabbling, humiliation and soggy discomfort. Fitzwalter and the leading nobles rode up to the gates of Northampton Castle in driving rain and demanded its surrender. Geoffrey de Martigny, in very bad English, told them that he held the castle by order of the King and he would surrender it only to him, and so the Army of God settled down outside the walls in the vague hope that the mercenary would change his mind.

He did not. And lacking the proper siege engines we could not hope to reduce this powerful fortress. I had truly forgiven Fitzwalter for embroiling me in his plot to kill the King, and I had grown to like, if not wholly trust him since our meeting at Alnwick before Christmas. But while he was undoubtedly skilled at cajoling and manipulating men into following his desires, he was far from a gifted general.

After a week of sitting before the walls, the Earl of Essex volunteered his men for an assault on the gatehouse. And the Earl of Locksley's men were to go in as the second wave in support of the Mandeville forces. We built ladders in the shadow of the towers, occasionally troubled by the crossbowmen taking long shots at us, but there was little blood spilt.

As the Earl of Essex's men lined up for their assault, the foremost men-at-arms carrying the long ladders we had built, I experienced once more the crippling terror of an impending battle. My mouth was dry as sand, my limbs trembled, and though I had made sure my bladder was empty before donning a suit of mail, I felt the desperate urge to urinate. We were formed up – fifty men armed with shield and sword – behind the block of a hundred or so Essex troops who would lead the charge. I thought I was going to vomit. What was the delay? I could barely stand it. If we were going to do this we must go now. I could see the mercenaries on the walls, their heads thick as blackberries behind the crenellations, waiting with their crossbows spanned, waiting to pluck our lives from us. We would all surely die – and for what? To take a castle that would make no difference to the war in the slightest? If we were successful – and I very much doubted that we would be – it would not force King John to agree to our demands. He would have lost a few mercenaries and one town. If we failed, even if we were not killed, we'd be finished. It was madness.

I looked to my right and there was Robin, conferring with Sir Thomas; to my left Miles and Hugh were talking quietly with their men. And I felt a sudden sense that something was wrong; something vital was missing.

And then it struck me. The massive form and ugly

battered red face of Little John was nowhere to be seen. His body was now lying in the earth of St Michael's churchyard in Hathersage, slowly turning to earth itself. My huge friend, who had always had some filthy, funny, bellicose comment to make on the eve of battle, was nowhere to be seen. And it occurred to me that his sacrifice at Bouvines, which had allowed Robin, Miles and Hugh to live, was all for naught. We would fight again and again until we were all in our graves. I missed the crude old bugger, how I missed his solid comforting presence on the eve of action. His absence was an ache in my heart.

Good God, I said to myself, what is this, Alan? Whimpering before action? You are a fraudulent knight! You may no longer boast of being a warrior. You are craven.

In the event, I played no part at all in the fighting that day. Thanks be to God. Robin held us back in reserve while Essex's men charged bravely forward with their ladders. The Mandeville men began to die before they had taken a dozen steps, sliced down by the wicked crossbow quarrels that came at them like black lightning. Three or four of the ladders actually made it to the walls, but the men climbing them were smashed away by chunks of stone hurled from the ramparts or skewered by javelins. It was clear within the time it takes to say an Our Father that the attack would fail. No ladders were up against the walls and Essex's poor men milled like frightened sheep below the gatehouse – and died like them too, in their scores. And to my utmost relief, Robin did not order us forward to join the crowd of staggering, falling men.

There was anger at the council that night. The Earl of Essex, his toad-like face purple with rage, accused everyone and anyone of cowardice and treachery. But Robin, who had come in for the worst of his tirade, merely said calmly: 'You do not reinforce failure. The attack had failed and I saw no reason to sacrifice my men's lives when there was no longer any chance of success.'

There was more uproar at that, but Fitzwalter checked it by shouting for silence repeatedly until the large pavilion in which we were meeting was a little quieter.

'My lords,' Fitzwalter said, 'I have news from Oxford.'

That silenced them.

'The King rejects our demands and denounces the charter as an abomination against God and his own sacred person.'

The crowd of barons muttered and groaned.

'This should come as no surprise; for we surely have not intimidated him with our prowess. The question remains, my lords: what shall we do?'

'You tell us – as you seem to have all the answers,' said Essex angrily.

'Very well. I say in for a penny, in for a pound. If we quit now, John will hunt us down individually and make us pay for our disloyalty – we will all die or, worse, be imprisoned for life and our lands will be forfeit and our heirs made destitute.'

'That's a cheery thought,' said the young knight beside me. I turned to look and recognised John de Lacy, the son of Roger, the man who had so bravely defended Château Gaillard a decade ago. Bull-headed Roger was now dead and this callow stripling held his lands and titles. God help us all, I thought.

'I say we make our message to the King as clear as crystal,' said Fitzwalter. 'We sign a document today, now even, that utterly renounces our allegiance to the King. We make the *diffidato*, stating that we no longer consider that we owe homage for our lands to the King.'

There was a stunned silence. 'You go too far, sir,' said the Earl of Winchester. 'We are in dispute with John, for sure, but he is still the rightful King.'

'What difference does it make?' said Robin. 'We are already beyond the pale. I agree with Fitzwalter. I say we make the *diffidato* today and cut our ties with John.'

I was a little surprised by Robin's stance; he had always made it a point of honour to keep to his oaths, but the general consensus was with Fitzwalter, and while we were waiting for the clerks to draw up the legal document I cornered my lord and asked if he really thought this was wise.

'We are outlaws again, Alan,' said my lord. 'We have been since we marched south in arms against John. I do not like to break my oath, but there comes a point when to continue to pretend to honour it becomes absurd. I feel that we have been more than patient with John – he could have met us to discuss the charter, to discuss the grievances of the country at any time, but he has refused us again and again. And this is John! He is not a man who honours *his* oaths. What was it you used to ask me in Normandy? It used to aggravate me beyond measure: Oh yes, "Why do we serve this King?" That's what you used to say. Well, from this day forward, Alan, we do not.'

In the second week of May we left Northampton, defeated, dispirited and with our strength ebbing away. The King had responded swiftly to our declaration of *diffidato*. He had not been even slightly perturbed by it, instead he had issued a general proclamation that the lands of all the rebels were now forfeit by royal command and any sheriff who so desired could seize them and any property they contained. A goodly number of knights and barons, on hearing the King's response, began slipping away from the so-called Army of God, many returning to their lands to gather provisions and fortify their castles. And John had gone further, he had announced generous grants of land to those barons who were wavering – bribes, in effect – to prevent them from joining our cause. It was a strategy that I had heard Robin call the stick and the carrot. For my part, I was filled with a sense of fear and dread as we tramped the twenty-odd miles to Bedford – we had decided

479

to take up the lord of that castle's offer of dry accommodation – for I realised that Westbury was now more than ever open to attack by the sheriff's men and Baldwin and a handful of men-at-arms would never keep out a determined assault. At least, Robert was with me. And for that I gave thanks to God.

After I had settled Boot and my son and my few men-at-arms in a snug hay barn just outside the town, I went in search of my lord inside the castle. Instead, I found Hugh in the vast inner bailey deeply involved in arranging food and beds for his exhausted men. He seemed to have little time for me.

'Where is your father?' I asked him.

'He's gone,' said Hugh.

'What?' I said. 'Where has he gone?'

'I don't know where he is, Alan, truly, I don't. Father told me only that he had an errand to make and that it would take a week or so and that I was to take command of the men until he returned. He didn't say where he was going, but he has left me with a great deal to do – so, if you don't mind, I am rather busy just now . . .'

I stumbled away in a sort of daze. What errand could be so important that it took Robin away from his men on the eve of battle, away from his sons?

I had absolutely no idea.

Robin was not the only man to desert the Army of God. Over the next few days at least half its numbers melted away as men fled back to defend their homes against their local sheriffs. I could hardly blame them – the King's vigorous response to the *diffidato* made every man of property vulnerable and, in my weaker moments, I even contemplated abandoning our cause and returning to Westbury myself. It seemed in those dark days that the flame of rebellion was guttering like a candle by an open shutter. King John, without doing anything much at all, had won – or so it seemed to me. I wondered if we had not made the greatest blunder of our lives in challenging him. His vengeance would be swift and merciless when the army was no more.

Then, as suddenly as he had disappeared, Robin returned. I found him one drizzly afternoon in the hall of Bedford Castle at a long table in conference with lords De Vesci, Fitzwalter and their host. The mood was black gloom and our defeat filled the air above their heads like a fine grey cloud. I came and stood behind my lord as he sat on a bench opposite the other lords and waited for him to notice me.

De Vesci was saying: '. . . and if we go now, and retreat to Alnwick, we can hold out against the King for a year or more. My Scottish kin will come to my aid, we can recruit more men, regroup . . .' He tailed off.

'You would abandon me here alone to face the King's wrath?' quavered Lord Bedford, clearly appalled at the prospect. 'I have fed you all these past days with no stinting, and this is how you repay me?'

481

'If we run back north, it is over,' said Fitzwalter. He seemed more angry than afeared. 'The rebellion is ended and our lives and lands are all forfeit sooner or later. Sooner, probably. There is still a chance that, if we hold on here, the other barons will come to our aid. They must want to see the charter sealed as much as we do.'

'The other barons will not come to us,' said Robin.

'Thank you, Locksley, that is most helpful,' said Fitzwalter. 'I suppose we must be grateful that you have condescended to return to us.'

'I say what I have always said – that the barons will not come to our aid, unless we show them that we can win. And, as I have always maintained, that will require a stroke of boldness.'

'But what can we do?' said Bedford. 'Every day more and more men desert in the night. They creep away like mice. We are weaker now than we have ever been.'

'That is why we must act now,' said Robin. 'We can have no more delays.'

'What would you have us do, my lord?' said Fitzwalter.

'I say we take London – and we take it now.'

Robin's words were met with a stunned silence. Then a tumult of angry words.

'Have you not listened to a word we have said? We have not the strength to take a well-defended pig-pen at present!' Fitzwalter was on his feet, his face beetroot red.

'But we can take London,' my lord said calmly. 'London

is rotten-ripe and ready to fall. I have spent the past few days there in consultation with my friends – and some of yours too, Fitzwalter. The merchants are with us – the money men want the charter of liberties and they are not afraid of the King. The Church, too, will not stand against us – my lord the Archbishop of Canterbury has seen to that. My cousin Henry has been working to this end for months and we have agreement with the guilds of the City, with the merchant princes and the bishops. If we can take the walls of London, they will rise against King John's garrisons across the city. London is ready to fall, I say. All we have to do is find the courage, the strength of mind to take it.'

'You are mad, sir! We have fewer than four hundred men,' said de Vesci.

'I could take London with twenty men,' said Robin. 'Sir Alan here could take it with a dozen.'

This was news to me, but I kept my mouth shut. So did the other men at the table – but out of sheer disbelieving outrage. Fitzwalter sat down again wearily.

'Listen to me. The key is Newgate,' said my lord. 'We don't need to fight all along the city walls, we don't need to take the Tower – all we need to do is take Newgate, one small unsuspecting bastion, and get the gates open in good time, then the rest of the army can ride right in across the bridge. Once inside, the city will rise – and London is ours. They are not expecting us. It must seem like an act of gross folly for us in our weakened state to attempt to seize the biggest prize in the land. But it is not folly. We can do this – and, if we do, at one stroke we will have won this war. The barons will come to us – almost all of them, I am sure of it. And then King John must capitulate and set his seal on the charter. All I ask is that we make one bold stroke, gentlemen, one bold stroke for victory. Are you with me?'

Fitzwalter began to laugh. A bubbling effusion of merriment, he clasped his belly and roared, tears streaming down his red face.

Robin gave him an icy stare. 'You find this amusing,' he said.

'No, no,' spluttered Fitzwalter. 'You are a devil when it comes to making fine speeches, Locksley – but I am with you. I am most certainly with you. What choice do we have but to accept this moon-crazed plan? There is no other course open to us. One bold stroke for victory!'

Three days later, at dusk, on the ides of May, Robin and I were in the chapter house of St John's Priory in Clerkenwell, half a mile outside the city of London. Some forty Kirkton men, mostly archers, and my handful of Westbury men-at-arms were waiting outside in the courtyard preparing themselves for battle in a variety of ways. The chosen men were blackening their faces with soot and goose fat, the bowmen were checking bow-cord and shafts, swords and daggers were being given one final sharpening. Robert had been sent to bed in the Prior's guest house. He had protested that after all his training with Thomas he was now ready for battle, but I had resolutely ignored his pleas. There was no need to risk his life along with my own. The Army of God was about several miles behind us, straggling along Watling Street in the line of march, and expected to arrive at the walls of the city by dawn; indeed, Fitzwalter had given Robin an undertaking that he and the whole army would be outside Newgate before the sun rose. The Prior of St John's had set out food and drink for Robin's men from the refectory and then had retired to his bed. But Henry Odo had been waiting there for our arrival. He was the bearer of bad tidings.

'The Earl of Salisbury is on the march,' he said in a breathless voice. 'The King's brother is coming to London with a force of mercenaries several thousand strong aiming to fortify the city and deny it to you. He is only a day's ride away.'

'Then we still have time,' said Robin. 'It will be tight, but we can do it if we go tonight. We must get Fitzwalter's men inside London by tomorrow morning or he will be cut to pieces on the road and that will be the end of all of us.'

'I have more bad news,' said Henry, as he waved over a young monk who was bearing a tray of cups of wine. 'The King's constable has reinforced all the gates of London, doubled the guard. I believe word of your plan has leaked out to the enemy.'

Brother Geoffrey's informant! Could this be his work? It would appear so. I had not done near enough thinking on this problem in recent days, not since suspecting my loyal friend Thomas and then deciding that it could not be him. But, as often happens to me, I found that not looking squarely at a problem allows the mind to come at it in other ways. I felt sure that Brother Geoffrey himself had given me sufficient information to work out who the informant must be. I was sure that there was something that he had said to me in that dank cell in Nottingham or at our meeting with the Marshal at Westbury that was of significance, but I could not put my finger on it exactly. No, it would not come, not while Cousin Henry and Robin were still disputing the attack on Newgate.

'I must advise, my lord, against making this stroke,' Cousin Henry was saying.

'No. We can still do it. We must do it,' said Robin.

We left the priory at midnight on foot. A sickle moon in a cloudless sky gave us light enough to see by – but also enough for the enemy to see us. Robin had persuaded me that a small stealthy force would stand a better chance of getting over the walls without raising the alarm, but I felt sick and shaky at the very thought of what we were about to attempt. He said that twelve men was the largest number that could make the assault but they would be supported as best they could by our archers from outside the walls, and stressed the importance of the gates: they must be opened by dawn so the Army of God could ride into the city. All other considerations were secondary.

We approached the huge bulk of Newgate, two massive square towers beside the double-doored gate, linked by a stone platform over the entrance and with walls three times the height of a man stretching away into the darkness on either side, and I felt the first now-familiar crushing sense of my cowardly fears. The gate loomed above me, thirty yards away, a stronghold packed with hundreds of men-at-arms, and my lord was asking me to assault it with a scant handful of comrades. I was battling a desperate urge to run. To flee from my friends and comrades and run blindly back into the countryside behind me. To run for ever, forgoing all responsibilities and debts of honour. To run until I could find some lonely corner of England where I could at last be safe and alone with my shame.

We stopped on the far side of a shallow, foul-smelling moat, in a sad huddle of ramshackle dwellings and workshops outside the walls – for the city had burst its bounds even then – and crouched down in the shadow of the old stone bridge. The moat had once been a formidable barrier, but over the centuries it had become filled with all the refuse of a vast city, and now it was a midden of noisome sludge only a foot or so deep. I could see the helmet of a single man-at-arms high above me, moving along the wall to the left of the gatehouse, and the glow of a brazier where the wall met the tower, but as far as I knew we had not yet been detected.

Behind me I heard Robin ordering the dispersal of his archers, each man taking up a position out of sight in the lee of a shack or craftsman's forge, or behind a bush or one of the few trees that had not been felled for firewood. The wide highway of Watling Street led arrow-straight away into the darkness behind us.

'Make ready,' hissed Robin. I began to unwind the bulky knotted rope that was wrapped around my torso, with three stout iron hooks welded together and attached to one end. My hands were shaking so badly that I could barely untangle the rope from the shield strapped to my back. I had never had the fear this badly before. I could barely control my body at all. Beside me, on my right, was Thomas, calm and cool. He saw I was in difficulties and deftly slipped the rope from my shoulders.

I found I was murmuring a prayer to St Michael, my protector, but in my heart I was screaming: 'God, have mercy on me and preserve my miserable skin this night. I beg you. Let me not be slain or maimed or put in unendurable pain and I will give you anything you require, my chastity, my lifelong devotion, anything.'

My whole body ached; I shivered, my legs quaked. A voice inside me was screaming: 'Run, run for your life.' It took all my strength just to stand there, waiting, waiting for the order to die. I thought I would vomit at any

488

minute; I felt a spurt of thick urine warm my legs and dribble stickily inside my mail-clad thighs.

On my left was a massive, dark presence and in my confusion I imagined that it must be Little John beside me. I think I must have been out of my senses with fear by then, for John spoke to me. I heard his deep familiar voice as clear as a church bell:

'Live, Alan, live like a man – until you die.'

And suddenly I was calm. Just like that. I felt as if the endless strength of my huge friend, or perhaps his indomitable spirit, had entered my chest and belly like a solid fire. My torso felt strangely warm, hot even. I looked down at my hands and saw that the trembling had completely stopped. My vision seemed clearer, my limbs seemed to glow with renewed strength, my legs were springier, my arms more powerful. My heart was light and free of fear. I breathed in deeply and the night air on my tongue tasted as delicious as a clear mountain stream. I felt I could conquer armies single-handed. It was nothing short of miraculous. Little John had told me that Gavin had spoken to him on the eve of our defeat at Bouvines and I had not believed him, but here, now, John himself was with me, giving me courage from beyond the grave.

I turned to my left to the vast dark shape to thank John for his wonderful gift, the gift of courage, and I saw in the moonlight that it was only Boot, a long, knotted club in his hands, looking down on me with a strange perplexed expression.

I made one more brief, silent prayer for the soul of my dear friend.

'Time to go,' Robin said in my ear.

'Yes,' I said, 'it is time. It is high time.' And I launched myself eagerly forward – into the bloody fire of battle.

Chapter Thirty-five

We ran, all twelve of us, with the ropes in our hands, splashing through the stinking sludge of the moat and up the other side. I looked up at the walls towering above me but there was no sign of the sentry I had seen before. It was well past midnight in the long lonely hours before dawn and I would not have been surprised if the sentry had found himself a quiet corner for a sit-down and maybe a snooze. I swung my hooks briefly in a circle and hurled them towards the top of the wall. Beside me I was aware of Thomas doing the same thing and further along Robin and a knot of Kirkton men swinging their iron hooks and letting fly. My hook bit into the top of the parapet with a dull metallic clang. And I was climbing like a monkey, buoyed up by a glowing strength from beyond the grave.

I was only halfway up the rope, my arm muscles aching, when I heard a loud shout of alarm from above and a surprised face under a broad helmet peered over the parapet and straight down at my climbing form.

The sentry had not been as vigilant as he might have been, but he had not been asleep at his post. He was three feet above me, shouting: 'To arms, to arms!' and I saw a blade flash in the moonlight – he aimed to cut my rope and send me tumbling to earth.

An arrow flashed through the air and smashed into the sentry's cheek, and the face above me was jerked away. I gave a final heave and rolled over the top of the parapet, the first man there. I hauled out Fidelity – and just in time. A second sentry rushed at me along the walkway on the inside of the parapet, a spear in his hands. He stopped out of range of my blade and poked at me with the spear. I seized the wooden shaft of the weapon and hauled forward; the man came staggering towards me and I crunched Fidelity into his upper left arm. The blade was kept from his flesh by his mail but I felt bone crack and he screamed like a woman in childbirth.

I stepped in and punched Fidelity's hilt into his face, knocking him backwards into empty air, and he fell kicking wildly and his back slapped on to the paving stones of the courtyard eighteen feet below. I paused for a moment to get my shield off my back and my left arm through the slings; my skin was burning, my heart galloping, a wild reckless joy running like white lightning through my veins.

An arched door at the end of the walkway, where the wall met the north tower, was swinging open and I saw half a dozen heads peering out. I snatched a glance behind me; there was Thomas, drawn sword in hand, and beyond him Boot, scowling like a fiend with a huge wooden club held across his chest. And beyond them Robin with two of his men. My friends were all with me. Little John was with me.

The enemy were now spilling out of the door and advancing along the walkway to me. The time for silence was over; the alarm had been raised all through Newgate. But I did not care a jot – I was lifted on the wings of battle. I roared: 'Westbury!' and charged straight into the pack of enemy men-at-arms by the tower.

The spirit of my friend possessed me bone and blood. I felt invulnerable, as mighty as a mountain and without the slightest shred of apprehension. I bowled into the men at the tower door, chopping my enemies down with Fidelity, punching them away with my shield; my blade was faster than a striking adder, more powerful than a thunderbolt – I burst through the half a dozen men cowering there, reaping lives like Death himself. Boot was at my back, swiping any man who escaped past me with his club, smashing skulls apart like rotten apples, and in one brief instant between the furious clash of steel and thump of metal on wood and the screaming of men, in one brief window of quiet, I realised that the big dark man was singing.

He was singing 'My Joy Summons Me'.

The enemy were running before my onslaught. Thomas was at my side now, cutting and lunging. The press of men fell away, scurrying down the spiral stairs of the tower, and Robin was shouting: 'The gates, Alan, make for the gates.'

I tumbled down the stairs after the fleeing foe, Thomas and Robin behind me, Boot behind them, his singing echoing like church music in the enclosed space of the stone spiral staircase. We shot out of the base of the tower and pulled up short – a score of men-at-arms and a pair of knights were formed up in the courtyard in a double line, rubbing sleep from their eyes, some still yawning, but armed and ready for battle.

I did not halt for an instant. I bellowed my war cry and charged them, throwing myself at the centre of their line, Fidelity swinging, a blurring silver streak. I chopped into the shoulder of one man-at-arms and he fell screaming at my feet. I lifted my shield high and took a sword-blow safely on the oak-rim. I felt a spear slide under the shield and punch through my mail at my waist. I had no sensation of pain. Just a feeling of a hard blow against my lowest ribs on the left. I surged forward, slicing my sword into the face of a screaming man; I killed another with a straight lunge to the throat, and cut the legs from beneath a knight at the back of the line with a low sweep.

Robin was killing beside me, and Sir Thomas, magnificent as ever, was cutting down foes left and right with a chilly precision. A rush of fresh enemy men-at-arms from the right was met square on by Boot, who swept them casually aside with great loops of his club, like a goodwife clearing cobwebs with her broom.

A knight engaged me: two fast blows at my head and upper body. I parried the first, stepped in past the second, in close to his body and smashed my helmeted forehead full into his face. He staggered back and I rammed Fidelity hard into his belly, punching the blade straight through his mail and into the soft guts behind.

I looked behind me at the huge oak double door and saw that Robin and John Halfpenny were struggling to lift the vast bar that kept it securely closed.

I shouted to Boot: 'Help them, man, help with the gate!' and saw the giant nod, discard his club and lumber over to my lord.

We had killed or incapacitated a goodly number of the enemy by now; the bodies of dead or broken men were all over the courtyard, blood was slick underfoot. But we had not won. There were more and more men debouching into the courtyard from the buildings that surrounded it and the south tower on the far side of the gate. Twenty, thirty, now fifty men. But they were wary of us and our bloodied blades.

I shouted: 'To me! To me!' And gathered as many men as I could around Sir Thomas and myself. We formed a thin line, just eight men, protecting the gate where Robin and Boot had finally managed to lift the bar from its brackets.

The enemy were coming at us now in earnest. A knight in a full-face helmet with a red plume was exhorting them to battle and about two score men were now running forward, spears and swords, raised shields and grim expressions. They were twenty yards away, and the certain knowledge dawned on me. They would charge and swamp us. And that would be the end.

So be it.

I lifted Fidelity and made ready to run at them. Our feeble line would not hold against so many and I wanted to attack, anyway. Live, Alan, I thought, filled with a searing, impossible joy, live like a man – until you die!

I opened my mouth, took a deep breath . . .

A swarm of arrow shafts hummed over my head and smashed into the advancing enemy. A dozen men fell in that one stroke. I looked behind me and saw that the gates were wide open and the archers of Sherwood were formed up on the bridge beyond. I saw Mastin drop his arm, and another lethal flight of shafts whirred through the air and smashed into the enemy. Half of them were now stuck with feathers, a quarter dead outright. And there were men-at-arms charging through the open gate by now, Robin's men, eager and fresh. But the battle was over. I saw the red-plumed knight make one last attempt to rally his shattered men, but they were all running for their lives – disappearing into the darkness between the buildings on the far side of the courtyard, slipping away into the shadowy bulk of London and safety.

The knight gave one last despairing glance at me and then he, too, turned tail and ran swiftly away into the shadows.

Chapter Thirty-six

The Army of God arrived an hour before dawn. They had been marching all night and were on the point of exhaustion. But their efforts were not in vain. We occupied Newgate and the surrounding fortifications and sent word with the dawn via Cousin Henry to Robin's friends and acquaintances all across London. By the time the church bells were ringing out the office of prime, a cheering crowd had gathered that stretched from Newgate all the way down Watling Street to St Paul's Cathedral. Within hours, the King's garrisons in the city gates surrendered their arms – all except the Flemish mercenaries who held the Tower of London. However, they could not recapture the city and it would have cost us blood to take the strongest castle in England. So, on Robin's advice we ignored the Tower, and left the Flemings, under watch by a company of Fitzwalter's men, to their own devices.

London was ours and a mood of general rejoicing gripped the whole city. Apprentices were given a half-day holiday, merchants closed their warehouses, artisans put up the shutters and the taverns were thronged with celebrants. The church bells rang out from dawn to dusk in celebration; the streets echoed with happy singing and the laughter of men released from their labours. Even when the Earl of Salisbury and his troops arrived the next day, the mood of defiant joy continued. William Longsword, Earl of Salisbury, was politely but firmly refused the city by Lord Fitzwalter and the Army of God, who manned the walls in a show of our strength, heavily reinforced with thousands of men from the city's militia bands.

Longsword did not stay long. He withdrew his forces to Windsor, a day's march away; for the King had finally quit Oxford and set up his headquarters in the castle there. The Earl was right to do so because, two days after the Army of God had entered the city, the first of the reluctant barons, those who had slipped away at Bedford, began to descend on London with their men, protesting that they had always been loyal to the rebellion, that they would gladly fight and die for the great charter. The waverers were flocking to our banner, just as Robin had predicted, and if Salisbury and his loyalist forces had not withdrawn, he would have been caught between two or even three vengeful rebel fires.

I missed most of the celebrations, however. The spear thrust to my waist had sliced through the skin and fat below my ribs but, praise God and all the saints, had not pierced my intestines. It was a long, deep, painful cut, that had required to be stitched up, and the learned London physician who did the stitching – a rich friend of Cousin Henry's – told me that I should not walk about or undertake any strenuous activity for some days and weeks. I spent the time at my former lodgings in Friday Street, where I was treated as a hero by my host, Master Luke Benning, a merchant friend of Lord Fitzwalter who had made his fortune in amber from the Baltic. Master Benning left me to myself but told me to treat the house and its servants as my own. I was, in fact, well tended by Boot, who bustled around me, bringing me potions and salves guaranteed to have a healing effect.

Robert had asked if he might lodge with Miles and Hugh at Robin's merchant friend's house in Queen's Hythe, and I had agreed. It is no fun for a youngster to be around an invalid. And Thomas, after dumping his baggage in one of the chambers on the second floor, disappeared for two days and nights and I assumed that, despite his promise to the pretty Westbury girl Mary, he had surrendered to his old vice. I could not feel angry with him for I judged that he had richly earned a reward.

My wound healed well over the next few days of idleness, while London celebrated and lords Fitzwalter, de Vesci and Locksley sent out messengers to all parts of the country urging great men to join our cause. The barons were still coming to our side in increasing numbers, now that we held London. And in other parts of the country, most notably in Lincoln and Exeter, but also in towns and manors from the Welsh marshes to the Kent coast, from the Humber to Hampshire, rebels were challenging the King's officials – particularly in the afforested areas – seizing royal castles, torching royal manors and executing sheriffs, foresters, verderers and other cruel and corrupt officials out of hand. After decades of oppression, it seemed, the whole country had united against the King. The English are slow to anger, I have always found, but when sufficiently roused an Englishman's ire is more terrible than any other man's. And during those joyous, victorious weeks in early June, England burned.

Meanwhile, I was snug in Friday Street. I swallowed the possets Boot brought me, drank down my potions and began to give the big man a few rudimentary lessons in the vielle – and found to my surprise that he had a natural aptitude for the instrument, an affinity with the notes and their combinations that was beautiful, indeed not all that far from magical.

I also had plenty of time on my hands to think.

Two questions were exercising my thoughts more than any other: who was this informant who had revealed to the Templars that we had given them the wrong Grail?

And was this person the same man who had told King John that I was planning to attack him outside St Paul's and so caused my arrest and downfall?

The second question was more easily answered. No. There was no reason to assume these were the same men. It was perfectly possible for two men to hate Robin and myself so much that they would wish our destruction – indeed, it was extremely likely, as my lord and I had made more enemies in our lives than either of us could easily contemplate. So I decided to treat the two questions as separate and see if that took me any further forward. Who had known that I would make my attempt on the King on that precise day in St Paul's Courtyard? Fitzwalter and De Vesci knew, and perhaps some of their men knew. No one else knew the exact time and place. I had told nobody what I was planning. Had I? A few others close to me such as Thomas and Robin might have guessed, but nobody else *knew*. I puzzled over this for the best part of a day and still could not find a solution.

The answer came from Robert's lips. He came to see me one morning, to see how my wound was healing and to show me his new dog. It was a lurcher bitch with almost the same colouring as the one that had died after the battle outside the walls of Westbury. He had bought it that very morning. I admired the dog, even after it pissed all over the floor of my chamber, and told Robert that he must take good care of it and make sure that he paid attention to its training.

'I will, Father,' said Robert. 'But it was no fault of mine that Vixen died. She was poisoned, I am sure of it. The swiftness with which she died, her death agonies, the wild contortions of her body. There can be no other explanation.'

Then everything fell into place. With a dreadful sinking sensation, I had the answer. I had been a blind fool. The person who had betrayed me to the King was the same person who had poisoned Robert's dog. I could hardly bear to think about it; indeed, for several hours my mind refused to accept it. But it was undoubtedly true, and there was no escaping the dismal truth.

When Robert had gone, later that same day, I turned my mind to the first question: the identity of the Grail informer. That proved almost as painful as the first. I was lying abed, it being long past nightfall, when the second solution came to me, more slowly this time but with equal surety. I did not sleep a wink that night as my mind wrestled with itself. For as I recalled exactly what Brother Geoffrey had said to me, the precise words, I knew who it must be who had betrayed us to the Order. I knew the informant must be one of two people – and that Robin dearly loved them both.

That long sleepless night, as I considered betrayal in all its forms, I also spent a number of the hours of darkness thinking about courage. I still believed that Little John had come to me from beyond the grave and given me his strength in my hour of need; he had killed all my fear and given me the power to face the blades of my enemies. But there are many kinds of courage, I reflected, and I knew that I was still sorely lacking in one particular kind. Would that my dead friend could grant me that. For I knew that in the morning, I had to go to Robin and give him the fruits of my sad deliberations, and I dreaded it. All that night I twisted the idea in my mind, trying to find a way to tell him that would not end our long friendship. I could not see one. In the end, sleepless, as I heard the cocks announcing the arrival of dawn, I prayed to God and begged Little John to stand beside me once more, as I pulled on my hose, tunic and cloak, and made my way through the quiet dawn streets of London to the house where Robin – and the informant – both lived.

A servant let me into the big house at Queen's Hythe – it was a wine merchant's abode and more than spacious – and he offered to take me to the hall where Robin was breaking his fast with his two sons and Robert. I demurred. I wished to speak to Robin in private, I said, and the servant, looking perplexed, ushered me into a small parlour and bade me wait there.

I helped myself to a cup of wine from the sideboard. It was only a little after dawn but I sorely needed the drink.

Robin came striding into the room in a gust of energy and happiness: 'Alan, there you are,' he said, 'I have no idea why Piers put you in here – don't be offended, I beg you. You look put out. I have news that will lift your spirits no end: King John has capitulated. He has agreed to the charter. Can you believe it?'

Robin's words wiped all other thoughts from my mind. 'Is this true? When did this happen?' I said.

'Well, he has not set his seal on the document yet – but he will. Archbishop Langton has worn out a dozen horses going back and forth between us and the King at Windsor, and John, of course, squirmed, prevaricated and protested a great deal – but finally we have an agreement. The archbishop put it to him that, the way things are going with the rebellion, he would surely not remain King for much longer if he refused to sign. Is that not wonderful? We have a meeting agreed: all the barons are to meet the King under a flag of truce at a place halfway between Staines and Windsor, by the river, someplace called Runnymede. I see you have already started celebrating,' he said with a nod at the empty cup of wine in my hand. 'Come through to the hall and have another drink and some breakfast.'

It was indeed the most wonderful news, but I had my painful duty to perform first – and once I had told Robin what I knew in my heart I did not believe I would be invited to breakfast or any other meal with him again.

'I must talk to you, my lord, in private,' I said.

'You seem awfully serious, Alan, what is it?'

'I know the identity of the informant – I know now

who told the Templars about the Grail, or rather I know that it must be one of two men. I must tell you now, with the greatest regret, that the informant must be either Miles or Hugh.'

'Hmm,' said Robin. 'That's what you truly think, is it? Tell me your reasoning, Alan. And this had better be good.'

I swallowed: 'The Templar Brother Geoffrey told me in Nottingham Castle that the informant was young – "our young informant", he called him. And the only people who could honestly be described as young and who also knew about the false Grail were Miles and Hugh. It must be one of them.'

Robin was very quiet then, but I took that as a good sign: he could have been calling for his sword or for armed guards to have me thrown into the street. He said: 'I suppose your reasoning is that Miles has long worshipped the Templars; he was even trained by some of the Brothers, and so he decided to betray me because he loves them more than me – is that it? And Hugh, well, we all know Hugh is illegitimate, the bastard son of Ralph Murdac, so he must be a villain. Is that your reasoning, Alan? Is that really it?'

It was, and in bed the night before it had seemed irrefutable proof. Now when Robin said the words out loud it seemed utterly fanciful and ridiculous. I nodded but said nothing.

Robin said: 'I think you are wrong. But even if you are

not – what has this wicked informant of ours actually done? Do you think he was the man who betrayed you to the King at St Paul's?'

I managed to say no; that I thought that was someone else.

'So all this informant has done is let slip that we played a trick on the Templars a dozen years ago. Yet the Order would have discovered our ruse in time, I am sure of it, I was sure of it then. So – to me – it does not feel like this informant has committed *such* a terrible crime. In fact, even if it were another man who informed on me, and not one of my sons, I do not think I would seek revenge. Perhaps I am getting old, but a little tattle-taling does not seem a worthwhile cause in which to spill a man's blood. And if the informant truly is one of my sons, do you not think I would forgive them? My own sons?'

'They did cause the deaths of several men when the Templars attacked Kirkton and Westbury,' I said.

I felt disconcertingly off-balance. I remembered a time when Robin would have had a man's tongue torn from his mouth for informing on him. Now, apparently, he merely shrugged it away. How my lord had changed with the blessing of time.

'Alan, Alan, those deaths were not fully the informant's fault. So he blabbed a little, the Templars got the wrong idea, we fought them and some men died. Fighting men die all the time, that is what they do. One day you and

507

I will die in battle. Is that a reason to take a sword to my sons, break Marie-Anne's heart with grief, and spoil the harmony of my household? I think not.'

I knew he was right. And it was slowly dawning on me that I had made a colossal idiot of myself yet again.

'I would like to know the answer to the riddle,' I mumbled.

'Very well, Alan, come and we shall ask them to their faces.' My lord strode from the parlour and along the corridor to the hall.

The three young men were seated at one end of the long table, all convulsed with some jest that Miles had made, or at least so I guessed. Miles had a sly satisfied grin on his face; tears were streaming down Robert's cheeks, and even Hugh was guffawing, and unusually loudly for such a normally sober fellow.

'Boys, I have a question for you,' said Robin, when the tumult had died down. 'As Miles and Hugh both know, some years back I played a low trick on the Knights of the Temple and exchanged a gold cup with them for our lives when we were in a tight situation. They believed it was the true Cup of Christ, although it most certainly was not. I have told you this story before, yes?'

Miles and Hugh both nodded.

'I also swore you to secrecy, if I remember rightly,' said Robin. 'So tell me honestly, and I swear I will not be angry so long as you give me the truth – have either of you told anyone else this tale?'

Miles and Hugh looked at each other. Hugh shrugged. But Miles turned to Robin and lifted his hand.

'You told someone, Miles?' said Robin.

'I did, Father,' said Miles, looking uncharacteristically shame-faced. 'I told one person – and I'm sorry for breaking my word to you. But I thought it would be all right – he being sort of family, in a way, and his father being involved, too.'

'He told me,' said Robert. I could see that he was trying to keep a bold face, but a corner of his mouth was wobbling.

'And have you told anyone else this tale?' I asked. 'Tell me truthfully, Robert, and I too swear I shall not be angry.'

'Oh, Father, I'm sorry, but I told some of the boys at Pembroke Castle. The other squires were all so nasty to me and I wanted to impress them. So I told them that my father had the true, the only Holy Grail in his possession. It was a black lie – I know it, know it was very wrong and I am so sorry, Father, but I told them the story of the Grail at Montségur, the wonderful tale that Miles told me; all the rest I just made up.'

The boy burst into anguished tears.

I had no difficulty in forgiving Robert for his boyish indiscretion. I understood entirely how it must have come about. Friendless in Pembroke and far behind the other boys in his military training, Robert, the newcomer, had sought to gain approval of the other squires with the only coin he had. The other boys had no doubt passed on the tale to Brother Geoffrey – mayhap taunting the Templar mischievously with his Order's blind stupidity over the affair.

We had our breakfast, a merry meal, all reconciled, and myself feeling greatly abashed. My fears that one of Robin's sons was secretly working against him had been proved groundless, and Robin's news that the rebellion was won and that the King would seal the charter lifted my spirits no end. I understood, too, who Brother Geoffrey had been indicating with a jerk of his chin when he had told me that the informant said we still had the Grail. Not Thomas. He had been indicating Robert. He did not know that the boy had simply been lying.

I asked Robert, quite casually, if he had told Brother Geoffrey about the Grail or if he had just told the other boys at Pembroke, and Robert's reaction startled me. His face went pale as chalk and he refused to meet my gaze.

'I would not tell that man anything willingly,' he said.

'Was he so very hard on you while you were there?' I asked.

'It is not that – he was a stern master, to be sure, but he was hard on all of us alike. It was not that. He did . . . other things. Sinful things. At night, he'd call me to his cell and then . . .' He stopped.

And after that I could not get another word out of him.

My heart had turned to ice. I saw that Robin was listening to the boy's talk with a face like stone. My lord said: 'Miles, Hugh, take Robert with you and see to the pavilion. It needs to be thoroughly aired before we depart tomorrow. And I want you to check the horses and also make sure the servants have packed suitable amounts of wine – if all goes according to plan with the King, we shall be celebrating.' And yet Robin's voice did not sound in the slightest as if he were planning a celebration.

'Alan, stay a while. I would like to have a private word with you, if I may.'

I had risen from the table, heedless of my lord's words, and I was making for the door. I had one thing on my mind and that was blood. The Templar would die screaming.

Robin caught my arm. 'Wait, Alan. We will do this thing together. We must not be hasty. Wait, I beg you, and I swear we shall have the truth out of this man And he shall pay, but you must not go off full of rage like this.'

'He . . . he hurt my son.' I could barely speak for wrath.

'Alan, look at me!' I stared into Robin's face, managing to find my focus.

'We will do this together. I swear it. You want revenge and you shall have it. But we need to plan. We need time. You will throw your life away if you go up against the Templars alone. And where would Robert be then? You and I will do this, quietly, without fanfare, but we'll do it after the charter is signed. Do you hear me?'

My lord was speaking good sense. And slowly mine

returned, too. For Robert's sake, I could not afford to be reckless. I would settle with this vile Templar calmly, permanently and with Robin's help after this business with the King.

At Runnymede.

Chapter Thirty-seven

There was nothing much to see at Runnymede – no castle, town or church: it was just a long meadow beside the meandering course of the River Thames; good horse country, lush, flat and green, with thickly wooded rising ground to the south. But Robin told me that this very piece of land had once been a place where the Witan, the council of wise men, would meet with the King of England in the days before the Normans overran this island. I doubt if more than a handful of the rebel barons of the Army of God knew that fact when they met King John there two days after the ides of June, on the fifteenth day of that month. For most of the lords who gathered there, it was not a place hallowed by the councils of ages past, but a place of victory today.

It was a sparkling, jewel-like morning, the first true day of summer, and the fighting strength of England paraded in its splendour in the sunshine on that bloodless field of victory. Robin and I and about a score of his men-at-arms spent the night before at St Mary's Priory on the other side of the river, but we were up before dawn and ferried across the Thames by local boatmen to set up our pavilion with all the others. Although we were meeting under a flag of truce, there must have been a thousand men in mail there that day, tearing up the green turf with the hooves of their galloping destriers. The field was already dotted with brightly coloured tents and pavilions and the banners of a hundred noble families fluttered above them in the perfect clear air.

The King arrived last, a little before midday, as was fitting for royalty, even such a tawdry monarch as he. He came downstream from Windsor by royal barge, a low gilded boat, rowed by two dozen brawny mercenaries, and he was accompanied by the Archbishop of Canterbury, who more than any man, except perhaps Robin, was the architect of the final agreement that had been hammered out between the King and Fitzwalter's rebels.

As the King stepped off the barge and on to the green turf surrounded by a screen of crossbowmen, he stumbled and a big bearded bowman in royal livery of scarlet and gold lunged forward and caught the royal arm to prevent John tumbling to his knees in front of the whole baronage of England. I was about five paces away, in the forefront of a crowd of Robin's men, and I caught the crossbowman's eye as he helped the King to right himself: it was Stevin, the garlic-loving lout who had given me so many beatings when I was his prisoner. I winked at him and grinned – he scowled in return, and quickly looked about him to see that the guards were in their places between me and the King.

John himself looked ill and tired. His hair had lost the red-gold sheen of his family and was now a washed-out browny-grey. His face was lined and pale, and there were circles under his eyes. He looked beaten, unslept and more than a little afraid.

The crossbowmen made a lane through the press of men-at-arms, and many of the watching men, even now, knelt in the presence of royalty. I did not. I looked on, standing tall and proud, as John was guided across the few hundred yards of flat green field with the Archbishop of Canterbury on one side and his brother the Earl of Salisbury on the other, and the crowd of barons, knights and men-at-arms following behind. The King raised his chin and made at least a pretence of dignity as he was shown to a dais which had been set up on the rising slope. He seated himself at a great wooden throne before a broad oak table and a priest began a loud prayer of thanks for the blessing of peace throughout the land.

The barons of England crowded forward around the King and the table at which he sat, and there was more than a little jostling from the big men in bright surcoats

515

and armour as they crushed in under the awning, eager to witness his humiliation. John closed his eyes, like a child wishing the rest of the world to be invisible.

The Archbishop of Canterbury took a large piece of almost square parchment from the table, held it aloft so that all might see it, and in a loud commanding voice he began to read in beautiful Latin the following resounding words:

'John, by the grace of God King of England, Lord of Ireland, Duke of Normandy and Aquitaine, and Count of Anjou, to his archbishops, bishops, abbots, earls, barons, justices, foresters, sheriffs, stewards, servants, and to all his officials and loyal subjects, Greeting.

'Know that before God, for the health of our soul and those of our ancestors and heirs, to the honour of God, the exaltation of the holy Church, and the better ordering of our kingdom, at the advice of our reverend fathers Stephen, Archbishop of Canterbury, Primate of All England, and cardinal of the holy Roman Church . . .'

There followed a list of the assembled bishops and barons, and as each name was mentioned I looked at the man who owned it: Master Pandulf, a tall austere figure in black, who served as legate to the new overlord of England, now sitting on St Peter's throne in Rome; Aymeric de St Maur, Master of the Templars, who was staring at me with a particularly intense expression; William the Marshal, Earl of Pembroke, was there too and I looked to see if his almoner was with him. Despite my promise to Robin that I would do nothing until after the ceremony, I did not know if I could keep my word if I found myself within striking distance of Brother Geoffrey. But there was no sign of that beast in human form. William, Earl of Salisbury, John's half-brother but a decent man at heart, was there; Hubert de Burgh, seneschal of Poitou, a severe hawk of a man whom I had known in Normandy, too; as well as the earls of Warren and Arundel, Oxford, Winchester and Essex and a host of lesser barons and knights. On the far side of the table I could see Lord Fitzwalter, who was glowing with his triumph, and Lord de Vesci leering with satisfaction. By my left elbow was Robin, serene and faintly smiling. On my right was Thomas. The knight had been absent for some days, and he had returned the night before the ceremony, looking tired and drawn but well pleased with himself. I asked him, a little sourly, if he had had a good win at the dice tables. But he looked hurt and said that he had not been gaming since he had promised Mary. I did not believe him. But I was too low in spirits to challenge his lies. It was in truth none of my business, either. And so I let it pass.

The archbishop read on through clause after clause that had already been painstakingly agreed with the King over the past few days. The archbishop spoke of the freedom of the Church, of the fair inheritance of lands, of the rights of widows and debtors, he spoke of scutage and taxes and the liberties to be enjoyed by the city of

London. Then he spoke the very words that had so warmed my heart in Alnwick:

'No free man shall be seized or imprisoned, or stripped of his rights or possessions, or outlawed or exiled, or deprived of his standing in any way, nor will we proceed with force against him, or send others to do so, except by the lawful judgement of his equals or by the law of the land.'

Once more those words made my heart glow: they meant that I could never again be slung into a gaol to starve my life away without fair trial, and neither would any other free man. For those words alone, I felt, the struggle had been worth it.

The clauses went on and on, dealing with the right of free movement for merchants and promises to reform the harsh forest laws, and just as I was growing a little bored, Robin nudged me and murmured in my ear, 'Pay attention to this one, Alan,' and I heard the archbishop read out the following:

'We will remove completely from their offices the kinsmen of Gérard d'Athée, and in future they shall hold no offices in England. The people in question are Engelard de Cigogné, Peter, Guy, and Andrew de Chanceaux, Guy de Cigogné, Geoffrey de Martigny and his brothers, Philip Marc and his brothers, with Geoffrey his nephew, and all their followers.'

I almost missed the name. But Robin made it clear to me in a low whisper. 'Philip Marc has already been dismissed as sheriff of Nottinghamshire, he left the castle two days ago, and I have arranged a new man for the position. He's called Lowdham, a mild-mannered, decent fellow, and I think you'll find him a good deal less demanding. You'll meet him in due course – we're to install him in his new post, help him settle in.'

I felt a lightening of my heart, despite the rage and grief that still gripped me. With Philip Marc gone, there would be no more danger to Robert or to Westbury over my unpaid scutage. If this Lowdham fellow was half as reasonable as Robin had suggested, I might not have to pay the tax Marc had demanded at all. A wash of gratitude filled my heart for my lord and his kindness.

I looked at the King and saw that his eyes were still tightly shut as they had been throughout the long recitation – but as the archbishop wound on and on and at last mentioned the council of twenty-five barons who would oversee the King's actions and whose duty it would be to seize the King's castles and lands if he broke the promises made today, I saw John's eyes snap open and a spark of some strong dark emotion burn in their faded depths.

King John is not quite so reconciled to this great charter as many suppose, I thought to myself. I found myself suddenly looking straight into the sovereign's eyes and he was looking into mine – and I realised that this was an expression that I could much more easily unravel. It was a look of pure and poisonous hatred.

At last, archbishop Langton was done. Silence fell over the assembled men. Clerks bustled forward. Hot green wax was dripped on a thick piece of tape attached to the bottom of the parchment. John had the Great Seal in his hand – and at the last moment he hesitated. A strong gust rustled the square piece of parchment, threatening to blow it away and hurl it into the crowd of men gathered around the table.

The archbishop slapped his hand on the charter, pinning it to the table. In the hush of expectation it sounded as loud and harsh as the crack of a whip.

'You must seal it, sire, before the wax dries,' Langton said.

John stared up into the churchman's face for a moment, then he swiftly stabbed the Great Seal into the spreading pool.

The King stood up abruptly. 'Are we done? Can I go now?' he said to the archbishop.

'Sire, you may, of course, do whatever you choose,' said Langton. 'You are the King. But first, perhaps, your royal highness might like to take the homage of the assembled baronage of all England.'

'Oh yes, the homage. The oath of fidelity,' he sneered. 'As if that ever stopped them doing whatever they damn well please.'

And with these gracious words King John of England took the oaths of allegiance from the noblemen of England, in which they lined up before the throne and one by one swore henceforth to be his faithful and loyal vassals.

Robin was one of the first to renew his allegiance. As soon as he was finished, we pushed our way through the throng and headed back to our pavilion.

'Do you think he will keep to the terms of the charter?' I said to Robin as we walked across that flat green space to our pavilion.

'For a week, even a month or two, maybe . . . To answer your question truthfully: no, he will not keep to it. But that is not the point, Alan. The point is that he has sworn to keep to it. He has given his sacred word in front of all the great men of the land. And even more importantly than that, the charter has been sealed into English law by the King himself. For the first time ever, the King has agreed to be bound by law like any man. And nothing John or his heirs and successors do can undo that. We have won, Alan, we have won a great victory: for ourselves, for our sons, for England.'

We celebrated with wine in the tent – Miles and Hugh and Robert making the gathering a raucous one with their youthful japes and pranks. Thomas, too, was in high spirits, jesting with the boys as if he were still a young gallant himself. Even Boot was mutely pleased and drank wine from a vessel that was either an enormous cup or a small bucket, depending on your point of view, smiling beneficently and silently at the gathering. I drank with determination. Only a vast quantity of wine, I felt, could wash away the sorrows that beset my heart even on that happy day.

I stood up, a little unsteady after my fifth cup of wine, about to make a toast to my lord and to thank him for his kindnesses, when I was interrupted by a commotion outside the tent and a strong, martial voice demanding entry of the sentry outside.

The flap lifted and into the heart of our merrymaking strode Aymeric de St Maur, Master of all the Templars of England.

'Sir Aymeric,' said Robin, 'I am so glad you could join us. A cup of wine?'

'I'll take wine, yes, thank you,' said Aymeric. He received his cup and lifted it in greeting to us all.

'I must admit,' the Master said, 'I was rather surprised to receive your invitation, Locksley. As you know, there is a grave matter that lies between us and despite several invitations I was beginning to think that you would not take counsel with us under any circumstances. I had feared that I might have to come all the way to your gates in Yorkshire just to make you speak with me.'

'You would be right to fear that,' I said, feeling the good wine rushing through my veins. 'When your men came to Westbury we taught them a valuable lesson; and we will gladly teach them another at any time you care to choose.'

'Alan!' said Robin, frowning at me. 'The Master is

our guest, do not give him cause for offence today, I beg you.'

'I know Sir Alan of old,' said Sir Aymeric, 'and I have admired him for years; it would take a great deal for a man of his courage and skill to offend me. And since he has brought it up – I must apologise for the events at Westbury last spring. Brother Geoffrey was a zealous knight, a true warrior of Christ, of course, and a fine priest, but he did sometimes overreach himself. Mistakes were made—'

'You said he *was* a zealous knight,' I said, my anger close to boiling over. 'Do you no longer consider him one?'

'Alas, my friend, Brother Geoffrey has been called to God.'

I was stunned. 'Do you mean he is dead?' I said stupidly.

'Sadly so. He was set upon by a murderous thief in London not far from the gates of the Temple itself just two days ago. Some blackguard lay in wait for him and cut his throat from ear to ear, nearly took his head off.'

'I am sorry to hear it,' said Robin, smoothly. 'The streets of London grow more perilous by the day. We really must do something about it.'

'Indeed, and it was a most curious crime. The thief must have been a man of prowess, for Brother Geoffrey, while advanced in age, was still a formidable fighter, and yet this thief defeated him with no great difficulty, or so it would seem. Poor Brother Geoffrey's purse was missing

– which is why it must have been a thief – but his body was also mutilated. His attacker cut his manhood from his body and left his male part in the poor fellow's mouth.'

Sir Aymeric's tone had hardened as he spoke these words. 'We will investigate the matter further and with all the resources at our disposal. And rest assured that we will find the thief, in time, and when we do Brother Geoffrey will be avenged.'

There was a long, awkward silence in that hot tent. Not a man spoke. I was frowning at Robin. Two days ago? Surely Robin did not know what kind of man Brother Geoffrey was before yesterday at breakfast.

'More wine, Sir Aymeric,' said my lord in a voice of silk.

'Thank you, yes. But perhaps we had better get to the crux of things,' said the Master of the Temple briskly. 'Do you have it? Do you have the Grail? Will you willingly surrender it to me?'

'No,' said Robin. 'I do not have it, and I will tell you why.'

'You say you do not have it,' said Sir Aymeric slowly. 'Why then did you invite me here today?'

'My lord, you know well enough that I am not – how shall I put it? – the most devoted of the Church's servants.'

Sir Aymeric made a coughing sound that might have been the beginning of a laugh.

Robin continued: 'I fully admit that I did not treat fairly with Guy d'Épernay outside the walls of Montségur.

524

I gave him a false Grail. I lied to him. But I had already made a solemn commitment concerning that relic to another man, an old priest and my friend, that I particularly wished to honour. Also, I am the kind of man who does not respond well to threats. I wished to save my men and also honour my promise to my friend, and so I played your Order false. I am sorry, I am truly sorry for my actions and yet, I might well do the same again if I found myself in the same circumstances. I gave the false relic to the Templars. But mark this: the true one, much later, was destroyed in a fire in Toulouse. It was an object made of very old cedar wood and I saw it burn, and so did Sir Alan, for that matter. The true Grail no longer exists and I will swear on the souls of my two children' – Robin pointed at Miles and Hugh – 'that now I speak only the truth in this matter.'

Sir Aymeric had his head cocked on one side and he seemed to be solemnly weighing Robin's words.

'The true Grail is no more,' said Robin, 'but I would make amends to your Order for what I have done. And this is what I will offer in recompense. I will grant one wish, one boon, any favour that it is within my power to fulfil, anything to you as Master of the English Templars, or to any of your successors. If you ask me to kill a man, even a close friend or relative, I will do it with no questions asked. If you ask me to bathe in the font at St Paul's or juggle apples at Nottingham fair, I will do it with no demurral or hesitation. For one time only, your Order's lightest wish is my command. That is what I offer you if you will put this matter behind us. One favour, for the wrong I did you.'

The Master of the Templars was smiling calmly at Robin.

'Three favours, my lord of Locksley,' he said. 'The true Grail, the Cup of Christ, is worth at least three of your favours.'

'No,' said Robin, his voice hard as stone. 'I will not change my offer. One favour is all I will give you. And I would remind you that I am not altogether defenceless. If you wish to make war on me and my friends – well, I believe we can withstand the force of your arms and even strike a few telling blows against the Order ourselves. If you choose war, so be it.'

'Enough,' said Aymeric. 'Let us not descend to vulgar bluster. I do in fact believe you when you say the Grail is destroyed – it was reported lost to fire by the Templars of Toulouse. I had hoped that it was not true, but now I believe I must accept that it is. I do not think you would swear on the lives of your children that it was lost were it a lie. I am also pleased that you did not increase your offer to three favours. If you intended to be dishonest in this regard, it is as easy to promise three false boons as one. So I accept your offer – on behalf of the Order, myself and my successors. And we shall call on you for it, you may be sure of that. But until that day, I will treat you as a friend and not an enemy, and I trust you will do the same.'

The Templar raised his wine cup and drank.

'I shall be honoured to,' said Robin, and he, too, raised his cup and drained it.

When Sir Aymeric has taken his leave. I asked Thomas to accompany me for a stroll around the field of Runnymede while the servants began to dismantle the tent and pack our gear. The wine had given me something of a headache and, much as I longed to lie down somewhere quiet, I could not rest until I had said my piece to the dark-haired knight. We walked down the bank of the brown, slow-rolling Thames and sat on a dead tree by the water's edge.

'I suppose I must thank you, Thomas,' I said.

'Thank me for what, Sir Alan?'

'For Brother Geoffrey.'

Sir Thomas Blood said nothing for a long while. And I watched as a pair of ducks flashed through the air and landed with a splash in the water just before us. Then Sir Thomas said: 'If you are glad that Brother Geoffrey is dead, I believe your thanks should go to this thief that Sir Aymeric mentioned, whoever he might be.'

'Thomas,' I said. 'I am not angry with you. I only learnt what that vile wretch did to Robert yesterday, and I would have ripped him apart myself. You have saved me a bloody task and it seems that you have accomplished it very neatly. So I thank you. I also apologise for accusing you of gaming when you were gone from my side.'

'Only a fool would admit to committing a murder,' Thomas said carefully, 'even to a trusted friend. And particularly when the mighty Knights of the Temple have vowed to track down the perpetrator of the crime and have their vengeance.' He stopped and tossed a scrap of bark into the water, frightening the ducks into flight.

'I do not wish to speak about this matter ever again,' Thomas said, 'either to you or to anybody else. But I will say this, and only this: your son Robert, whatever his shortcomings, whatever his strengths, is my friend. And any man who deliberately harms my friend will always suffer the consequences while I have strength.'

Chapter Thirty-eight

Lord de Lowdham proved to be an amiable fellow, as reasonable as Robin had said, if slightly plump and near-sighted and, in my opinion, not overloaded with intellect. He seemed utterly determined to make everybody he met like him, which made him charming company, to be sure, but made me wonder whether he would be able to shoulder the burdens of the office of High Sheriff of Nottinghamshire, Derbyshire and the Royal Forests with any degree of competence.

'I am sure I shall find it a most taxing position,' said Lowdham, with a chuckle and a glance to see if I appreciated his hilarious jest. Then he saw my pained expression and said: 'But my lord of Locksley tells me that if I find myself in any difficulties I am always to seek your counsel.

If you won't mind me constantly badgering you for advice, Sir Alan . . .'

I said that I did not mind and that I would be at his disposal whenever he needed me. Privately I thought that it would be satisfying to have the ear of the sheriff, and for once in my life not to be in conflict with the man in that powerful position.

We were riding north from London to Nottingham with Robin, Miles, Hugh, Sir Thomas, Boot, Robert and all Robin's men, plus a hundred men-at-arms in the red, blue and gold de Lacy livery, who belonged to Lowdham. He was a relative of the powerful de Lacy family, a nephew of old Roger, the stubborn defender of Château Gaillard, and cousin to the new young lord, his son John.

John de Lacy had supported the rebellion almost from the start and he was now a power in the north. He had been allowed by King John to choose the new sheriff of the county, ably assisted by Robin and other northern magnates, and his amiable cousin Lord de Lowdham had been selected by popular acclaim – Robin was not the only one to realise that a pliable royal official at Nottingham would be a boon.

Our official task was to escort Lowdham safely to Nottingham and install him as the new constable of the castle there. But there was another urgent matter that I wished to settle as soon as possible.

We left Runnymede that same afternoon the great

charter was sealed and I confess that I hurried our party north. I wanted, if possible, to outstrip the news of John's humiliation, though it soon became apparent that it was a vain hope. Word of the charter travelled faster than lightning across the land and when we arrived at the town of Nottingham, at dusk on the second day, it was clear that the news had arrived well before us. As we rode our horses through the dim streets, Robin was recognised by many, and we were besieged with questions about what the new charter would mean to ordinary people. Would all tax debts be forgiven? Would no man ever be imprisoned again? Were the cruel forest laws abolished? The answer to all these questions was no. Indeed, I knew that for many English folk the extraordinary event that had occurred between the King and his barons in a Thames-side meadow would have very little or no impact on their daily lives.

We were swiftly admitted to the castle of Nottingham, even though it was past curfew, simply by announcing the presence of Lord de Lowdham, and showing the parchment that confirmed his new position as sheriff.

I left Robin and Lowdham in the main hall, where the new lord of the castle insisted on meeting all the hall servants. Taking only Boot with me, I hurried to the great tower, a massive square fortification between the inner and middle baileys which housed the sleeping quarters of the castle's more senior knights.

I ran up the stairs and sped down a corridor and stopped

dead outside a large oak door, my hand poised to turn the handle and ready to barge straight in.

What stopped me was the sound of a voice.

A female voice. And it was speaking about me:

'. . . whatever they have agreed to, this silly charter they have made the King agree to, there is no reason I can see for us to give up the fight against *him*,' said Tilda, the loathing in her voice thick as curdled milk.

'It's not so easy, my darling. Dale has the luck of the Devil,' said Sir Benedict Malet. 'I had him here, in my hands, chained like a dog, and I was ready to pay him back for all the humiliations he has heaped on us – and what did he do? He persuaded that monster to help him escape. His luck is scarcely believable.'

Boot was a looming shadow behind me. I controlled the urge to order him to charge straight through the doorway.

'Do not upset yourself, my dear,' Tilda said. 'Dale is a hard man to kill, as I know myself. I informed the King that he was planning to murder him – he practically admitted the plot to me himself, the love-struck cretin – and even though he was caught in the act of murder, he somehow wriggled out of that crime.'

At St Paul's, I thought. Yes, I told her myself. And yes, I had been a cretin.

Tilda was still speaking: '. . . I gave him poisoned meat when he was at the very door of death after some illness and the big lump didn't even seem to notice – he actually got better. The Devil's luck once more. But we must not give up, my love. We must not. He is vulnerable through his son, you have proved that here at Nottingham, so if we can get to the brat—'

That was when I pushed open the door. But once inside I stopped, frozen with sorrow. For all that I had suspected for the past few days was now proven to be true. I had hoped, with a mad, tiny part of my soul, that I had been mistaken. But there was no doubt. I stood there transfixed, just staring at the two figures in the big bed on the far side of the room, naked but for the linen bedsheets. Tilda, I saw with a pang, looked more beautiful than she ever had before, her black hair falling in curls over her perfect bosom, her lips blood-red, her blue-grey eyes huge in the candlelight. Benedict, doughy and white as lard, looked like a shaved pig in the bed beside her.

I could think of nothing useful to say, except: 'Boot, take that man down to the hall, now, and keep him under guard.'

As Boot lumbered over to the bed and hauled a protesting Benedict out from under the covers by his foot, I gazed at Tilda's naked white flesh and realised, quite suddenly, that I felt nothing at all for her. Not the slightest stirring of love, nor even lust, just a chilly acknowledgement that she possessed a great and flawless beauty.

At least on the outside.

'You had best get some clothes on and quickly get yourself back to Kirklees,' I said to her. 'And if you ever come near my son or me again, I will tell Mother Anna how exactly you spend your nights when you come to visit Nottingham.'

'You understand nothing, Alan Dale,' hissed Tilda, her eyes blazing now. 'You have never understood a single thing – about me, about Anna, even about Kirklees.'

'I understand that you are my enemy, that you have always been my enemy, and that you posed as my friend in order to beguile me and open me to your revenge. I also understand that you pose a danger to my son. But you should understand this, Matilda Giffard: if Robert comes to any harm through you or through your agents, if a single hair on his head is touched, I shall come to Kirklees and burn the place to the ground with you inside it. Do you hear me? You touch my son, and you die in flames.'

There was nothing more to say. I turned on my heel and left, following the sounds of Benedict's cries as he was carried helpless on Boot's shoulder down the corridor and towards the stairs.

I wanted to gut Benedict there and then, to sink my blade in his belly, rip out his intestines and watch him bleed to death before my eyes. I wanted to do it as a payment for his threats to Robert. I wanted to do it for his treatment of me in that castle cell. If I am honest, I also wanted to do it because Tilda was his lover, and had been for many years, and although I no longer wanted her myself, I still hated the sweaty pig for debauching her perfect body. However, it was Robin who dissuaded me from taking my vengeance there and then.

'We fought for the rule of law, Alan,' he said, as we stood over the weeping, shivering, naked lump in the main hall of Nottingham Castle that night. Indeed, I actually had my misericorde unsheathed in my hand, ready to strike.

'We fought for the principle of freedom under the law. We fought long and hard for an end to the arbitrary violence and the rule of the strongest man's whim,' said my lord. 'Now we have Benedict in our power, we cannot abandon that principle, can we, Alan? Can we? Think about it. It must be legal or all our struggles have been for naught. He must be tried for his crimes in a proper court of law and have a fair and appropriate sentence passed on him by a duly empowered royal official.'

Eventually I agreed.

'Good,' said Robin. 'I know just the right man for the task.'

Sir Benedict Malet stood trial for his crimes the next day before a court convened by the newly appointed High Sheriff of Nottinghamshire, Derbyshire and the Royal Forests, the noble lord of Lowdham. Benedict stood accused of misappropriation of royal funds, namely a goodly quantity of tax silver that had never found its way to the King. He was also accused of the murder of eighty-six men and women from the county of Nottinghamshire, executed for failing to pay trumped-up tax demands.

No one spoke up for Benedict except himself; he made a quavering, mumbling, tear-splashed speech about merely obeying orders that was almost an admission of his guilt – I had half-expected Tilda to speak for him, and was dreading seeing her again, but there was no sign of her either at the trial or anywhere in the castle.

She had vanished.

I gave evidence against Sir Benedict, along with a dozen or so townsfolk whose relatives had suffered under his and Philip Marc's regime, but it was Boot's eloquent testimony that sealed his fate. The big man spoke for nearly an hour about the men he had executed, naming as many as he could remember and attesting to their innocence of any crime save failure to pay over the outrageous sums demanded by the sheriff. Benedict was found guilty by a jury of twelve good men of the county, a unanimous verdict, and it fell to Lowdham to pass sentence.

I happened to be standing by his bench when the new sheriff was ready to pronounce. He leaned over to me and whispered: 'Do you think, Sir Alan, that I should show some leniency in this case – I really do not want the people to think I am a cruel fellow. He *was* merely following the orders of Philip Marc and the King, after all. Perhaps a stiff fine, or banishment . . .'

'I don't think so, my lord,' I whispered. 'I think it would

be wise to set an example in this case. It must be death, I'm afraid.'

'Oh very well, if you really think so, my dear fellow . . .'

They hanged Benedict Malet in the courtyard of Nottingham Castle the next day at dawn. I came out to watch, as did Boot. The big man had offered to perform his old grisly duty one last time but I told him no.

'Those days are over, my friend,' I said. 'I hope you may never have to kill again. I very much hope the same for myself.'

But as I saw Benedict slowly strangling in a hempen noose, his fat, white, urine-drenched legs kicking and jerking in the empty air, I felt pity well up in my heart. I do not like a hanging, I never have. And so, after a few moments, when Benedict's face was purple as a plum, and his tongue was sticking out like some grotesque red snake, as he twitched in his death throes, I gave him mercy.

I stepped forward, slipped the misericorde from its sheath, plunged the keen blade deep into his belly, then sliced sideways through the thick rolls of skin and fat, tumbling his bluish-white guts to the castle courtyard floor in a spew of hot blood.

I did not stay to watch him die.

Instead, I gathered my people, stepped up into the saddle and pointed my horse towards Westbury, towards home.

Epilogue

My back is bloody but my heart is full of joy. On the eve of our expulsion from Newstead, Brother Alan and I were saved almost, it seems, by a miracle. I took my beating like a man, I like to think, although I am not used to such overwhelming pain. I tried to show as much courage as Brother Alan would have shown in his prime. And a few hours later, as I was nursing my lacerated back and slowly gathering my meagre possessions, God showed his mercy. A cavalcade of knights, all gaudy plumes, bright flags and huge snorting horses, clattered into the priory courtyard. It was Lord Westbury himself, the grandson of Brother Alan, son of his dead son Robert, and a dozen of his followers. A tall, muscular blond man in glittering silver-chased mail and with a fine long sword at his waist leapt off his horse and insisted on seeing the prior immediately. I had not known this, and I am certain that Prior William was equally ignorant, but Alan Dale the younger, the newly ennobled Lord Westbury, has risen high in the service of our beloved Henry of Winchester in recent years, he has the King's ear in all things – not least the appointment of bishops.

After a private audience lasting less than an hour, the news was announced. Prior William is to take up the vacant see of Durham – he is to be a bishop at last, and I – oh, I can barely inscribe these words for my joy – I am to be the next prior of Newstead. Brother Alan, of course, is to remain with us for as long as he is spared.

My happiness is tempered by the knowledge that this cannot be for long. I told my friend the good news and he rejoiced with me. And Lord Westbury came to his cell soon afterwards and they spent a happy hour together discussing the fortunes of the realm and the doings at Westbury. But seeing his grandson completely exhausted him. And Brother Alan is now so reduced in strength that I fear he will not last out the week. Perhaps even the night.

As I write these words, sitting quietly at the table in his cell, Brother Alan is asleep. He gave me a nasty shock just now: he gave a hard gasp, his eyes closed and he fell so utterly still that I confess that I pressed my ear to his slack mouth to check that there was still breath in him. There is, praise God, but very little. He is pitifully weak and I believe I will lay down my quill now and tiptoe away. But I shall return in the morning, if my friend lives through the night, and take this goose-feather in my hand once more. For there is one more story to tell, the ancient warrior told me fiercely just before his eyes closed this evening.

'Do not think your task is finished yet, young Anthony,' he whispered. 'The tale of the great charter and the rebellion of the barons is not quite done. There is one more adventure involving my lord of Locksley that I must recount, and I cannot rest easy in my grave until it is told. It is the most terrible tale of all, a tale of blood, betrayal and pain; a tale of good men slaughtered and bad men triumphant. It is the tale of the death of Robin Hood . . .'

And that was when he closed his eyes.

Historical Note

On the third page of *Outlaw*, the first novel in this series, I had Alan Dale recalling his deeds as a young man and setting down these words about his friend Robin Hood: 'I will write his story, my story, and set before the world the truth about . . . the great magnate who brought a King of England to a table at Runnymede and made him submit to the will of the people . . .'

When I wrote those words more than a decade ago, I knew roughly where my heroes Robin and Alan were headed, that King John would be their long-term enemy, and that Magna Carta would feature in one of the books towards the end of the series. But I have a confession to make: when I typed those words, I had only the vaguest idea of what Magna Carta actually was. I hadn't read it, nor had I read much about it except in passing. In fact, I thought that the Great Charter that King John was forced to set his seal to in June 1215 would be rather like the Declaration of Independence or the Gettysburg Address, a document filled with ringing oratory, brimming with fine and noble sentiments, that it would be no less than a pledge of proto-democracy from a beleaguered absolute monarch to the ordinary people of England for ever.

I couldn't have been more wrong.

Magna Carta is actually quite dull to read. It's repetitive, full of medieval legal jargon and often rather awkwardly phrased (at least the English translation of it is – I never got much beyond *amo*, *amas*, *amat* in my Latin classes at school). It has little in the way of structure or even a theme. It reads, in fact, like a bucket list; as if a group of exuberant and slightly drunken lads had got together and all told the scribes what they wanted in no particular order, all shouting at the same time:

'Hey, how about we get rid of those bloody fish weirs in the Medway!'

'I want a free pardon and my hostage sons back home – now!'

'Yeah, and how about those dirty mercenaries – send them back where they came from!'

Nowhere is there any mention of anything truly democratic. It is, actually, pretty much all about money. It's about reliefs and dues and scutage and inheritance, about widows' rights and debts owed to the Jews. It is mostly about restricting the King's right to mulct cash from his barons whenever he wished in the form of taxes of one kind or another. And yet the group of bellicose aristocrats who got together and forced the King to stop continually ripping them off did something extraordinary. They created a precedent: a document that curbed the actions of the richest and most powerful man in the land and made him submit to the law, just like anyone else. That is sort of democratic, in the loosest sense of the word; the idea that no one is above the law, even a king anointed by God to rule over his subjects.

It also re-introduced the old Saxon idea of a council of men who would advise (and implicitly control) the King and make sure that he behaved himself. It wasn't a parliament, not even close, and the great council of twenty-five barons never actually came into being, but the 'democratic' – if you want to call it that – genie was out of the bottle. Finally, the idea that no free man should be taken and imprisoned without a trial by his peers warms my heart, too. Even though it leaves the unfree serfs out in the cold. It's a fine principle and in these terror-ridden times, as the power of the state swells alarmingly, I think it is a principle that we should all vigorously defend.

The true importance of Magna Carta, however, is as a symbol. The document itself, close-written Latin in fading black ink, full of complaints and grudges, arcane bickering over rights, duties and taxes, is not the point – it is the idea that it represents that has endured these past eight centuries. Magna Carta is a talisman against the over-weening power of princes, a shield against tyranny, a bulwark against absolutism – even if it was compiled by a group of self-serving and privileged professional warriors. Without Magna Carta there would be no Bill of Rights and perhaps no general concept of human rights either. Magna Carta symbolises freedom under the law, the idea that the individual should have as great a degree of liberty as is consistent with a well-run state in which all can safely live and prosper, and that magnificent idea, I think, is worth celebrating in this year of its eight hundredth anniversary.

I should also confess, at this point, that I played a little fast and loose with the historicity of the Magna Carta ceremony. I have King John himself petulantly sealing the document with his personal seal before the assembled barons, and this is most unlikely to have happened. In fact, there was a special machine, rather like a small press, which was used for affixing the official royal seal on to important documents and this mundane task may have happened anywhere from Windsor Castle, John's head-quarters in those weeks, to the Priory of St Mary's at Ankerwycke on the other side of the Thames from Runnymede. The affixing of the great seal to the charter would have been done by John's clerks. The meeting at Runnymede was not about the sealing of Magna Carta but its proclamation and the subsequent act of homage by the barons. The document – or rather the many copies of the charter – would have been sealed and sent out to royal castles in the four corners of the country at some point between mid-June and mid-July by John's efficient bureaucrats. The King himself may never have even handled the final version of the charter, he may never even have laid eyes on it. For this small but deliberate deception, I plead guilty and offer as my defence the novelist's privilege to make a scene as dramatic as possible.

Magna Carta might never have come about at all were it not for the military disaster at Bouvines at the end of July 1214. The battle occurred much as I have described it except, obviously, without my fictional heroes – Robin, Alan, Little John, Robert, Thomas and the rest – playing their parts.

The allied army coming up from the south through the woods of Cysoing caught the French in the middle of crossing the bridge at the hamlet of Bouvines and if they had attacked them at that time with all their strength they might well have won the day. Instead, they lined up their troops in three battles in the traditional formation opposite the French and gave Philip the time to get his men back over the bridge. The French King did burn the bridge once his men were across and, if the allies' performance was lacklustre, Philip Augustus played his weaker hand remarkably well. He was slightly outnumbered and caught in an awkward situation but he managed to turn the tables on his disorganised foes and win the day. The Count of Flanders' forces in the south were destroyed by the French cavalry and the Count was captured, Emperor Otto in the centre ran away, and in the north of the field the Count of Boulogne and the Earl of Salisbury did indeed form a sort of forerunner of the nineteenth-century redcoats' square, or the Scottish schiltron, an impenetrable hedge of infantry steel surrounding their cavalry, although it did not do them much good. They too were ultimately destroyed and Boulogne and Salisbury were captured. The non-noble prisoners, many of them Flemish mercenaries, were butchered by the French.

Bouvines destroyed for ever King John's chances of recovering his lands on the Continent, and this for many of his noble subjects was the last straw. A victorious king – such as, say, Richard the Lionheart, who was also no slouch when it came to squeezing the country for cash – is a good king, as far as the medieval military caste was concerned. If the King could lead his barons to victory, the accompanying tide of wealth in ransoms of captured enemies, seized lands and booty from a ransacked countryside was likely to keep all of them quiet and happy. If the King lost, the nobles were likely to find themselves or their relatives in chains and faced the very real risk of financial ruin. War was business in the thirteenth century, you might argue that it still is. I find a parallel between medieval warfare and the way we see the economy in the twenty-first century. When a modern economy is doing well, house prices rising, unemployment low, governmental sins are more readily forgiven. But when recession bites, ministerial heads roll and the government of the day is likely to be kicked out. In the thirteenth century, so it was with war. Much would be forgiven a successful warrior-king but woe betide a man like John who consistently lost crucial battles.

The medieval historian J. C. Holt famously wrote that 'the road from Bouvines to Runnymede was direct, short and unavoidable', and while some might quibble with 'unavoidable', the defeated king was in a far weaker position after the battle, militarily and financially, and his barons were, as a result, far less intimidated by him. If Bouvines had been a great victory, or even just a very lucrative one like the successful raid on Damme the year before, I think it unlikely that the English barons would have rebelled and there would have been no Magna Carta.

Incidentally, Bouvines – which is a scarcely remembered engagement in the English-speaking world – has huge recognition-value, even fame, in France. It was fundamental in the development of the French kingdom and confirmed the French King's sovereignty over Normandy and Brittany. It was, perhaps, the most important battle that most British people have never heard of.

If you would like to read more about Bouvines, Magna Carta and King John's struggles with his barons I would thoroughly recommend W. L. Warren's superb *King John*, Sean McGlynn's excellent *Blood Cries Afar* and Danny Danziger and John Gillingham's very entertaining *1215: The Year of Magna Carta*.

Of course, the issuing of Magna Carta in June 1215 was not the end of the story. Nine weeks afterwards, at King John's behest, the Pope annulled the Great Charter and excommunicated all the rebel barons. Civil war immediately broke out once more all across the land . . . but that is a story for another day, another book.

Robin and Alan may not rest on their laurels just yet.

Angus Donald
Tonbridge, March 2015

Read on

for an exclusive extract from
Angus Donald's next and final instalment in the
OUTLAW CHRONICLES:

THE

DEATH OF

ROBIN HOOD

Available for download and Sphere hardback
in August 2016

I humbly pray that whomsoever wishes to read these parchments in the years to come shall indeed be able to do so, for in parts my falling tears have caused the black ink to run and the words to mingle together on the page. I am not a lachrymose man, I believe, but this tale is filled with so much sorrow that it would make the angels weep – yet also laugh, perhaps, and maybe even rejoice in the courage, strength and resourcefulness of mortal men. The words contained herein are not my own, they have flown to me straight from the mouth of Brother Alan, one of our most venerable monks here at Newstead Priory, and it has been my task to copy them down as faithfully as I am able.

Brother Alan is too frail now to write himself. Indeed, he is very near to death and spends nearly all his days in his cell, wrapped in blankets and furs, despite the first warm breath of spring in the air. And yet his mind is still clear and his memory sharp. Some might argue that this task is beneath my dignity – I am after all the Prior of Newstead, in the county of Nottinghamshire, and lord of a community of a dozen monks and a score of lay workers and servants – but Christ taught humility and Brother Alan was the man who taught me my letters when I first came to this House of God nearly ten years ago. I have never forgotten his kindness and now that I have been elevated above my fellows, I shall endeavour to make some repayment of that debt.

Christ also taught us to hate the lie – and I must not pretend that I undertake this task solely from piety and gratitude. Brother Alan's past as a knight, as one of the most renowned fighting men of his day, and the stories he tells of battle and bloodshed, of comradeship in combat, give me a thrill of pleasure that is not entirely godly. Yet I believe I am doing God's work in recording his story, for it sheds light upon the last years of the reign of King John and the accession of our beloved Henry of Winchester, his son and, by the grace of God in this blessed year twelve hundred and forty-six, our sovereign lord and King – long may he reign over us.

This work also aims to reveal the stark truth about the crimes and contributions of another great man, one who was Brother Alan's friend and comrade for many years, about whom much has been said and sung, and most of that false, up and down the land. To expose these lies and calumnies – that is God's work, indeed; as it is to reveal the true nature of this strange man, the rebel baron who fought for an evil King, the former outlaw who used the law to bring justice to the land, the unrepentant murderer and thief, the loving father and loyal husband, the friend of the poor and champion of the oppressed. It is the Lord's will, I do earnestly believe, that the whole truth shall be known at last about the man called Robin Hood.

Chapter One

The square bulk of the keep of Rochester Castle thrust upwards into the twilight, ominous as a vast tombstone, and cast a long black shadow over the outer bailey, the cathedral beyond the walls and the sprawling smoke-wreathed town around it. From my post, at the centre of the old wooden bridge over the River Medway, the keep was almost due south and about three hundred paces distant. Shading my eyes from the glare of the westering sun off the water, I caught the silvery glint of the sentries' helmets as they patrolled the battlements, and on the dark, eastern side of the massive stone walls, the first slivers of candlelight leaking from arrow slits.

It was a forbidding fortress, one of the mightiest in England, built to guard this crossing of the river on the road from Dover to London, the most direct route an invading enemy would take to attack the largest and richest city in England. Yet the castle's dominating stone, its implacable solidity, was of great comfort to me. Battle was surely coming – a day or two, a week at most, and it would be upon us in all its blood and agony and fury, and then, when the arrows began to soar, the steel to scrape and men to scream in pain, I knew I would be more than grateful for the castle's twelve-foot-thick walls that climbed a hundred feet into the air.

The east wind was freshening, wafting a light mizzle from the cold waters of the estuary a couple of miles behind my back, and I pulled the damp green cloak tighter around my shoulders. My stomach gurgled unhappily – it must surely be almost time for supper and my relief – and I rubbed my reddened hands together and stamped my numb feet. By night's fall I should be snug in the guard-house on the southern side of the bridge – there would be hot mutton broth and fresh bread and butter, a cup of warm spiced wine and the company of old friends. But where the hell was Sir Thomas Blood? The sun was already squatting on the western horizon.

I looked hopefully to my left towards the stout two-storey wooden box arching over the planks of the bridge on the southern bank. Was I imagining it or could I already smell the broth? A pair of thick-set men in green cloaks, long yew bows in their hands, were propped against the rail staring silently over the water, vacant as cows at a gate. I looked right, past the piles of boulders, each roughly the size of a human head, collected below the rail in little cairns of three or four rocks every ten feet, and saw a young, slim, fair-haired swordsman, similarly green-cloaked, fifty paces away at the northern end of the bridge. He leaned over the rail and lowered his head, and I saw a gobbet of spittle shoot from his mouth and disappear below. Perhaps inevitably, echoing up from underneath, came the faint roar of a complaint, its maker at first unseen from my vantage point. A slim rowing boat emerged, heading upstream, with a red-faced bald fellow mopping his pate and shaking his fist at the handsome young devil laughing above him.

'Don't do that, Miles,' I bellowed. 'It's churlish, it's unseemly . . . it's plain disgusting, for God's sake.'

The young man turned to look at me. His long, lean face seemed lit from within, like the All Souls' candle inside a hollowed-out turnip, illuminated by a mischievous almost child-like delight.

'I'm bored half to death, old man,' he shouted back. 'Bored as a boy-loving eunuch in an all-girl brothel. Surely our watch must be over by now. Besides, that baldy fellow sells bad fish. He's a cheat. Father says so. That basket of carp he sold us yesterday was mostly mud, skin and bones.'

His father, of course, was my lord, the Earl of Locksley, my old friend Robin, who on this chill October day was, no doubt, sitting in the warmth of the guardhouse toasting his boots by a brazier. But, even if Miles's father had not been my lord, I would have been loath to scold the youngster – despite him daring to call me an old man. Not only because I liked his irreverent high spirits, which cheered the hearts of our whole company, but also because he was a fine fighting man in his own right, a quicksilver fiend with a blade and utterly fearless in the storm of battle.

Apart from the angry fisherman, now pulling away at a pace, leaving a stream of ripe insults in his wake, the river upstream was as placid as a pond. A few ancient craft lay hauled up on the slick banks and two old salts sat on boxes, their heads bent together, knitting their nets slowly, rhythmically, from time to time pausing to pass a leather bottle between them. I turned around, full into the cold breeze, the drizzle spitting directly in my face, and looked towards the curve of the river where it disappeared into the low pasturelands. Nothing but slow brown water and low grey fields, and a few scattered sheep casting monstrous shadows, as the sun nestled down behind me. Not an enemy in sight. Not a sniff of danger either. I could have been safe and snug at home in my manor of Westbury in Nottinghamshire rather than doing sentry duty on a mist-sprayed bridge in the flatlands of east Kent.

I heard a discreet cough. 'Sir Alan,' said a deep voice behind me and I turned to behold a short, powerfully built, dark-haired knight in full mail, helmet under one arm, smiling up at me.

'About time, Thomas,' I said. 'About bloody time. All quiet. Nothing to report. This godforsaken bridge is all yours.'

As I stepped into the guardhouse, I saw my lord seated at the long table in the centre of the room, spooning the last drops from an earthenware bowl. A battered, soot-blackened steaming cauldron had been placed in the middle of the board, next to a basket of bread, a jug of wine and a stack of crockery.

'Report?' said Robin.

'There is nobody out there,' I replied, reaching for a bowl. 'If John really is coming here, he is taking his own sweet time about it.'

'Oh, the King is coming all right,' said Robin cheerfully. 'He has to. His new men, his Flemings, will surely cross the Channel and land at Dover, and we bar the route to London. He must take Rochester, if he wishes to take London from the Army of God. And he must take London if he wishes to win this war.'

The so-called Army of God, under the command of the less-than-saintly Robert, Lord Fitzwalter, did indeed hold London. Robin and I had stormed the walls for him just over three months ago and as a result we had captured the capital and been able to force the King to set his seal on a great charter at Runnymede, a document that was supposed to guarantee the rights of free Englishmen for ever. But, despite solemnly swearing to abide by the charter, calling for peace in the land and renewing the oaths of loyalty with his barons, the King had renounced the agreement a mere handful of weeks afterwards. The Pope in Rome, at the King's behest, had damned the charter, too, as shameful and illegal and had excommunicated all the rebel barons.

We had struggled and suffered and bled for that square piece of smoothed calf skin, and wrangled day and night over the terse Latin words it contained. Yet despite Robin's insistence that by forcing the King's hand we had struck a blow for liberty that would be remembered for generations to come, I sometimes wondered what all the strife and bloodshed had achieved. If it had, in fact, achieved anything at all. King John, that cowardly, murderous snake, had simply ignored the great charter and spent thousands of pounds in tax silver recruiting fresh mercenary troops from Flanders and northern France. War had broken out again almost immediately between the rebel barons and the King's new continental hirelings.

Nevertheless, our position was not hopeless. Since the sealing of the charter, many English barons who had previously been fearful of resisting the King had rallied to our cause – the Pope's mass excommunications notwithstanding. Indeed, the constable of this very castle, Reginald de Cornhill, once a staunch King's man, had opened its gates to Lord Fitzwalter and his men not two days before and declared himself a lover of liberty, before departing with unashamed haste and all his men for his lands in Surrey.

Yet we rebels held London, and Exeter in the south-west, and a scatter of small castles in the north – and now we held Rochester too. And, while Fitzwalter prepared the defences of this mighty fortress with his grizzled captain William d'Aubigny, Robin's detachment of twenty archers and a dozen men-at-arms had been given the task of holding the bridge. For the King was surely coming up from Dover. And I knew it just as well as Robin.

The door of the guardhouse crashed open, impelled by an impetuous boot. 'Do I smell yesterday's mutton broth?' said Miles, striding inside and unfastening the golden clasp to drop his wet green cloak on the dirty rushes of the floor. 'Isn't there anything a bit more substantial to eat? I could make short work of a bloody beefsteak or a dripping roast chicken – God's bones, that would suit.'

'It's broth or nothing,' said his father, with an edge in his voice. 'You know as well as I that we are on short commons, all of us, till the supply train comes through from London. We must tighten our belts till then. And do try not to whine quite so much, son.'

'Not whining. Just making polite dinner conversation.'

Miles plonked himself down on the bench next to me, helped himself to a clay bowl and filled it to the brim. 'Mmmm. Mutton broth. Nice and watery. And plenty of gristle, too, I see.'

I could actually hear Robin grinding teeth. But my lord held his peace.

'What news from the castle?' I said, after a long uncomfortable pause.

'D'Aubigny has it nicely in hand, I believe,' said my lord. 'He says the fortifications are sound, the walls in good repair throughout, and he has enough men and arms to hold it for months against a determined assault – providing of course that sufficient food stores can be brought in.'

William d'Aubigny was a bear of a man, immensely strong and quick, and with a reputation for ferocity in battle. He was lord of Belvoir Castle, a fortress in Leicestershire about fifteen miles east of Nottingham. As a not-too-distant neighbour of ours, he was well known to Robin and to me.

'Fitzwalter is planning to leave us, though,' Robin said.

'What?' I said, swallowing a mouthful of hot soup too quickly. 'Why?'

'He says he's needed in London. A grand council of the barons has been called. They're to discuss recruiting aid from overseas and Fitzwalter says he must attend or who knows what foolishness will occur.'

'So our gallant commander is deserting us on the eve

of battle?' said Miles. 'Scuttling back to London. Hardly inspiring behaviour in a leader.'

Robin ignored his son and concentrated on wiping clean his bowl with a crust but I felt called on to defend Lord Fitzwalter's honour. My relationship with the captain-general of the Army of God had not always been cordial but since the war began I had grown to like the man.

'He is our leader and it makes sense that he should attend this important council with all the other senior barons,' I said.

'Were you not invited to attend this vaunted gathering then, Father?' said Miles. 'How strange! Perhaps they feel that playing watchman on this ancient bridge is more your mark.'

I could have punched the lad off the bench for that insult. Indeed, I felt my right fist clench and rise from the board. But Robin beat me to it.

'The sentry on the roof has been complaining of the cold this past hour,' said Robin serenely. 'When you have finished that nourishing bowl of broth, Miles, get yourself up there and take his place. I'll be sure to send someone up to relieve you at midnight' – Robin pretended to think – 'or perhaps at dawn. We'll have to see. I'd like all the serious fighting men to get a good night's rest.'

'But, Father, I had plans to visit the town tonight. There is this girl I want to see and as I'm not on duty—'

'Well, you are on duty now,' said Robin. 'Off you go.'

'But it's not fair . . .'

'Don't whine, lad,' I said, perhaps a touch smugly. 'Obey your lord's command.'

Miles opened his mouth to argue but before he could speak the door swung towards us and we all three looked up in surprise at the dark entrance, now wholly filled by Sir Thomas Blood's short form, broad shoulders and steel-helmeted head.

'Boats, my lord,' said Sir Thomas. 'Boats on the river. Scores of them.'

From the roof of the guardhouse, we had our first glimpse of the enemy, of the feared Flemish legions of King John. At least fifty rowing boats, downstream, three hundred yards away. Each boat was showing a single pinprick of yellow light, a lantern or open fire-pot, enabling us to see them against the blackness of the water in the failing light, and every vessel was pulling hard for the centre of the bridge.

'Miles, get back to the castle now. Alert Lord Fitzwalter – tell him . . . tell him that the bridge is under attack by several hundred of the King's men and that we will hold as long as we can. But it cannot be for long. Tell him to come with all speed.'

'But I want to fight. If you send me away, I'll miss everything—'

'For once, Miles, just do as you are bloody well told!' My lord did not raise his voice above a murmur but there was a whip-crack in his tone that sent his younger son scurrying for the wooden stair.

'Now, Alan, let's see about discouraging these Flemish fellows, shall we?'

DISCOVER
Angus Donald's **thrilling**

OUTLAW CHRONICLES

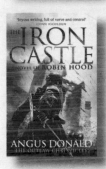
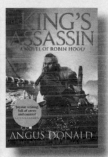

'A **gloriously entertaining** reboot' *The Times*
from
'A **master of adventure**' Robyn Young